The most

t

Christmas
in his bed

Three all-new red-hot
Christmas stories from

SAMANTHA HUNTER
CARRIE ALEXANDER
ALISON KENT

Christmas
in his bed

SAMANTHA HUNTER

CARRIE ALEXANDER

ALISON KENT

M&B™ and M&B™ with the Rose Device
are trademarks of the publisher.
Harlequin Mills & Boon Limited, Eton House,
18-24 Paradise Road, Richmond, Surrey TW9 1SR

CHRISTMAS IN HIS BED © Harlequin Books S.A. 2009

Talking in Your Sleep © Samantha Hunter 2007
Unwrapped © Carrie Antilla 2004
Kiss & Tell © Mica Stone 2008

ISBN: 978 0 263 88316 9

009-1209

Harlequin Mills & Boon policy is to use papers that are
natural, renewable and recyclable products and made from
wood grown in sustainable forests. The logging and
manufacturing processes conform to the legal environmental
regulations of the country of origin.

Printed and bound in Spain
by Litografia Rosés S.A., Barcelona

Talking in Your Sleep

SAMANTHA HUNTER

Samantha Hunter lives in Syracuse, New York, where she writes romance full-time. When she's not plotting her next book, Sam likes to work in her garden, quilt, cook, read and spend time with her husband and their dogs. You can check out what's new, enter contests, or drop her a note at her website, www.samanthahunter.com, and at her blog, www.loveisanexplodingcigar.com

Don't miss *Hard To Resist* by Samantha Hunter available in February 2010 from Mills & Boon® Blaze®.

For all my readers, old and new, thank you for your support, e-mails, cards, notes, comments and kind thoughts. I wish you all the happiest and most wonderful of holidays, that you find your passions and that the magic of it will stay with you all year long!

1

RAPHAEL MOORE TENSED his body then relaxed it one inch at a time. He began with his toes, moving up his calves to his knees, and concentrated on releasing the strain in his lower back. Breathing evenly, he imagined floating on a warm, soothing ocean current, the heat of the sun hypnotically beating down on him, and drifted off into a dreamy half consciousness that soon would lead to sleep.

"Oh, that's so good.... Touch me right there...."

"Dammit!" he cursed as his eyes shot open. The agitation of being wrenched out of his relaxed state doubled his shock. Taking a deep breath, he closed his eyes again, trying to control his heartbeat. He flexed his fingers in an attempt to catch hold of what had almost been his—a good night's sleep.

"I love how you kiss me. I want your mouth everywhere...."

He sat up, swinging his legs over the side of the bed, planting his palms tightly against his ears, attempting to block out the woman's voice. He could still hear her moans and sighs.

Obviously she was having a very good time, and he had no problem with that, but couldn't she do it with the window shut? He felt like some pervert, for Chrissakes, listening in.

The action happening a few yards away wasn't the only thing that was hot. A freak heat wave had temperatures up near ninety for Christmas in San Diego. It was inducing weird behaviors in everyone, the unusual weather combined with the usual holiday madness. His neighbors, however, seemed to enjoy being all sweaty.

After just having left the bitter cold of New York, he welcomed the heat, too. Summer was his favorite season. Even the smothering, humid city air in July and August didn't faze him. He'd happily embraced the West Coast, which didn't look at all Christmassy to him, in spite of the holiday decorations.

It felt like August, not December, and Rafe knew he'd made the right decision taking Warren up on his offer to stay here while his buddy was on his honeymoon in Thailand. Warren had grown up in the same Brooklyn neighborhood as Rafe. As kids they'd been inseparable and had served time on the volunteer ambulance together before Warren had decided that life wasn't for him. Now he had his own consulting business in sunny California. He'd been bugging Rafe to come out for a while, so Rafe had flown out for the wedding, then stayed to house-sit. It was great timing for both of them. Rafe had the place to himself for a month until Warren and his bride returned on January third.

If only for the neighbors, it would have been perfect. Warren had bought this little fixer-upper on a small residential street in North Park, and after the renovation the house was going to be fabulous. Rafe liked working with his hands, and it helped to have something to do. He was used to working, and he'd go nuts sitting around all day. He'd remodeled his entire apartment in Brooklyn, a relaxing activity in his off hours. Warren was happy to have him do some work on the house.

This was Rafe's first time in California, and he'd taken to it immediately. The sunshine and heat had lightened his mood as soon as he'd hit the tarmac. A native New Yorker, he hadn't been sure about leaving his home, but San Diego was heaven by comparison, at least at this time of year.

"A little lower...please...." a sexy woman's voice begged.

Rafe experienced a stirring in his groin that he had no business feeling, but hell, he was a man and he'd been listening to this monologue for three nights running. How many months had passed since a woman had talked to him like that? Insomnia was a libido killer.

Before his sleeplessness, his job had ruled his life, including his sex life. Being an emergency medical technician was all he'd ever wanted to do.

He'd thought about medical school, but he wasn't interested in the years of training it took to be a doctor. He liked the action of emergency services over being camped out in a classroom. Instead of spending the last twelve years studying how to help people, he'd been able to do it every day.

Despite the constant stress and pressure, for years he'd thrived on helping people when they needed it most. That was until this past year. Suddenly he couldn't sleep. Nothing helped, save the pills that he refused to take. Pills might address the insomnia issue, but they wouldn't solve the larger problem— why he'd burned out on the job after all those years, and why he couldn't handle it anymore.

All he could see was the endless stream of people in trouble and that they'd lost far too many of them. His last loss had been a five-year-old girl with asthma, alone at home in her tenement apartment. No one had been there to help her when she'd suffered a serious attack, and her parents hadn't been able to afford the costly medicines. Though the girl had been smart enough to dial 911, Rafe had gotten there too late.

Over the years, there had been so many cases like that he could barely keep count. Lots of good stories, too, but the bad ones were catching up with him. Like the husband and father of six children who had died right in front of him after being hit by a drunk driver, or the teenager shot on the street for no apparent reason while coming home from a graduation party. Their faces haunted Rafe as he lay awake in the dark hours of the night.

Something critical that had kept him sane seemed to have broken. The result was he'd lost his sense of purpose, his drive to do the work.

The insomnia might be a cause or a symptom, he still wasn't sure, but it had messed up his life for good. When he'd almost crashed the ambulance—with a patient on board—he'd been put on paid leave, and he couldn't argue with that decision. The company had taken his record into account and hadn't fired him— they were treating his break as accumulated sick and vacation time. However, if he couldn't solve his sleep problem, he knew he'd be in for permanent retirement.

The prospect made him feel hollow inside, and he pushed it away, knowing it would torture him for the rest of the night, at least. That was part of the problem, the endless thoughts that wouldn't stop, and the more he tried, the more they barged through, keeping him awake even when he was exhausted.

"Oh, yes…again…"

Rafe fell back on the bed, groaning, but not in pleasure. How long were they going to keep at it? It wasn't normal—these people went at it for hours every night. He wanted to be cool, to say, "More power to ya," but in truth he wanted them to shut the hell up and go to sleep.

Grabbing a pillow and heading to the sofa in the

living room, even though it was about eight inches too short for his six-foot frame, he walked out of the room, slamming the door behind him.

"DAD, I'M SORRY, I just can't—I know, it's yours and Lois's first Christmas together, so maybe it's better for you to spend it alone."

"Joy, we'd love to have you. It would be good for you and Lois to get to know each other."

Joy Clarke closed her eyes, exhausted, counting to twenty before responding. She'd met her new stepmother at her father's wedding, and liked her well enough. Lois was a nice woman who made her father happy. Still, Joy wasn't particularly interested in bonding. Her own mother had left them when she was nine. Since Lois was only ten years older than Joy, she was hardly a maternal figure.

"I know, that would be nice. Maybe in summer."

"That's what you said last spring."

"Work is crazy, Dad. I'm up for a promotion, and I can't afford to take time off now. Holidays are crazy in the toy business."

In truth, Christmas was a year-round holiday in her industry, everyone competing to get a jump on what the next hot product would be and making sure marketing and distribution was in place if they found it.

"I'm proud of what you've accomplished, Joy. You work hard, like I taught you, but I hope you'll be able to take some time off to come home. Perhaps once you get that promotion."

"Yeah, Dad. I have to go. Duty calls."

"Okay, sweetheart. Work hard, now."

"Always do," she said, hanging up the phone on the familiar exchange they'd shared since she was a child. He always told her to work hard—as he had—and she always did.

Joy settled her face in her hands, permitting herself a moment of quiet. She wanted a nap, badly. But a two-minute power-nap wasn't going to replace all the sleep she'd been losing thanks to restless dreams that were bothering her as much when she was awake as when she was asleep.

For several weeks, she'd had strange, muddled sexual dreams that left her edgy and restless. At first, they weren't about anyone in particular, just a shadowy figure who brought her to the edge of pleasure, but denied her real satisfaction. Then her neighbor, Warren, whom she barely knew, caught her by her car one day and told her a friend of his would be house-sitting over the holidays. She'd listened dutifully though honestly she had so much to do she didn't keep track of her neighbor's comings and goings. Warren told her the friend's name—Rafe Moore—and a general description. She hadn't thought twice about it at the time, until she'd seen the house sitter moving in, hauling his bags from the taxi that dropped him off.

Ever since…well, suffice to say her vague dream lover had taken on a real face. The experiences were getting much more intense, more explicit, and even more satisfying, but she woke up every morning exhausted. It was aggravating—why was she dreaming about this guy every night? She'd never even spoken to him, just watched him walk from the car to the house, puttering in the yard, in all his shirtless glory….

She groaned, trying to shake away the thoughts. It was bad enough he was in her head every night, let alone starting to obsess about him in the daylight hours. She had to work. She'd managed to dodge the bullet of having to go to her father's house for Christmas this year, using the one excuse her dad always gave merit: work. Never failed, but she wouldn't be able to put them off forever.

Her excuse was the truth though—she really was buried under work. The piles of papers and file folders stacked up all over her desk was proof of that.

As the public relations officer in charge of handling recalls, which happened fairly regularly in the toy-manufacturing industry, her responsibility was to make sure that the company's image didn't suffer when a product didn't work. God forbid anyone got hurt or worse, but sometimes it happened. Her whole life was about spin control, but she also legitimately tried to make sure that customers were taken care of, and would continue to buy Carr Toys.

She was good at doing that. Still, as corporate bottom lines became more pressing, manufacturing was forced to lay off more workers. The remaining staff had to pick up the slack, taking on more and more work. That had inevitably led to the making of more production mistakes. The result of those ended up in her lap. Her life had become a parade of broken toys and apologies on behalf of her company.

It wasn't what she'd pictured when she'd chosen PR as a major in college, where her classes had always been fun and exciting. Her professors had said she had talent, and she'd believed them. When she'd taken a job with a toy company, somehow she'd expected it to be fun. Six years later though, turning the corner of her thirtieth birthday, she knew better.

Carr was a multibillion-dollar company with three manufacturing locations, worldwide distributors and hefty competition within a troubled economy where customers were more than willing to sue when a product had a defect, especially a dangerous one.

Thanks to the triple punch of corporate downsizing, performance testing, and the replacement of older, more experienced employees with younger ones at lower pay and benefits, the work atmosphere had become increasingly cutthroat. She was up for a promotion, but she was also going against three other department managers who would be happy to sell their grandmothers for the same job.

Pressure, not fun, had become the name of the game. *Fun* was only a marketing strategy.

Joy could work under pressure because it was required of her, but it was something she'd had to become accustomed to. When things got tough, she remembered all the years her dad, who had been a utilities lineman, had worked weekends, holidays and whatever else he'd had to do to support them.

He never complained about it, and that taught her the value of hard work. She'd learned from his example. She took pride in what she did, but lately, in weak moments, she wondered if it was enough.

She straightened in her chair and turned her attention to the nearest pile of folders, picking the top one off and opening it. Then eyeing the calendar, she pursed her lips.

Two weeks before Christmas.

Joy felt no connection at all to the season, taking little part in the decorating, partying or shopping. Who had time? Her dad hadn't been much for Christmas after the year her mom left, and who could blame him? Joy had quickly learned that getting excited about Christmas was just setting herself up for disappointment.

She needed to focus on the reports she had in front of her, get ready for a meeting and prepare for a news conference on a recent toy recall. Later today she'd be standing in front of a group of reporters all waiting for her to slip up and give them something juicy to print, but she'd represent her company well. All she needed was a good night's sleep and to get her sexy neighbor out of her mind. Easier said than done.

2

RAFE HAD ACTUALLY MANAGED to doze on the sofa for a few hours come early morning. Waking to the sound of car doors slamming as people left for work, he'd made himself get up and had spent most of the day scraping the wallpaper from a small side room—nasty work in the heat—but it had kept him busy and active, and he'd accomplished something.

In spite of his lack of sleep and the hard work, he was charged with energy so he decided to go for a run. Endorphins, or the sun. Or a hint of his returning sex drive, maybe.

Though he'd shut the voice out last night, the simmering, sensual responses it sparked had lingered. He'd had to walk around the house several times to lose the morning erection that didn't seem to want to disappear. It was good to have blood pumping to those particular body parts again, though it would be nice if he had someone with whom to expend that excess energy.

The late-afternoon sun was setting low, and it still hit him as odd, but appealing, to be seeing summer sunsets in December. The news back home said the northeast was getting its first real snowstorm. Ambulances would be busy putting in extra hours; accidents, fires, all increased with the snow and ice. The kids would have a white Christmas, but for himself, he was content to have a sunny one. He heard the wail of sirens several times a day, and it never failed to make him look up for a second and wonder.

The beaches were a few miles from his neighborhood, and Warren had left a map in the car. San Diego was pretty easy to navigate, and he hopped in the car, taking the coastal highway a few miles north. He pulled off to the side and watched some late-day surfers decked out in neoprene paddle out into the water. He meant to look into taking some lessons—surfing seemed fun, and that was what he was here for: fun, recovery, relaxation. Hopefully a month of all three would get him back in shape to return to New York, and to his job. He got out of the car and started walking down the beach, falling into an easy jog.

He passed a group of young women in bikinis, their gazes following him as they watched him over the tops of their sunglasses. One smiled and offered a little wave. He nodded back and stopped jogging for a moment.

"Hey, why not?" He posed the question to himself under his breath and approached the beach bunnies, smiling at the girls as he neared.

"Hey, ladies."

"Hi there."

The one who'd waved had somehow claimed dibs, since the others backed off and let her take the lead. She was pretty—the kind of girl the Beach Boys sang about, what every New York man imagined California girls would be like. Blond, young, tanned all over.

"You talk like the guys on the *The Sopranos*."

"No, I don't." He laid on his New York accent a little heavier since they seemed to like it, though in truth it sounded more like the accents of the Italian kids he'd always hung out with, and still did. City accents weren't so much defined by where you were, but rather who you were, your ethnicity. As it turned out, Rafe was Italian-Irish, but he had more Italian speech patterns than Irish because of the neighborhood he'd grown up in.

Not that the beach bunny would care about the subtle distinctions of New York dialects. Or that Tony Soprano and his crime family actually lived in Essex County, in New Jersey.

They giggled again, and he was hopping from foot to foot, suddenly antsy instead of interested, ready to take off. The girls—and there was a world of difference between these girls and women his own age— were in their midtwenties, but seemed much younger. He was only thirty-three, but it seemed like a century from where they were. This had been a bad idea.

"You here on vacation?"

"Nope, just a regular working Joe, I'm afraid."
He scowled—why did he lie?

Bunny pouted. "Too bad. You could blow off
work and come party with us."

"Us?"

"All three of us, honey, if you're up for it." Her
tone and the look she gave him left him in no doubt
of what she meant. The prospect left him astound-
ingly cold. No doubt it would be the solution to his
lack-of-sex problem—it could also potentially kill
him—but he wasn't interested.

He had a certain sexy voice replaying in his mind
like a TV jingle that wouldn't stop. His neighbor. Her
voice seemed to get him going more than these girls.

"Sorry, gotta long day tomorrow, and have to get
home. You ladies have a good evening."

He tipped an imaginary hat and walked away,
thankful for an easy escape, and mentally kicking
himself for stopping in the first place. Falling back
into a run, he headed toward where he'd left
Warren's car parked. He'd just been offered a deal
most red-blooded, single men would have seriously
considered. Instead of jumping at the opportunity,
he was running in the other direction. Insomnia was
neutering him.

Twenty minutes later he was driving through
Balboa Park, taking a shortcut he'd found over to
his neighborhood. Pulling into the driveway, he saw

his neighbor, Ms. Talk-Dirty-To-Me, unloading something from her car. He was going to talk to her and deal with at least one of the things keeping him awake at night.

Taking the opportunity, he stopped by the curb near her driveway, got out and jogged up to where she was lifting bags out of the trunk. He checked her out—she had that natural look he liked on a woman, no makeup, pretty reddish-brown hair. A blue business suit disguised curves he could tell were hiding under its severe cut.

Her hair was clipped back tightly in a bun, though a few silky strands teased her neck, curling naughtily. His breath caught a little. What the hell? Was he having naughty-librarian fantasies about his neighbor? He cleared his throat, keeping his voice normal and friendly.

"Hi. Need a hand?"

He winced, hoping the simple question didn't sound like a pickup line.

Her gaze shot to him and then bolted away—she was working overtime not to make eye contact. Clearly she recognized him, but she was pretend-ing not to. Why was she acting so weird?

"No, thanks."

"I'm your new neighbor—for a month, anyway."

"Yes, I know."

Wow, she was rude. Annoyed, considering it was *her* nighttime activities that were keeping him awake, he persisted, not willing to be pushed away so easily.

"Here, let me get that one—it looks heavy."

He reached to get the last paper sack, and she tried to beat him to the punch—the result being a large tear in the bag they both grabbed for, through which several canned items fell to the pavement, one narrowly missing his bare foot.

She was clearly agitated now. "I told you I didn't need you to do that—now look at what you did. These are all dented!"

He was going to apologize, hoping she found the accident more charming than angering, like something out of a romantic comedy. No such luck. She appeared truly distressed. Was she obsessive-compulsive in some way and couldn't tolerate dented cans?

"Does it taste different if the can is dented?" he joked, bending to help her pick them up, then stalled when her hand shot upward in a "stop" signal, halting him.

"These were to be donated to people at the local food bank. I don't want the families receiving them thinking someone would only donate damaged goods."

Her tone was scathing and Rafe stepped back. He had truly been trying to help. However, she had told him to back off, and he hadn't.

"I'm sorry. I'll tell you what, I'll take these and

replace them with new ones. Do you need them tonight?"

She was quiet for a moment, not meeting his eyes as she stood. "No, that's fine. Thank you. I can get some new ones in the morning."

"You and your boyfriend do a lot of charity work?" he asked, looking at her hand and not seeing a ring. "I can buy some groceries to contribute to the cause. To make up for being such a klutz." He tried the charming smile that he'd used at the beach. It didn't work on this woman. She glared.

"My boyfriend?"

She seemed confused, and that made him question his certainty.

"I assumed you were...involved." He decided to plunge forth with the conversation, taking the opportunity to address the issue he'd come to talk to her about. "I heard you two *talking*...you know, last night."

He put some slight emphasis on the words, trying to make obvious what he was really saying, but not wanting to embarrass her if he could help it. Though he'd like to see how she'd blush, what the effect would be on that pale skin. She shook her head, hitching her armful of bags up a little higher.

"I wasn't talking to anyone last night."

"Around two in the morning? It's why I hoped to catch you, actually. It was kind of loud, and I had a hard time sleeping. My bedroom window is right across from yours, so I, um, heard every word. I wasn't trying to eavesdrop, it was kind of unavoidable."

If she'd looked confused before, now she was staring at him as if he were certifiable.

"Listen, I don't know what you're going on about, but I wasn't talking to anyone, especially at that time of the night. I was dead asleep. The noise you heard must have been coming from somewhere else. Probably out on the street."

Now *he* was confused. Maybe she was embarrassed. That made sense, he figured—and hoped she was embarrassed enough to shut the window tonight.

"Hmm. Well, okay then. Are you sure I can't help you with those…?" He left the end of his sentence open, so she might fill in the blank with her name, the way most polite people would. Instead she frowned and turned up the walk.

"Yes. I'm sure."

Well, that had better solve his problem. Rafe went back to his house and hoped for the best.

THEY WERE WRAPPED in white satin, and everything was scented of rose petals and sex. Joy laughed—she was having the time of her life. *He* took a length of the smooth material and twisted it tight. Her heartbeat quivered in anticipation—what was he going to do?

"Hold out your arms," he commanded in a husky tone as smooth and hot as the undulating pleasure that was coursing through her bloodstream.

"Are you going to tie me up?"

"Yes. I want you helpless. *Mine.* To do whatever I want."

She quivered from head to toe, holding her hands up to him in supplication, but her thoughts were wicked.

"Do whatever you want to me—I want everything from you. Anything."

He laved her skin with his tongue as he wound the satin rope around her wrists in a soft figure eight, and then proceeded to bind her to her elbows. Gently, he pressed her back down, pushing her arms upward and attaching the ends of the material to the headboard.

"Anything?"

"Anything." She was daring, adventurous—she wanted to be the lover he'd never forget.

He rose up on his knees, glistening and perfect, his erection jutting out toward her belly as he swung one leg over, straddling her waist.

"You're so beautiful," he crooned, looking at her with eyes burning so fiercely she couldn't glance away. "You may be tied up, but I'm your slave. I'll do whatever gives you pleasure."

She writhed, arching upward, needing the contact he was promising, wanting the torture.

"I want to taste you. I want you in my mouth. You're so hard…. I love wrapping my lips around you when you're like this." The short, uneven pants of desire chopped her words into uneven phrases, but she didn't care.

"I think we can make that happen…. Your breasts are so full, so soft…."

He reached down, cupping her breasts. Leaning in, he sucked both nipples at once until she was nearly screaming with need as he licked her, wetting her skin all over, making her slick.

Straightening, he kept her breasts tight between his hands, torturing her nipples with his thumbs as he slid his cock in the pocket between, groaning, squeezing himself tighter as he thrust forward, toward her mouth.

She loved it, watching him start to lose control as he pumped faster. She dipped her chin to dart her tongue out, sliding it over the tip of him every time he moved forward, reveling in his guttural moan. He came fast and hard, and she drank in his excitement, helping him milk the last drop of ecstasy from his orgasm. She was so turned on she couldn't think straight.

He leaned in, kissing her forehead, and then moved down her body—she knew he wouldn't leave her unsatisfied. He never did.

Glancing up from between her parted thighs, one hand lightly pet the hair between her legs, the feathering touches almost making her beg. She fought her satiny restraints for the first time, wanting to gain control, to make him hurry.

Instead, he drew warm, wet trails up the inside of her thigh with his tongue, and then she did beg. Pleasure and need seeped from every pore as she strained toward him, her flesh parted for his invasion, exposing her.

His finger grazed her clit, drawing her body into one long shudder. He knew how to hold her back, laughing against her before his mouth descended. Her body bowed in taut anticipation of the release that was mere moments away, and she couldn't hold back a scream when she came, the name of her lover ripe on her lips. "Rafe."

RAFE WAS RIPPED AWAKE by the scream. He bolted out of bed, trying to discern the source—had he imagined it or had the woman's voice screamed his name?

The window—it had come from next door. Without much hesitation, he yanked on jeans, ran down the stairs and through the front door. Vaulting up his neighbor's steps, he banged on the door, yelling.

"Hey! You in there? You all right? Answer the door!"

He cursed that he'd left his cell back in the bedroom—if she didn't answer, he was calling 911.

He considered going down the side of the house and entering through the window, but he didn't know the situation. If things had gone bad—as they sometimes did between lovers, and who knew what his tidy and prim neighbor was into—he'd be walking blind into a crime scene. It could make a bad situation worse.

No one answered. He started back down the steps to go call the police when the door swung open, and he braced himself to face the guy who likely had caused the scream.

Instead he faced all five feet six inches or so of his neighbor, wrapped in a short terry robe that definitely showed off things the suit had been hiding earlier, including an absolutely gorgeous pair of legs. Her hair was wild, her face flushed. She looked as if she had been having sex; but she also looked furtive, and maybe a little frightened.

"What are you *doing?*" she demanded, taking a step back, closing the door slightly as if afraid of *him*—or blocking his sight of someone else standing there with her.

"I heard you scream—you called for help. You called my name."

It was dark on her porch though the light was on in the entry hall behind her. He squinted, taking a step closer, searching for bruises or any evidence of harm. Moving away, she started to close the door.

"I didn't scream, and I certainly didn't call for *you.*"

He didn't know why she would deny it, maybe she was embarrassed or maybe she was afraid. He knew from prior experience that someone could be behind her in the doorway, and she could be telling him to leave under some kind of duress. He had to see for himself that she was okay.

Clearly panicked, her voice rose. There was no way he was going anywhere until he knew what was up. "Leave me alone! I'm fine—are you crazy, coming to my door at this hour, causing trouble—"

"Okay, have it your way." He glanced at her, communicating his intention to get help, and went down the step.

"Wait."

He turned, watching her run a hand over her face. He wondered if she was covering for someone trying to escape from the back.

"Why should I let you in here when I'm alone— I don't even know you. For all I know this is some ploy to get inside the house."

He looked at her steadily. "Do intruders usually bang loudly on your door, shouting for everyone in the neighborhood to hear, and then talk to you on your front porch for a while?" He blew out a breath. "If I wanted in for some nefarious reason, believe me, this wouldn't be my method."

"I've seen stranger things on the news."

"I'm a friend of Warren's—doesn't that tell you something?"

"Not much. I don't know him that well."

"He lives right next door."

"So? Am I required to be best friends with my neighbors?"

Coming from a close-knit neighborhood, he shrugged—he'd always known his. Sometimes too well. Maybe things were different out here.

"Listen, I'm Warren's friend, and I'm also an EMT—though I don't have any ID at the moment—if you're hurt, I can help you, and you can call the police or I can, before I step foot in the place."

"Why do you keep insisting on thinking I'm hurt?"

"I told you, I heard you scream. It woke me up."

"I'm telling you, it wasn't me." She bit the words out, increasingly agitated, but he knew what he'd heard.

Had she really screamed his name? Out loud? The thought had her cringing inwardly.

"It *was* you. What I want to know is why you're lying. It's either me or the police, sweetheart, take your pick."

Furious, she threw open the door, challenging him, and he had a moment of doubt. Still, he needed to follow through—he had to make sure she was okay, then he'd leave.

JOY WATCHED HER NEIGHBOR—she still didn't even know his name—as he prowled around her home. He'd given her one of the most intimate visual inspections she'd ever experienced before he'd started checking out the house. He said he was an EMT, and she supposed his survey was strictly clinical, though it hadn't felt that way. Given what she'd been dreaming about, that could be her fault, but she wouldn't admit it.

He hadn't laid a hand on her; he'd done nothing inappropriate, but had looked her over so thoroughly, apparently searching for signs of abuse, that she'd nearly squirmed. He was in her bedroom now, convincing himself she was safe. Her cheeks went up in flames.

She was mortified and impressed all at once that he was so concerned about her safety. Not all neighbors were willing to get involved. She never was. It wasn't anything personal, but she worked a lot, and had never really gotten to know the people living around her. Still, had she really been in trouble, she was glad to know there was someone who would help.

However, this situation was getting more embarrassing by the minute. She must have screamed in her sleep the way she had in the dream—in her dream about *him*—but there was no way she was admitting that. She supposed she could have claimed to have had a nightmare, but that wouldn't explain screaming his name. She wasn't exactly good at thinking on her feet in the middle of the night. She hoped that once he saw there was no one else in the house, he'd believe her that he'd heard a voice from some other source.

As he ran up the stairs, two at a time, she couldn't stop the rush of heat that flowed right down her spine to her core as she watched the muscles in his back flex, and she almost sighed over the perfect masculine shape of his rear. This man was even more handsome up close than he was in her dreams.

And, in her dreams, he had been perfect.

She shook her head, trying to clear her mind.

When he came back down, he gazed at her with curiosity and announced, "You seem to be here alone."

"Yes, I told you that."

"So why'd you scream?"

"No, I... It wasn't me. It must have been someone out on the street."

He shook his head, and then his eyes narrowed. She held her breath—what was he thinking?

"Do you talk in your sleep?"

It was as if her deepest secret had been revealed—which in a way it had—and she shook her head in denial.

"No. No one's ever said so, anyway."

"That has to be it. You must have been having a dream or something—do you remember?"

She crossed her arms defensively. "No, I don't. I was sleeping soundly until you came slamming at the door, demanding access to my home, threatening me with the police."

There. The best defense was a good offense, right?

"I thought you were in trouble. It was a pretty loud scream. Woke me out of a...a halfway decent sleep." His tone took on a tenor of astonishment. "I can't believe I was actually *sleeping,* and then you woke me up," he accused.

Her "good offense" strategy was suddenly on the ropes. "Listen, I don't know what it was, but I'd like to get back to sleep, and I assume you would, too."

They were standing about a foot apart, and all she had on was her robe and underwear. From what she could tell, all he had on were those jeans, and they weren't even zipped up all the way. She had to get him out of here before she almost swooned for crying out loud, feeling a surge of lust for him.

"I won't be able to get back to sleep."

"Why not?"

"I have chronic insomnia, and the nightly chatter hasn't been helping. I can't remember the last time I actually was sleeping as soundly as I was before your scream ended that."

"I. Didn't. Scream," she ground out between her teeth. "I don't talk all night. I don't talk in my sleep."

He ran a hand though sandy hair that was cut just the right length, and the gesture made her lose her train of thought for a moment. He had perfect arms. Nicely toned, muscular but not ridiculously so. They were manly arms. She didn't like the body-builder type, though she had no doubt he was strong. What on earth was she doing? She never—or rarely—ogled men like this.

"Listen, fine. You probably don't snore either, but—"

"Hey! I *don't* snore," she declared stoutly. This much she knew for sure.

"Fine. Still, on the very small, almost impossible chance that it's you, and that you don't realize it, could you do me a favor and close your window? Just in case."

The sarcasm of his tone put her off, but even if it hadn't, she wasn't about to change her habits for a stranger.

"No."

He blinked, standing there looking luscious and confused. Images of what he'd done to her earlier in her dream ran through her head like an X-rated movie, and she had to drop her gaze.

"*No?* Just like that?"

"It's hot."

"Use your AC."

"I don't have AC. There's only one small window unit in the house and it is too noisy. Why don't you close your window?"

"Why should I close my windows? You're the one screaming in the middle of the night."

She squared her jaw, supposing there was no reason not to tell the truth on this one. "Well, I'm not closing my window either—it's too hot."

"Fine."

"Fine."

She stifled a yawn, moving toward the door. "I don't know who you've been hearing at night, but people are out on the streets all the time—it was probably something out there."

"It's the same voice, saying the same things. In fact, it's your voice. I'm sure of it."

Sending him what she thought was the coldest look she could manage, she yanked open the door. "You're imagining things. Thanks for your concern, but I'd like to go back to bed."

He moved toward the door, shaking his head, and looking at her with a smile that had her knees buckling. Then she caught herself.

"I'm Rafe by the way. Rafe Moore," he said slowly, watching her closely as if to catch her up, and she hoped she gave nothing away.

"Good night, Mr. Moore."

She didn't offer her own name, and simply arched an eyebrow when he paused, waiting. Blowing out a breath, he nodded once, his lips tightening. She almost felt bad, but she didn't want to give him one ounce of encouragement.

"Call me Rafe. We're neighbors, after all. Good night."

Joy sank down by the door, utterly mortified. She'd held her own, but her dreams were obviously getting out of control.

Rafe wasn't the only one who wouldn't be going back to sleep tonight. In truth, she hated that she was contributing to his insomnia. He seemed nice, really, and was obviously a good guy, concerned about his neighbors, ready to help. He had a really cute accent, too….

Shaking away thoughts of her hunky neighbor, Joy couldn't risk going back to bed and the dreams starting up again. Not tonight. She didn't know why she was having them—she didn't even care for sex all that much. The few serious relationships she'd had had proved that. Of course, maybe if sex in reality was as terrific as it was in her unconscious, she'd revise her opinion, but in her experience, it hadn't been.

Eyeing the armchair and ottoman by the TV from her sitting position at the base of the door, she smiled. At least if she fell back into her lusty dreams no one would hear her from there.

3

RAFE SEARCHED THE CROWDED shelves of the garage in the corner where Warren kept his tools. He was looking for the laser level Warren had bragged about, but couldn't find it anywhere. His pal was not a slob, exactly, but he was a pack rat. Everything from old electrical tape to plastic bags with every spare part you could think of was crammed three-deep on the narrow shelves.

While Rafe hadn't been able to fall back asleep, the couple hours he'd managed had given him a boost of energy. He was intent on repainting the small kitchen for Warren and his bride—Rafe's version of a Christmas/wedding gift—but he had to put up the wainscoting first, and that required the level.

When he yanked free a box from an upper shelf, what he found was more interesting—an older model camcorder. He recognized it in an instant— Warren had gotten it for his eighteenth birthday, and they'd had a hell of a time with it.

They'd pestered Rafe's sisters particularly, fol-lowing them around with the camera until his eldest sister, Becky, had threatened to crush it under her car wheel if they didn't stop. Rafe was the fourth after three sisters, and though he loved them dearly, and they all had close relationships now, back then, he had been a major pain, as younger brothers aim to be.

Taking the camcorder out, Rafe saw there was a tape inside and for the heck of it, hit the play button, wondering if he might stumble across one of those old adventures. Within seconds, he was hitting the off button, a little shocked—Warren and his new wife had apparently been having a little fun with home movies back before they were married and had forgotten to remove the tape. Of course, they probably hadn't expected anyone to be rummaging through their garage, either.

His embarrassment at discovering the video of Warren in flagrante delicto was muted by the sudden brainstorm that hit him—this could be just what he needed to prove his case.

If his neighbor, name still unknown, wouldn't believe she was talking—and loudly—in her sleep, he could tape her and prove it. Then, she wouldn't be able to deny it was her.

He took the tape out. He could buy a new one and replace this one later, after he accomplished his purpose. There was a place downtown that converted old tapes to compact discs. If he went to the local hardware store now, he could buy a new tape and a level to work on the kitchen.

However, grabbing Warren's keys and heading out to the car—which always stayed in the driveway because the garage was far too packed with everything for it to fit—Rafe was distracted by an older woman teetering on a ladder across the street, hanging some Christmas lights. He jogged over, looking up and calling out, "Hello. That ladder seems a little rickety—could I give you a hand with those lights?"

The woman suspiciously looked down at him. "Who are you?"

He smiled. She reminded him a lot of his grandmother, whom he especially missed at Christmas. This woman seemed tough and independent as well; Rafe recognized the look.

"Rafe Moore, ma'am, at your service. I'm watching over Warren and Trudy's house while they're on their honeymoon."

"Oh, I have seen you. Warren, he's a good boy."

Watching her twist around on the ladder Rafe got nervous.

"If you would like, I could give you a hand with those lights. That ladder doesn't seem too stable. Warren has a good one in the garage. Why don't you come down and let me go get it?"

She smiled. "That would be wonderful."

Rafe moved forward, holding the ladder firmly as she started to step down, relieved he'd come outside when he had—if she'd fallen, it could have been serious, even from only six feet up. On the job, he'd frequently been called for older people who'd taken simple falls in their own houses, falls that had caused their deaths in some cases.

"What's your name, ma'am?"

"Oh, sorry, I'm Bessie Woods." She lowered herself slowly. Finally with both feet on the ground, she smiled up at Rafe, shaking her head at the ladder. "My husband passed on last spring. I didn't really plan to do much for the holiday. My family is worried and doesn't want me alone, so I just found out they're all coming here next week to spend a few days before Christmas. I'll go home with them for the New Year. I couldn't have the grandkids showing up with not a single Christmas light on the house."

She sounded a little grumpy. Rafe nodded, straightening the ladder, silently cheering her family for not abandoning their matriarch. She might not think she wanted the Christmas cheer and the company, but she'd be happier for it once everyone was around. The holidays were so hard for people who'd lost loved ones.

"Well, let's see what we can do about that."

She patted his arm and moved to the side so he could remove the ladder from where it leaned against the porch.

"We'll do that, and then you can come in and I'll make you some lunch." She didn't ask him, she told him, and he chuckled, not even bothering to argue. She looked up at the ladder.

"My Butch had that ladder for years. I was always yelling at him to get a new one or he'd break his neck. He never did, so I figured it must be good enough. Have to admit, though, I miss him every day. He used to take care of all these things, and…" Her voice faded, choking slightly, and Rafe's heart squeezed.

"How long were you married?"

"Fifty-seven years. Four children of our own, eleven grandkids, four great grands," she declared proudly, and Rafe was doing some quick math in his head.

"They're all coming for Christmas?" He looked at the small house, wondering how they'd fit.

She laughed. "Oh, no, just my youngest son's family—he lives the closest. The rest are scattered all over the country, though I see them often enough."

"Good to have a close family," he stated and realized for the first time that he actually was spending the first Christmas without his own. For some reason, his urge to escape the city, and the job, had blanked out that realization. He knew they'd understand—he'd missed several holidays when he'd had to work—but he'd never been away, completely, for the entire time. His sisters were busy, too—two of them were married; the other, a single lawyer, didn't seem to have much interest in marriage.

The four of them were always in and out of their parents' house, around the neighborhood, several times each week. None of them had ever considered leaving New York. It had been a shock for them when Rafe had announced he was heading to California, if only for a little more than a month. They'd been apprehensive, but supportive. They knew he was having problems, and he knew they were only a phone call away.

His eyes drifted over across the street, to his neighbor's house. Did she have family? People who cared? She appeared to be very alone. He felt a twinge of sympathy if that was the case.

"Where are you from, Rafe?" Bessie interrupted his thought.

"New York City."

"Ah, been there once. Too loud for me."

He laughed. "Bessie, what do you think about giving this ladder to the Goodwill—they'll repair it for someone else's use, and we can get you a sturdier stepping stool, though not for outside jobs.

"That sounds like a smart idea."

He looked over at the house next to Warren's where nothing was stirring.

"Can I ask you a question, Bessie?"

"Depends on what it is."

"Do you know the name of the woman across the street?"

She eyed him shrewdly. "That's Joy Clarke."

Joy, he thought, liking the name. He'd never known a Joy before.

"As far as I know, she's free as a bird," Bessie added knowingly. "Used to be a young man who visited pretty often, stayed some nights, if his car in the driveway is any indication, but that was a while ago. I didn't like him."

"You met?"

"No, but I didn't like how he came speeding up the street in his fancy car, the radio blasting. A real man doesn't need to draw attention to himself like that. She doesn't have much to do with anyone, from what I can tell. Probably has her reasons. She does come around collecting for charity now and then, but that's about it. I don't know much, but I do know you look like a man who's interested."

He pulled back. "No, no…not *that* way. There's a neighbor issue I need to talk to her about. Thought it would go easier if I knew her name, at least."

"Whatever you say."

It was clear Bessie wasn't buying his story, though he took her teasing in good humor. She hustled in to make the promised lunch—and to get more lights now that she had someone to help hang them. He went to get Warren's ladder, and wondered about Joy as he strung the lights. He noticed there wasn't a single holiday decoration in her yard.

Bessie served him one of the best bowls of chicken soup he'd ever had, even if it did make him sweat in the sweltering heat. Cooling off, relatively speaking, he sat on the step out front untangling some outdoor extension cords he'd found in Warren's garage. Joy emerged, looking as if she were going somewhere, keys in hand, and he decided to make another approach.

"Joy!" he called from across the street, setting the cords down and seeing she was surprised he knew her name. Crossing to meet her, he tried to ignore the way she tensed up when he neared.

"Sleeping in late on Saturday, huh?"

"I've been busy. How'd you know my name?"

"Bessie mentioned it."

"Bessie?"

He tilted his head toward the house across the street. "Bessie? The older lady who lives there, in the white house—just lost her husband?"

"Oh, yes. Right."

"I caught her trying to hang some Christmas lights and almost killing herself up on a ladder, so I'm helping her out. Wondered if you might want to come over and give us a hand? I could use someone on the ground to feed me the extension cord while I'm up on the roof. She makes a mean chicken soup."

"Sorry, I have to get going. I need to replace those groceries." She didn't bother hiding the stiff accusation in her tone. "And run some errands."

"Don't you ever relax?"

She was clearly taken aback. "I beg your pardon?"

"You're always so tense, so tight. You'll give yourself high blood pressure."

She arched an eyebrow. "I guess you're an expert, seeing as you're an EMT?"

He smiled. "You remembered."

"Impossible to forget conversations with men who storm in my door in the middle of the night."

"I hardly stormed your door. Though I probably would have if you hadn't answered."

"That's not comforting."

"I thought you were in trouble. I didn't know you were talking in your sleep," he added, his normally easygoing personality giving way to the urge to taunt her.

"I do not—never mind. I have to get going."

She stepped around him, and he let her go, shaking his head, but thanking her silently for the reminder that he still needed to go to the store to pick up that tape.

"I DON'T KNOW WHAT I'D DO without you, Joy— you're a total lifesaver."

"I had fun. The guys did most of the heavy lifting, and I can't wait to get back and get those chairs and dressers cleaned up—they're really gorgeous. You might want to consider selling them rather than using them—I think at least one is an antique."

They'd been moving some furniture donated by

an estate sale into the Second Chance shelter that Pam ran, and were taking time out for a late lunch. It had been a busy afternoon.

"Oh, I don't know. I kind of like the idea of replacing some of the crappier stuff, make the rooms nicer."

Joy grinned, relaxed for the first time in days as she sat with Pam Reynolds at the cheery sidewalk café, munching panini sandwiches and talking. Pam was the first friend she'd made in San Diego after she'd moved. The people who had owned Joy's house had left some old furniture, and Joy had been looking for a place to donate the stuff. She'd discovered a shelter a half mile away and when she'd called Pam, she'd not only taken Joy's donations, but had ended up talking her into doing some volunteer time at the shelter.

It was a great place. Second Chance did more than give people a meal or a cot for the night; Pam was really trying to change people's lives. The shelter housed up to twelve residents at a time. The men came from all walks of life, but they all wanted a second chance, and that was what she gave them. Pam had arrangements with local colleges, employers, businesses, high schools, doctors…. Whatever it took to give a break to those who were willing to work for it.

Joy had been so inspired by the project that she'd become a regular volunteer and supporter. Even when she was involved in the most menial tasks, Joy

was doing something real, something worthwhile.
She was contributing to people's lives. She spent a
lot of her weekend and weeknight time at the shelter,
helping out how she could, but also visiting with
Pam. They'd become close friends over the years.
Though Pam was about ten years older than Joy, the
age difference meant nothing to their friendship.

A San Diego native, Pam hardly looked her age
either; her curly hair, almost black, framed skin
kissed by the California sun. Pam's family lived in
an exclusive neighborhood northeast of the city,
and she'd been born into privilege that no one would
imagine given her no-nonsense clothes, almost
always jeans and T-shirts. She was pretty, but didn't
bother with makeup; she almost didn't need to. Joy
envied her strong features and flawless skin.

"Any chance you can cover me tonight for a few
hours?" Pam asked tentatively and then waved her
hand. "Never mind. You've been working all day,
and it's Saturday night."

"You have a hot date?" Joy teased.

Then the most amazing thing happened: Pam's
beautiful skin turned beet-red. Joy's jaw dropped.

"You do! You're seeing him again, aren't you, this
mystery man you've been stealing away with...."

"Oh stop that—we're not 'stealing away'
anywhere. It's simply a Saturday night out."

"With the same guy?"

Pam seemed very tense, and Joy didn't get it.

They usually talked about everything, including men, but on the topic of her love life, Pam was unusually silent. Joy didn't push, but it was the single snag in their friendship that she worried about; why wouldn't Pam confide in her? Wasn't that what best friends did? Joy told Pam everything, not that there was much to tell—she'd dated some guys from work, but nothing much ever came of it.

"Sorry, I didn't mean to push. I just want you to know you can talk to me if you need to."

Pam smiled. "I know that. I will tell you about him, once I know how it's all going to work out."

"It's been going on for a while—you guys getting serious? Wait—sorry—I didn't ask that," Joy said, holding her hand up, and they laughed. "If you want a night off, I can cover for you. I don't have any plans tonight," Joy offered.

"I wish you did." Pam made the comment offhandedly as she polished off the last of her salad.

"What's that supposed to mean?"

Pam sighed, pushing her plate back. "Joy, you're a jewel and I'm so thankful we met I can't tell you. It just seems like you don't do anything but work and volunteer at the shelter. It's not healthy."

"I do plenty of other things."

"Like what? I think you've only been out on a dozen dates in the entire six years I've known you."

"I date now and then, but I can't seem to meet anyone who catches my interest. They're all so…I don't know, they're just not guys I want to go out with more than once or twice."

"Maybe because you worked with most of them and you ended up talking shop most of the time. You should be fishing in different oceans. Find someone new, with a different job, different interests?"

"Maybe. I don't know, Pam. I've tried the whole dating thing, but I don't seem to have the same wiring as other women."

"Meaning?"

"You know. I've told you." Joy lowered her voice and leaned across the table. "I'm no good at any of it. Dating, men, sex...I never have been."

"You're being too tough on yourself. You just haven't met the right guy."

Joy pushed her own sandwich away, unfinished, and met Pam's eyes. "You don't want to talk about your love life, I don't see why mine has to be under the microscope."

"Now stop being like that. I'm your friend. I want what's best for you. I told you, I'll tell you everything soon, but for now, I want to hear if you've met anyone new."

"Not really, I mean... Well," she hedged, thinking of her sexy neighbor.

"C'mon, I know there's some dirt you're not telling me. Fess up."

Joy sighed and relented. "I, apparently, talk in

my sleep. Loudly and clearly," she added with sarcastic gusto.

"What does that have to do with—wait—is this something a man told you? Someone who might have spent the night, perhaps?"

"Yes, no—I mean, not exactly."

"You only had a soda with lunch, right?" Pam teased, and Joy stuck out her tongue at her.

"It's complicated."

"It always is. Do you always talk in your sleep?"

"I'm not sure, but…"

Fighting a strangling sense of mortification, Joy went on to tell Pam about the dreams—and her sexy neighbor's visit in the middle of the night. She hoped for some sympathy, but by the time she was done relating the tale, Pam was smiling broadly, and…laughing.

"This isn't funny." Joy wrapped her arms around her middle and became mulish, not enjoying her friend's amusement at her expense.

"I'm sorry, honey, but it kinda is. I mean, you've been losing sleep dreaming sexy dreams about this guy, and he's hearing it through his window. He's getting a blow-by-blow, er, you know what I mean. Now he shows up at your door, your knight in shining armor? Ready to take on the guy who made you scream—and that happens to have been *him,* at least in your dream? No, this is *very* funny. It's exactly what you need."

"You're losing your mind. No one needs this. I'm exhausted, I forgot a meeting the other day, and Ken was completely pissed. I'm up for that promotion, and that didn't help. I do not need another guy in my life right now."

"Maybe not in your life, but you could definitely use one in your bed. There is a difference. Is this new guy hot?"

Joy made a face. "Very. He seems like a nice enough guy, too—he did come over to 'rescue' me when he thought I was in trouble. He was helping the older lady across the street with her Christmas decorations. I think I heard him working on Warren's, my neighbor's, house."

"A real live Boy Scout."

"Would make sense. He's an EMT. Used to saving people."

"Sounds like he's always prepared," Pam added naughtily, and Joy couldn't resist laughing, her bad mood melting away as she joined in the joke.

"He did do a good job with tying knots in my dream."

The two women dissolved in laughter.

"I think you should go for it."

"Go for what?"

"He heard you talking—and we can only imagine what you're saying—and he's coming around, trying to strike up conversations, hoping to save you from dastardly deeds…checking to see if you're attached. He's *interested,* Joy. So be interested back. Have a fling. Give yourself a hottie for Christmas."

Heat invaded Joy's face. "No way. Just because I'm having these dreams, that doesn't translate into reality."

Pam shoved her chair back and stood, leaving a tip on the table. "Maybe it should. He sounds like a perfect man—hot, willing and temporary. If you're doing him instead of dreaming about him, maybe you'll actually get some sleep. In fact, scratch tonight—I want you to get some rest."

"Please, keep your date. I'm fine, and I love being a part of what you do," Joy said with sincere emotion in her voice, trying to avoid the temptation to think too much about Pam's idea.

"I do, too, in spite of the problems lately. We lost a major source of funding last week. All the businesses are strapping down the coffers with the economy in the shape it is. They have less to give, even at this time of year, and you know this is when we count on receiving our big donations."

"Is it serious? I can't imagine this place closing—it's too valuable to the community."

"No, we won't close, but we might lose some essential resources if I can't pull something together."

"I guess asking your folks…?"

Pam shook her head resolutely. "No. They never approved of me doing this. While we manage to have a halfway decent relationship, there's no way I would ask them for money, and they wouldn't give it anyway."

Joy's heart went out to her friend. "I'll do whatever I can to help, Pam."

"You're a sweetheart, Joy. I wish I could afford to put you on as paying staff at Second Chance for all the work you do, but it's not possible at this point."

"I don't need the money—that's why I have a job. I'll pound the pavement, do whatever I can to help you get this place in the black."

Joy teared up. She didn't know why this was affecting her so strongly.

"Thanks, I'll take you up on that. I hope you'll also think about doing whatever you need for yourself, as well. Give yourself a gift."

Joy rolled her eyes, realizing Pam was back on their previous topic.

"I promise I'll think about it," she said, knowing that she likely wasn't going to be thinking about anything else.

4

EARLY MONDAY MORNING, Rafe slipped the disk he'd had converted from the camcorder tape into a paper bag and rolled down the top of the bag with determination. He'd leave it for her with a note. She'd find and listen to it. Then there would be no denying that she was not only sleep-talking, but she was dreaming about him.

Why she would be, he had no idea. Joy was pretty, and he'd admit she wasn't hard to look at, but she hardly seemed interested—in fact, she seemed the direct opposite of interested. Yet, she had screamed his name in her sleep. He was sure of it. He'd tried to replay it a thousand times, wondering if he misheard or imagined it, but the next night had told the truth—she'd done it again, and he'd gotten the evidence.

He eyed the bag, thoughts simmering in his brain. His major goal was to win—to prove to her that he was right, and that he wasn't just harassing her. Her attitude toward him all but made him sound like a liar or a perve, and he didn't like either one.

Still, there were other possibilities. What if she dropped the argument, and apologized? What if she admitted the truth? What if she really was attracted to him—that would explain the nighttime fantasies, right? Question was, was he interested back? Maybe. It had been a long time since he'd had sex, or had even been in the mood. When Joy Clarke was in dream mode, her sexy talk got him going, and he might be willing to explore that, if the circumstances were right.

A zing of interest worked through him, unexpected, but welcome. This kind of thing was exactly what vacations were for.

He finished the note and smiled. All set. He didn't have any plans for today, so he'd hang out here, work on the house and see what happened. Peering out the window, he saw her car in the front drive—she hadn't left for work yet. Good.

Quickly darting out the door and across the short yard, he left the package on her step, inside the screen door so she wouldn't miss it.

He thought he heard her singing some top-forty song through the open screen, her voice becoming slightly louder, definitely off-key. Cute.

She was walking toward the front door. After running back to his own porch, he ducked behind a tall plant, watching her come outside, notice the package. She picked it up and looked around, pausing for a moment; he swore she was looking right at him, but she couldn't possibly see him through the thick foliage.

She opened the envelope, read the note with a roll of her eyes and shoved the disk into her bag. *Score!*

Smugly satisfied that she would be stopping by later to apologize and imagining how graciously he'd accept, Rafe thought he might invite her out to get a bite to eat. From there, the possibilities were endless.

IT HAD BEEN A COMPLETELY crappy morning.

Joy slid her fingers through her hair as she worked on news spots for the recall follow-ups and knew her mind wasn't on it. She kept making stupid spelling errors as she composed an e-mail form response to all the angry customers writing the company. She looked at what she'd written in a fit of pique:

Dear Valued Carr Toys Customer:
We at Carr Toys value your business and continued patronage. As complaints go, the wheels falling off a toy is not an earth-shattering problem, so please get over it and stop bothering me. I haven't had a decent night's sleep in weeks, and I'm really getting tired of your constant complaints about such a trivial issue. Have a nice day, and we hope you'll continue to shop Carr Toys.

Yeah, that would probably need to be heavily revised.

"Problem?"

Ken, the PR director, peeked in her office door, and pasting on a smile, she shook her head.

"No, no problem. I've been working on the latest e-mail response to the Toddler Tank complaints."

"Didn't I tell you? Barb's handling that since she was in that meeting you missed."

The slight note of censure was there, and Joy hated herself for being unnerved by it.

"I'm sorry, Ken. It won't happen again."

He stepped inside her door, looking down at the folders in his hand, then back at her.

"Joy, you've been acting strangely lately. You should take a break. You've got a lot of vacation time piled up."

"Ken, I'll get back on my game. I have no desire for time off. I wouldn't know what to do with myself." She laughed lightly, hoping he was buying it. "I live for my work."

Her boss eyed her speculatively, as if he were about to say something, and then nodded.

"Okay, if you say so. I'd rather have you take some time off than not be able to give one hundred percent."

As if she didn't usually give one hundred and twenty? Wasn't she due an eighty-percent day now and then? She nearly had to bite her tongue to stop from reminding him that she'd missed one meeting—one, in the entire time she'd worked there. Exhausted, she'd overslept and hadn't made it in until noon. Yes, that was bad, but it wasn't as if she made a habit of it.

"Gotcha. No problem." She forced a smile.

When he was gone, she sagged in her chair. It was lunchtime, but she had too much to do, and she wanted to catch up and get back in the swing. It had to be the loss of sleep; she'd never been so dragged out.

Maybe saying she lived for work was an overstatement, but she certainly wasn't as on top of things as she should be, and she wanted that promotion—more money, a bigger office, more job security, and her father would be very proud of her. Maybe once that was accomplished, she could take a vacation. After she'd established herself in the new position, of course.

Her stomach growled. She should see if there were any bagels left in the snack room down the hall. Grabbing her purse, she walked to the outer offices. Reaching inside it to find some change, her hands touched something unfamiliar. Then she remembered shoving the disk in there earlier.

Sitting down at a computer kiosk, she heard muted voices behind her and turned. The representatives of some new potential distributors were congregating outside Ken's office, getting ready to leave for lunch.

She glanced at the masculine scrawl on the plain white paper, frowning. It was obviously from her neighbor—what was he up to? The note simply read: *Play this when you get a chance. Thanks, Rafe. PS: I'm flattered.*

It was mysterious and annoying, and she flipped the shiny disk out of its package and slid it into the computer in front of her. What could her neighbor be up to now? Why couldn't he just leave her alone? Still, curiosity got the better of her. He said he was flattered—flattered about what?

Squinting, it appeared to be a video, though not a very clear one. There was no image, only a dark smudge that looked like some kind of night shot, and the picture wasn't good at all, but the sound was exceedingly clear.

"Oh, God, yes...there...harder..."

The sultry voice filled the room, and Joy sat back in total shock—it sounded like *her.*

"You're so hard.... Rafe, I need you inside me...."

Realizing it *was* her, she sprang furiously into action, hitting the keyboard frantically and trying to shut the damned thing off, but somehow, due to the magic of computer technology and recalcitrant fingers, she ended up turning the volume up even louder instead. The room was ringing with moans and sighs. The sound triggered a memory, and she knew exactly what was coming next.

"Oh, no! Stop! I said stop!" She yelled at the console, hitting the button on the little disk slot repeatedly, trying to extricate the disk before it was too late.

Finally the slot popped open, and she removed the disk with shaking fingers, thankfully cutting short some of the more graphic descriptions of how much she loved Rafe's…equipment.

My God, she thought, totally mortified. She'd never even thought half of the words she'd heard coming out of her mouth, let alone *said* them.

Disk in hand, she didn't look up for a few minutes, afraid of what she might find. When she did, her first reaction was gratitude that most of the people had left for lunch. However, the few lingering workers—including one freshman college intern—were all staring at her.

Words of profuse apology forming on her lips, she recalled the distributors and closed her eyes in mortal agony. The sound of someone clapping loudly startled everyone back to life. A sick sense of dread punched her in the gut. She turned to find the men all staring at her, too, some smiling widely. Ken looked horrified.

Unable to process what had just happened, Joy fumbled the disk back into her purse and headed for her office. Slamming the door behind her, she leaned against her desk, trying to catch her breath, but finding it difficult. Ken came in behind her.

"What the hell was that?" Then he backed off, looking at her more closely. "Joy—what happened? Are you going to faint?"

Joy wasn't sure, actually—she'd never fainted in

her life, but she was tempted to give it a shot. The black world of unconsciousness was pretty appealing right now.

"I d-don't know," she panted, trying to get hold of her panicked breathing.

"How can you not know?"

"I don't know," she bit out. "Someone left me that disk and I didn't know what was on it." She could at least tell the truth about that much. Her PR instincts kicked in. She had to find a way to make this better.

"You should call security."

"No, no. I think I know who it was. I'll handle it. It was a joke, I'm sure."

"A pretty sick joke. I'll support you in placing a formal complaint against whoever gave it to you."

"No. I mean, it wasn't anyone here—it was at home. I found it in my mailbox."

Ken stood gaping, unsure what to say. Obviously he hadn't equated the voice on the recording with her, which was no surprise. When people thought of her, they didn't exactly think "sex kitten," and her normal voice was nothing like the sultry, sexy voice on the recording. Even she had trouble believing it was her, but it was. No need for Ken to know that, though.

"Ken, please, I'm okay. You have people waiting," she reminded him. She just had to get him out of there.

"Shit, yeah. I'll tell them it was a bad joke, and we're handling it."

"That's good. That's about right. Extend my deepest apologies."

"I'll do that." He looked at her for one moment longer, and she started messing with the folders on her desk, waiting until he walked back out the door.

Crisis averted, hopefully. Still, it was akin to when the jury heard evidence that they weren't supposed to—someone could tell them to erase it, but she knew this would become part of office lore, and remain on Ken's mind for a while. She was going to have to kick butt on her presentation to get that promotion.

Armed with that resolve, Joy tried to get back to work. Her concentration lasted about five minutes.

How could he have done this? Her neighbor seemed like such a nice guy, but apparently he was a big pervert who taped women in their sleep.

Well, okay, maybe not a pervert, she admitted grudgingly. She supposed she had pushed him into proving his point, since she wouldn't cowboy up about the sleep-talking. Yet what he'd done was wrong, and intrusive, and it had given her some bad moments at work. She was going to get through this afternoon and then she planned on making her neighbor her first order of business when she got home.

RAFE WAS HAVING a great day—one of the best he'd had in a long while. After a relaxing morning run, he'd finished up a few projects. He wondered what

Joy was thinking as she listened to his video. Sure she'd grouse about being proved wrong in her denials of sleep-talking, but he hoped she'd be good-natured about it.

In the late afternoon he decided to wash Warren's car. Several kids were playing football in the street. When the ball was tossed into his driveway, he pretended not to notice, but then turned the hose on the kid who bravely came after the ball. A frenzied water fight ensued. The kids abandoned their game in search of supersoaking water pistols, camping out behind the bushes, making sneak attacks as they plotted to get the best of him.

Though he adored his sisters, Rafe always loved the horseplay with his male buddies that he didn't get at home. The kids' eyes shone with delight when he blasted them with the hose. Kids loved water, and they loved play-combat, and that was the same no matter what coast you were on.

When he heard a sound behind him, he growled playfully and swung around. Gripping the trigger on the nozzle, he hosed the figure standing on the other side of the driveway—but it wasn't one of the kids, and he released the hose trigger immediately, the jet stream of water flagging to a drizzle. Too late.

"Oh, shit…Joy, I'm so sorry…." He heard the chuckles and catcalls of young boys behind him as they delighted in his mistake. "I thought you were one of the kids…. You know, we don't always think in the heat of battle."

She stared at him silently, her lips pressed tightly together, her eyes cool—no, make that frosty. She was soaked from the blast; water was dripping down her cheeks.

"Are you okay? I, uh, didn't see you there."

She choked out a little laugh, one that didn't sound humorous—this woman looked as if she was teetering on the edge. What he knew from growing up in a house with three sisters was that her black cloud of temper was centered on him, and it was about far more than getting soaked with a hose. His mind zipped to the tape and he intuited that it might not have gone over as well as he'd hoped.

A few silly comments were still floating around the yard, and he waved his hand behind him, shooing the kids away. They complied, groaning about their fun ending, but Rafe was focused only on Joy and how she was continuing to glare at him.

"How could you?" she finally said, her voice tight and low.

"I told you, I didn't know it was you…."

"You *know* that's not what I mean. This—" she looked down at her sopping-wet suit before continuing "—is adding insult to injury. What were you hoping to accomplish? Embarrass me? Get me fired? Is this some kind of sick revenge for your sleep problems?"

He frowned, dropping the hose and stepping forward. "Revenge? For what? What are you talking about—why did you get fired?"

"I didn't get fired, but no thanks to you and your stupid...that awful...that..."

She couldn't seem to say the words. Much to his dismay, she choked back a sound that was half sob, half moan, which only seemed to add to her embarrassment as she lifted her hands to her face, her shoulders starting to quake.

"Oh, no! Joy—you played that at *work?*"

He thought back, remembering how she'd popped the disk in her bag. Never in his wildest imagination had he thought she'd play it anywhere public. He looked up—she made next to no sound, holding it all in, but her stiff shoulders hunched and he knew she was deeply upset. It struck him that what he'd done had been thoughtless, and he'd been so smug about it all day. He was ashamed about that; what had seemed like a good idea now appeared so stupid. Taking a step forward, he started to speak, and when she lowered her hands, her eyes were blazing.

"Yes, I took it to work, you son of a bitch! I didn't know what it was. I didn't know some low-down Peeping Tom had videotaped me sleeping— what are you, some kind of sicko?"

Low-down? Peeping Tom?

"Now hold on just one second—I never intended for you to go and—"

"Oh, so now this is *my* fault?" She wiped the tears from her eyes furiously, and he didn't know what to say. This wasn't exactly the end he'd imagined.

"No, but I didn't know what else to do, you were being so stubborn. You were all but accusing me of harassing you, and you were calling my name in your sleep, so I felt like I had to do something. I didn't know how else to get you to believe me."

"Why? Why did you have to do this? Who cares if I sleep-talk, even if it is about you! That's an accident, I don't know why I'm dreaming about you, it just started, it's just…I don't know what it is, but it's not a big deal. Believe me."

"Then why deny it so much? Why not just laugh it off?"

"It was embarrassing."

"I would have understood. I told you, it keeps me up at night. I know about sleep problems. I know how difficult it can be. But you know, for the last night or two, it kept me awake for completely different reasons."

"Because you wanted to tape me and prove you were right."

"In part. But also because you're turning me on, to be honest. I kind of like being in your dreams."

He thought a little flirting might help, but saw the disbelief and fury flash in her eyes. He took a step back as she took a step forward. *Bad move, Raphael.*

"How dare you?" she shrieked, then she turned

and stomped away from him, her shoes squeaking from the water, one heel sticking into the lawn and pulling from her foot altogether. She didn't even stop to pick it up. Her bad day was his fault, even if he'd never meant for it to happen that way.

"Dammit," he cursed under his breath. "Joy!" he called out, not wanting to leave things this way. "Hey, come back. Let's talk this out."

She kept walking to her car, grabbed her bag out, and didn't even cast a dirty look in his direction as she marched up the steps and through the front door.

"Well, that went badly," he said, slamming his hand down on the hood and then checking to make sure he hadn't dented Warren's car.

She'd said she hadn't gotten fired, but apparently someone had heard that tape who shouldn't have. He ran a hand over his face. While he'd never anticipated anything like that happening, he did share in the blame. After all, he'd made the tape and left it there, watched her take it to work. He'd guessed either she'd ignore it or listen to it when she got home, but that was no excuse. He'd screwed up big-time.

He had to find a way to make it up to her. He didn't know why, but he couldn't let things stay as they were. When she'd stood there, furious and crying, it had been all he could do not to cross the driveway and take her in his arms, wipe away her tears.

He didn't know why the impulse was so strong— if he felt guilty, if he was really attracted to her, or just responding to her sexy nighttime chat. Either way, he knew he had to try to make things right. Maybe earn another chance with her.

Most of his talents included life-saving techniques of some sort, and he'd never been accused of being the most romantic guy in the world. As he'd learned from the women in his household, when a guy screwed up this badly, comfort was a big necessity. With that thought, he knew exactly what to do.

JOY LEFT HER SOAKED, wrinkled blue suit on the bathroom floor. Demoralized by the day and by breaking down in front of Rafe when she'd meant instead to be cool and intimidating, she stood in the shower relishing the feel of the hot water pounding down on her. In spite of the warm weather outside, the sweltering soak was good. Her muscles were more relaxed, and her headache had receded somewhat.

She reassured herself the office gossip would quickly pass. As soon as something new came along, this incident would be forgotten—that was how office environments worked. If she made herself scarce, she'd weather the storm. She wasn't used to being the subject of office gossip because she tried to be professional in every way. She'd always gotten along with everyone, and didn't make a spectacle of herself at parties or public events, and then today she'd done so in spades.

She closed her eyes as the thought triggered an awful reminder: the office Christmas party was next week, the day before they closed for the holiday.

Great. It was like never-ending torture. She always hated the Christmas party; the food was bad, everyone drank too much, and Ken always insisted everyone stay until the end to exchange their gifts.

She hadn't even picked up a gift for her "secret Santa" contribution, and she wasn't sure what to get. She'd pick up a gift certificate to one of the local stores or restaurants. It was a safe, neutral gift that someone might actually use—unlike the sensual massage kit for two that she'd somehow garnered the year before. It still sat boxed up in the closet.

Wrapped in a thick terry robe, she searched the kitchen, realizing she didn't have any ice cream or much junk food around at all, but neither did she want to go to the store, so she settled for a bowl of cereal. Plopping down in front of the television, she clicked through the channels, groaning as Christmas shows, Christmas music, Christmas ads appeared on every single one of them.

It was insanity. Couldn't they broadcast a show that wasn't about Christmas? There were millions of people like her, sane people who didn't celebrate the holiday.

She clicked off the television, opting to read for a while instead. She searched for the romance novel she'd been consuming in bits and chunks for what seemed to be forever, never sitting down with it long enough to get to the end. She needed a happy ending right now and was determined to enjoy the one between the pages.

The room darkened, and as she reached for the light by the side of the sofa, she blinked at the flash of red then green on the wall opposite where she sat. At first she thought it might be a fire engine, but the green flash killed that thought. Walking to her front window, she saw the house across the street blinking and flashing madly, twinkling its Christmas cheer right into her dark windows.

She couldn't escape. It was *everywhere.*

In the blinking red-and-green assault, she saw the shadow of a figure turn up her walk, heading to her porch. She frowned, squinting to see as the figure came closer.

"Unbelievable!" she huffed, sliding away from the window. There was no way she was dealing with this man again—ever.

The anticipated knock came, softly at first, then louder. He rang the bell, once, not giving up.

She stood still, silent, only breathing when he turned and she heard his footsteps walk away.

Her shoulders relaxed and she grabbed her book from the table, trying to escape the flashing lights by retreating to her bedroom. She'd cuddle up in bed and read, away from everyone. She took off her robe and crawled in under the cotton blanket, not bothering with a nightgown.

Relaxing, finally, she settled back to open her

book when some delectable aroma drifted through the window. Her stomach grumbled, clearly not satisfied with her bowl of cereal.

"Joy?"

She heard his voice and clutched the sheet, tugging it up close under her chin. She parted the curtains, peering through the crack—he was right there, right under her window. She turned off the light so he couldn't see her.

"Joy, I know you're in there. I want to talk—to apologize. Will you let me do that?"

She didn't say anything, obsessed with the fact that he was only a few feet away from where she lay stark naked underneath a sheet in her bed, and while she wanted to be angry, her nipples pebbled against the soft fabric, warmth invading the space between her legs at the sound of his voice—this time it wasn't in her dreams.

"What do you want?" she snapped, disturbed at her own physical response. "Go away."

"No, not until you let me apologize correctly. I made you something. Let me bring it over—you can't be going to bed yet, it's only seven."

"I'm tired. I had a hard day, as you know," she said accusingly.

"I know. Don't you even want to know what I made for you?"

She blew out a breath, gathering the sheet up double and yanking the curtain aside. There he was,

standing below her window like a beach-boy
Romeo with his sexy eyes and ruffled hair. However, he wasn't offering her a serenade or poetry.
Her eyes drifted down to the foil-covered dish in his
hands.

"What's that?"

So she was curious. It didn't mean anything.

"It's manicotti. Homemade."

"Really? By whom?"

"By me. My mother taught me, and she's been
known to acknowledge, though not in public, that
it might even be slightly tastier than her own."

She remained silent, not knowing how to respond.

"I made it for you, Joy. I know it's not enough to
make up for what happened today, but I hope it's a
start. Let me come in? I'll drop it off for you, apologize and leave. Okay?"

The seductive aroma of the pasta was her undoing—her stomach was listening to Rafe even if
she didn't want to.

"Okay. I'll meet you on the porch."

No way was she letting him step inside.

She yanked on a pair of jeans she had thrown
over a chair and grabbed a tank top, then headed for
the door. She could still smell the manicotti. If she
were a stronger woman, a less hungry woman,
maybe she could have resisted, but she hadn't had
homemade manicotti in, well…ever. Her father
hadn't had much time to cook, and she followed in

his footsteps in that way, too. Taking a deep breath, she opened the door.

She wasn't sure what made her knees weaker— the smell of the food or the image of Rafe standing there in jeans, a white T-shirt that said Little Italy in faded letters and oven mitts up to his elbows as he held out the hot pan. He slanted a charming smile that she found far too sexy, though his eyes communicated nothing but sincerity.

"It's hot. You got somewhere I can put this down?"

So much for not letting him inside.

"Uh, yeah. Here, follow me to the kitchen."

As she walked, she realized she hadn't thrown on a bra in her haste and she covered her chest with her arms, nodding to the butcher block near the stove. She had little counter space and made up for it with added pieces, the butcher block, the small table in the center with two chairs, though she rarely used both.

"You can set it there. It will be okay on the wood."

He did and stripped off the oven mitts as he did so, revealing strong, tanned forearms. All of her hunger signals were getting mixed up—did she want manicotti or the guy who'd made it?

Stop, she ordered herself, shifting from foot to foot as they stared at each other quietly. She knew she was supposed to say something, but she didn't.

"Okay, well, listen. I hope you enjoy it—it freezes well, so when it cools down, you can cut it up into portions and have dinner for a month. I just wanted to say I'm sorry—about the tape, and the hose, uh, mistake. I didn't mean any harm, and you know, I'll leave you alone now," he said with an air of finality and turned toward the doorway, grabbing his mitts as he went.

She stepped forward, unsure why, but words were coming out of her mouth before she could stop them. "Um, this is an awful lot of food—have you had dinner?"

He turned, his smile brighter, his eyes more hopeful. Dammit. He had gorgeous eyes, a velvet-brown that drew her in, fringed with the long, thick lashes men were so often unfairly graced with.

"Thanks—I am starving, but I wanted this to be a gift. You sure you want to share?"

He was offering her an out. But he had made her a nice dinner, and she'd invited him. So they'd share some food, make nice conversation, and her day would end on a better note than it had started.

"Yes, please, let me get the plates, and you can serve. I don't have any fancy kitchenware, but what I've got is in the drawer there," she babbled, pointing and then turning away in order to compose herself while she got some plates. She rarely had guests for dinner, meeting people out in restaurants instead.

"As long as we can lift out a few pieces, I think that's the basic requirement. My mom says the TV cooking shows have been great for gadget sales, but they make people think that working in a kitchen is more complicated than it needs to be."

She smiled, her spirit lightening as she reached into the cupboard.

"I know," she added, taking out two plates. "Same with the organizational experts—you know, the people who go on the morning shows and clean up someone's messy office by stacking all kinds of new bins and baskets and labeling everything? Like that does any good," she said as she turned back to where he carefully lifted the manicotti from the pan.

Her mouth literally watered while she watched the cheese stretch as he put a large helping on a plate.

"Exactly," he agreed.

The heady aroma nearly brought her to her knees, and she blanked her mind when she started to calculate calories. Fat content be damned.

"If people aren't organized in the first place, adding more buckets and shelves for them to put stuff in will only make the initial problems worse in the long run," he continued.

She stood holding both plates of manicotti, staring at him as if she was seeing him for the first time. Not as the guy who was bugging her about sleep-talking, not as the erotic lover of her dreams, and not as the idiot who'd almost gotten her in deep trouble at work.

She saw a nice, handsome guy with whom she was actually comfortable for more than five minutes at a time. Someone who didn't act as if she had to prove her worth or meet some invisible expectation. Someone who'd brought her dinner. Who had *made* her dinner.

"Are you okay?" he asked, breaking her out of her fugue. "Let me take those, they have to be getting heavy—you want to sit down in the other room or here?"

She blinked as he took the plates. "Here at the table is good. That smells so good I could cry," she said sincerely and then caught his eye as he put the plates down. His face had become far more serious suddenly, and the atmosphere shifted between them.

"I don't want to make you cry again, that's for sure, Joy. I couldn't be sorrier about the first time."

He sat, indicating that he wanted her to start first, his hands at his sides as she took a bite and closed her eyes in bliss.

"Let's not talk about that. This is so good I can't even begin to tell you."

He grinned. "Thanks. Mom would be pleased. Well, maybe not that I helped screw up your day, but that her cooking lessons worked."

"She must be a fabulous cook."

"Straight from heaven," he agreed, digging in to his own dinner.

"Are you an only child?"

"Nope, three sisters, and Mom insisted we all

learn to cook, and Dad insisted we all know our way around a toolbox and a car engine."

"Sounds like a great family."

"I love them, but I'm biased," he said, grinning.

She set her fork down, taking a breather and reaching for her glass of water, frowning as she looked at it. "You know, I think I have some wine in the other room—I'll get it. It was a gift, and I haven't had a chance to open it. Food this delicious deserves more than water to accompany it."

"Sounds good," he added, smiling as she stood to leave the room.

She walked away, weirdly light in her step— after such a terrible, horrible day, she was almost… happy. Reaching to retrieve the wine from the top of the cabinet where she'd set it six months before—she didn't often drink by herself—she didn't question why she was so happy, and returned to the kitchen, stopping short of the table.

"Oh…damn."

"What?"

"I don't have a corkscrew."

"No problem—do you have a toolbox?"

She eyed him warily. "Uh, sure. My dad gave me one when I bought the house."

"Nice thinking. Grab it and we'll have this open in a jiff."

She did and came back to watch him poise a pointy-looking tool over the cork, aiming with the hammer over the wooden handle. He smiled at her, full of mischief, and her heart somersaulted, just a little.

"Move back—in case I miss."

"Maybe we shouldn't—"

Before she could object, he'd brought the hammer down in three expert taps, never missing a beat, and she watched as he pushed the cork down into the wine, drew back and gently levered the sharp point of the tool from the floating cork. Then they were back at the table, finishing their meal and drinking a spicy pinot noir that had only a few bits of cork floating in the bottle.

"Rafe," she started, sitting back in her chair, stuffed and not sure how to broach the conversation. He looked at her curiously, but didn't speak, taking a sip from his glass. The memory of what his mouth felt like—in her dreams, anyway—made her lose her breath for a moment. What was going on?

She never reacted this way to men, even to men she liked. Joy never got the jitters, the quivers and goose bumps other women talked about—in fact, she didn't experience many of the things with men that other women talked about. It was her nature, and she'd come to accept it, but Rafe was throwing her off.

"I really appreciate this—the food and the company, and the apology, though you know, I've been superstressed at work lately. It wasn't your fault, not really—I don't know what possessed me to listen to that disk in the middle of the main office. I guess I didn't think, and that's my fault, not yours."

His eyes darkened. "I'm sorry for my part in it anyway. Are you in serious trouble?"

She shrugged. "I managed to save it at the last minute. I came up with an explanation that was more or less true, sorta." She smiled a little, and he smiled back. "I'm up for a promotion, and I don't know if it's going to happen. I deserve it, I've worked hard for it, but I've been so tired lately, and it's been hard keeping up with everything that's landing on my desk."

"What do you do?"

"Public relations for Carr Toys."

"Cool! You work for a toy company?"

"Yeah, I thought it would be cool, too. It's not. Carr is just another big business trying to make its bottom line. There are some really interesting departments, like the toy design or marketing, but my work involves a lot of pressure, arguing and such."

"How so?"

"I handle toy recalls and company-image issues. You know, like now, with the Toddler Tank, the truck?"

"I saw that story in the paper—that's you?"

"Well, yeah, I'm the lead on customer relations and media communications. It's been a disaster, the wheels falling off of the truck that every little boy wants for Christmas, wheels that present a potential choking hazard. Parents hate Carr toys, and I have to somehow make them happy—the parents and the company."

"That doesn't sound fun," he admitted with a frown. "I never really thought about what happened on the company end of one of those recalls."

"You mentioned you're an EMT, like for the fire department?" she asked, taking the focus away from herself. The wine was making her warm. She studied the slight sheen of perspiration on Rafe's brow, finding it sexy, and licked her lips unconsciously, the taste of wine and sauce still lingering there. She wondered if he tasted as he did in her dreams....

"Yeah, in New York City, for a hospital, not the NYFD. Best city in the world, no offense." He grinned again. "But the insomnia has been dogging me for months—I finally had to take a leave of absence when I almost crashed my ambulance. So, here I am, trying to get over it. Thought a vacation somewhere new, away from the job, might help."

She groaned. "Only to find a loud woman next door keeping you up all night...I'm so sorry. I wish there was something I could do about it. I keep having these dreams," she said emphatically and then remembered whom she was talking to— and exactly whom she was dreaming about—and stopped short.

"When did they start?" he prompted softly, but

the mood changed between them, crackling with sexual tension. She swallowed hard.

"I was having them for a while, but they were just fuzzy, indistinct, frustrating…. Then when you moved in, I saw you…. Suddenly they were about you. I don't know why."

He nodded, and her face turned even hotter, though it wasn't the wine anymore. She was incredibly embarrassed at what she was revealing—the wine was loosening her tongue a little too much, and she pushed the glass away.

"Hey, don't be embarrassed. I'm flattered, personally speaking, but on the other hand, somniloquy is a real sleep disorder."

"Som—what?"

"Somniloquy—talking in your sleep. I know what hell a sleepless night can be. Are you having any other problems, lost sleep, etcetera?"

She wanted to kiss him for understanding—or maybe she just wanted to kiss him, period—and nodded emphatically. "Yes, I'm exhausted. I sleep all night, or seem to, but I am dead tired in the morning."

"Your body is sleeping but your mind isn't—you're probably waking up more frequently than you realize, and lack of sleep will catch up with you."

"You know a lot about sleep."

"That's what happens when you don't get much of it—I've been through the grinder trying to solve my own disorder."

He was being so kind, and that he understood and was so sympathetic made everything far too intimate between them for some reason. She stood and took their plates to the sink, needing to get up and put some distance between them, but it didn't work. He stood and followed her with the remainder of the table's contents.

"Have you tried a sleep clinic, or taking pills?"

She grimaced, leaning against the sink. "I don't think pills will help me stop dreaming about you." She clapped a hand over her mouth too late, sputtering, "I mean, uh…"

He chuckled, reaching past her to turn on the faucet, filling the sink with soapy water. He was way too close, she observed, inhaling his masculine scent, but she didn't move away.

"I know what you mean," he said, leaning against the sink, facing her. "I guess the question is what can you—or we—do about it?"

RAFE WATCHED THE ROSES bloom in her cheeks again. He was fascinated with every little thing about this woman and far too turned on. He shifted slightly, crossing his legs casually and hoping he could mask the hard evidence of his interest as they stood contemplating each other by the sink.

"Joy?" he prompted as she managed to look everywhere around the kitchen but at him.

She stepped away from the counter briskly,

wiping her hands on a towel even though they hadn't actually done any of the dishes. Her expression and her smile were overly bright.

"Hey, thanks for the manicotti. Maybe you should take some home? It's a lot of food for one person."

Suddenly he wasn't aroused, but plenty confused.

"Am I being dismissed then?"

He knew he sounded ticked off and regretted it as he saw the flare of panic in her gaze. She set her hands on her hips, facing him.

"Listen, I don't want you getting the wrong idea—and I think you were."

He crossed his arms over his chest. "What wrong idea would that be?"

He didn't say another word and watched her wrestle with her own discomfort, trying to answer his question without answering it. She mumbled something and he leaned in. "Excuse me? Didn't quite catch that."

She glared at him. "I didn't want you thinking that I was coming on to you—you know, with the dream thing. They're only dreams. That's all."

It made him itch to find a way to show her how prim and proper she wasn't. Whether it was coming out in her dreams or not, he glimpsed the passionate woman who lived beneath the uptight facade. For some reason, beyond his own denied libido, he wanted to bring her out.

"Joy, maybe you need to loosen up. I know you

take your work seriously, and you have a lot of stress, but do you ever have any fun?"

She looked up, frowning. She hadn't expected that, he could tell.

"Of course I do. I have plenty of fun."

"Doing what?"

"I like to read and watch TV, when I'm not working. Sometimes I go to a movie, or go out. Walk on the beach."

"Do you do those things often?"

"When I can, like most people. Work takes up a lot of my time. You don't get promotions by working forty hours a week."

"You sound like you're good at your work, but sometimes people get too wrapped up in their work. I love being an EMT, but it's my job, not my life. I think knowing that is what allowed me to be good at it. Do you love PR?"

"You don't have to love your work to be good at it. I love being good at it."

"Why would you do something that doesn't make you happy?"

Her eyes widened. "Uh, because we're adults and we work, we pay bills, and do what's expected of us. Keeping my house makes me happy."

He blinked—the way she'd said it sounded like someone else talking, not her. He wondered where someone got the concept of work that Joy obviously clung to so strongly.

"Well, that's true, but you can be happy in the meantime."

She shoved her fingers through her hair, and he found himself wondering how soft those strands were.

She yawned. "I'm sorry, I'm tired. It's been a tough day and I have to be up early. Not all of us are on vacation, able to stay up to all hours debating the nature of life and happiness," she said sarcastically but without bite.

"Listen, I have an idea," he said, deciding to ignore the fact that she was withdrawing from him again.

"Does it include walking toward the door?"

He grinned, liking her smart-ass side, even if it was being directed at him at the moment.

"Eventually. You know, if you go to bed now you're only going to be screaming my name in an hour or so," he said teasingly.

"That's not funny."

"No, it's not, but I know a little something about sleep disorders, and maybe yours is caused by all this stress."

Her eyebrow quirked up in the sexiest way he'd ever observed. "Oh, and I suppose you'd like to help me relax?"

He took a step closer, close enough to catch the scent of her soap and shampoo. Her eyes widened, but she didn't look away as he responded.

"Yeah, actually. I'd like that. I have time, I like

you. I think you like me, even if you won't admit it. We could have some fun."

"Exactly what kind of fun are you talking about?"

He didn't bother hiding his attraction as he spoke. "Anything you'd be open to."

"So you did all this, tonight, just to come on to me," she accused, but he shook his head.

"No, I didn't. I promise. I'm honest enough with myself to know that I'm attracted to you—how could I not be? Look at you," he said. "You're a beautiful woman."

"Give me a break," she huffed.

"I'm serious—I haven't been able to get your hair out of my mind since I saw you by the car with the groceries, how you had it all wrapped up tight. Even now, it's pinned back, when you're here alone, at home. Don't you ever want to let it down?"

He tugged a random strand and it fell forward across her ear. He rubbed it between his fingers, and he went hard again. Her gaze was fixed on his, and her lips parted.

"I—I like my hair like this. It's out of my face," she said, her voice catching as she tucked the rogue strand back behind her ear.

He smiled. She wasn't unaffected by him, and that gave him the signal to push a little harder. He wanted her. Maybe it was her dreams that stoked his imagination, but he wanted to loosen her up.

"Joy," he said softly, moving a little closer. "Just let go for a minute."

Before she could stop him, he had tugged off the band that held her hair back, and watched the silky sheet of auburn fall forward, sweeping across her cheek, then back to settle along the gentle curve of her chin. He was entranced with the motion, and touched her hair again.

"Rafe." Her tone held objection, but she didn't step away.

Instead, she closed her eyes, as if she couldn't bear to watch as he slid the palm of his hand underneath the curtain of her hair and curled his fingers around the nape of her neck, pressing slightly before threading back out through her soft tresses. The strands felt like fine ribbons, and he swallowed hard, his hand trembling.

"It's like silk, or softer, actually," he said.

She hadn't opened her eyes, and he took advantage of the moment. He leaned in, stealing a kiss. She startled, and he murmured something, sounds, reassuring her. He darted his tongue out to taste her closed lips, asking for passage beyond. When she opened her mouth, he misinterpreted and took the plunge, moving in for a deeper taste, groaning as he drew her closer, only to find her hands planted between them pushing him back.

"Rafe, no…please." She was breathless, flushed, and it took a minute for his pulse to settle, her words cutting through the fog of passion that had enveloped him so quickly he was amazed.

"I'm sorry," he said, dropping his hands but not stepping back. He looked deep into the blue depths of her eyes. "What's wrong?"

The stiff mask she wore for the world slid back into place, and she wrapped her arms around her middle as if she were cold.

"I was trying to—I was going to say, you have to understand…this won't work. It shouldn't happen."

"Why not?"

He followed her gaze outside the kitchen window toward where the lights strung on Bessie's house blinked and twinkled merrily. The sight still seemed odd to him in the summerlike weather. Finally, Joy spoke, though she kept looking out the window, instead of at him.

"Because I don't like it."

"What? Kissing?"

"No. That…the lights. The decorations, the music, the gifts. Christmas."

"You don't like Christmas?"

"No, I don't."

He frowned. "Okay. Well, I don't think you're alone in that, but what does it have to do with us getting together?"

She aimed a cool, direct gaze at him. "It has to do with us because I don't feel any of it. I'm annoyed by all the clutter and the lights—all of it. As you observed, I hardly know my neighbors, and they don't know me. I don't like my job, particularly, but I like what it gets me. I don't do presents or cookies or carols, and I'm not really into casual sex, either, or sex in general, so you're barking up the wrong tree, okay? I'm not that type of woman."

She'd traveled a long distance in that little monologue, and while he didn't quite get the bit about her not liking Christmas, or why that mattered, the latter comment caught his attention.

"Why would you say you're not the type of woman who enjoys sex?"

She shrugged, trying to look nonchalant, but he could see the burden of past pain in her deliberately calm gaze.

"Believe me, I've gotten feedback on the issue, and I'm just not very…warm. I'm not a warm person."

"You're right," he agreed, garnering a flash of surprised hurt from her before adding, "You're not warm—you're *hot.* Everything about you is hot, and you've got me hot, as well. I hear you at night, and—"

"Those are *dreams,* Rafe—they're not *me.*"

"It is you. Maybe it's the real you trying to get out. Have you ever considered that?"

She looked absolutely miserable at the possibility, and he took a chance, moving closer to her again.

"Listen, Joy, I don't know why you have the picture of yourself that you do, and I agree, you've closed yourself off from some things in life—no, let me finish—I'm not criticizing, and I don't want to be your shrink. You have reasons for what you do and how you do it, and I'm not really about changing that. You're losing sleep, so am I. I'm here for a few weeks, and I like you. I think you might like me. Maybe we can have a little fun together."

"You mean sex."

"I mean fun. If that includes sex, great. I'd love the chance to show you how hot you are. How you affect me," he said honestly. That she could even believe she was a cold fish was beyond him.

"Thanks, but I don't need you to save me," she said stubbornly. He could have been offended, but instead he looked straight back at her, and while he didn't know where the words came from, he knew they were true.

"Who knows? Maybe I need you to save me."

6

"Hey—good work today," Ken said, popping his head in the office door and grinning. Joy had been up to her ears regarding the last-minute release of a new and improved Toddler Tank, which was being shipped out to families with recall certificates that very day, a full seven days before Christmas. Manufacturing had done triple-time fixing the problem, and the tide of negative feedback was starting to turn. It was costing the company a fortune, but it would pay off in the long run. Joy had been all over the media all day, making sure everyone knew what a good job her company had done.

"Thanks." She took the time to look up and smile back at Ken.

"Um, how's that other thing going—you know, with the problem you were having, whoever's leaving you those, uh, materials?"

She blushed, his comment taking a little of the shine off the moment. "It's fine—I made sure it was addressed last night," she said.

The relief on Ken's face was palpable. No doubt

he was glad he didn't have to deal with it internally. "That's good. Well, you really stayed on top of things today. I was impressed."

All was forgiven, and everyone was in a great mood with the great save they'd managed to make. This aspect of the job was much more gratifying than all the negativity she'd been wading through before.

"You've been at it all day—it's six—you heading out soon? I thought I could buy you a congratulations drink," Ken proposed.

"Six? Oh, crap—sorry, I mean, thanks for the offer on the drink, but can I take a rain check? I have somewhere to be, and I lost track of time."

"Hot date?"

Ken was happily married, so she knew he wasn't coming on to her. "No, volunteer work I do in the evenings."

"You're a wonder, Joy. Not everyone would work all day and then volunteer at night. Make sure that's noted on your employee profile."

"That's not necessary. It's something I do because I enjoy it."

"Still, can't hurt to keep building that résumé. Joy?"

"Yes?"

"You really did a great job on this recall—I'll be sure to make that known to the board when we're making the promotion decisions."

She smiled, nodding. "Thanks, Ken, I appreciate that."

She practically danced to the parking lot—she was back on track, and in line for the promotion. At the moment, she had to grab some dinner and get to Second Chance. She'd offered to do the night shift there and had her change of clothes in the backseat, ready to go.

When Pam had called that morning asking her to cover at the last minute because Rashid couldn't make it, she'd jumped at the chance, maybe a little too eagerly. There was the small—teensy, really—chance that she was avoiding going home since Rafe might be tempted to come over and see her. The events of the previous evening had been thrumming through her brain and her body all day long, and she didn't know what to think about it, except that she didn't want to think about it.

However, Rafe had been wrong about one thing: she hadn't gone to sleep and dreamed about him because she'd been up, tossing and turning and trying not to think about how he'd tenderly touched her face, the heat in his gaze, or the gentle kiss he'd offered—with the promise of so much more.

If she'd dared let herself fall asleep she would have spontaneously combusted, having been so close to him, his presence following her into sleep. So she'd stayed awake, his words echoing in her mind as she realized she didn't need to go to sleep to have Rafe Moore—he was offering himself to her on a silver platter. Maybe she was crazy, but it scared her to death.

In her dreams she was a different woman, uninhibited, sensual—not her ordinary, uptight self. She meant what she'd told him—she dated, sure, and she'd liked a few of the guys she'd seen over the years well enough to take things to their inevitable conclusion in the bedroom. She'd dealt with the sting of more than one breakup, as well. None of the men had said she was awful in bed or anything, but what else was a girl to think? She obviously didn't have the sex appeal she did in her dreams. Dream sex was usually more satisfying for her, too, sadly. Even so, she hoped it would cease soon—her sleep deprivation was wearing her out.

Rafe was interested in her because he'd heard that sexy version of herself, not the real Joy. Joy was willing but awkward, generally not knowing exactly how to respond to a man's touch. She didn't want to be like that, but even when she wanted to participate, she never felt natural or carried away by passion. It was a self-perpetuating problem that had converted a rather boring sex life into a bona fide dry spell. Rafe was offering to help her end it, but his interest was based on false information.

That was why she'd pushed him away—he had a fantasy of her and it was so far from reality that it could only lead to disappointment for both of them. Rafe might like her hair down, but it would take a lot more than freeing her hair to thaw out whatever made her so boring in bed. The one thing she was sure of was that she couldn't face seeing disappointment in her performance mirrored in yet another man's eyes.

Especially not in Rafe's hot-chocolate eyes.

She hoped he'd take the hint and back off. Better to nip this in the bud, she thought as she drove into the Second Chance parking lot.

Cheery multicultural holiday decorations were on display in the windows and on the lawn. People who stayed at the shelter came from varied backgrounds. There was a menorah in the window circled by Christmas lights. A Santa stood on the small scruffy patch of front lawn beside a makeshift manger. Joy smiled, realizing this was the only time looking at all the Christmas decorations hadn't made her wrinkle her nose.

Maybe it was because here the decorations meant something more than the suburban competition to outdo one's neighbors. Here, this little pastiche of holiday cheer represented hope...and home, if only for the moment. For people who lived here and were working so hard to improve their lives, this was a sign of their belief in something good. Bolstered, she got out of the car. She was avoiding Rafe, but even that couldn't dim her optimism as she walked through the doorway, looking forward to her evening.

"WOW—LOOK AT YOU!"

Pam spun around, surprised. She hadn't even

heard Joy walk up. She also wasn't decked out in her usual jeans, T-shirt and Padres cap with a pen stuck behind her ear.

"This looks okay?" Pam asked hesitantly, smoothing the sides of her deep green formfitting dress down for what must have been the fiftieth time, flashing looks in the mirror and then at Joy for reassurance. Pam's fortysomething curves were still holding up, and she didn't look half-bad, but she hadn't dressed up like this in such a long time. She just wasn't sure.

"Okay? You look amazing. I love your hair that way—that pretty little holly clip is a nice touch. That dress is to die for. I don't think I've ever seen you this dressed up—or this nervous."

Pam smoothed her dress yet again. "I have a date, but I'm thinking twice about it."

"Is this about your mystery man? You know, I promised not to push, but if he has you this nervous, he must be terrific, or is something wrong?" Joy prompted.

Pam knew she wasn't being fair, keeping her relationship a secret. Besides, tonight everything would be out in the open anyway, so she certainly should tell Joy, whom she considered her best friend. She was so afraid of recriminations, especially since Joy meant so much to her. What if when Pam told her, Joy thought she was a total skank? Still, she had to take that chance.

"He is…terrific. This is our first dress-up date, and I don't know. I had this event, a Christmas party with the local chamber of commerce, you know, because of all the business connections I have with the shelter, and so I go every year, and this time I thought, well, maybe I won't go alone. So I asked him."

Joy nodded approvingly. "Sounds like a good plan. But. Who. Is. He?" Joy insisted playfully, and Pam bit her lip, drawing up the courage to answer her question.

"It's Ted."

"Ted?" Joy repeated, her brow furrowed. Then her eyes went wide with realization. "*Our* Ted? Ted Ramsey?"

"Yeah, that's the one," Pam said, tensing as she mentally braced herself.

"Wow. I can see that—I mean, I didn't see it, but now it seems so obvious. You guys would be great together. How long have you two been, you know…?"

Pam sagged against the desk. "We had an immediate attraction—I knew it shouldn't happen, but we gave in after he'd been staying here about six months."

"You and Ted have been together for almost two years and no one knows? This is your first dress-up date?"

"Well, we were on and off—some long off periods while he got his life back on track, and we both knew it was against the rules. Can you imagine how it would look if anyone knew I was sleeping with one of our residents?"

"I guess I can see where you'd be concerned, but it's not like he's a child, or incapable of making his own decisions, Pam. You're two adults who are attracted to each other. What's wrong with that?"

Pam's eyes shone with tears and she tried to dab at them before she ruined her makeup, but she was losing the battle. "I was so worried you'd think I'd crossed the line," Pam said, sighing with relief.

"It sounds like you've been keeping it in for so long, you probably just let it build up in your mind—why would anyone care?"

"I run this place, and I love it. It's my life. The people who come here are adults, yes, and they have to take responsibility for their lives, but they're also disadvantaged with the odds against them, and I wouldn't want anyone thinking I took advantage or, you know, that anything…unsavory was going on here."

Pam tried to find words, but her face simply flamed hot. "I tried to stick to the rules, we both did. Flirtatious or sexual behavior here is very strictly prohibited for good reasons, as you know. But it was like every time we saw each other, or spoke to each other, we couldn't think about the rules."

Joy smiled a little. "You want my honest opinion?"

Pam nodded.

"I think it's really romantic. Ted's a great guy—

he was what? Around thirty-nine when he came here? He'd had a tough break that nearly ruined his life, but he didn't let it, and you helped him make it the rest of the way—but look at him now. I'm surprised I never saw it before. It makes total sense, since you spend most of your time here anyway. It's no different than meeting someone at work."

"I suppose," Pam agreed tentatively.

"He's been so happy. I guess I figured it was natural for him to be so jovial. He's gotten his life back together and he's almost completed his college degree—but I think you're the one who put the sparkle in his eyes."

Joy laughed and Pam blushed again, though she was also pleased that Joy hadn't reacted badly.

"Thanks. I can't tell you what a load off it is to be able to tell you."

"I was wondering what was going on, I have to be honest. I thought maybe you didn't trust me or something."

"How could you think that?" Pam was shocked. "I trust you completely. This was… Well, I don't know. I didn't know what to say. Ted and I swore we wouldn't tell anyone until we were both ready."

"So how come it took you so long to go out on a real date? I mean, I can understand why you'd want to keep things under wraps, but you could have gone out long before this, couldn't you?"

"Oh, we do, we go out all the time, but just the

two of us. But those were small, private dates, nothing fancy. Nothing with other people. You know, where people would know us."

"So that's what you're nervous about?"

"I don't know." Pam looked in the small mirror she had hanging over her desk, grabbing a tissue to fix her slightly smudged makeup. "I guess I'm worried what people will say."

"Like your parents? Do they know?"

Pam rolled her eyes. "No. Haven't hit that hurdle yet, but they're bound to have a coronary. After I rejected all the 'eligible' bachelors they wanted me to marry for all those years, I think they finally assumed I was probably gay, and were happy not to know if that was the case or not."

"I never understood why they don't support this cause—their picture is in the paper often enough in connection to other charity events."

"It's hard to explain. That's when they can donate large checks, not get their hands dirty. They wouldn't mind if I supported causes, they don't approve of my level of…involvement."

"I'd think they'd be proud of you."

"Well, we've maintained a truce about it over the years, since they could see I wasn't about to stop my work. My relationship with Ted will be the real test. I can't allow anything to threaten this place—we're already struggling enough. A harsh blow like someone saying I act inappropriately could be a disaster."

"I guess I can see that, though this is personal—it never interfered with the work you do, so it's really no one's business."

"Well, we'll see. Tonight is our first public event together. Ted wanted to wait until he was out on his own, and he's almost completely moved into the new place. We're going to move in together after the New Year."

"How wonderful!" Joy crossed the room and gave her a congratulatory hug, and Pam smiled, her happiness at the prospect shining through her concerns.

"Yeah, and he's been really instrumental in coming up with some good business strategies for Second Chance. He's as devoted to it as I am, you know, and I guess, I don't know…"

Pam was relieved when Joy seemed to read her mind.

"You don't know if you want that? This place is yours, and now you find you're sharing your whole life, including the shelter?"

"It's mostly that, yes, but I also want him to have his own thing."

"I can see what you mean, though. You've built this place. It is yours, but I can also see why he'd want to be involved, and use his talents to help you out."

"I want to make sure that he follows his own goals. He's worked hard to be where he is, and maybe he should go after his MBA or start his own business or do something…I can't quite figure out if this is really what he wants, or if he's only being…grateful."

"Even if he is, is there something wrong with that? I think it's sweet that he wants to be part of your life, and to help out. Ted hardly seems like the type not to go after what he wants—after all, he got you," Joy teased.

"There's a good point." Pam smiled, shaking her head. "I don't know—meeting here muddied the waters, I guess. We knew who we were when he was here, but now, well, some of the rules have changed. We're into a new stage of our relationship. I don't know how to separate it all out."

"You love him."

"Yeah, I do."

"Then you'll work it out."

"You're right, we will. Thanks. So how about you?"

"What about me?"

"Any news about the hottie next door?"

"Oh. I can't believe I forgot this—or I suppose I should thank you for helping me forget it, at least for a little while," Joy groused.

Pam listened to Joy's story about the tape, so engrossed that she forgot her own troubles.

"Oh, honey—that's terrible. Sounds like he made up for it, though."

"Yeah, he did, but I'm so foggy from not getting any sleep I can't seem to tell left from right anymore."

"Well," Pam said slyly, "I think we discussed that the solution to your sleep problem might be right next door."

"He said the same thing," Joy said, sighing.

"Okay, I have to go, so make this fast—what happened? Don't edit," she warned.

Pam was intrigued. She'd wished for Joy to meet someone wonderful for so long, and now it sounded as if she'd met someone truly different from the boring corporate types she usually dated. Maybe it was true that people in love wanted all their friends in relationships, too, but Pam truly wanted to see Joy happy. She worked hard and was a devoted friend. Over the years though, Pam had come to see that Joy held something back in her life. There was something deep inside she kept locked up, and Pam had always hoped the right man might come along with a key.

"After dinner, things got a little…heated. He kissed me, he said he wanted more, maybe."

"So what's the problem? He's cute, and you're available—go for it."

"Go for it? Of course I can't go for it—he's just some guy who's in town for a few weeks looking for some action."

Pam tilted her head to the side. "Yes? Exactly what do you see wrong with that scenario? A fling is ideal—you have some fun, don't take it all so seriously. You don't have to worry if this guy meets anyone's standards but your own—he's temporary. It's not like you'd be bringing him home to meet your parents."

Joy frowned, perplexed. "I guess I figure when I get involved with someone, it's for the long term, and I do tend to measure men by what my dad would think of them. I think that's natural. He raised me."

"You measure everything that way, Joy, and while your father is a good guy, maybe you need to start measuring things with your own stick. Including yourself. What do you want? What makes you happy?"

Joy frowned. "I—I'm not sure. I thought I was happy. I guess I haven't thought about it much."

"Well, think about it. Some rules are meant to be broken. Believe me, I know." Pam smiled.

"Speaking of which, when's Ted getting here?" Joy asked, not so subtly changing the subject.

"He's not—no one here knows about us yet, and I don't think they should until he's no longer living here, so we're meeting at the party."

"It must be hard, keeping it secret."

"It has been, especially from you—but I care about your opinion, and I was so afraid you would disapprove."

"Why would I? I love you and Ted."

"I know. I wish I'd told you sooner, but we thought it was better this way."

"That's fine. It probably added that whole forbidden-lust factor, huh?" Joy teased, laughing as Pam's cheeks stained red again.

"You're bad. Anyway, thanks for standing watch tonight."

"No problem."

As they walked out to the main room, Pam took a few bows and curtsies as she received compliments on her dress. Both women were surprised when Rashid, the night-shift staff, came in the front door.

"Rashid! I thought you weren't able to be here tonight?" Pam asked.

"I had my schedule wrong—I'm due at the warehouse tomorrow night, so I'm good for tonight. Sorry if it messed you up," Rashid said.

"I don't know how you do it all, Ras," Pam commented and Joy echoed the sentiment. Rashid ran the teen shelter across town and also worked a third shift in a home-improvement supply warehouse, on top of finishing his grad degree in social work. He'd spent his childhood on the streets, and Pam respected how he'd changed his life through sheer determination to do so. Growing up in the privileged environment that she had, where everything came so easily, she found it inspiring to know the people she did.

"If you still want the night off, Rashid, I'll stay. I was prepared to, anyway," Joy offered.

Rashid shook his head. "Thanks, but I'm good. I want to talk with some of the guys tonight."

Pam looked at Joy, grinning. "I guess that means

you get to go home early. Maybe check in on your neighbor, see what he's cooking tonight."

Joy glared, and Pam laughed, her friend's excuse to avoid her neighbor flying right out the window.

7

RAFE HUNG UP THE PHONE, deflated and lonely. First he'd called his parents, who were missing him, and his mother had done a primo job trying to get him back home for Christmas. It was hard for them to understand why he wanted to be so far away, that he needed to be far away from the job. If he was back in the city, all he'd be able to think about was work, and that wouldn't help him.

Of course, then he'd returned a call from Steve, the guy he'd been riding the ambulance with for the last three years. Steve's wife had just given birth to their second child, and Steve had called to share the good news. Rafe was happy for his bud, but the conversation inevitably had turned to work.

Rafe missed it the way he would miss one of his limbs. He'd started college thinking he wanted to be a doctor. In his junior year he'd volunteered as an EMT and was hooked. He'd worked his way up to being a registered paramedic, and he loved it. The rush, the speed, the immediacy of helping people when they most needed it—it all made his blood run and his heart beat.

Until he'd started having nightmares and losing sleep. Gradually, he'd found he was getting frazzled, not handling the stress as well, not processing the emotions that came with the job. Classic burnout, his colleagues had told him—it got everyone eventually, and he'd lasted longer than many.

He'd thought he could handle it, thought it would pass on its own, but when he'd realized his pride could have cost Steve's kids a father the night he'd nearly crashed the ambulance, Rafe knew he couldn't keep going. He couldn't do the job he loved, and he would never be able to do it again if he couldn't solve this problem.

The sleeping pills had side effects that could be as bad as not sleeping, so drugs were not really an option. So here he was, two thousand miles away from everything he knew, staring out Warren's window into a December evening that looked more like the Fourth of July.

Needing some air, he broke away from where he was sitting on the side of the bed and went out the front door, no destination in mind, just needing to get out. Standing out on Warren's front walk, he relaxed his breathing, chasing the stress from his mind as he started working through a series of stretches. The sun dipped and the lights on the houses around him clicked on.

As he leaned over, his eye landed on the single unlit spot on the street. Joy's house. The windows were dark, the car gone, not a creature was stirring in that lonely little house. He'd heard her car leave that morning—before the sun had come up, even though they'd been awake most of the night before. Where could she be now? Working late? Out with friends? Volunteering at the shelter she obviously loved so much? Avoiding him?

Why did he like Joy Clarke so much, exactly? He barely knew her.

Didn't matter; he couldn't keep his mind off her.

Straightening, he looked at the dark facade of her home again and contemplated her dislike of Christmas. She'd said she didn't like it—that the lights annoyed her—but maybe she needed someone to share it all with? He'd asked her to hook up with him, essentially, and she'd shied away. Maybe there was another way to reach her.

Jumping in his car, he made a quick trip to the local home-improvement warehouse. Since he'd been working on Warren's house, the staff recognized him. Several eager young female clerks helped him pick out decorations, and encouraged him when he told them his plan. As he drove home, the more he thought about it, the more determined he became.

Back at Warren's, he grabbed his ladder, brought it over to Joy's yard and got started. He'd have to work fast, as she could be home any second. The more he had done, the harder it would be for her to tell him to undo it. He smiled devilishly to himself.

An hour later, when he was up on the roof and nearly finished, he heard a car's motor and looked down, watching Joy pull into her driveway, stop, then drive forward the rest of the way.

He swung down over the edge back to the ladder and heard her car door slam.

"What the hell are you doing?"

He was prepared for her temper and turned around calmly, greeting her politely.

"Evening, Joy. Putting up some lights—you're the only house on the block without a single light on," he answered, nonplussed. "It's not a lot—a bit around the edge of the roof and corners—you won't even be able to see them from inside."

She glowered. "I don't want to see them at all— you have no right to have your way with my house!"

He couldn't help but grin at her phrasing—her house wasn't the only thing he wanted to have his way with.

"Stop smiling at me like that! I'm serious!" she said between clenched teeth.

"I know you are. I'll make you a deal. You help me finish putting up these lights, and we'll turn them on, and if you still don't like it, I'll take them down. Though I've been working on them for quite a while, so it may have to wait until tomorrow," he said with a sigh.

"It's been a long day, Rafe…."

"All the more reason for you to do something fun at the end of it. With me," he said, bending to hand her a coil of wire and lights. "Hold these and feed them up to me as I clip them, okay? This is the last bunch."

She sputtered for a moment, but he hopped back up the ladder, not giving her a chance to object. Sure enough, she walked to the edge and fed him the lights as he neatly clipped them into place.

"Did you end up working late?" he inquired casually, filling the silence between them.

"No. I went by the shelter."

"Hmm," was all he said, earning another curious look.

"What's that supposed to mean?"

"I thought maybe you were trying to wait me out and come home late, so I might get the hint that you're not interested."

"It didn't work, apparently."

He looked down, catching her eye unabashedly. "That's because I know it's not true. Just like I know you're not going to hate these lights, even though you're going to want to."

"You're pretty cocky for a guy I just met." The comment was dry, but not angry, so he figured he was making progress.

"I have a good sense of people. I had to in my line of work."

"You're wrong about the lights—you're going to end up taking them all down again."

He gave himself a mental high five as he realized she hadn't denied her interest in *him*.

"Could be. Maybe you need to look at having these lights up here from a different perspective," he offered, hanging the final string and making his way back to the ground.

"How so?"

"Plug that in over there, and we'll see."

She shook her head but did go to the corner of the house to plug in the cord. Immediately, her house was outlined in soft white and red lights.

"I liked the red and white—like peppermint," he said, standing back to admire his work.

"I guess. What did you mean, a different perspective?" she asked finally.

"Well, I wanted to do this for you. However, even if you don't enjoy Christmas decorations so much, there's a neighborhood of people here who will. The kids, especially. I used to walk the streets back home and look at all the lights when I was a kid." He was quiet for a moment, letting his words sink in. Joy obviously had a sense of social purpose or she wouldn't volunteer at the shelter. He figured all he had to do was appeal to that part of her.

"Now, when they walk by your house, it will lift their spirits. It makes you part of the neighborhood, part of the community. When Bessie looks out her front window, she'll see your lights the same way you see hers. It'll make her smile, and you know, she needs that. The holidays are difficult for people who've lost loved ones."

He could tell from her quiet contemplation of the lights that he'd made her reconsider. Joy obviously cared about others—maybe more than she cared about herself.

"If you think I can't see how you're being so clever with manipulating me, think again," she said tartly. "I guess they're pretty. It's not too much."

"So they can stay up?"

"Yeah, I suppose."

Cheerful about his victory, he grabbed her and kissed her, not allowing her time to put up her defenses. Instead, much to his surprise, she put her hands around the back of his neck, tentatively at first, and then with more commitment as she opened her lips and let him explore further.

Delighted to comply, he tasted her thoroughly, rubbing his tongue along the contours of hers, teasing every satin inch of her mouth. He eased his arms around her, taking in the graceful sway of her lower back, the curves below, and kept himself busy memorizing every nuance of her mouth.

She sighed against his lips, kissed him back gently, but mostly allowed him to find his way around her, and he didn't mind that one bit. Though when he drew back and gazed at her face, taking in flushed cheeks and her lowered eyelids, he couldn't help but wonder what had changed.

"I guess you really liked the lights more than you thought you would," he said teasingly and saw a hint of a smile at the edge of her well-kissed lips.

"I think I like you a little more than I thought I would," she confessed, surprising him.

Not wanting to let the fires die out, he dipped down, nuzzling the warm skin of her neck. She shivered even though it was far from cold outside.

"I'm glad about that. Want to go inside?"

She hesitated, as if weighing her response, and then nodded. Without a word, she took her keys from her pocket and he could see her hands tremble. Desire or something else?

He followed her in. As the door closed, her keys fell to the carpet along with her bag, and he didn't waste a moment.

"I love how you taste," he shared before devouring her mouth again, urging her to respond, to take him as much as he wanted to take her. He licked the thundering pulse in her throat, knew that she liked it by the soft sigh she couldn't hold back. "Touch me back, Joy. Kiss me back," he said against her mouth.

She did, and when he slid his hands up under her shirt, she moaned into his mouth as his palms closed over her breasts, kneading through the fabric of her bra, teasing her nipples to fine points that he enjoyed playing with.

Rafe pressed his erection against her hip, rubbing gently. He was close, ready to explode. It had been a long while and he was starving for release.

She seemed to notice, intuiting his need to be touched, and slipped her hand down inside his jeans. He caught his breath audibly when her fingers closed around his length and he pressed into her harder. They dove into each other's kisses enthusiastically and within seconds he gave in, groaning as he came, unable to hold back. It was one of the most erotic things he'd ever experienced, so much so that he remained hard, barely finished but ready to go again.

"Uh-oh, we're one-nothing now—want to go to bed early and even the score?" he asked teasingly, weaving his hands through her hair and nuzzling her warm skin.

He could taste the sheen of perspiration that had formed there, turning him on more. This first time had been fast, taking the pressure off, but when he got her upstairs he'd show her that her dreams paled compared to reality. He wanted to make her scream with pleasure while she was completely awake.

"Oh, no, I don't think so. That's all right," she said quickly, extracting her hand and slipping away from him, hitting the light switch by the door.

He blinked in confusion, watching her bend to pick up her keys and coat, putting her keys in her pocket. She smoothed her shirt and hair, as if, well, as if they were done.

"Excuse me?" He walked over and tugged her up against him, looking down into her eyes, her face only inches from him.

The desire he'd experienced with her in the semidark by the door vanished, however, the only hints of it remaining in the color of her cheeks, her swollen lips and the musky smell of sex between them. He could see the stemmed desire in her eyes, the tautness of her features, as if she were under stress. He'd be happy to relieve it for her, but had no idea what she was doing.

"What game are you playing, Joy?" He was still on edge, his body hot for hers and his emotions scrambling. He didn't like how she just shut it off, the passion. It made what had happened, well...cheap.

"No games." She put her hands on his arms, pushed back, getting some physical distance. "I...I don't know why I did that. It was nice, it's okay—you don't have to, ah, even the score. It was a mistake, obviously."

"Why?" He wrapped his arms around her even though she gasped an objection and tried to push away. But he held her there, moving his hands firmly around her back. Her resistance was nominal, as if she were fighting herself more than him. Finally, she looked up at him.

"You're only here for a few weeks. This won't go anywhere. I don't know you."

What he'd interpreted as distance he now

realized was not that at all, but instead closer to fear or anxiety. He loosened his hold, but stayed close.

"So you'll spend a couple weeks getting to know me, and we'll have some fun. Remember fun, Joy? Have you ever really let yourself go and not worried about every little thing?"

"Easy for you to say, you're on vacation, you don't have a career that needs your attention, and you—"

"You said you don't know me—and you're right," he reminded her tersely. "You don't. This isn't completely a vacation, Joy. It's a leave of absence because I couldn't do my job. A job I happen to love, and which has been my whole life. So don't say I don't understand that. Now I can't do it, because I can't get a damned night's sleep."

He stepped back, wiping a hand over his face, lowering his voice when he saw her stunned expression. Great. She'd hit a nerve, and their emotions were running high, but that didn't give him the right to lash out.

"Listen, maybe you're right, I'm sorry—"

She took a step forward. "No… You're right. I don't know you, so I shouldn't make assumptions. I didn't mean to do that, I didn't know…" She drifted off as if searching for the words, and he waited.

"You're right. I haven't had fun in so long…. Maybe that's why my blood pressure's up—"

"You have high blood pressure?" he asked, slipping into his EMT role without a second thought.

She smiled. "Slightly. The doctor wasn't concerned, but she did tell me to find ways to relax more. I guess I didn't really follow that prescription."

He took another chance. "Maybe I could help with that?"

His stomach actually did a little flip when her cheeks turned hot as if merely thinking about having fun excited her, and he experienced the corresponding stir in his lower regions again. They could have a little fun together.

"I don't know, Rafe, I can't make any promises about...*that.*" She glanced meaningfully toward the door, and he knew to what she was referring. "I've never been very good with, uh, sex. I don't seem to enjoy it much."

Saying the word made her cheeks burn even hotter and he watched her flailing, wondering how she could think such a thing about herself.

"Coulda fooled me, honey, but a lot of people are insecure about sex and—"

"No, take my word for it—that's why I keep dreaming, like I do—that never happens in real life. Ever. It's never been my...thing." Her hands flew up, covering her red face as she moaned with embarrassment. He pried her fingers away.

"Listen. Part of having fun is no pressure, so there isn't any. There's fun, and then there's *fun,* and I'd like to have both kinds with you, but you lead the way, okay?"

She took a deep breath, obviously relieved, though her hands were ice cold in his. He was going to make it his personal challenge to warm her up.

"Okay. Thanks," she said.

"Who knows?" he said, pulling her against him. "Maybe we'll end up making a few dreams come true."

8

"THIS IS ONE OF THE MOST magical nights of my life," Pam whispered, a delicious shiver running down her spine as Ted's big, powerful hand touched her gently at the spot where the back of her dress scooped down past her shoulder blades.

"Every night is magic since I met you," he responded in the husky drawl that she loved. If they weren't at a business-oriented event, she would have snuggled even closer, thrilled that their first public appearance together was going so well.

Her forty-two-year-old hormones were dancing right along with them. Who knew love and passion would find her at this point in her life? Being with Ted made her feel as if she were twenty again. They couldn't seem to get enough of each other. The flames of desire were licking at her again.

"I wish we could be open about everything so that everyone could admire you as much as I do," she said regretfully, and he squeezed her hand in response.

"It's better that they don't know how we met, for the sake of the shelter, but for me, too, Pam. I don't want people looking at me for where I came from. I want them to see me as I am, now. With you. With my degree in hand, my new place, my new job… The past should be left in the past."

Pam didn't completely agree, if only because Ted had picked himself up from such a low point and had not only defeated the odds, but beat them senseless. She loved him; she was proud of him and she knew his story would give other people hope. Unfortunately, it would also raise suspicion and cast a jaundiced eye on her reputation as a non-profit manager. While they were two consenting adults, they couldn't make their history general knowledge. It was too risky.

They couldn't even have people at the shelter know—it would open too many doors that should stay shut. After a while, when Ted was out on his own, established in his work and his life, they could let everyone know, saying they'd gotten together after the fact.

Still, it bothered Pam so much to have to lie.

The music ended and she didn't realized how tense she'd become in Ted's arms until he looked into her eyes with concern. She blew out a breath, laughing softly.

"Okay, sorry. I know I should leave work at the office." She dropped her hands from his shoulders as they walked from the dance floor. "I love that tux—you look right at home in it."

"Pays to buy quality."

She stepped back in surprise. "You bought that? It's yours?"

He grinned. "I wasn't taking you out in a rented monkey suit, and I plan to get a lot of use out of this over the years. Clothes make the man," he reminded her, a quote from one of their favorite goofy movies, *Joe Versus the Volcano*. She grabbed his hand and tugged him down close.

"No. I think in this case it's very much the opposite."

"Well, thank you ma'am," he said, his eyes sparkling with desire. "How about one more drink, and then we can take the party home?"

"That sounds like a perfect plan," she agreed.

She'd stayed a respectable time, had fun, mingled with the people she needed to mingle with, catching them up on the shelter's latest doings and making sure they knew how critical their donations and services were to the shelter's success. She'd even managed to convince the manager of a small local grocery chain not to drop their program asking customers to donate at the cash register. Every small victory counted.

Glancing toward the bar to see if Ted was making his way back to her, Pam caught the eye of Martin Solese of Solese Construction. She hadn't seen him earlier, and he was one person she was trying desperately to hold on to—the shelter needed new front steps in the worst way and she didn't have enough cash on hand to pay full cost. However, Martin had become so in demand in the local housing market that she never really saw him anymore. His secretary said she forwarded Pam's calls, but Pam never got a response.

She thought it might have to do with the fact that he'd asked her out once and she'd said no, definitively. She didn't mix business with pleasure as a rule, and she'd explained that to him; she hadn't wanted to jeopardize his support by going out with him. She'd also just met Ted at that time and hadn't been interested in anyone else. She pasted on a smile as Martin approached the table.

"Pam! How are you? You look too gorgeous to be here all alone—didn't I see you dancing with someone?"

She nodded as he took a chair close by her side, Ted's chair, wishing he'd taken one a few seats away. "I am here with someone. He's getting drinks now. I didn't see you here earlier."

"Ah, got off to a late start tonight, waiting for my date."

"Anyone I know?"

"Probably not. She's a model from L.A.—we met when I was hired to do a summer house for her father. We've been seeing each other for a few months now." He delivered the news in a tone that subtly suggested that Pam had missed out. If he was serious about someone else, it would make it much easier to ask him to do some work on the shelter.

"Listen, Martin, I wanted to talk to you about some work we need done—"

"Here we are…. Martini for you and, oh…hello," Ted interrupted them, and Pam looked up, glad he had returned.

"Thanks. Oh, Ted, I wanted to introduce you to—"

"Ted… Don't I know you from somewhere?" Martin interrupted, his expression surprised as he stood and shook Ted's hand. Pam noticed that Ted had gone a little pale and set his drink down on the table with a shaking hand.

"No, I don't think so," Ted responded gruffly. And then it hit her and she felt slightly panicked— of course, Martin had been working on installing new windows right at the time Ted had arrived at the shelter. It seemed unlikely that either man would remember the other, so much time had passed.

"I remember," the contractor said, tapping his forehead now, "you helped me put in windows when I did that job at the shelter. Weren't you…you know, uh, weren't you staying there?"

Martin stumbled and Ted caught Pam's eye as the two other couples returned from the dance floor— one of them being the grocer she'd convinced to keep supporting them.

The three stared at each other as the implications struck them all simultaneously. Pam hoped against hope that Martin wouldn't make anything of it. As he turned his narrowed gaze on her, she saw the anger tighten his jaw and she knew she wasn't going to be that lucky.

"So…I asked you out at the time and you said you didn't want to date me because we had a conflict of interest due to my donating work to the shelter—however, it appears that you didn't feel the same conflict of interest in getting involved with one of your charity cases? Is Ted special or do you take care of all your male residents that well?"

Pam recoiled but heard Ted growl from across the table.

"You'd best take that back and apologize, Solese," he warned in a tone of voice she'd only ever heard him use when some of the guys at the shelter got out of line. She looked up to see him towering over Martin.

Mr. Douglas, the grocery-store owner, broke in, confused. "What's going on here Ms. Reynolds? What are these two men fighting about?"

People around them in the country club had started milling about and observing the two men angrily staring each other down. It was too late to save face—the best she could do was to try to keep them from pounding each other.

"Ted, stop—Martin, back off—you're out of line."

Martin laughed, looking around at his audience.

"Oh, I'm out of line? I think you're the one who's out of line, dating your male residents.... How many people here know? What do you think they'd think if they did?"

"That's enough, Martin," she cautioned in her own icy tone, reeling with anger. How *dare* he call her out like this? "I don't owe any explanations to you or anyone. I can date whomever I like. It just so happened not to be you. The conflict of interest was an excuse—I wouldn't have gone out with you anyway, so accept that fact and deal with it."

Every person's eyes were trained on her, including Ted, who had lowered his fists, thank God. Martin was so outraged he was beyond words.

Mr. Douglas broke the silence. "If I am not mistaken, am I to understand that you, Ms. Reynolds, have been dating this man, and he is one of your residents at Second Chance?"

"Yeah, that sums it up nicely," Martin added nastily, and she shot him another glare before turning her attention to Mr. Douglas.

"Mr. Douglas, this is a terrible misunderstanding. Martin is only upset because I turned him down for a date, that's all, and maybe everyone has had a few too many martinis," she offered, trying to lighten the mood, but it wasn't happening.

Douglas was old school, and she knew he already had reservations about Second Chance as it was— he'd heard some news story "exposing" homeless people as con men and layabouts who would rather live off the system than work for a living. It had taken her a while to convince him that that was not the case, at least not in her program.

"Ms. Reynolds, has your date been a resident of your shelter or not?"

"Mr. Douglas, this really is not the place for this discussion. If we could make an appointment to talk in private—"

"I'll happily make that appointment if you can tell me he was *not* one of your residents."

Pam chewed her lip, painfully aware of all the people watching them now. This was the nightmare she'd been trying to avoid. She tried dancing around the truth, knowing before the words were out of her mouth that it wasn't going to work.

"He isn't—in fact, he has a nice town house on—"

"But he *was,* wasn't he, Pam?" Martin sneered.

"That's enough—enough already," Ted stepped in. "What's wrong with you people? I lived at the shelter, yes. I got myself together at a point where I needed some help. Maybe you all have had it easy, but it's not like that for everyone. I have a job, and a home, and a wonderful woman to share my life with. Besides that, I don't see how this is anyone's damned business but our own. Pam's done nothing she needs to explain to any of you, and neither have I."

Pam looked up at Ted, shaking her head, the

questions in her mind bursting out before she could stop them.

"Why? Why would you say all that?"

Ted jerked back as if she'd slapped him. She wanted to take back the words—or maybe not. The public declaration left her no wiggle room, no place to hide. Everyone knew now, and while that might be fine and dandy for Ted, the lives of twelve other people who hadn't quite gotten their feet under them still depended on her.

Now that the cat was out of the bag, she knew they'd be losing donor support left and right. How would she manage to keep the shelter open? What would happen to those people who lived there? This was terrible.

"I'm sorry," Ted offered in an overly controlled tone of voice that didn't quite mask his hurt. "I said it because it's true. Why should they be attacking you because you didn't want to date *this* guy?" He glared at Martin again. "We're consenting adults— we don't owe anyone explanations."

She nodded, not knowing what else to do, unable to say a word. Mr. Douglas solved that problem again.

"Well, while that may be the case, and you certainly are free to date whomever you wish, you can forget what we talked about earlier, Ms. Reynolds. I had questions about supporting your organization as it was. Considering this new development, I know that I for one do not want to be associated with such a scandalous arrangement."

"Mr. Douglas, you don't understand—"

"I understand very clearly."

With that, he turned and left. People started clearing away from their table, murmuring and whispering, leaving only Ted and Pam looking at each other hopelessly.

"What now?" Ted asked miserably.

Pam shook her head. "I don't know, Ted. I just don't know."

JOY DIDN'T WORRY ABOUT her dreams that night because she didn't fall asleep. Even though she'd assured Rafe that she didn't want to engage in any more sensual explorations that evening, they'd shared a glass of wine, a tentative kiss good night, and he'd left.

She wanted to be relieved, but she wasn't. All she could think about was how his erection had weighed in her palm, how thick and hard he'd been, and how his desire had touched her at depths of need she hadn't known she had.

She could recall the nuance of every moment, how he'd kissed her, the sounds he'd made, as if he was really enjoying himself, really turned on by her—and the end result seemed to imply that was the case. Still, that wasn't so unusual for guys, right? It was easier for them.

It was much more difficult for her to think about giving herself over that way. The incident by the door was easy—it was all about him. Though she couldn't fault him for offering to do his part—truth was, she was scared.

She was also excited.

She was a mess, actually.

Though she'd sent him home tonight, she'd agreed to *fun*. She was hoping maybe she really could reach down and find the key to loosening up with a guy like Rafe. Could she enjoy being with a man who appealed to her, and her alone? Someone who tempted her to take a chance? She blocked the recurring thought that her father would give her "that look" if he knew she was carrying on with an unemployed ambulance driver.

Her father wasn't here, and she was an adult woman, making her own choices. Pam was right— Joy needed to take control and stop worrying so much about what her father would approve of or not, or if her dates met some weird, invisible standard of perfection. That way of thinking hadn't exactly led to a stellar love life so far.

Tossing to the other side of her bed, she threw the blanket off, sweating, though cool night air was drifting in from the screen. She hesitated, wondering if Rafe was watching her. The erotic possibility had her squeezing her legs together, trying to quell the need that pulsed through her.

Was he over there, as hot as she was? Lying awake, wondering about her? Wishing he was here with her? Or did the satisfaction she'd helped him find earlier lead him to the night's rest he so ardently desired? Selfishly, she hoped he was wide awake.

She sank her teeth into her lip. *Fun.* It might be fun to pull the curtain to the side and switch the low light of her closet on, illuminating the room slightly, enough so he could see. Could she do it?

Do you ever have any fun?

Rafe's question taunted her in the darkness, and she thought maybe she could have some fun right now. She could tempt him from the window. If he was watching, maybe he'd come back over and help her ease the ache that was keeping her awake, and they could have some fun together.

Her heart beat erratically in anticipation, and she turned the light on low, knowing no one else could see down the side of the house unless they were right outside. Or in Rafe's house. It would be a private show.

Slipping her nightgown from her body, she crawled back onto the bed, lying back and drumming up the courage for what came next, when she heard a knock at the door.

"Wow, that was fast," she commented with a grin, launching herself out of bed and grabbing her robe on the way downstairs. As she belted it, she wondered if maybe she should abandon it and answer the door naked—that would be fun, right?

It would also mean standing in her doorway with nothing on—while it was the middle of the night, you never knew who might be walking down the street. It was enough that she was naked underneath.

Her hands trembled slightly as she turned the burnished brass knob, feeling like the naughtiest girl alive for beckoning a man from her window. Swinging open the door with a smile, she stepped back, her mind blank with surprise when she didn't find Rafe, ready and willing, but Pam, sobbing and miserable.

"Pam! What happened? Come in. Oh, my god, honey, what's wrong?"

Pam's makeup was streaked and her hair was disheveled, as if she'd run her hands though it repeatedly.

"I broke my shoe on your stair," she said between sobs, and somehow Joy knew that wasn't the source of her friend's unhappiness.

"Come here, sit down. I'm sorry about your shoe, but what happened?"

Joy grabbed a box of tissues on the entry table and handed them to her.

Pam blew her nose noisily and took a few gulping breaths, then managed to croak out a few clear phrases, not looking or sounding like the canny, self-assured woman Joy had always known.

"Oh, Joy." She took another deep breath, her body shaking with the effort to control her sobs. "I don't know what's going to happen now…."

"Listen, how about a glass of wine and we can talk?"

"I—I'm s-so sorry, to w-wake you up…."

"You didn't—I was awake anyway, and you probably saved me from making an ass of myself."

Pam looked at her curiously through bloodshot, tear-filled eyes, and Joy shook her head. "Not worth discussing—let me get the wine, and don't worry, you're sleeping here tonight."

Joy knew her friend's sudden appearance had saved her from making a colossal error in judgment. She didn't like seeing Pam so upset, but she'd almost made a huge mistake.

She'd told Rafe that she wanted to take things slowly and see what happened. Five hours after saying that, she'd been ready to do a naked peep show for him from her bedroom window. Her wants, needs and desires were seriously confused, and rushing matters wasn't going to help any.

She poured two glasses of wine, emptying the bottle that she and Rafe had opened for dinner, and handed one to Pam.

"Okay. Now, what happened?"

Joy could swear she'd never seen anyone in this much emotional pain since her mother had walked out the door on her father. Pam was usually so stalwart and strong, not letting much get to her, and Joy had always admired that. Right now, though, her friend looked completely done in.

"Oh, God, Joy. Everything is such a wreck. It was all so perfect twelve hours ago. Well, not perfect, but perfect enough, you know? If only I hadn't gone to that stupid party…"

Joy leaned in, trying to make sense of the stream of comments.

"Something bad occurred at the party?"

"It was a disaster—well, at first it was wonderful to be out with Ted, dancing, and the place looked beautiful, with all the lights and the tree…." Pam stopped, gulping to control breaking into sobs again.

Joy grabbed more tissues. "Here. Cry away, then talk."

Through her sobs, Pam managed to tell Joy, in detail excruciating enough that Joy completely shared her friend's embarrassment and pain.

"That Solese! He's such a pig—he came on to me, too, back then!"

Pam's astonishment stemmed her tears. "Are you kidding?"

"Nope. He caught me in the kitchen at the shelter one day, I was packing some lunches, and he got in my personal space a little too much. When I asked him to back off, he asked me out. I turned him down flat, of course. He didn't like the rejection—I think he might have gotten mad at me, but one of the residents came in, and he left."

"Why didn't you ever tell me?"

"I never thought about it again, to be honest. He was so annoying."

Pam nodded. "Well, his annoyance translated into a big scene tonight, and that scene might make some serious trouble for me—we could be shut down by the end of January if people stop their donations. If the papers get hold of this, maybe faster."

Joy threw her hands up. "I don't get it—it's not like you house teenagers or vulnerable populations. These are grown men. Ted's an adult, and you have an adult relationship. How is he doing in all of this?"

Joy knew she'd hit the big nerve when she saw fat tears rolling down Pam's cheeks.

"H-he… We're not together anymore." The last word was choked out on another sob.

"What do you mean you're not together? How can that be?"

"We were so angry with each other, I guess. We left, and drove down to the Seaport and walked, and he was in his 'too bad about them, what do we care?' mode, and I had to remind him that twelve other lives are depending on me and keeping that shelter open right now. His open declaration threatened that—who knows how bad it will be if word gets around?"

Joy sat back, pensive. Pam was in a terrible spot,

and she didn't know exactly what to say to make her feel better, so she chose her words carefully.

"I can see how you were both pushed into impossible corners. I don't blame him for wanting to come out and say you're together—he's right, why should you be ashamed?" Joy said, holding a hand up to stem Pam's quick response. "I can also see that you're right, too—it's about more than the two of you. You have worked so hard to make Second Chance what it is, and it's directly responsible for how successful Ted has become. He should have realized that."

Pam raised a hand to her face, quieter now, but seeming almost emptied out.

"He does know, which is making him feel guilty for what he did, though he shouldn't—you know? It also means the people at the shelter will probably find out, and that could screw things up there. You know how they see me as a mother, or like a boss, at least. This could diminish me in their eyes."

"Because you fell in love? How can they miss how wonderful this is? They would all be inspired to work for the same in life, I think."

Pam smiled wanly. "That's true, but as you know some of them aren't 'there' yet—they've faced such hard times, and they rely on me as the steady presence, the rock…. If they think I might leave, abandon them, well… Or there could be any number of responses I could imagine, none of them good."

"All the more reason for you and Ted to provide a united front. You should talk to the residents together, explain, and Ted could make sure they understand. I think they'd be happy for you."

Pam shrugged, draining her wine.

"It's all too complicated. That may or may not be the right way to go. I have some people I can ask, counselors at other agencies. They can help. I don't know if Ted and I will be getting back together—he was hurt, I was hurt, a lot of angry things were said."

"Oh, Pam, that happens in the best of relationships. People overcome worse all the time—you know that. What's your motto?"

Pam closed her eyes, shaking her head.

"No, come on. You know every single one of those guys who has come in has lost hope and then they find you. What do you tell them?"

"There's no challenge so huge you can't take it on one step at a time," Pam repeated tiredly, a phrase she'd used a million times with others.

"And?" Joy prompted.

"Okay, okay. Sheesh. And if you argue for your limitations, you get to keep them."

Joy smiled, setting her glass on the table.

"I never knew how annoying those sayings were until now," Pam muttered, and Joy laughed.

"A joke! All is not lost if you can make a joke!" she cheerfully offered one more of the many motivational truisms she'd heard Pam share over the years. Corny as they were, they cut to the truth of things, and they worked.

"This may be more than we can—"

"Stop—no arguing for your limitations, remember?"

Pam sighed heavily, giving in. "Okay. Okay. I'll find out tomorrow how bad it is, and we'll get started trying to save face."

"Maybe it won't be as bad as you think. You could start by adopting some of Ted's attitude—while he made an error in making his announcement when he did, he's right. You don't have to apologize for the fact that you're with him. You shouldn't."

"I know. I'm used to giving everything I have to the shelter. I've done that for years, and I don't know how to separate it all out."

"You could start by calling Ted. You two need to talk more now that you're calm."

Pam nodded, her eyelids drooping.

"Time for sleep. Tomorrow is a new day," Joy quipped and offered Pam a blanket.

"Please, stop. I can't take any more motivation now."

"Okay, see you in the morning."

Pam burrowed down into the large sofa, and Joy milled around for a bit, making sure she had settled down before heading to bed.

Looking out her window, she saw the lights on in Warren's house. Rafe was up at this late hour. Her notion of acting the temptress had her shaking her head as she crawled back into bed. Something was tipping all of their worlds sideways lately. Hell, she'd almost opened the door stark naked to her friend tonight. Poor Pam had saved her from seriously embarrassing herself. She'd have to tell her that when she was feeling better. Maybe.

As Joy lay in bed, she mulled for long minutes on whether she had actually experienced a ping of disappointment when it hadn't been Rafe at the door, but sleep saved her from having to admit it.

9

RAFE HADN'T SLEPT AT ALL, his body and mind wired from the interaction with Joy. He'd meant what he'd said. He wanted to get to know her, to have some fun, to help her loosen up. No pressure. He'd have someone to share the holidays with, and maybe they could exert a little physical energy together. All good things.

Glancing down at the insistent morning stiffy he had thinking about it, he hoped they might be able to do that sooner rather than later. She was as wound up as he was, and ready to explode. The repressed desire inside of her and the hungry desperation of her kiss told him that they could share a very merry Christmas together, indeed.

After making his way to the shower, his eyes tired from the lack of sleep though he wasn't as groggy as usual, he stepped under the hot water and thought about the moment by Joy's door.

He had no doubt they would be good together, in spite of her worries. He soaped himself, wondering who had instilled such doubt in her mind about her own sexuality, and why it had taken such deep root. Whoever it was, the guy must have been a bastard. Joy kissed like an angel, he thought, remembering how soft her mouth had been, arousal shooting through him. Rinsing off, his palm curled around his cock, which was demanding attention.

As tempting as it might be, he resisted, backing off. Taking off a little steam never bothered him, but in this case, he wanted to wait—he wanted to stay in this suspended state of arousal, looking forward to what it would be like when he finally could show Joy how much fun they could have together.

His fingers moved instead to the shower dial, switching the water from hot to cold, solving the problem the old-fashioned way. Within moments he was back out, drying off and reaching for his jeans with a keen sense of expectation about seeing Joy later that day. Tonight would have to be soon enough, and in the meanwhile, he had enough house projects to keep him busy and pass the day.

As he was about to leave the house, however, Joy pulled into her driveway. He stopped and got out of the car, crossing the lawn to meet her.

"Hey—what are you doing home?"

She looked tired, as if she'd been up all night, as well. "I was going to go in late, but Ken actually told me to take a personal day—we had a great day yesterday, and he's in a generous mood, so I took him up on it. Pam came by in the middle of the night with a problem, and I'm exhausted after staying up with her."

"Who's Pam?"

"Oh. A good friend. She runs the organization where I volunteer."

"Is she still here?"

"No. She left before I got up, but I thought I'd justify my day off by making some cookies for the shelter, so I went to get some supplies."

"That's nice. Want help?"

She'd been talking to him over her shoulder as she was taking grocery out of the car, and finally she turned, their eyes meeting in a flash of heat.

"Um, sure," she said, smiling. He nearly cheered out loud. Progress. "I haven't baked anything for a while, so I can't guarantee how successful this will be—do you know how to make cookies?"

"I know how to eat them," he joked, taking two of the bags and walking with her toward the house.

"You can be the taste tester then. That way we'll know that no one at the shelter will die from eating my cookies."

"Oh, thanks, that's just swell," he responded with mock sarcasm, chuckling as they went inside. "So," he said, following her into the kitchen and noticing the blankets still thrown over the living-room sofa where her friend must have stayed. "What kind of crisis did your friend have?"

"Oh, it's with her love life, but unfortunately it could also mean trouble for Second Chance."

He frowned as her voice broke on the last, and he realized she'd stopped unpacking things from the bags.

"You okay?"

She shook her head. "Sorry. I'm worried about the shelter. Pam has some potentially serious trouble, and I want to help. Maybe I could pass some thoughts by you, get your take?"

Rafe was surprised, and flattered. "Sure. Go ahead."

"I want to find a way to offset the rumors circulating about the place—undeservedly—maybe some sort of event to show people how much good Pam does for the local community."

Rafe took over unpacking the groceries, leaving items on the counter and said, "Why don't you tell me what the problem is?"

Joy related most of Pam's dilemma as succinctly as she could. To her relief, Rafe didn't particularly see the issue with two consenting adults getting together, regardless of their backgrounds. However, he also knew the world could be far more judgmental, and said so. She warmed to him even more for being so accepting.

"I'll give you what feedback I can, but it sounds like you're already on the right track."

He held out his hand. She took it, and there was

a spark of something in her eyes that he liked very much.

No one was more surprised than he was when she launched herself forward into his arms. He was taken off guard, but not about to argue. Joy had a lot of emotion riding under the surface, and he wondered what it would be like when she really let go.

"Hey, I like this," he teased.

She drew back, looking at him seriously, the way she always did, but her eyes were brighter.

"Thanks, Rafe. It's nice to have someone to spend the day with, making cookies, bouncing ideas around. I'm so used to being by myself, but I like your company. A lot. The whole thing with Pam, with this guy she likes, well, it has me wondering how much we miss if we worry too much about what other people think."

"That's a good point. You have to make decisions that are right for you," he said in a low tone, his eyes dropping to her mouth.

He knew what a huge step it was for her to be open with him, to share her thoughts and ask his opinion, and the urge to kiss her was killing him. When she didn't move away, he gave in, dipping forward to taste her lightly, then more deeply until they were winding around each other, breathless. He walked her backward a few steps until she bumped into a chair and lost her footing. Steadying themselves, she laughed and pushed the hair back from her flushed cheeks.

"Maybe we should make those cookies."

He nodded, his heart pounding from the kiss, his erection straining against his jeans. He could think of better ways to spend the day, but that wasn't what Joy needed right now.

"Tell me what you want me to do, and I'm yours," he said, knowing she'd pick up on the not-so-subtle innuendo in his offer. He meant every word.

BY FOUR O'CLOCK, the house was hot from the oven, as well as the sun shining in all day. Cookies surrounded her and Rafe on every side—all surfaces of the kitchen were covered with cooling, decorated or soon-to-be-decorated cookies.

Baking hadn't been that difficult, really, and it had been fun. They'd worked together easily while brainstorming ideas to help the shelter. Rafe actually was a wonderful sounding board, and he was very creative, and told her what he thought honestly. She was even more excited about her ideas now and couldn't wait to tell Pam. She felt so good to be doing something, not sitting around worrying.

Joy peeked at Rafe while he stood sprinkling sugar in a very precise, male fashion over a tray of frosted goodies—he was gorgeous, inside and out. He was so easygoing, happy to help. He genuinely seemed to like her company, too. Warmth stole through her, and she bit her lip, watching him. The T-shirt he wore was a little damp from the heat and stuck to his skin, revealing the strong muscles of his back, and she lowered her gaze to other delectable regions.

Rafe might be surrounded by sweets, but he was a sexy confection all by himself. She chuckled out loud, and covered her hand to her lips a moment too late. He turned, looking at her, a dab of green sugar at the corner of his lips.

"What's so funny?" he asked, unaware.

"You've been sampling again," she accused, her eyes transfixed on the sugar.

Following the direction of her stare, he started to lift his hand to remove the evidence, but she stepped forward, halting him. She shut off her mind and followed her instincts for once. It was about time she started taking some of the opportunities for fun that came her way.

"Let me," she offered, her heart beating furiously as she slipped a hand behind his neck and lifted up to dart her tongue out and lick the sugar away.

He lasted for two strokes of her tongue against his skin until he pulled her up close with a groan and took over, backing her into the counter and kissing her so hard and so thoroughly that she couldn't breathe, but air was highly overrated anyway. If she'd thought the temperature was hot in the kitchen before, it was rising by degrees as he kissed her.

"Joy, I want you something fierce," he murmured

in her ear, pressing the promise of his erection against her hip. Tension twisted inside of her, invading the moment—should she?

His hand slipped under the T-shirt she was wearing, finding her breasts, closing and rubbing, plucking and caressing the sensitive tips into hard points against his palm. Oh, my, he knew what he was doing, and her body responded to his dedicated, confident touch.

"You like that? How about this?"

Pulling her shirt off right there in her kitchen, he had her topless before she could object, not that she planned to. It was scandalous—the windows were open; she could hear voices out in the yard where a woman next door visited someone else across the fence. They couldn't see…but they were there, and she and Rafe were…*ohhh.*

He suckled her so sweetly she dug her fingers into his hair and she managed to quell her moan to a whimper, lest she be heard through the screen door. When he drew away, lapping her skin with his tongue, she objected with a muted groan.

"Come here," he said, his eyes wicked as he grasped a bowl of frosting they'd been using for cookies.

She held perfectly still, unbearably aroused as he used the soft spatula to completely frost her breasts. Her skin was so hot she figured the confection would melt right off her skin. Rafe smiled devilishly, reaching for some red cinnamon sprinkles. Her eyes went wide.

"Rafe, what are you doing?"

"Decorating you—you are plenty tasty enough all on your own, but this is fun—isn't it?" He looked at her intently, and she had no choice but to agree.

"Yes, it is."

He took great care in "decorating" her, and she thought she would go crazy, dying for his mouth on her, waiting interminable minutes before he stepped back to admire his masterpiece. He yanked off his own shirt and hauled her against him for a deep kiss.

"You ruined all that hard work," she whispered breathlessly as he released her, icing and cinnamon candies smeared all over his chest now, as well.

"Now we get to share," he said with an evil wiggle of his eyebrows, making her laugh, then moan, as he began licking away the frosting with dedicated thoroughness, his tongue washing every inch of her clean, her body on fire and writhing as he did. She was short of begging him to take her by the time he finished, and she knew he could tell that when he looked at her.

"Do you want this, Joy? Do you want me?"

She'd never wanted anything more. He was like every dream she'd ever had—literally—coming true. But even her dreams, while hot, hadn't been this fun, this real.

She held his gaze, nodded, and he smiled in

heartfelt relief, as if he'd been poised on an edge, waiting. The fact that he seemed to have held his breath for her answer made her feel special. Within seconds he was naked and so was she. A tray of cookies slid noisily to the floor as he made room for her on the counter, his movements sure but urgent.

She couldn't believe a man, let alone a man like Rafe, wanted her this badly. She could see in the way his eyes raked over her, in the hardness of his body and the tremble of his hand, how much he needed her.

"I've never done this before…on a kitchen counter, I mean," she said hesitantly, watching him grab a condom from his wallet and slide it over his shaft. She was on the pill, but didn't protest. The next thing she knew, he was flush up against her, that delicious part of him sliding against her heat, though he didn't make his way inside.

"I hope you'll find this worth sacrificing a few cookies for," he teased, planting his palm on the crease of her hip and thigh, his thumb rubbing the hot slit of her flesh, making her gasp in delight. His hand was large and warm, his fingertips slightly rough, probably from the work he was doing on Warren's house, and the sensations his touch brought forth were mind-blowing.

"What cookies?" she joked breathlessly, arching against him. She curled her fingers around the counter's edge, positioning herself and opening for him as he eased inside of her, big and hot, filling her completely. She trembled with the completeness of it. Yes, this was better than her dreams—and her dreams had been pretty damned good.

"Definitely worth trashing the cookies," she said, hearing him chuckle as he began to move, rocking his hips in a steady rhythm, finding her mouth with his and parrying his tongue with hers in the same way.

There was a delectable pressure building inside—something she couldn't remember experiencing with another man, ever.

Rafe couldn't seem to stop kissing her, her mouth, her face, her neck, murmuring hot words now and then, but mostly his lips were engaged in kissing every spot of her he could reach as he drove himself forward with increasing speed, touching her everywhere, urging her to come along with him.

She wanted to—she honestly did. Satisfaction hovered on the edge like a lightning bolt on the horizon, ready to strike, but the moment she became conscious of it, the brightness disappeared.

She groaned in frustration—why, *why* couldn't she do this simple thing? Her body was obviously willing, though her mind wouldn't let go. Sex was in the brain, so they said, and she seemed like living proof. Her brain was completely out of sync with her body.

Knowing it wasn't going to happen, she didn't intend to risk Rafe's disappointment. They'd had a perfect day, and she wasn't going to let on that she couldn't live up to his expectations.

Turning her attention back to the moment, she relished the strong grip of his hands on her backside, how his fingers pressed in as he buried his face in her neck. Following his gentle cues, she lifted her legs up over his shoulders, increasing the intensity of the vocals she made, indicating she was reaching her climax, and loving how he responded by hammering even harder into her, throwing his head back. She watched him, not entirely minding that she wasn't completely in the moment; it was worth it just to observe the wild intensity with which he made love to her.

She'd never seen a man so utterly open and uninhibited—and with *her*. The idea that he reacted to her this way touched a chord deep inside. She couldn't stop watching him.

No sooner had she become aware of the glimmer of possibility than his jaw clenched tight until he let out a grown of release, fitting himself so tightly into her that she was sure even air couldn't move between them as he finished. He pulled her against him, his chest heaving breaths of spent passion.

Her body slid against his, both of them sweaty and slick as he lifted her back down to the floor. She cuddled against him, enjoying the moment. He felt so good to her, there was no denying that.

As their breathing settled, he rubbed her back

and stepped away a little, looking down into her face. He looked more relaxed, more handsome, if that was even possible.

"That was wonderful," he said, and she nodded, not quite meeting his gaze, kissing his shoulder.

"Yes, it was."

He backed up another step, framing her face in his palms and looking at her with a gaze so penetrating she nearly had to turn away. "Joy, I know a lot about the human body, and about women. What I don't know is why you'd fake it with me."

"What do you mean?"

"Joy," he said in gentle admonition, and she moved away, bending to reach for her clothes.

"Fine, I faked. So what? It was nice anyway, I enjoyed it—I think I might have come close, but I typically don't...I've rarely been able to, uh..."

"Orgasm," he stated bluntly.

She looked away stubbornly, pulling on her underwear and her shirt. "Yes."

"Why didn't you tell me instead of pretending?"

"I didn't want to make it bad for you—I didn't want you to be disappointed."

"Why would I be disappointed? How could it be bad? It was incredible. A lot of women have trouble in that department, and if you'd told me, I could have done something else."

His voice lowered to a sexy pitch when he said the simple words *something else,* making her flutter all over in response, but she also didn't know what to say. No man had ever talked to her this bluntly before—none had cared, happy to enjoy themselves and go on their way. She'd gotten used to it, and Rafe's penetrating gaze and questions made her squirm, awkward and exposed.

He put his hands on her arms, making her face him.

"Listen, okay, fine," she said blusteringly. "I know this is a guy thing, you like to know you can make us respond, and I did respond, Rafe, as best I could. I loved what you did, but I'm too uptight. I think too much, and I can't turn it off. It's not you, it's me," she joked lamely.

Joy felt on edge, probably because her body was still riled up. Rafe didn't make it easy; he didn't let her off the hook, and she didn't know exactly how to deal with it. Rafe didn't want spin, he only wanted the truth.

"Joy, we can try lots of different things, whatever you want," he said quietly. Leaning in to kiss her, she didn't kiss him back, but didn't draw away, either. "Let me show you—we can experiment, play, whatever."

Joy wanted to believe that, but she knew…she just *knew* that as long as her mind was engaged, she wasn't going to be able to loosen up enough to find satisfaction. The wheels in her mind spun around an idea, one she wasn't sure she should speak out loud. Would he think she was a total freak?

Regardless of her doubts, she wanted badly to be

with Rafe—she wanted so much to believe what he was saying, and there might be one way they could both enjoy their time together.

"You're open to anything?"

"As long as it doesn't involve serious physical injury, animals or shaving off my body hair, yes. Anything."

She laughed. He made her laugh so easily. That was a good thing, wasn't it?

"My doctor told me my little problem wasn't anything physical—I'm mentally blocked. I can, uh, you know…help myself," she admitted, and saw his eyes blaze with interest. "Then there are my dreams…. Nothing holds me back in dreams, so it's only a problem when I'm awake, apparently," she tried to joke, but it fell flat.

"That's good to know," he said, not laughing, either, touching her face gently.

"So I'm thinking, maybe we should try being together at night. You know, if you come over and sleep here, and I start to dream…I think I would be less…repressed, just then."

His brow furrowed, and she held her breath, afraid he would refuse.

"I'm all for spending the night in your bed, Joy— but are you saying you want me to have sex with you while you're sleeping?"

She fidgeted, but decided to boldly state her case, since he had said he'd do *anything*.

"Well, I mean, I have these hot dreams, and they're about you anyway, and maybe if you're there, then if things start up, and maybe my mind would be as receptive as my body. I do want you, Rafe."

He pulled on his jeans, taking a moment to think.

"I see your point, but I wouldn't want to startle you, or worse, while you're sleeping. Chances are those dreams are about more than sex. Maybe if we spend some time during the day together, and get to know each other a little, that would help, too. You know, the Japanese sometimes make foreplay last all day long, or longer, before actually having sex." He smiled naughtily. "I think we've gotten a good start in that area."

"Oh," was all she could say. The thought of all-day foreplay with Rafe made her knees weak.

"So why don't we clean this mess up and take a shower—" he looked down at the frosting dried to his chest "—and then we can head down to the shelter to talk with your friend."

"You want to come to the shelter?"

"Sure, I want to help if I can."

Joy chewed on her lip, thinking. "I don't know. It's probably not anything you really want to bother with, seeing as you're just here for—"

"Joy," he said, cutting her off.

"Huh?"

"Don't close me out, and don't make what's between us low—I'm not just here for sex."

She cleared her throat. "I was going to say, as you're just here for a few weeks."

"Oh. Whoops." He slanted an embarrassed grin, but recovered quickly. "Well, I want to help, if I can. It's less than a week before Christmas, and you have an ambitious plan, so I'll be another set of hands. I'd like to be part of this with you, even if for a little while."

She didn't know why having him come to the shelter was so difficult, as if she were sharing more with him now than her body. Still, his appeal was sincere. He'd listened to her all day and had some good ideas.

"Okay. I appreciate that."

"Thanks. It'll be a fun day. And then…" His voice trailed off, but he was smiling in a way that made her blood warm and her muscles loose.

"And then?"

"I want to spend the night with you, Joy—I'd like to spend every night that I'm here with you. I've got enough of an ego that I'd like you to be awake when I'm inside of you. I want you to know you're with me, not just in your dreams, flattering as that is. I want you to know it, remember everything I do to you."

The way he said it made her melt. She remembered quite well what it was like when he filled her body with his own, and she would like to be awake for that, too.

"I know. Me, too. Maybe this is a way to get to that point?"

He pulled her close. "Sure…but first let's go take that shower."

10

JOY SAT IN THE MEETING, trying to concentrate, but her focus was not on the job at hand. She made eye contact with Ken, nodded, scribbled down a note, and then her thoughts wandered off. She couldn't wait for this endless meeting to cease. Who really cared about what colors of certain toys sold better than others? Did she?

Not really.

However, she did care about being able to pay her mortgage, so she made another effort, listening intently to what was being said, only to find her mind drifting off yet again.

The routine tasks in her work bored her to death, if she were to be completely honest. She had more important things to think about, like the fund-raising event at Second Chance. Pam had loved the idea, but they were all busting their backsides to make it work—it was five days to Christmas and counting.

Christmas had suddenly taken over her life. Rafe was decorating everything in sight—including her, she thought naughtily, knowing she'd never think about frosting the same way again.

Along with Pam, they were throwing a Christmas bash at the shelter for the community at large, as well as businesses and organizations they wanted to reconnect with. It was a more personal way to put a kibosh on the rumors that might be spreading about Pam and to show how much good the place did in the community. Joy knew people would be impressed if they came and saw the place, met Pam and met the people who lived there.

She had so much to do to get ready. She also had to polish her final presentation for her official interview with the board for the promotion, and yet she found herself curiously less excited about that prospect. With Rafe, the holidays, Second Chance... there was so much going on, she was losing track of her priorities, she thought. Or they were shifting, which was a much more disconcerting prospect. She'd always known what she wanted, hadn't she? Rafe was showing her a whole other side to herself that made her think maybe she should want more.

Between the sheets of paper that comprised her notes, she sneaked out her list of people to contact, reviewing it, strategizing the best way to approach each one. She planned to purchase formal invitations—bought with her own money—to send in the mail as well. She didn't plan on accepting a refusal from anyone, if it meant she had to drive them to the party herself.

For the first time in as long as she could remember, she had an attitude resembling Christmas spirit. A sense of anticipation was in the air, though she knew that was mostly due to the prospect of seeing Rafe soon. They'd spent a cuddly night together the evening before, and she'd slept better than ever, wrapped up in Rafe's arms as he stroked her back. No dreams had come to her—she'd been so exhausted that she had been too tired to dream. Unfortunately, she'd apparently been too tired for anything else, as well.

When she'd awakened, Rafe had been propped up in bed, fully clothed, reading. He'd had shadows under his eyes, and she knew he hadn't slept. For the first time, she'd realized the extent of his problem—people talked about losing sleep, having insomnia, but she realized that Rafe really was awake, all day and then all night, unable to sleep. She couldn't imagine it. How did he maintain any energy at all? Yet he'd gotten out of bed and had gone for a run as she'd left for work. Astonishing.

He'd left her with a kiss so hot she could still taste him; she closed her eyes and relived the moment. She wanted to rock his world, to ride him into exhaustion and give him the best night's sleep of his life—it had become a personal goal.

She grinned secretly as she played out the

naughty fantasy in her mind, imagining what it might take to exhaust Rafe. When a vibration buzzed softly in the pocket of her suit jacket, she jumped, emitting a little squeak of surprise, her face flooding with heat as everyone turned to look at her.

She plucked the cell phone out, smiling in apology and peeking at the most recent hot text message from Rafe. He'd been sending them all morning, part of his "all-day foreplay" plan. It certainly had spiced up her day, that was for sure.

Reading the current message, she wiggled a little in her chair, completely blanking out on the fact that she was being addressed.

"Joy? Are you with us?"

She blinked, setting the cell phone down on the table. Then realizing the people next to her might see the text message, she quickly snatched it up, fumbling it in her fingers, nearly sending it spinning across the table. Holding her breath, she managed to finally stick the phone back into her jacket pocket as it started vibrating again.

When she looked up, she saw that Ken was watching her impatiently.

She hadn't been caught in a situation like this since she'd been bold enough to pass notes in fifth grade and had had hers read aloud to the class. She wondered if Ken would have read her text message aloud if he'd grabbed her phone, and her naughty smile twitched again.

"I'm sorry, what?"

Ken cleared his throat. "I know it's the holiday and everyone is distracted, but I asked if you had worked out the media campaign for the Pearson project?"

"Oh, yes, of course," she said, pulling herself together and distributing her copies around the room, then quickly starting to review the main points, when Ken interrupted her.

"Joy," he started, and she looked up quickly.

"Yes?"

"What is this? This isn't the right paperwork."

She glanced down and realized that she'd made copies of the party-planning list for the shelter, not her media plan.

"Oh, I'm sorry—this is for another project...." she apologized, her naughty humor disappearing as she gathered the papers. "I can go over the budget verbally, I know it like the back of my hand, I'm so sorry for this, there's a lot going on this time of year you know—"

"What project is this? I didn't know we were planning a Christmas event," he inquired.

"It's pro bono work for a homeless shelter on the north side."

Ken looked completely baffled. "Pro bono? What do you mean pro bono? We don't do pro bono."

"It's a personal project."

"How much time have you been putting into it?"

"It's on my own time—I'm running event organization for them. It hasn't cost you anything," she reassured, trying not to sound too biting.

"Apparently, it costs us your focus on our work, and the projects we've put in your lap, I'd say," Ken offered, and she sighed, having no real answer to that.

"You're right. Sorry." Yet was she? She didn't feel sorry. She felt annoyed. She irrationally wanted to tell Ken to cram it, but she knew he was right.

"Well, mistakes happen. You can tell us the high points of the media plan, and we'll want copies directly after the meeting."

She didn't know how she managed to do it, but she did, and when the meeting was over, she couldn't have been more relieved. Ken didn't leave the room, however, but went over to the door, closing it before she had a chance to escape. *Shit.*

"Ken, really, I'm sorry but—"

"Joy, you're one of our best. Maybe the best among your peers at the moment."

She hadn't seen *that* coming and blinked. "Um, thanks."

"I mean it. You're a strong contender for the new position, certainly the most qualified, but the question I need to ask you, is this the best job for you?"

"What?"

"There's no debating you're good at this work, Joy, but do you really want to do it for the rest of your life? The new position will take up even more of your time and energy, and while I don't doubt that you have the mind and the talent for it, I do wonder if you have passion."

"Passion?"

"Yes. You're good at what you do, but I don't often see you excited about it. Lately, that's even more evident. I've worked with you for a while now, and you're competent, efficient, but…it's like you're still holding something back. Honestly, if I had to choose, I'd go with someone who had more passion and fewer qualifications, because passion is what takes you the distance."

She tensed at the criticism. "I didn't know *passion* was a requirement."

"It's not, but it's something we all think about when we're hiring someone to join the executive staff. A passion for the job, the company, the product. A personal connection. If you want this job, Joy, before we make a final decision, I need to know you really want it, and for more than the bigger paycheck. If this is what you want to do day in and day out for years to come. If you have—"

"Passion," she finished for him, flatly.

"Yes. Exactly."

Joy withered, sinking back into her chair, thanking Ken as he left. What could she do? It seemed passion was the thing lacking in her life overall, and she had no idea if she'd ever had it, or how to find it.

RAFE WAS GRINNING ear-to-ear as he pulled into Warren's driveway. He stepped out of the car to see Bessie getting out of her own car across the street, starting to take out sacks of groceries from the trunk. Rafe trotted over to give her a hand. He liked Bessie, and she always fed him when he came over—it reminded him of his own neighborhood back home, where someone was always trying to feed him something. Thankfully his job and time at the gym worked it off.

"Hey, let me give you a hand with those," he said, lifting the bags out of her arms.

"Well, now, they don't make many like you anymore, Rafe. I hope that young woman across the street knows she's found herself a real gentleman," Bessie complimented him. He acknowledged the words with silence, secretly thinking that if this nice old lady knew what plans he had for Joy later that night, she might not think he was much of a gentleman.

"Lots of groceries here," he commented, changing the subject as they walked up the steps. "Doing a lot of cooking this week?"

"Oh yes. Baking for church and for friends— among which you may count yourself—and of course my family will be here soon, so I need to start now. They all have good appetites, and I like to make everyone's favorites," she declared.

Rafe felt a little twinge of loneliness for his own

family. His mother did the same. His favorite was the manicotti that was standard Christmas-Eve fare, along with the homemade custard-and-cheese cannoli. His mouth watered thinking about it.

"You can put those down on the table, thank you very much. Can I make you some lunch?"

He smiled and then shook his head. "Don't tell my mother if you ever meet her, but your soup is as good as hers, Bessie. There isn't much that would keep me from it, but I have a Christmas tree tied to the top of Warren's car, and I need to get it down and inside the house to surprise Joy."

Bessie's eyes sparkled. "Oh, you're a romantic one, too. I'll send some soup over later—enough for both of you."

"We won't say no," he assured her with a wink.

He returned back to his car, and before long had hauled the Christmas tree into Joy's house, along with a boatload of decorations he'd bought at the store. He wasn't going to decorate it for her, but they'd have some fun—and some *fun*—doing it together.

Still, he looked at his watch and wondered where she was. Time had slid by while he'd put up the tree, and he hadn't realized it was already a half hour later than Joy normally came home from work. He knew this was a busy week. Maybe she'd gotten caught up in something. He was willing to wait.

Still, she hadn't replied to any of his text messages after the first few, and he hoped he hadn't ticked her off again. He sat with an old magazine and the undecorated tree until the sun went down and the Christmas lights were all blinking outside the windows. Finally he gave in to his worry and called Second Chance. No, Joy wasn't there, and Pam hadn't heard from her.

By the time he called her cell and left a message, a little chunk of fear had lodged itself in his gut. He'd seen the results of too many times when someone didn't make it home one night, and it was hard for him not to imagine the worst.

Still, what could he do? He didn't really know Joy all that well, certainly not enough to expect her to check in with him.

Worry turned to annoyance, which transformed into irritation and near anger again as he saw her headlights turn into the driveway, then relief took over. She was fine, just late. Going out on the porch, he met her on the steps.

"Hey, you're home late," he observed, unable to keep the slight accusation out of his tone.

"You were waiting for me?"

Something about that stung; they hadn't had firm plans, but he thought it was pretty clear they were getting together that evening. The fact that she obviously hadn't even given him a second thought put a big dent in the masculine ego.

"Not really, I just stopped by," he lied, his pride digging in.

"Oh, I'm sorry, Rafe. I was out driving."

"Where?"

"Around. I had to think."

Rafe's irritation dissipated as he detected the tone of confusion in her voice, and he went the rest of the way down the steps and took her hands in his.

"Think about what? Us?"

"No... Sort of. Related. I had to think about why I have no passion."

What the hell?

"This sounds like a conversation we need to sit down for. Did you eat?"

She shook her head and they entered the house. Rafe ordered some takeout and then took her coat, leading her over to the sofa to sit with him. Gathering her in his arms, he drew her near and was gratified when she curled in a little.

"You bought a tree."

"I thought we could have some fun decorating it."

"I haven't had a tree in forever. Never as an adult."

"Really? You did say you aren't that into Christmas."

She twisted to face him. "I'm not, and don't you see, that's it."

"What?"

"At Christmas, when everyone is excited, when

there's shopping and gifts and all these celebra-
tions, I don't get into it. I'm left flat."

"Why is that?"

"My father pretty much gave up on Christmas the
year my mother took off with her lover. He would buy
me a gift each year and leave it on the kitchen table,
but we didn't do trees or any of those things. I think
it was too painful for him—it all reminded him of her."

Rafe paused, absorbing what she'd said. "She
took off at Christmas?"

"Yeah. He—the man she was seeing—was
taking her to Paris for the holiday. So she went. We
never heard from her again. I don't even know if
she's alive, or where she is," she stated matter-of-
factly. She didn't really have any emotional trauma
over the issue anymore.

"That must have been a huge blow."

"Yes, it was. Dad was never the same. He worked
hard, made a decent living and we had a good life,
but I guess our life wasn't glamorous enough for
her. He worked a lot, long hours—"

"I meant for you, Joy. Sure it was hard on your
father, but he was an adult. What about you? To have
your mother leave you like that. How old were you?"

She shifted uncomfortably. "Nine."

"Old enough to know what was happening."

"I understood as much as I was able, yes. I heard
them arguing the night she left. I took care of him the
best I could—we took care of each other, I guess."

"It sounds like it was difficult for both of you, but to never have Christmas again? That's harsh for a kid."

She shook her head. "I didn't want it either. If I had asked, he would have done it, but it reminded me of everything bad, too, so why bother? I guess I still feel that way about the holiday."

She was partly lying. A few years after her mother had gone, she had often wished her dad could celebrate Christmas with her. She would sometimes sit in school and fantasize what gift he would buy her, or how they might decorate the house or send out cards, the way other kids did. Those things had never happened, and she'd loved him enough not to ask for them. She hadn't wanted to cause him more pain. So she'd shut down her own emotions and memories as well, learned to temper her expectations.

"It wasn't right, Joy, and it obviously affected you—question is how long are you going to let your past dictate your present?"

"Rafe, Christmas is one thing, but I'm not passionate about anything! I'm good at my job, but I'm not wild with excitement about it. I was in a meeting today about the best color for new toys and I could not have cared less. I don't have hobbies or boyfriends, and I'm not even that good at sex, because I'm lacking basic passion. That's it. That's the bottom of it."

Rafe was stunned at the tirade, and not entirely sure how to respond.

"You were led to this conclusion because?"

She dropped her head back, groaning. "Ken, my boss, he told me I was a strong contender, maybe the best, for the new position I wanted."

Rafe smiled, unsure how this fit in, but going with it. "That's terrific news!"

"Yes, but he also suggested that while I am very good at my job, I don't have passion for it. Ken says maybe I should rethink if I want the new position, because it demands *passion*."

She made a face when she said the word, crossing her arms tightly in front of her in what Rafe recognized from life with his sisters as a classic female defensive posture. "This is the one thing that I do not have, apparently, across all areas of my life. I'm passionless."

Rafe wasn't sure how to respond, but he took in her deflated, disgruntled posture as she slumped away from him on the sofa, and did the only thing he could do, under the circumstances. He burst out laughing.

He laughed, in fact, so hard that he started to tear up, and could hardly defend himself against the repeated thumps with the bolster pillow that Joy was hitting him with.

"What is so funny, exactly?" she demanded, up on her knees and lording over him with the pillow, her face fierce, which made him laugh all the more—she made quite the picture.

"You—you are. The fact that you think you don't have any passion is one of the most ridiculous things I've ever heard."

"I don't have it, Rafe, I really don't. It all makes sense now—the job, the sex, everything."

"I personally disagree, especially about the sex, but do you think maybe you might have grown up thinking passion was a bad thing? Passion was the reason your mother left your father, and took off to Europe with another man. So it got a pretty bad rap even when you were a kid."

She sat up straight, and he could see the thought take root in her mind.

Joy sat back on the sofa, stunned by the revelation. She was a thirty-year-old woman who'd spent her life, even as a child, holding tightly onto any emotion, not letting anything squeak out, lest it lead her down the same path her mother had gone. She'd been living her life by rote, and she'd never even known it.

"Joy?"

"Oh, God, Rafe…I've been so stupid. I never even realized what's been missing in my life, how afraid I've been of everything that's asked me to make any small emotional investment. It's all been locked up inside, all this time…."

"Coming out in your dreams, though…I guess it was time for you to have this realization. My mother always says things happen when we're ready for them to happen."

"I don't know how I could have lived this way for so long, not really caring about anything, just going through the motions."

"Well, maybe it's not quite that drastic. You cared about your father enough to set your own needs aside, and you care about your friends, like Pam, obviously, and you care about Second Chance—you seem pretty passionate about that to me. You've been really excited about the party, and even about Christmas, the last few days," he offered.

"I do feel differently about my work at the shelter. I never thought about it as work, per se, so I didn't make the connection to how much more involved I am there than at my regular job. I guess that's what Ken means about passion. I had it, have it, I just didn't see it."

"Well, it can go both ways—I loved my job with complete passion, and I think I might have been a little too obsessed with it, to a degree that I burnt out, and now I have nothing else to do. It's not a great feeling."

She lifted her eyes to his, and the zap of heat in her gaze, of understanding, sympathy, and *passion,* had his heart thumping madly.

"I think you were probably astonishing at your job, but maybe when one passion flags, there's a reason, and it's time to find another," she said softly, reaching up to touch his face. Something good—

something very good—was happening between them, and for the moment, Rafe didn't care to talk about work anymore.

"I never knew passion before. Until you," she confessed.

Rafe rubbed his hands lightly up and down her arms. "You're a passionate woman, Joy. I've known it from the moment I...heard you. Definitely when I touched you."

"Rafe," she whispered as he eased back the jacket from her arms and started unbuttoning her shirt, dragging his knuckle along her collarbone.

"You're so soft.... Your skin is like butter, but you're strong, too. It's very sexy," he added, unhooking her bra and working it downward.

"Rafe...how can you be thinking of sex right now? When we're having this serious talk?"

"I think of sex whenever I look at you, think about you, and most definitely when I'm next to you. You're the first woman to turn me on in a long time, Joy—you have no idea. The insomnia, and the stress from the job...I haven't been with anyone in a while. My passions were robbed from me, too, but you've helped bring them back to life."

His hands covered her breasts, massaging gently, and her heartbeat quickened.

She wound her arms around his neck. "Really? You haven't been with anyone since you started losing sleep?"

"Before that, even. I haven't been in the mood. I don't know why. I still can't sleep, but I sure enjoy being awake more than I have for a long time," he said against her skin as he bent to plant kisses across her midriff. "I am most definitely in the mood."

"Rafe, what about the tree?" she asked, relaxing into his touch and encouraging him to continue his exploration.

"Later," he said as he pulled her close in a deep, promising kiss.

11

RAFE HAD THE MOST gorgeous shoulders she'd ever seen. She loved running her hands over them, squeezing them, watching the muscles bunch and relax as she stroked his skin. A physique like his was built from the hard work of carrying stretchers and lugging heavy equipment. He was solid… everywhere. She slid her hand down between his taut thighs and rested it against the ridge in his jeans, sighing. Yep, solid.

"Tempt me all you want, lady, I'm bound and determined to hold out against your feminine wiles," he quipped, tugging the firm tip of one breast between his lips. When he sucked the tender flesh, darting his tongue over her as he did so, the sensations ignited a desire so fierce that she couldn't think clearly.

"I don't think either of us will hold out for long," she panted. Her clothes gone, she could finally glory in the touch of his lips and hands on her skin. He scraped his beard-roughened cheek against the side of her breast, and she loved it. She wound her hand around the back of his neck, urging him on.

She'd never had sex on her living-room floor— or any floor—before. Lame, but true.

"Hey, what about you?" she asked since he hadn't taken off anything but his shirt.

"There's time…. I want to explore you first," he murmured against her skin, and she moaned when he ran his hand up her leg. Suddenly her mind clicked in again, making her feel too exposed, too much at a disadvantage.

"You could undress, too," she suggested, but when he looked up at her, shaking his head, the hot intentions in his gaze shut her up.

"I don't want to be tempted to go too far. You tempt me, Joy, to the edge of reason. Just lay back, relax… Let me enjoy you…and I want you to enjoy me doing it. I want to show you how much passion you really have," he said gently.

"Oh!" she gasped as his mouth traced a path from her navel down to the slick opening between her legs and back again; every muscle in her body clenching in exquisite expectation.

"You fine with that?" he checked. He did it again, and she could only moan out her agreement.

It was so fine that she widened her thighs, inviting him in. The uncomfortable sensation of exposure had passed, replaced with need.

One delicious lick of his tongue on the oversensitized flesh of her sex had her shuddering. She focused on the sensations as he deepened the intimate kiss, stroking his fingers over her skin, urging her along.

She was more than willing to comply, and wiggled a little. She was even so daring as to raise her hands to her breasts, touching herself. He must have noticed and muttered his approval as he brought her closer and closer to the edge. Yet a part of her still held back. Whatever he wanted her to give, she didn't seem to be able to do it. She was having a hell of a lot of fun, but was unable to release the tightly coiled tension.

Then Rafe withdrew his hot touch and began trailing kisses down her thighs, then back up, bringing himself beside her. He gathered her against him, but she pushed back.

"Rafe?"

He put his lips to hers, the taste and scent of her own essence mingled into the kiss, and a wave of excitement washed over her. She clenched her thighs together, hiding her face in his shoulder, unabashed and yet embarrassed by her own raw neediness.

"I—I want more, Rafe," she begged, planting kisses from the column of his neck to his shoulder, pressing herself into him wantonly. He was still erect, still excited; the heat emanating from his skin was more than she thought a human being could generate.

"I know. Me, too. Now isn't the time."

She looked down over her naked, aroused body. "You stopped because I tensed up," she whispered, dismay replacing her arousal.

He got to his feet, putting his hand out to help her up.

"Yes—because I want you to enjoy it. We have plenty of time. That was nice, and we'll pick up where we left off, don't worry," he promised with a wicked smile. Confused, she reached for her clothes.

"Wait. Don't get dressed," he ordered.

"Why not? It's obvious you don't plan on getting *un*dressed," she said grumpily.

"Don't worry, I will…but we're going to have a little fun first—remember, foreplay all day? No need to rush. We can draw it out, see how long we can last."

"Yeah?" she said, annoyed, but halted with her shirt in her hands, not putting it on. "So what did you have in mind?"

"It's almost Christmas. I brought you a Christmas tree. The traditional thing to do is decorate it."

She'd forgotten about the tree. She hadn't had a tree since she was a child; she didn't have any decorations, even.

Then she spotted the bags on the floor.

Rafe went over to them, and she forgot about the tree again, watching the lovely interplay of muscles along his back, butt and legs, as he moved. She was definitely experiencing some passion.

In a flash, he lost his own clothes. "Naked Christmas-tree decorating," he turned to her and said with a sly grin.

"I *don't* think so," she said, grabbing at her shirt again. "There's sap. Those needles are sharp."

"Nope, I thought of that already. This is a Fraser fir, very soft to the touch. We're completely safe. As for sap, well, that shouldn't be a problem if we're careful, but if you get sticky, I'll wash you off," he said flirtatiously, and she rolled her eyes.

He stood assessing the room, a glint of excitement in his eyes, his hands planted on his hips. She was speechless—this was surely the oddest day of her entire life.

"We can close the curtains while we're decorating."

Joy didn't really care about the tree, but she watched his naked form with great interest. He had a beautiful, sculpted backside, and his front, well, she knew how nice *that* was. He was still semihard as he pulled boxes from the bags without an ounce of self-consciousness. To avoid standing there like a moron, she joined him in the task.

He smiled up at her and she was unexpectedly moved.

"That's the spirit," he said agreeably. "I got all types of decorations. I wasn't sure what you'd like."

"Thank you. I'll pay you back," she said, unsure what else to say, but his hands froze over his task.

"That's not the point, Joy," he said quietly, and she knew she'd stuck her foot in it. "It's a gift."

"Oh, I mean, I didn't mean... *Shit,*" she said, dropping to sit on the sofa. Her body was still throbbing from his abridged seduction, and her brain was on overload trying to process the things happening to her. Now here she sat, naked in her living room with Rafe and a Christmas tree. Freakishly, she didn't seem to care as much about her job at the moment. Was she in denial? Shock?

"Joy?"

"Hmm?" She didn't look up.

"Relax. Unpack the decorations, we'll decorate it, and see what happens. Maybe you'll have fun. Stop thinking it to death."

She sighed heavily into her hands. "Okay. Okay, you're right. Old habits are hard to break. None of this is normal to me."

"Maybe that's a good thing, right?"

"I suppose."

She rooted through the bags and pulled out boxes of lights and decorations.

"First, the lights," Rafe declared.

She looked over at the tree. Staring at it, she could almost imagine snow outside. The image evoked memories and emotions she'd thought were gone, and she wrapped her arms around her middle, shivering.

"Are you okay?" Rafe asked.

"Yes, I'm fine…. I forgot how pretty the trees are."

"They are pretty. I can't imagine Christmas without one."

"I used to have some favorite decorations—they're probably still up in the attic at Dad's."

Rafe was gazing at her with such warmth, concern and understanding that she had to glance away as he spoke. It was as if he knew what was going on inside of her clearer than she did, and she didn't know how she felt about that.

"You ever go back?"

"Not for a while. He remarried last year. He's happier than he has been since I can remember. I think Lois has been good for him, and I know she's insisting he celebrate Christmas. I'm glad for him."

"That's good. What about you? Don't you want to be happy, too?"

She didn't say anything, his words landing home. She looked at the tree again, picking up a string of lights.

"I don't know. I figured if I made the right choices, did the right things, worked hard, then I would be happy. It doesn't seem to always end up that way, does it?"

"Maybe they weren't all the right choices."

She blew out a breath. "Could be," she hedged. "I think we'd better get back to decorating this tree."

He smiled, taking the string of lights. "You're the boss."

Somehow, with Rafe, who had blustered into her life, had her decorating trees and walking around her house naked, among other things, she doubted that, but wasn't about to argue.

They worked in concert, placing the lights, then

moved on to the ornaments. Rafe had bought enough for two Christmas trees, and they'd be lucky if this one didn't topple over once they were done. She was enjoying herself more than she'd anticipated.

"Help. I can't quite reach this branch," she said, stretching to hang a heavy Santa ornament on a thick, stubby branch close to the top. Rafe stepped behind her, slipping a hand around her waist and snuggling close as he took the ornament and hung it from the branch she'd been targeting. She almost dropped the damned ornament, raw desire making her knees weak.

He didn't move away when he was done hanging the decoration, but instead wrapped both hands around her front, his hands doing wicked things to her breasts as he kissed the back of her neck. She leaned against him, the hardness of his cock slipping into the pocket of heat between her thighs as she issued an unmistakable invitation for what she wanted him to do, right now, right there, standing by the Christmas tree. He didn't do anything more than continue to kiss and rub, shifting back and forth with a gentle friction that had them both panting with need.

"Rafe," she said breathlessly, reaching up to touch his face, "let's go upstairs. We'll finish the tree later."

He murmured his agreement, then suddenly the doorbell rang, yanking her out of the spell with a groan.

"Ignore it," she said.

"It's the food," he said, pulling on his jeans and grabbing his wallet. "Just take a sec. I'm starving," he added, dragging his eyes down her form as he said it.

They hadn't had dinner, though she wasn't hungry for anything but more of what Rafe was doing to her body. When he went to the door, she made sure she was out of eyesight, and shivered, missing his heat.

After he set the food on the table, he turned her around in his arms and took her mouth in a kiss so carnal her toes curled into the carpet, and she thought hazily that she might never wear clothes around her house again.

His tongue stroked hers repeatedly before sucking her into his mouth, tasting her deeply, touching her as she wanted him to touch her elsewhere. She'd never, ever, in her life been this turned on by a man's touch. She had a hard time coming, yes, but she was damned near the edge from what he was doing to her mouth, and she wanted more, saying as much when he released her from the kiss.

"We will…after the tree is done. Then we can have some dinner and admire it."

"I don't want to wait," she pleaded, her frustration reaching a fevered pitch. He kissed her again, and her body fit itself to his.

"Just a little longer. Don't be so bossy," he teased, kissing her nose before stepping away to reach for the last few ornaments. Joy wanted to scream but helped him nonetheless, placing the last ones much less thoughtfully than she had at first.

She was hot all over and craving whatever relief Rafe could offer. She'd never been this aroused in her entire life, and while it was all good, she was simultaneously afraid of losing the buzz, as if too much teasing would backfire, like overinflating a balloon and having it burst.

One look at Rafe's very aroused body and she knew her fears were probably baseless. This horny phase she was in wasn't likely to pass until she had him—maybe repeatedly.

PAM WOKE UP SUDDENLY, jerking her head from the desk with a cramp in her neck. Papers she'd been working on were plastered to her cheek. She peeled them off, casting a glance at the clock—it was 11:00 p.m. Another night on the cot in the back. She had to finish working on the budget first, though. Maybe if she crunched the numbers again, she'd find a way to squeeze more out of them.

Even with Joy's help, they would barely be able to afford the kind of party they were trying to give, and every cent counted—it was a last-ditch effort at keeping Second Chance open, outside of taking a loan that Pam had no idea how she'd ever pay back. She hadn't told the current residents what was going on, and didn't intend to, not until it was absolutely necessary.

If the worst happened, she'd already been in contact with some other shelters, and she would make sure her people had places to go. The problem was that the other places offered lodging, but they didn't necessarily offer as much support to get people started in new lives, new jobs, with a new sense of self.

Second Chance was about giving people a step up, not just a place to stay. She'd put everything in her life for the last fifteen years into building this place, and her vision had worked. She wasn't going to lose it without a fight.

The determination to fight was good—it was what she needed to keep herself from thinking about how much she missed Ted. They'd talked a few times on the phone, but the conversations had been stilted and touchy. She was hurt, so was he.

They weren't sure how to approach each other anymore, and she hated it—they'd been comfortable around each other since day one, and now it felt as if there were a huge wall between them. All she wanted was his touch, his kiss, and to be able to lean on him right now, but it wasn't possible.

Well, she'd stood on her own before, and she would now. Her thoughts drifted to her parents, and if she were honest, she'd been tempted to ask them to bail her out. They might do it, but then there would be strings, and she couldn't deal with that. They'd never give her the money without conditions, and that was why she'd never asked. They were good people, basically, but they had a different set of values, and they'd always wanted something different for her than what she wanted for herself.

As she turned her bleary eyes back to the pages spread all over the desk, she jumped when there was a soft knock at the office door. She got up— everyone was usually in their room by now, but someone must have noticed her light on.

As she opened the door, her heart plunged. Ted's large form filled the doorway.

"What are you doing here?" was the first thing out of her mouth, and when she saw him flinch, she instantly regretted her harsh welcome.

"I miss you," he said, his tone raw, matching the emotion in his eyes. "I know I screwed up. I want to make it better, I want us to make it better, Pam. Whatever it takes."

She stepped away, hearing what he was saying, but taken aback by the unexpectedness of it. He looked exhausted, haggard, even in his new suit. He must have come directly from the office. Still, she couldn't deny the happiness that surged inside of her. Maybe the wall between them was crumbling somewhat; maybe there was hope.

"I'm sorry, I didn't mean to snap. I'm tired, and I was just startled to see you so late. I've missed you, too," she admitted, closing the door behind him. "I was going over the budgets."

"Are things okay?"

"No," she said honestly, and she hoped without blame. "It's going to be tighter than tight, but we're throwing everything into a Christmas fund-raiser. We're hoping to turn attitudes around, get things back on track. If not, we won't make it long past the new year, unless I take a loan, but I don't know how the hell I would pay it off if I did. Douglas caused some damage, and Martin didn't exactly help—both of them were more than eager to talk to people around them, and of course they made it all sound so...bad."

He met her gaze, his own lighting with determination. "Let me help. I'm doing okay now, I'll get a raise soon—take the loan you were considering. I can shoulder the payments until you get back on your feet."

She shook her head. "No, I can't do that—you just bought the house, the car.... You have enough—"

"Stop," he said firmly.

She looked up and saw the fire in his gaze. Not anger, but something else, something close.

"If I tell you I can handle it, I can handle it, Pam."

Before she knew it, he was across the room, hauling her up against him. She didn't really have time to think. It felt so good; he was so tall and solid against her, she forgot what she was about to say, anyway.

He gazed down into her face, his large, rough hand stroking her cheek, then her hair. Desire for him throbbed straight down to her core. He'd affected her like this ever since the first time he'd touched her, and it had only grown stronger between them.

"You drive me crazy, Pam. I can't stand being away from you," he said, then lowered his lips to hers and took her in such a deep, erotic kiss that her eager responses spiked and she wound her arms around him, giving as good as she got.

Still, as their mouths mated and their bodies sang with the renewed contact, she became distracted by the bitter aftertaste of beer on his kiss, and drew back.

Ted, thinking nothing of the pause in their contact, took the moment to walk away, take off his jacket, his powerful back and arms visible beneath the white dress shirt. She took in his short brown hair, cut in an almost military style. She knew for a fact that the body under the clothes was as strong and virile as his movements suggested.

"Ted, have you been drinking?" she asked tentatively.

He took off his tie, pausing to look at her. "Yeah, I stopped for a beer after work."

"Oh, and you drove here?"

He threw the tie down on the desk.

"Alcohol was never my problem, Pam, as you well know. It was one beer, with dinner, and I sat and thought through what was happening with us. Then I drove over here. Would you like me to sign in? Take a Breathalyzer?"

She'd never been the brunt of his sarcasm, and it stung her. She'd stepped over the line. She'd insulted him, and tried to soften it.

"Stop, I'm sorry, I didn't mean it that way, I want to make sure you're okay is all."

"That's exactly it—you need to stop taking care of me, at least in that way you do with people here who need the guidance and the counseling. I'm your lover, Pam, I'm the man who loves you and wants to be your husband, have a life with you."

The anguish in his eyes tore at her, and she tried to respond, but nothing she could think of sounded right. He went on. "That's all I want you to see when you look at me, but I know there's always some part of you that sees the guy who came in here with nothing—the homeless bum all those people at the party saw, too."

The accusation was like a slap.

"No! How can you say that? I've never, ever thought of you like that. I don't think of anyone here like that, Ted, but especially not you."

He crossed to her again, taking her in his arms and giving her a heady demonstration of his desires—she had no doubt about the emotion that was between them by the time he spoke again.

His face was flushed, his eyes dark with desire, and she melted when his hardness nudged into her stomach. She wanted him so much it almost hurt. It was clear they were in sync on that. There was something about him—something steely that she hadn't really noticed before. Something new. It sent a shiver of excitement down her spine, but it also made her wary.

"If you mean that, then good," he said against her ear. "I want to help you with the problem here, because I know I was part of causing that problem in the first place, shooting my mouth off at that party. I allowed my needs to take precedence over yours, and I want to make up for that. Like any equal partner would."

"I know, I just…I don't know. I guess I have to get used to us being different now."

"Pam, the only thing different is that I'm independent again, I've gotten my life back, and want you to be part of it. Why is that hard for you? I can work all day, go for a beer, and it doesn't mean anything. It's what people all over the world do. I would have picked you up and we could have gone together, if I'd thought you'd have come."

What he was saying made perfect sense—so why was she still apprehensive? Had she been treating him like one of the residents without realizing it? The people who stayed at the shelter were strictly forbidden to drink, but those rules didn't apply to Ted anymore; it had been a knee-jerk reaction on her part, but what did that say about her?

Was she having problems thinking about him outside of the shelter, as an independent man who loved her? Did she only know how to navigate their relationship when he was defined by the rules of the shelter? Did that make things safe? Did she even know the Ted Ramsey who existed outside? She thought she did, but at the moment, it was all confusing as her mind spun with a thousand new questions.

"I don't know, Ted—I love you, too. I do think of you as my equal, of course I do—but I don't feel right allowing you to take on that kind of burden for me. I can't explain it right, but I can't do it."

He looked incredulous and hurt. She wanted to make it right, but she didn't know how to do that. She couldn't lie to him, but the truth was murky, even to her.

"So you would rather risk losing this place than leaning on me the way I had to lean on you so many times? Let me help, Pam."

"I...I can't. Not like that."

The door that had been opening between them shut again.

Ted shook his head, the pain he was obviously in clear in his voice, though he stood tall, proud. "I miss you like hell. I love you, and I want you so much I ache. Life is empty without you, but dammit, I won't be less than a whole man to you, Pam. I won't go through life that way. So you decide... and if you think you can lean on me, let me love you the way you've loved me, let me be there for you like you are for everyone else, then you call me. I have my pride, too. I'm not going to settle for less than everything from you."

He was out the door before she could respond, not that she knew what to say. Her heart went with him, ripped from her chest and leaving her alone with cold confusion.

Lost, she wrapped her arms around herself. She didn't know what to do—her world was unraveling and she didn't know how to make it stop. Ted was gone, and she was on the verge of losing the shelter, as well. So she did the only thing she could—she sat down and went back to work.

12

RAFE LAY AWAKE, sighing heavily as Joy slept. She'd passed out in his arms after a couple glasses of wine. His body was aching for hers after the torturous hours of sexy teasing. Had he been crazy to suggest the all-day-foreplay idea? *Nah.* They'd enjoyed every minute of it.

Still, their timing might have been a little off. She'd had an emotionally exhausting day, and he was frustrated beyond reason. They'd made some progress. He was getting to know the real Joy, and she'd actually loosened up a little. The idea she had about herself as passionless was crazy, but he also knew there was no way to convince her except by demonstration. If given the opportunity, he would be happy to oblige, but her pleasure was paramount. As turned on as he was, he wasn't about to engage in any more one-sided sex.

If only he could sleep as well, there'd be no problem. He closed his eyes, knowing it was a useless pursuit, and opened them again moments later, looking out the partially opened window into the side yard. He enjoyed having the bed next to the window, as well—it was a luxury that he'd never thought about in the city, where it was too noisy and hot.

Though, as much as he loved holding Joy next to him, there was something about being in bed with a deeply slumbering partner that made his insomnia even more excruciating. It was as if she'd gone somewhere he couldn't follow, which was pretty much true. He'd been left behind, and that added a new layer of stress to being awake. Now he was awake *and* alone.

Sleep was an experience that couples shared as much as anything else, not that he'd ever had a relationship last long enough to know. His job hadn't exactly been a good one for carrying on long-term relationships. He wanted nothing more than to be able to fall asleep right now and wake up tangled with Joy, and then they could pursue other pleasures, rested and relaxed.

She stirred in his arms, breaking his train of thought—thankfully—since thinking too much was the enemy in the middle of the night.

She curled close and planted a sleepy kiss on his chest. One simple touch and he was instantly hard and ready. Great. Now he was awake and turned on.

When she murmured something softly against his skin and moved her hand over him, stroking his length, he groaned her name and nudged her face up toward him. Her eyes remained shut. She was smiling, though, and wanton in how she arched against him, sliding her leg over his, bringing his cock in direct contact with her core. He gasped, his body seeking the contact even as his mind knew he should back away.

She was dreaming...and fast asleep.

He placed his hands on her upper arms to try to lever her away. Before she could do what he knew she was about to, he shifted, and she landed on his hip instead.

She was kissing and touching him all over, and he wondered if he should do this—she was asleep.

She dipped her head down and drew the head of his erection into her mouth and sucked, circling him with a velvet sweep of her tongue. He cried out, fisting his hands into the sheets so tightly he heard the elastic snap as they loosened from the edges. She was driving him insane with her mouth.

"Hon, are you awake? Joy?" he said roughly, trying to wake her, but then thought better of it. She was enjoying herself, and she knew she was with him—she was repeating his name with every kiss down the inside of his thigh. She had suggested using her dreams as a means of bridging into real-life sex, so he tried to get more comfortable with the idea. After grabbing a condom off the nighttable and sheathing himself, he lay back, relaxing.

He would let her do whatever she wanted—act out her dream, her fantasy, and play it by ear. If she stopped, God help him, he would stop, too.

"Do you like this?" she said sexily, brushing the ends of her silky hair over his sex, making him dizzy.

"I love it. I love everything you do," he said truthfully, and it occurred to him that he'd rarely been the passive recipient of lovemaking in his life. He was used to taking a more active role, setting the pace.

It was different—and nice—having her take the lead. He also suspected in real life she wouldn't be as bold or as aggressive. He swallowed hard as she ran a finger lightly over his sac.

When she looked up again, her face was illuminated by desire and need. She leaned over him slowly, emerging from the dark like a succubus, his lover who only came awake at night. It was incredibly sexy how she moved so sensuously, and for a moment he questioned if it was her dream or his. Even though sleeping, she was intriguingly accurate in her movements as she touched him everywhere and then gently drew her hand over his eyes.

"No looking…just feel," she commanded in a husky whisper, at once sounding like the daytime Joy he knew, but also not like her at all. He couldn't repress the erotic thrill of his sight being denied. She slid down his body, straddling him. He literally held his breath as he waited for what she'd do next, hoping.

She didn't take him right away, but moved along his shaft, riding the length of him without penetrating, her nipples grazing his chest as her moans became more and more excited—as did he.

Finally, when he thought he might lose it if she kept on, she enveloped him in one deep, downward thrust. She rode him hard, her palms planted solidly on his chest as she took what she wanted and gave so much in return. He'd been waiting so long to be with her like this that he tried to slow down, to make it last, but she was driving him over the edge with her.

He hung on, unsure how much longer he could last. The hard spasms wringing his cock told him in no uncertain terms that she was coming—and he let go and drove up inside. His orgasm triggered another one for her, much to his delight. She collapsed against him as he pulsed inside of her, enjoying the vestiges of his own climax.

"Joy?"

"Mmm. That was nice," she said sleepily against his chest, cuddling in. As far as he could tell, she hadn't woken up at all.

JOY STRETCHED OUT IN BED, more rested and satisfied than she had been in a long while. A glance at the clock told her it wasn't morning, yet she was alert and awake. However, something felt off—sitting up, she looked around, disoriented. She was completely nude for one, but that wasn't what was bothering her.

Rafe had come to bed with her, and now he was gone.

Grabbing her robe from the chair, she wondered if he'd left. She'd had another dream—a fantastic dream. The memory of it was wonderful, though she wished yet again that she could tap into that kind of passion when she was awake— it was obvious she was capable of it, so what was the problem?

As she hurried down the hallway, she stopped midstride, noting a particularly pleasant soreness between her legs. Her muscles were loose and relaxed, as they might be after a good workout. Something was definitely different.

She'd dreamed about Rafe, but she suspected she hadn't been completely dreaming. At least that wasn't what her body was telling her.

Entering the kitchen, she saw the back door open—she never left her door open like that.

"Rafe?"

"Out here," he responded in a quiet voice, and she stepped outside, tugging the robe more tightly.

"What are you doing?"

He was sitting on the swing on her backyard deck, quiet in the dark of the early morning.

"I couldn't sleep. I needed to get up, get some air. Sometimes when I'm laying awake for too long, it's like the dark is closing in on me. I have to get out."

"I understand, I just wondered where you went."

"Nice to be missed."

She heard the smile in his voice and went over to join him on the swing. "It must be close to morning."

"Another hour or so before sunrise, I'd say."

"Rafe…"

"Hmm?"

"Did we… I mean, did I…uh…?"

"Yes. You did. We did. Do you remember?"

"I remember the dream. My body remembers the real part, if you know what I mean. I can feel the, uh, after effects."

"Are you okay with that?" He turned to her, sounding curious.

She thought for a moment, then nodded. "I'm glad…. In my dream, I, uh…"

"Took control, rode me like the wild hussy you obviously are," he teased and she thumped him playfully in the arm.

"Smart guy. I guess I did that for real?"

"You sure did. It was awesome."

She was ridiculously pleased at his words, and relaxed. "It's a little weird, to think I could act it out so precisely, but I don't remember, not really. It's like a, well, like a dream."

"Do you remember how you got on top of me, and drove me to the edge? Do you remember coming…twice? I love how your face looks when you let go—you're beautiful anyway, but right in that moment, it's awesome," he said reverently.

Her face flamed. She did remember, though she wasn't used to the intimate flattery, and hadn't expected it.

"I do remember. I didn't know I'd actually done it—I'm not usually that forward."

"You can be that forward with me anytime you want, Joy. It was incredible."

"You still couldn't sleep."

"No, the two things aren't related. Lack of sex wasn't ever the reason I couldn't sleep," he said, and then, as if realizing how he'd sounded, tried to backtrack, but she put a finger to his lips, smiling. She had no doubt that Rafe had had lovers whenever he'd wanted them, but for some reason it didn't matter—he was here with her, now.

"I mean, uh, in other words, lack of sleep killed my sex life, not the other way around. I think it all stems from stress caused by my burnout."

She rushed to reassure him, not wanting to lose the mood. "No, I know what you mean. Don't worry."

His hand snaked around the back of her neck, drawing her in for a kiss that quickly turned hot. Caught up in the kiss, she gasped when his hand was suddenly under the flap of the robe, caressing her nipple into immediate hardness, and desire flooded her.

"Rafe, my goodness, we're in my backyard," she protested on a half laugh, half sigh, but he kissed her again, and she put her hand against the front of his jeans—he was as hard as a rock, and she moaned in pleasure at the discovery.

"I know."

"Would you like to go back inside?"

"Why don't we just stay here?"

"Out here? On the deck?"

"Sure. Why not? It's cool and dark, and I think that your dream life is telling you to be more aggressive, more adventurous, Joy. Find your passions, and run with them. Let go. As great as it was earlier, I'd like to share that with you when we're both awake. What do you think?"

She bit her lip, looking around—Warren's house was empty, obviously, and the next house was a full yard away, and her trees and hedges provided some privacy. No lights were on; the street was silent—they were completely alone.

"Okay." She took the plunge, her heart racing as she undid her robe, opening it, though not taking it off. It was enough exposure, more than she would have ever indulged in before. The idea of what they were about to do sent shivers of anticipation down her spine.

"Oh—wait, no protection," he said.

As he started to get up, she placed a hand on his arm. "I'm protected. I've taken the pill for years, and I'm okay, you know, health wise," she said, knowing that she didn't want him to leave her right now unless there was very good reason, since she might lose her nerve.

"Aw, babe, I'm good with that. The thought of being inside of you with nothing between us is a dream come true," he said roughly, releasing the snap on his jeans, and she wasted no time diving her hand inside, stroking him gently.

"You always feel so good, Rafe. I love touching you," she whispered, telling him she was as turned on as he was. She was, completely and utterly turned on. Rafe was right—she did have passion, particularly for him.

"You drive me crazy…the way you put your mouth on me earlier, then took control, I loved it," he responded and a thrill of excitement ran through her.

"You liked me taking control?"

He looked her in the eyes, utterly serious. "I loved it. I love watching you do me, sliding over me, touching me everywhere…. I'm yours for the taking, babe. Anything you want, I'll give it to you," he said, sliding his hand down between her legs and rubbing his thumb over her clit until she was shaking with need.

"Rafe, sit…. Sit back on the swing," she said in a trembling voice, aroused beyond all measure. The cool morning air played over her hot skin, and she watched as he did exactly as she said, pushing his jeans down his long legs to the floor of the deck and sitting back on the swing, watching her, but not moving a muscle.

"Want to sit on Santa's lap?" His mischievous tone sparked something playful and naughty inside of her, and she laughed, feeling like the sexy woman she was in her dreams.

"I do. I know exactly what I want for Christmas."

"Come on over and tell me."

"I'd rather show you," she said seductively, poising herself before him as if to sit, raising the bottom of her robe and lowering down, taking him in deep, until the base of his erection pushed against her pubic bone. She snuggled her backside against his lap, finding her balance, and leaned back on him.

"That's perfect. You fit against me, around me, so absolutely perfectly," he said, his voice ragged, and she knew he was as aroused as she was. His arms came around her, holding her in place as he pushed the swing in motion, the sway creating a gentle rocking motion without either of them actually moving.

"Is this what you wanted?" he asked, his voice thick with excitement.

"Yes," she gasped, winding her hands up around the back of his neck, holding on, kissing his jawline. He kept her still, and didn't thrust or urge her to move, the swing levering them against each other, his shaft buried so deeply inside her she embraced every inch of him and yet wanted more.

"What about this?" he asked, sliding one hand down between her legs as he parted the slick flesh there to rub his long fingers over all the right spots.

"Oh, yes…especially that," she agreed. The swing's movement deepened the motion, and she began to tighten unbearably.

Rafe gave up the Santa game, his face against the back of her neck where he investigated the taste of her skin quite thoroughly. She closed her eyes, the swing moving them together like a single, undulating wave.

The swaying motion was so slow, so deep, and she was hypnotized by the onslaught of sensations that she had no control over. Groaning in ecstasy as he uttered guttural, raw words in her ear, she gave herself up and was lifted out of herself, the world around her, traveling to some special, magical place with Rafe.

He filled her so completely, she wasn't sure she could breathe. Her core was hot and slick, the friction unbearable, and she needed to find relief, though the thought of stopping was also unbearable.

At precisely the right moment, he tipped his hips up from the seat of the swing, ever so slightly, thrusting deeper and catapulting her over the edge. The powerful climax took her so thoroughly by surprise that she cried out, regardless of their semi-public location.

His lips caught her exclamations, swallowed them with his own groans of satisfaction as he pulsed inside of her. She knew she'd never experienced anything quite so miraculous as they drifted down from the heights together, wrapped around each other as intimately as two people could be.

They sat together, still swinging gently back and forth, and she knew something had changed for her. Something deep, something more than desire or even gratitude tugged at her. She didn't want to think. She hated to even get up and have to separate from him at all.

Still, as she opened her eyes, flashing lights against the trees and Warren's roof caught her eye.

"Those Christmas lights look funny," she commented.

Rafe jerked upright, keeping his arms around her as he stood, stabilizing her so she wouldn't fall.

"Shit—those aren't lights—it's a fire."

13

JOY RAN INSIDE. Frantically searching for her cell phone, she found it on the counter and dialed 911. Rafe had taken off like a shot, clad only in jeans and bare feet, yelling after her to call for help as he bolted across the street to the house that was burning. She'd called after him—what did he plan to do? Her hands shook as she reported the fire and raced around the house grabbing her clothes, anxious to go find Rafe.

She knew the house belonged to the older lady he always talked with, Bessie, whose lights he'd helped string. The elderly widow whose lights Joy had grumped and groused about, and whom she'd refused to help when Rafe had asked her the week before.

She hung up—she didn't exactly have time to indulge in guilt—and ran back into the street. Sirens screamed in the distance, and the neighbors emerging from their homes were milling about in various states of morning dress, but she didn't see Rafe. Where was he?

She watched the flames engulf the house, black

smoke pouring out of the windows, and knew in her heart where he was. He'd gone in. That was why he'd run off so quickly—Rafe had gone inside to try to save Bessie. She felt utterly helpless, and sick with worry.

Finally, fire engines and a rescue unit ripped up the small street, an ambulance on their heels, pulling to a quick halt in the front yard. The outside air was acrid and thick as the sun rose in a halo of smoke over the house. Joy was hit by the intense heat when she ran up to the firefighter closest to her and grabbed his arm, shouting to him that Rafe had gone inside.

He and three other men dragging heavy hoses headed for the porch as Rafe appeared in the door, an archway of fire framing them all. Joy held her breath as two of the firefighters took the body of the small woman from Rafe's arms, and another helped Rafe away from the house as his body clutched in a fit of choking coughs.

All of a sudden, the arch over the front porch collapsed, Christmas lights and all, right where Rafe and the other men had stood moments before. Police arrived, and they corralled people back to the other side of the street, but Joy stayed in place, all the action happening around her as if she'd become invisible. No one bothered her, or she didn't notice.

She couldn't see Rafe at all, and that snapped her back to life. She rushed forward to where she'd spotted him last. The sounds of flames, rushing water, loud engines and louder shouts surrounded her, but she had only one focus: Rafe. A fireman blocked her path and she pushed past him.

"You have to let me by. My, uh… My husband is hurt—he went in the house." She shook his arm, making him listen. "He's the guy with no shirt—I saw him come out, but I can't find him—I have to make sure he's okay. Please," she pleaded desperately.

The fireman nodded. "Your husband saved that woman's life, ma'am. He's over there." He pointed her in the direction of a rescue vehicle where Rafe sat on the edge between the open doors, an EMT handing him an oxygen mask. She took a few steps and stumbled, tears blurring her vision.

"Rafe, oh, my God," she cried, throwing her arms around him. "What on earth…I didn't think you were going to go *in* there when you ran off," she said, holding on tight.

His chest rumbled against her, and she didn't know if he was coughing or laughing, but he squeezed her tightly and then gently disengaged her arms from his neck, waving away the EMT who was hovering.

"I'm fine—I knew the house since I'd been in there a few times, and I found her easily. Just sucked up some smoke is all. It was only a minute or two I was in there, no big deal."

He coughed again, and she drew back, looking

into his face, something powerful arcing between them. This was more than a two-week fling. She knew it, deep inside her heart.

He caressed her cheek. His tone had been reassuring, as it must have been for hundreds of people before her, people he reassured and saved every day. Suddenly she didn't want to be the one being protected—or rather, she didn't mind his concern, but he was the one who needed the help right now. Why hadn't she seen it before?

"I'm okay, Joy. Not even a scratch, see?"

"It could have been a lot more than a scratch."

"But it wasn't. Bessie's okay, and I'm okay."

The image of his handsome, soot-stained face was engraved into her memory, and her heart, and she couldn't find words, so she simply held on to him a little longer. When his arms slipped around her, too, hugging her close, in spite of herself she fell in love with him right there on the spot.

Too bad he would be out of her life in a little over a week. He planned to head back to New York right after New Year's.

She loved Rafe, but he was leaving. What had passed between them a moment ago was something stronger than lust, but did he love her, too?

Rafe's gaze followed the movements of the people around him, the firefighters getting control of the blaze, the onlookers talking among themselves, the police keeping people back. The ambu-

lance roared past them, whisking Bessie away—
whose life Rafe had definitely saved.

Joy could see how much it all meant to him, and
how painful it was for him to be on the outside
looking in. Rafe was about helping people; that was
who he was. He saved lives; things like running
into burning buildings came as naturally to him as
breathing came to everyone else. Somehow, he'd
even managed to break down the walls Joy had built
around herself and help her, too.

She'd never been more sure of herself in her life
than she was right at that moment—more alive,
more in love—and it was about more than sex. Who
was helping Rafe? She was immediately ashamed,
her life and her problems having been the center of
their focus to this point. Whether he loved her or
not, she knew what she had to do. This time, it was
about Rafe.

Everything crystallized; all the concerns she'd
had, all the neuroses, pressures and worries that
had plagued her life fell away, meaningless. She'd
spent her life withholding the best of herself, afraid
to give in case someone should take what she was
offering and walk away. Ever since her mother had
left, she'd held the most vulnerable parts of herself
back, determined never to let anyone else hurt her
that much again.

With everyone except for Rafe. Maybe it was different for him because he was the opposite. He opened

himself to life and he wasn't afraid of anything. He did what he did because it mattered to him.

What mattered to her?

Certainly not the toy company, their profit margins or the promotion she'd been so determined to get. None of that mattered.

There was the shelter. That mattered. Maybe she'd been going about everything the wrong way— she wanted her work to make a difference, the way Rafe's did. She wanted to use her talents to help people who needed it, like Pam and the residents at the shelter. She wanted to throw herself out into the world and see what happened, and if she got hurt, well, there were worse things. Like the numbed life she had been living.

There was more than enough help to go around for clients who could afford to pay for it, but what about everyone else? While financial security had always meant a lot to her, she could see it wasn't the cornerstone of life, nor should it be.

Her dreams of Rafe had been pushing her to risk, to take more chances, to go after what she wanted and to make things happen—and not only in bed, but in life.

As the meaning of the moment dawned on her, it was as if a latch opened up inside of her and she could breathe freely for the first time in her life. There wouldn't be any more dreams, no more talking and acting out in her sleep. She slanted a gaze at Rafe's sweaty, dirty, lovely chest and smiled—she'd be plenty able to live out her fantasies wide awake from now on. All of them.

Boldly taking his hand as they crossed the street back to her house, she knew she wanted to start her new lease on life by helping him as much as he'd helped her.

The question was how?

RAFE WALKED ALONG the hospital hallways, following Joy, who knew her way around the place better than he did, though in his experience all hospitals more or less looked the same.

Garland and fake Christmas trees, menorahs and other holiday items were scattered throughout the stark yellow-white hallway. As much as the decorations aimed to offer holiday cheer, for many of the people in here, and many of their loved ones, it was not a happy season, and no amount of decorations would make it one.

It had often been difficult to get through the holidays when he'd been riding the ambulance—the holidays were a time of year when people could be at their best, or their worst. Loneliness and hardship, poverty and loss were often highlighted, the contrast sometimes too much to bear. Rafe had usually turned to his family to remember what was good and happy about this time of year.

As for right now, two days until Christmas, being

in the hospital reminded him of the sadness he'd had close personal contact with over the years, though there were happy stories, too. The Christmas babies born, the lives saved, the tragedies averted, as was the case with Bessie, whom they'd come to see. Focusing on the upside was how he'd gotten by as long as he had, though apparently he'd lost that ability somewhere along the way.

He'd rarely seen people after he'd brought them to the hospital, and even though he hadn't acted in an official capacity with Bessie, he felt off balance. He held a bunch of flowers in one arm and clasped Joy's hand in his other. She was walking at a slightly faster pace, looking for the room, full of cheer.

To be honest, he'd been surprised when she'd told him she wanted to go with him to the hospital. He'd had the impression that she didn't connect much with her neighbors, but then, a lot of things seemed to have changed with Joy. In the two days since the fire, she'd been far more energized, unbelievably sexy. In bed—and out of it—she was rocking his world.

She was also busy, working on something every minute, usually associated with the shelter. They'd both spent every free minute getting the fundraising party planned, which was why they were late to see Bessie. Christmas was two days away, and Rafe knew how much keeping that shelter open meant to Joy. Still, the changes in her demeanor since the fire were considerable, if a little mysterious to him.

Among other things, she'd taken to wearing her hair down instead of tied back, and she seemed more relaxed. He found it hard to believe that getting over her sexual inhibition had led to such a personality shift, but it didn't really matter. What did matter was that she was happy. He liked to think he had something to do with it.

The more time he spent with Joy, the less he thought about going back to New York, and maybe not even going back to his job. Working hospital shifts and driving ambulance was tough on relationships, and he'd made his work the center of his life for so long because nothing else more important had presented itself. Joy was changing all of that.

As they reached the end of the long hallway, nurses and activity buzzing around, he teetered on the edge of a huge decision. He was technically on a leave of absence, but he was considering making that leave permanent. In fact, maybe he'd already made the choice.

He wanted more time here in San Diego and Joy was the reason for that. Going back to New York without her was quickly becoming a nonoption, but he wasn't sure what she would think about that. Would she want to tie herself down to a relationship with him, when he had no idea what was next?

Stopping by the door of Bessie's room, he heard

voices, and knocked softly, making sure it was okay to enter.

"Rafe! My hero, you come in here," Bessie exclaimed, holding her arms out. She wasn't alone, he could see, a younger, well-dressed couple were sitting at her bedside.

As he hugged Bessie and stood back, he handed her the flowers, aware of Joy right behind him. Reaching back for her hand, he drew her next to him.

"Hey, Bessie. You're looking chipper—glad to see it."

"Yes, well, thanks to you, I'm around here to tell the tale," she said, her eyes moving to Joy. "I see you brought a friend."

"You know Joy, Bessie, from across the street. She called 911 when we saw the fire that morning," he explained and nudged Joy forward.

"Well, I can't thank you enough for that, Joy," Bessie said, her eyes tearing up. "You both saved my life, and the firemen got there in time to at least save many of the things on the second floor— there's smoke damage, but so many of my memories, my wedding pictures, my husband's things, were upstairs," she said, choking up, and couldn't continue.

Joy bent over and hugged Bessie, reassuring her.

"I'd be happy to help get them out and clean things up, if you'd like me to do that. I wish we could have seen it sooner, is all, but Rafe is the real hero. I only made a phone call," Joy said, releasing Bessie from the hug.

She wiped away a few tears and nodded. "They told me as much, and I can't believe you came into that burning building for me," Bessie scolded Rafe gently in an emotional voice, and Rafe stayed silent, not knowing what to say.

"I can see you don't like being told you're a hero, but you are. Anyway, this is my son Charles, and his wife, Melinda. They came as soon as they heard, and I guess I'll be staying with them for a while until the house can be taken care of."

"So you'll be rebuilding?" Joy asked politely, and Bessie nodded.

"The old place needed a lot of repair—it was an overheated circuit that started the fire. I left a Crock-Pot on all night, and I guess the fire started in the wall where it was plugged in, so they say."

"That's awful, Bessie, but at least you're okay," Rafe added, shaking hands with Charles and Melinda, who looked both relieved and concerned as they chatted. Rafe didn't want to intrude on the family moment—he was used to being on the outside of such things.

"We'd love for Mother to come live with us permanently, but she likes being on her own. It's nice to know she has such good neighbors," Charles said.

"There aren't many who would run into a

burning building to save someone," Bessie added with blatant admiration.

"What do you do for a living, Rafe? Mom said you were here on vacation?" Bessie's daughter-in-law asked.

"I'm a paramedic, back in New York," Rafe said casually and tried to change the conversation to focus back on Bessie, but his attempt failed yet again.

"Well, you're a hero to us—I hope you'll let us do something to show our appreciation," Melinda said, and Rafe waved away her offer.

"That's not necessary, really."

"We insist. Please." Charles met his gaze, and Rafe knew it was important to the younger man to do something to show his gratitude, but Rafe wasn't about to accept any personal payment for doing what anyone could have done.

"I'll tell you what. If you're all in town, there's a Christmas fund-raiser at a local homeless shelter tomorrow night that we're helping out. We'd love it if you could come, Charles and Melinda, and Bessie, if you're up to it."

"We're probably taking Mother home tomorrow morning, but we would like to make a donation. I wish we could do more," Charles said. "You saved my mother. After having lost Dad, this could have been the saddest holiday ever for our family, and you changed that. We can't express what that means to us. Thank you."

Rafe nodded, accepting the thanks awkwardly. Joy's hand was on his back as they all shook hands and said their goodbyes. Walking down the hall, Joy turned to him as they waited for the elevator.

"Rafe, in all the years you did your job, did anyone ever say thank you?"

He shrugged. "Sure. Some people sent cookies, or dropped a note."

"No one ever personally thanked you for helping them?"

"New York is a big place, Joy, and we handled so many cases every day…. There were several ambulance companies, even more drivers. It was a daunting number of people. Patients couldn't tell us apart let alone know our names, especially when they're in crisis. It was our job to help them. Thanks isn't necessary," he explained.

The elevator doors opened, and as she stepped inside, she raised her emotion-filled eyes to his.

"It's something you deserve."

"Knowing we've helped is enough."

Or was it? he asked himself, though somewhat ashamed of the question. What he did wasn't supposed to be about recognition, but had the endless stream of people whom they'd helped and never seen again finally gotten to him? Was it the source of his burnout and insomnia?

Rafe didn't like that idea. Maybe it was more about never knowing how most of those patients ended up—he only saw them at their worst, but never, as he'd had the chance to do with Bessie, when things turned for the better.

In the shelter, Joy and Pam could see someone move from destitution to success, from being dependent to self-sufficient, and that was a reward he'd never had. All he'd seen was the never-ending moments of crisis. It was a reality he'd never acknowledged before.

Joy murmured her agreement with what he'd said, but Rafe kept his other thoughts to himself, considering them less than noble. Having Joy think anything less of him bothered him a lot. Still, did he always have to be the hero? Was his ego so bound up in what he did that he didn't even realize it? He didn't like to think so, but maybe.

As they left the hospital, Joy was distracted, lost in thought, even through lunch.

"You're quiet," he observed, toying with his own food and caught up in his own thoughts. It was nice that they could be quiet together, but he wondered what was on her mind.

"Sorry, going over party stuff. Thinking about Bessie, and how happy I am about how it all turned out—I hope the same happens for Pam."

"It was good of your boss to give you these few days off before the holiday."

"Uh, yes—" she looked down at her soup "—I

told him about the fire and everything, and he was very supportive."

"So things are working out there," he prompted, picking up on some weird sense that she was holding something back from him.

"Yeah, things are working out very well, but really, the shelter is what I am focusing on right now. That's where my real passion lies, and I guess I never realized that."

"That's wonderful, Joy—they're lucky to have you."

His thoughts circled back to his own situation. Maybe getting his old sense of purpose back wasn't the right move—maybe it was time to try something new. Instead of trying to find the meaning his life used to have, he should look for something new, much as Joy was discovering. He'd always assumed he'd drive ambulances forever, but now he was questioning that. The prospect of returning to the job brought him none of the anticipation and excitement it used to. That was something he had to accept. It was over.

When they returned home, Joy headed off to run some errands for the shelter party, and Rafe sat by the phone for a long time. Finally, convinced he was doing the right thing, he picked it up and dialed his boss. It was time to leave his old life behind him.

14

"IT'S CRAZY—I CAN'T believe all these people showed up! This is miraculous!" Pam swirled around to face Joy, nearly dropping her punch on the person next to her, more thrilled and happy than she had been in weeks. The party was packed; music was playing; residents were decked out in their Christmas best and making contacts and showing the employers, supporters and community members who had come to the party that they were good, decent people who deserved a second chance. It was all she could have dreamed of and more.

Still, her cheer lapsed slightly as she noticed one gap in the crowd; Ted hadn't come. She hadn't been sure if he would or not. She'd left an invitation on his phone, but he'd never responded. She'd been too busy to brood on everything that had happened between them. One thing for certain—she knew she still didn't want him taking financial responsibility for the shelter. Not because she didn't think he could handle it, but because, well…this place was *hers*. She didn't want to have the burden placed on anyone else but her.

However, at least for the moment, it looked as if they were becoming financially secure again. Donations were pouring in faster than they had in a long while, and she'd already set up several new contacts for services. She thought this Christmas party would be an annual event—thank God for Joy.

"You really saved us here, Joy. I know the social and counseling aspects of this business inside out, but I guess I was never a great publicist—I never really thought about bringing the community inside, opening the doors and letting them see the place, who lives here, how we work," she said, giving her friend's hand a squeeze.

"I'm so happy for you, Pam, that this is going so well. The shelter is going to benefit big time, in spite of the rumors—no one is talking about it, or even cares. It's so obvious you do good work here, and that the place is an asset to the community."

"Thanks—it's more than I ever dreamed of. Thanks to you and your help—you are a PR goddess. Speaking of which, what about your promotion at Carr? Have you heard anything?"

"I actually…I called Ken today and turned it down—in fact, I quit."

Pam was obviously shocked.

"You quit? Your job?"

"Yes. The corporate life isn't for me. Never was. I worked hard and I was good at it, but I was never happy. Not really. One side benefit is I saved and invested a good bit of money. Now I can afford time off to find out what I really love doing, and I have a feeling it's going to be finding some career through which I can help support organizations like yours."

"That's fantastic! That's such a huge step, Joy."

"It's wonderful. It was time for me to make a move."

"You do seem like a load has been taken off, though. You seem happier. Lighter."

"There is some other news, though. I need you to keep it between us."

Pam leaned in, noting how Joy's gaze had traveled over to Rafe, and she wondered if her friend was about to share wedding plans.

"I may be moving to New York."

"What?" Pam said loudly, drawing the attention of some people nearby. "What? Why?"

"I quit my job to be with Rafe. I want to help him work through this sleep problem and get back to his job. He loves it, Pam. You should have seen him at that fire, and with Bessie afterward. It's his life. I want to share that life with him, hopefully. So I'm going to tell him later that I want to go back to New York with him when he's finished his vacation here. I'd like to explore new career options for myself, and help him get back on his feet."

"Wow. That's not what I was expecting, but *wow*. That's huge! Are you sure? I mean, it's clear you two are crazy about each other, though—and

I'm happy for you. It's nice to be madly in love, but you know, that's a big chance to take," Pam said, happy for Joy, but unable to keep a wistful note from her voice.

"Well, we haven't actually said anything about love yet—in fact, we haven't said anything about anything, but it's time—I'm crazy about him. I have to take a chance. There's just something…"

"Special. I think you're right. There is. You should do whatever's necessary to hold on to it."

Joy hugged her. "Pam, thanks. I know you mean that. I know it's especially difficult because things have been rough between you and Ted lately, but—"

"No, please. Not tonight. It's killing me what's happened with us, but I think it's over. I haven't heard from him since our blowout the other night, and he's not here now, so, you know. I think that's it," she said, trying to sound brave, but her voice quavered, giving her raw emotions away.

"I don't think so. Honey, I know you love Ted like crazy, and he loves you, too—but you both let your pride get in the way. Rafe has taught me that relationships are about helping each other, leaning on each other, and maybe you might have a teensy bit of a hard time doing that with Ted?"

Pam started to bristle, but then gave in, her shoulders slumping. "Maybe. I guess it's because I'm used to standing on my own."

"You're the heart of this place, Pam, no doubt,

but you can't be afraid to lean on the people who want to help you."

"I know. I guess in my heart I didn't want this place to fail, and I didn't want anyone—including Ted, especially Ted—to think I'd failed, as well. When he wanted to take on the loan, I wasn't protecting him, I was protecting *me*. I wanted to save the place on my own terms."

"You did."

"No, I did it with help from my friends—and I should have let Ted help, too."

"It's never too late."

"It may well be. I don't know how to make Ted understand. I really hurt him."

Joy smiled, her gaze sliding to the door. "Actually, I think you're in for a surprise."

Pam followed Joy's gaze. There was Ted standing tentatively by the door, a group of people around him as they all dealt with their coats and said hellos. The world dropped away as Pam's eyes met his and she started breathing again—had it only been a few days? He looked so handsome, and she knew Joy was right—pride and ego were no reasons to throw away the best thing in her life.

She started to make her way through the crowd, to go to him, but Joy's hand was on her arm.

"Wait. Just a minute."

Pam stopped, puzzled, as Ted and the group he'd apparently come with went forward to the platform at the front of the room. As they did so, Pam realized that she knew the four men who followed along with Ted—though they looked so different now. She held her breath, realizing what was going on and not quite believing it. Ted took the podium, appearing a bit apprehensive as he cleared his throat, using his booming baritone to get the room's attention.

"Hello, everyone, happy holidays. I'm Ted Ramsey, and I used to be a resident here, not so long ago. I was thirty-eight when I lost everything and ended up on the street. I used to live in New Orleans, where I worked as a handyman in the building where I lived. Because of Hurricane Katrina, I lost my home and my job, and the building was never rebuilt. For me, everything was gone. Absolutely everything," he said, clearing his throat again. The room was completely silent, listening, and he continued.

"I was evacuated to San Diego. I didn't have any family, and my friends were all in similar situations, so I lived in alleys, didn't eat or sleep for days in a row sometimes. I tried to find jobs, but I didn't have money for new clothes, no address, and the more you're out there, the less anyone wants to give you a chance. To most people, I was a bum. I was arrested for sleeping in a park and the cop who let me off told me about Second Chance."

Pam put her hands to her mouth, seeing the admiration among the listeners as Ted continued.

"Thing is, anyone can end up homeless—you think it can't happen to you, but it can. The world can take you to some pretty low places. However, because of this shelter and people like Pam, there are second chances. All of us here—" he gestured to the people standing proudly behind him "—found a new life though this place, and some of us found even more than that," he said, his eyes meeting Pam's, his tone husky with emotion. She'd never loved him more. He smiled then, as he wrapped up, and her world lit brighter.

"We're hoping you'll listen to our stories, and support this place well into the future, in any way you can."

Ted stepped down to a deafening level of applause and cheers, the audience turning their attention back to the stage to listen to the other members of the group. Joy hugged Pam, her own eyes teary.

"Ted did this on his own—he told me, but he wanted it to be a surprise. He contacted every person he could find to come back here and share their stories. They flew in from all over. He did it for you, most of all though, Pam, because he loves you. Make no mistake about that," Joy said, and Pam could only nod, emotions bunching any words she might have spoken into a soundless knot in her throat as Joy stepped away.

Then Ted was there, large and handsome, close and warm, and all she could do was throw her arms around him in front of God and everyone without thinking twice. She didn't care what anyone thought, only Ted. She loved him, and she told him so, needing him to know that he'd always come first with her. When his arms wrapped around her and their lips met, Pam knew it was going to be one of the best Christmases ever.

JOY SHRIEKED AS SHE and Rafe ran from the car to her house, lugging bags of gifts and goodies from the party, laughing as they got soaked anyway, not moving nearly fast enough as the rain poured down in dark sheets. The heat wave that had been baking Southern California for weeks was finally giving way as cooler weather settled in for Christmas.

It wasn't snow, but she'd take it.

Dropping the bags safely on her porch, she looked at Rafe—quite the stud, decked out in his suit. Laughing with glee, she ran back down the steps and began dancing out into the yard, arms spread, glorying in the cool wash of the rain.

With a laugh, he joined her and pulled her up against him, taking her mouth in a drugging kiss as the rain poured over them and they swayed back and forth in a slow, wet dance. It thrilled her that Rafe was able to get her so hot, so fast, and most of all it thrilled her that she'd discovered such a deep well of passion in her life, and she wanted to share it with him.

"Want to take the party inside?" she asked seductively, tugging at his tie.

"Absolutely."

Arm in arm they walked back up the porch and in the door, peeling off their wet clothes layer by layer until they were nude and shivering up against each other.

"I think a hot shower is needed," she said, her teeth chattering. She squealed as Rafe picked her up in his arms and climbed the stairs. In the shower, he returned to kissing her, turning the hot water on high without breaking their lip-lock even for a second.

Joy was in heaven as the steamy water and Rafe's touch chased away the chill. He was so solid and warm, her hands drifting over every inch of his skin was a pursuit of which she could never tire.

When he hoisted her up, pressing her back against the tile and sliding home, deep inside her welcoming body, it was all so right and natural, as if their bodies were made for each other and no one else. She gave herself up to him, completely trusting, more than happy to follow his lead as he made her body soar with pleasure she hadn't known she was capable of.

Joy hoped she'd get a lot more chances to make up for lost time in the physical-pleasure department, but what she was experiencing with Rafe was also deepened by emotions she'd never felt for any other man.

Coming down from their interlude, they soaped each other from head to toe and then rubbed each other dry with soft towels. Rafe trotted off to grab some wine and agreed to meet her downstairs. It was late, but what the hell? It was the night before Christmas Eve and she wanted to celebrate.

She couldn't believe she'd quit her job, or how good it felt. She knew it deep inside, in her gut. It was new to be so sure, so confident. She liked it.

She'd have to find something else eventually, but for now she planned on enjoying an extended vacation, hopefully with the man of her dreams. Joy paused, a little riff of nervousness running down her spine as she contemplated what she'd say. What if Rafe was still in favor of their original plan? A few weeks of no-strings fun that she now very much wanted to attach some very hefty strings to?

Donning a sheer nightgown, Joy found him on the sofa where he sat quietly, lounging only in a pair of flannel house pants, his beautiful chest bare, and her heart fluttered at the picture he made. The rain poured outside, and he didn't seem to notice her arrival as he studied the twinkling lights of the Christmas tree with an intense expression that didn't seem to fit with their light-hearted evening.

"You're staring a hole in that tree—everything okay?"

He looked up, smiling. "Fine. Just thinking. The tree is pretty. I notice you snuck some gifts underneath."

She sat down close by his side, cuddling in. "A few."

"I have some things for you, too, though I have to wrap them," he confessed.

She swatted him playfully—they'd said no gifts, but now that she was in full swing with the Christmas spirit, she couldn't resist putting some prettily wrapped packages under the tree. Working up her courage, she stood up.

"I have one thing I want to give you now, actually."

He smiled flirtatiously at her. "Again?"

"Not that, at least, not this minute. A real present."

"You don't have to do that, Joy," he said. "We should wait until Christmas morning. It's only one more day."

"I really want to. I really want you to have this now, because I have some things I want to tell you, and it's all wrapped up, so to speak."

"Well, okay. I'm never one to turn down a present," he teased as she walked to her desk on the other side of the room and took a folder from under the large calendar that rested under her computer.

She sat, placing the folder between them, and explained in a rush, "It's not a gift like the ones under the tree, but it's something I wanted you to have for Christmas. I got the idea from Ted, you know, how he contacted all those people for Pam and the shelter, and from our visit to Bessie the other day. I thought, I don't know…that it could help you get over your burnout problem. Just open it and stop me from continuing to babble, okay?"

Rafe looked at her quizzically and slowly reached to open the folder, then pulled out a thick pile of e-mails.

"What is this?"

"Your boss helped me get in touch with some of the people you've helped. When I called them, they were so enthusiastic to finally have a chance to contact you and say thank-you—like you said, at the time someone is picked up, they don't know who you are, and time passes—but so many people jumped at the chance to tell you what your help meant, Rafe. I wanted you to know, too."

He waded through the stack, smiling at some, remembering others very clearly, caught up in a string of memories that he shared with her as they went through the e-mails together, and when they'd reached the last one, he looked at her, his heart in his eyes.

"Joy…I don't know what to say." He lifted his hand to her face, his expression solemn and emotional. "Thank you. This…this is beyond words."

"I did the legwork, but you've done these wonderful things for all of these people, and you've made a huge difference in my world, too, Rafe. I need you to know that. In fact—" She took a deep breath, started to speak, but then stopped.

Her hands were shaking as she knew she teetered on the edge of something wonderful or potentially terrible in her life. What if she was jumping the gun? What if her instincts were off and he didn't want her as much as she hoped he did? Telling Rafe her true feelings, what she wanted, was an enormous risk. The words clogged in her throat. Was she ready? She'd quit her job, turned down a promotion and was determined to start a new life. Only this time, it wasn't her job, but her heart that was on the line.

Rafe looked deeply concerned, as he always did when something troubled her.

"Hey, what can be so horrible? You can tell me anything, Joy."

He took her hands, cold from nerves, and warmed them in his own. She stared for several long moments into his face, the blinking lights of the tree creating a cheerful backdrop that bolstered her courage. It was Christmas, after all. The time for miracles, right?

She took another deep breath, getting the rest of it out as quickly as she could. "How you saved Bessie, and those e-mails, talking to the people you've helped—what you do is so important, so meaningful. I want to have that meaning in life, too, work I can be as passionate about as you are about yours."

"That's wonderful, Joy," he said sincerely. She

knew he meant it, but he also looked guarded and drew back from her slightly. Fear lodged in her chest, but she pushed herself forward. She had to tell him, for better or worse.

"So…I quit my job. I'm not going back to Carr. I love you, Rafe. I love how you make me feel, how you care for others, and how terrific and brave you are. I want to go to New York with you and help you get back to your job. We can work it out together. I want…I bought a…ticket, already," she finished lamely, gripping his fingers tightly because he hadn't let go and she needed something, anything, to hold on to.

"You bought a ticket? To New York?"

She nodded, not particularly encouraged by his incredulous tone.

"You quit your job?"

She nodded again, wishing he would stop repeating everything she'd said, as if she weren't skittish enough already about laying her heart on the line.

"Um, well, okay. I don't know if you'll need that ticket, but—"

Her heart sank and she pulled her hands away quickly. "It's okay, I know, I dumped all of that on you out of nowhere, and if you don't want me to go back with you, I won't. God, I'm such an idiot, I don't know what I was thinking—"

"Joy. Stop," he said softly as he pushed her still-damp hair back from her forehead.

"Huh?"

"Let me finish." He blew out a breath, relief evident in his expression. "For a moment there, I thought you were going to tell me it was over, and I needed to hit the highway. Good thing you didn't, because I love you, too. Utterly and completely."

Confusion stopped her cold. "You love me? You thought I was going to break it off? I don't get it— you said I don't need the ticket...."

"Right. You don't. Because I quit my job, too. I thought I'd stay here in California. Be with you. To start a new life."

Nothing he said could have surprised her more. She sat back, stunned.

"You... You quit? I thought your job meant everything to you. The letters..."

He looked down at the sheaf of papers. "They're fantastic—I'll always treasure them. They're also a goodbye of sorts, I guess."

To say she was stunned was an understatement. "No, Rafe, you can't give up! We can go back to New York—you can be with your family, we'll solve this insomnia problem, and we'll get you back on the ambulance."

"I'm not giving up, I'm letting go. There's a difference."

"Rafe, but," she started to argue, and he held up a hand to stop her.

"The longer I stayed here, the more I was with

you, and away from work, the more I realized I didn't want to go back. It's time for a new phase. A change. I guess I knew that, it was why I got so burned out in the first place, but I wasn't able to accept it until now. I'll find a job here, maybe something new, I don't know yet. Maybe I'll go back to school. Are you willing to take that risk with me? To jump into the future, not knowing what it holds for us?"

"I think…yes…I'd like that," she said, still processing the turn of events.

"I'd love for you to come back and see my city and meet my family, but here you have the shelter, friends, and a life, and I'm getting used to this climate. I want to meet your family, and I think I'd like to try surfing," he finished with a grin.

She stared at him as if he were speaking a language she didn't understand, and he tried to make his case a little more clearly.

"We have time—we can decide what we want, where we want to go, what we want to do, together. There's no rush. I will, however, need a place to live. I was kind of hoping I could move my things in over here." He ended his sentence on a big yawn and shook his head as if to clear it, bringing both of her hands to his lips.

She took a few minutes to absorb what he was telling her—he'd quit his job to stay here, and she'd quit hers to go with him.

It was perfect. They had their whole lives before

them. A real adventure with the man she loved. Her heart raced with excitement at the prospect of her new future, and of sharing it with Rafe.

Finally, she spoke. "I like that idea a lot, you living here. I guess we got each other the same gift," she said, chuckling, leaning her forehead against his.

"Looks like," he said on another yawn, and she looked at him in amazement.

"I can't believe you quit your job for me."

"I'm delighted that you quit your job for me. We have a fresh slate now, a new beginning for both— excuse me," he said, interrupted by a yawn.

"Hey, you're yawning," she observed.

"Uh-huh," he said, rubbing his eyes.

"You look absolutely exhausted."

The import of her words finally dawned on him.

"Joy…I *am* tired—really *tired*," he said in surprise, the sudden need to sleep almost overwhelming.

Whether it was the finality of making a decision about his job, making peace with the past, or having found his place in life with Joy, the tension that had always pulled tight, keeping him awake night after night, seemed to have disappeared. "I guess there's only one way to tell—we have to go to bed."

She stood, holding out her hand to him. "I like that plan. If you're not tired enough to pass out immediately, I bet I can find a few ways to make sure you are," she promised seductively.

He stood and took her hand, pulling her up close, then ran his hand down the length of her back and around the swell of her backside, then back up again. She gloried in his touch, focusing on the hot trail of desire he created, and leaned in for a kiss.

"And to all a good night…."

* * * * *

Unwrapped

CARRIE ALEXANDER

Carrie Alexander is the author of several books for various Mills & Boon® lines, with many more crowding her imagination, demanding to be written. Carrie lives in the upper peninsula of Michigan, where the long winters still don't give her enough time to significantly reduce her to-be-read mountains of books. When she's not reading or writing (which is rare), Carrie is painting and decorating her own or her friends' houses, watching football and shovelling snow. She loves to hear from readers, who can contact her by e-mail at carriealexander1@aol.com.

_1_

"WHAT'S YOUR FAVORITE DIP?" Debby Caruso asked, her brown curls bobbing as she bounded from the kitchen of Sutter Chocolat carrying a tray of triple-dipped strawberries. Each plump berry had been enrobed in layers of white and milk chocolate, then finished off with a sinfully rich coating of the shop's signature brand of dark Swiss chocolate. "I can't quite decide between strawberries and cherries, though I used to favor apricots, for some ungodly reason."

As Karina Sutter opened the display case, she smiled at the telltale juice that had trickled down Debby's round chin. The head confectioner was prone to sampling. "What about banana?"

"Too mushy. I like the squirt of juice in my mouth." Debby slid the tray inside, then set her hands on her ample hips. Her tongue swiped up the trickle. "You'd think I'd have more dates, huh?"

"Especially since you swallow," Karina teased, then reached into the glass-fronted case to straighten the decorative paper lace edging at the front of the tray. She rearranged the back row to cover the gap made by the missing strawberry.

A bemused Debby watched her fuss before closing the door on the display of decadent fruits in their pleated gold paper cups. "Not even tempted to try one? I'll never understand you."

"I may have one for dessert after lunch."

"Me, too, if there are any left by then," said Debby. The triple-dipped strawberries were a fast seller. "That's the difference between us. I'm a double helpings girl and you—you're disciplined." Debby screwed up her face in disgust, betrayed by the generous grin she couldn't contain for long. "You realize that your perfection is very aggravating to the rest of us."

Karina was only half listening, toying with the heavy gold chain at her neck as her gaze shifted outside. "I'll try to do better at being bad."

Debby watched her employer gaze at the upper stories of the apartment building across the street. "Oh, really? He's home? Is today the day?"

Karina backed off. "Maybe not *today*..."

She turned to smile at a customer ogling the marbled chocolate scallop shells, offering the woman a sample. The store handed out a lot of samples. One bite of any of the array of fine chocolates and assorted sweets and most people were hooked. Karina had been accused of being personally responsible for a mass neighborhood weight gain, although the accompanying improvement in her customers' sex lives more than made up for the calories.

"Why not today?" Debby asked. "It's been three weeks."

"I don't want to rush into creating a situation I'll regret."

"What's to regret?" Debby put a hand on Karina's arm and nudged her toward the window, away from the twin cash registers and the workers busily filling orders from the walk-in traffic. The December cold snap hadn't slowed business at all. Nothing went so well with a frosty winter day as sex and chocolate.

"You feed him the chocolates," Debby continued, "you show up at his door naked beneath a trench coat, you have a weekend of fabulous sex."

"Shh." Karina darted a look at the customers, even though it was likely that none of them would be shocked at the titillating talk. In fact, sex was probably foremost on their minds, second only to their chocolate cravings.

Debby lowered her voice. "We're not talking *relationship* here. You want him only for a fling, right? One torrid fling to give you memories that'll keep your bones warm when you're a little old lady married to a little old man who can't get it up without a crane."

Yes, that was what she'd convinced herself that she wanted after her first glimpse of the mystery man, though she'd never put it as colorfully as Debby.

Karina had followed the rules all of her life, aside from one major exception when she'd tossed out her degree and the offer to teach at a prestigious small college to open a chocolate shop instead. Her parents had been dubious, especially as she was taking advantage of the family recipe handed down through the generations. But the shop had become a rousing success as word of mouth spread about the amazing amorous side effect of the chocolate. Before long her supplies and staff could barely keep up with demand.

She was devoted to the shop, as well as making a home from the bi-level apartment above it, newly renovated now that she owned the building. But she was also careful to make time for a proper social life. She took advantage of New York's cultural and sporting amenities. Connections to family and friends were duly maintained. And she'd dated a selection of fine, up-standing young men. Eventually she'd choose one to marry, now that she was approaching thirty, the ideal age to get serious about a husband and children.

However...

Karina pinched the tip of her nose, but there was no distracting her from the plan.

Often, especially during the past several weeks, she'd wished she could be as natural and spontaneous as Debby—and many of her customers, thanks to the cocoa beans that stimulated sexual arousal. But she doubted that it was possible to change her true nature.

Even with the help of the chocolate, even when she was halfway gone with lust for the man who'd recently moved into the building across the street....

Debby, Karina's closest confidante, had been push-ing the idea that for once she should take advantage of the secret Sutter family recipe for personal gain. A *very* personal gain.

She was reluctant. Manufacturing an interest from her intended partner seemed cheap. Almost like cheat-ing. Then again...how many opportunities presented themselves so perfectly? She couldn't use the chocolate on any of her male acquaintances, the prospective groom pool. That might lead to a false romance it would be awkward to remove herself from. She didn't want complications. She only wanted...

Hot sex.

Just this one time. Sure, she was naturally a con-trolled person, but she could be spontaneous. After some thought and planning, granted.

Karina's eyes strayed to the city street outside her shop's window. The mystery stud should be walking by any minute now. He didn't keep to a schedule, but after watching him for three weeks she'd picked up on his tendencies. At some point during the day he went for a walk, frequently returning with a newspaper, a coffee or take-out food, but rarely staying away for more than an hour.

He always returned alone.

She glanced at her watch. Fifty-two minutes and counting since he'd exited the street door of his building.

"It's too complicated," she said to Debby, knowing that she'd get an argument—and probably wanting one. "With him living so close and all. What if the plan goes wrong? I'd still have to see him every day."

"Only from behind a window," Debby replied. "It's not like he ever comes in."

That point had been nagging at Karina. What kind of man could walk by a chocolate shop filled with women exuding obvious carnal appetites and never even hesitate?

Only once had he so much as broken stride—the day that a frequent customer, an adorable blonde, had been away for two weeks without her usual rations. She'd run headlong out of the shop with her mouth full of fudge, practically orgasming with relief right there on the sidewalk. The aphrodisiac effect packed more of a wallop after deprivation. The customer had swooned into the stranger's arms, all feverish and dewy-eyed, babbling about how hot she was. He'd merely set her back on her feet and continued on his way.

"We don't know that it would even work," Karina said. "He seems to have no interest in my chocolate."

Or me. As humiliating as it was to remember, a week ago she'd undone the third button on her blouse and provocatively positioned herself as she rearranged the front

window display during his coffee run. Mystery man's
eyes had skimmed right over her.

"True, men don't tend to be as susceptible to the secret recipe." Debby wasn't about to let that stop the
plan, bless her. "Luckily, I've got a double-strength
batch of Black Magic truffles cooling in the kitchen. I'll
make you up a gift box. He won't know what hit him,
but he'll be grateful forever."

Karina glanced at her fervid patrons. Bright eyes and
flushed cheeks prevailed. Those who were new to the
shop looked a bit startled at the jittery excitement in the
air. "What if this goes the other way, and he becomes
addicted?"

"Hmm." Debby pooched out her lips. "What if?
You'd end up with a gorgeous guy who wants you day
and night. I don't see the problem."

"You know I don't want a romance founded on a trick
of chocolate. Besides, this one has no long-term potential. He's a loner and he's unemployed."

"You don't know that for sure."

Karina shrugged. "I've never seen him with another
person. He doesn't seem to own a suit or be interested
in finding a job. Most of the time, he's home all day." And
all night, but she wasn't ready to tell Debby about *that*.

"Maybe he works out of his house, on the computer
or something."

"Maybe…" Except that she could see into his apartment from hers, and she'd never noticed him spending
much time at the computer. Of course he kept his blinds
closed an awful lot, even during the day.

"Doesn't matter anyway. When you've had your fill
of his Christmas package, you cut off his supply of
chocolate and be done with him."

Karina shook her head. "That's too calculating." Besides, the chocolate was only a stimulant. It couldn't control libidos quite so neatly.

"But that's the point! I can't imagine that he'd have any problem with the plan. Even a grouchy loner won't say no to a blonde who wants to use him as a boy toy."

"I suppose." Karina smoothed her hair, although it didn't need smoothing. She kept it in a tight bun or braided knot at work. "I'll think about it."

Debby rolled her eyes. "Uh-huh. I knew you'd chicken out again."

"I'm not chickening out. I'm—" Karina tilted her nose into the air, trying to suppress a grin. "I'm being careful."

"Yeah, well, be careful you don't wind up delaying so long he gets snagged by one of our customers on an afternoon sugar high."

Karina watched a trio of women rush into the store, along with a draft of cold air from the open door. They stamped their boots and pulled off gloves, hungrily examining the display cases. The avaricious gleam in their eyes said that no man nor truffle was safe from their potent hungers.

Karina was taken aback. "You do have a point."

Debby knew when to let Karina ferment in her own juices. She returned to the original topic—dipping fruit. "Since strawberries are out of season, I'm planning to switch to pears for the holidays. Strictly fresh. Dipped in dark or milk chocolate and topped with a dollop of custard. Except that wouldn't be very portable. Caramel, you think? That might work."

Karina let Debby's musings slide over her. She didn't need to respond except to offer an encouraging murmur now and then. The head confections chef was worth double her weight in cocoa beans.

While Sutter Chocolat had been prosperous from the start, business had tripled in the past three years under the combination of Debby's brilliance in the kitchen and Karina's painstaking management. They now had two full-time workers behind the counter, another to answer phones and handle shipping and deliveries, a handful of part-timers who filled in as needed, plus the kitchen staff. Each employee had been selected with utmost care, as they had to be entrusted to handle the secret supplies and knowledge of a recipe that would be worth a fortune to the big candy makers.

With the steady flow of revenue, Karina could have easily expanded into a chain of stores or a mail-order business, but that would have gone too far against the family's preference for moderation. The secret recipe was not meant for mass consumption on a grand scale. Nor were there enough of the rare, ultra-expensive cocoa beans—grown only on a western-facing slope in the shadow of a remote Brazilian mountain—to handle such volume.

"I'll experiment with the different varieties," Debby rambled on. "Anjou might do. I'm not so sure how well pear slices will keep and I can't bring myself to go the dehydrated route…."

"No worries. We'll sell them fresh every day, like the strawberries." A pedestrian caught Karina's eye—a head of dark brown hair moving above the rest of the crowd. She leaned toward the front window, bracing herself on the display counter. *Yes. It was him.*

Oh, yes.

He was striding along the opposite side of the street,

oblivious to the wintry weather with a gray scarf dangling around his neck and a long brown leather coat flapping open in the breeze. Tall, tanned, fit—by the looks of him, no one would ever guess he was a mole who spent most of his days huddled in a closed-up apartment.

Not for the first time, Karina mulled over where he'd come from. A tropical climate would be her first guess, though he didn't look like an island bum except on the surface, with the deep tan, the ruff of overgrown mahogany hair that sported natural highlights, and the way he usually managed to have a five o'clock shadow by noon.

Otherwise, there was a restlessness about him. His gaze roved, rarely lighting, always sharp as flint. He never smiled. The somber mouth and hollow cheeks spoke of an intriguing air of experience. A city vibe, not an island one.

Merely the sight of him gave Karina interesting tingles, and she'd had only one nibble of a new employee's molded ganache medallions that morning, so she certainly couldn't blame her arousal on the chocolate.

"There he is," she murmured to Debby. She sighed. "*That's* my favorite dip."

Debby chuckled. "How would you know until you've sampled him?"

"I just know. He's delicious."

Surprisingly, the man didn't return directly to his building, but veered off to cross the street, nimbly dodging traffic with one hand raised to stave off a cabbie blaring his horn.

"He's coming this way," Debby said.

A hot self-awareness flushed through Karina, especially as she realized that she'd walked out from behind the counter toward the windows without realizing it. She wadded her apron in stricken hands. "Oh, no. He can't. I'm not ready."

They scrambled to get her out of the linen apron with eyelet trim. "Knot's too tight," Debby said, working on it.

"Over the head." Karina pulled the apron up past her face, but the tie had been crisscrossed twice around her waist and it caught beneath her breasts. She tugged. Her blouse pulled out of the waistband of her skirt. "Help."

"I'll get scissors." Debby bustled away to search the supply shelves hidden below the display cabinet.

Karina gave another yank and the apron popped past her breasts. She ripped it off over her head, only to discover that the man was directly outside the shop window, looking inside as he walked by. More than looking. Staring wide-eyed.

She was so startled by his unusual interest that she stood stock still. Strands of loosened hair floated around her face, her clothes were in disarray and the crumpled apron hung off her left shoulder and arm.

For once, his gaze didn't skim her. He didn't halt either, but he continued to stare directly at her, his stride slowing as his eyes ignited her with their intense, lingering appreciation.

Karina went hot, then cold, then even hotter as her skin was shot with prickling needles of arousal. She blinked once and the man was gone.

And there was Debby, wincing. She waggled a finger. "Uh, your blouse…"

What about it? Karina's head floated like a helium balloon until she put a hand up and touched skin. *Pop.* Her blouse—

Was hanging open.

Wide open, in an inverted *V.* All but the top button had come undone when she was struggling to get the apron off over her head. The mystery man hadn't been looking at *her,* he'd been leering over her breasts, almost fully exposed by the lace-trimmed cups of a dainty demilune bra.

Stunned, Karina looked down. Her nipples were as hard as bullets. Worse, they peeped over the lace edging, winking naughtily at the passersby.

She grabbed both sides of the blouse and wrapped them across her torso. "Oh, God."

Debby chortled. "You sure have his attention now."

"This is terrible." Karina tossed a weak grin at the gawking customers and quickly slipped behind the counter, heading for the swinging doors that led to the back of the store and the kitchen and office areas. On the way through the first short corridor, she shook free of the apron, clutching it to her chest, needing the extra covering.

"He saw *everything,*" she said to Debby, who followed her into her private office, past a startled Janine Gardner, the young woman who'd been recently hired as their receptionist and shipping clerk.

Debby shut the door on Janine's inquisitive stare. "Aw, hell, Kare. Maybe not." She gave her employer's shoulder a comforting rub. "I mean, your blouse was sort of draped open across your breasts, so…"

"But my arms were raised." Karina dropped the apron on her desk, then lifted her arms, letting the blouse hang open again from its lone button. Hard to tell how much of her had been exposed, except that when she'd looked down the first time, it had seemed like plenty. More than enough to attract the attention of even a detached, brusque loner.

She collapsed into the chair behind her desk. "This is just *terrible.*"

Debby eased into the visitor's chair. "Not really."

"I flashed him!"

"And he enjoyed it."

Karina nudged her breasts deeper into the bra cups where they belonged. She didn't normally go around with her nipples out. The struggle with the apron must have lifted them an inch or two, just enough to poke out of the skimpy bra.

At the most inopportune moment. She mentally cringed while rebuttoning her blouse.

"You know what?" Debby said. "Putting aside your embarrassment, this might be the best thing that could have happened." She waved off Karina's flustered denial. "Look at it this way—he's *got* to be thinking about you now. Probably even fantasizing." Debby smirked. "You have great tits."

Karina groaned.

"They're so perky. Mine are, you know—" Debby stretched the scoop neck of her neon-pink top and peered into her deep cleavage "—pendulous."

"I'm pretty sure men prefer pendulous."

"Sometimes." Debby smiled. Regardless of the contemporary preference for skinny, she was not neurotic about her voluptuous figure. She frequently said that being thin wasn't worth giving up chocolate.

Karina envied her friend's confidence in herself. She diligently worked to maintain her weight through diet and exercise, which was also a good thing. Just not very freeing. "I don't care if he liked them. I never intended to—"

"Put 'em on display?"

"I'm humiliated." Karina squeezed her eyes shut. "I can't face him now."

"You have to. As soon as possible."

She shook her head. "Oh, no. No. Absolutely not."

"But he's thinking about you. Wanting you."

"Probably thinking I must be desperate. Wanting me to leave him alone."

"I really doubt that. And I'm sure he realized that you didn't mean to flash him. He had to have seen you trying to get the apron off."

Karina cracked an eye. "You think?"

"Yep. And I *know* you, Kare. You're gonna use this as an excuse to retreat for another month." Debby stood and slapped her palms on the desk. "I won't allow it. I'm going to the kitchen right now and putting together that assortment of truffles. Get your coat on. You're delivering them personally."

Karina pressed a couple of fingers to her mouth. "I can't."

"Sure you can."

"No, I mean—" She searched for an obstacle that Debby would accept. Other than her personal humiliation. "I don't know his name. Even if I can get in, there's no way I'm knocking on the door of every apartment in his building. That would be so obvious there'd be no doubt remaining about how desperate I am."

"Like I said, I never met the man who cared, but you do have a point." Calmly, Debby walked behind the desk and flicked on Karina's computer. "Take me to the store's customer list please."

Karina typed in a password to access the protected files and called up the database. "He's not a customer."

"But Annie Rittenouer is, and she lives in the same

building. I bet she'll know who our mystery man is and what apartment he lives in."

"Oh." Karina frowned. "Um, wait. Do we really want to ask Annie? She's the chatty middle-aged woman with short bleached hair, right? The one who sends her husband over for a new supply of peanut clusters every Friday morning."

"That's Annie." Debby scrolled to the *R*s and read out the customer's number as she lifted the desk phone and dialed. Karina made frantic motions and grabbed the phone away as a woman's voice said, "Hello, hello?"

"Good day, Mrs. Rittenouer. This is Karina from Sutter Chocolat, calling to tell you that we're running a holiday sale for our regular customers. Twenty-five percent off peanut clusters, today only."

Karina hushed Debby while the customer made ecstatic noises. "Oh, really? Your favorite? Shall we have a box delivered on account? My pleasure, ma'am. Thank you."

"But you didn't get any information," Debby said when Karina hung up.

"I'm into the building. That's enough. I'd rather keep the rest of it quiet."

"Then you're actually going?" Debby was clearly surprised by Karina's initiative.

"I'm going." An intoxicating flutter in the pit of her stomach made Karina pinch the end of her nose to sober herself. *Toughen up. It's only a sexual attraction, not a peace treaty at Versailles.* "Because you're right. It's now or never."

"Now. Absolutely." Debby clapped her hands and squeaked a *yippee* sound before she swung around in the small office, reaching for the knob. "Give me five minutes."

"No hurry."

"Yes, hurry. There will be no backing out." Debby threw open the door, catching Janine hovering. "Back to your desk, missy," she said, sailing by with the tails of her apron flapping.

Janine's nose twitched. "Can I help you with anything, Ms. Sutter?"

"Thank you, no. Oh, wait—how about getting me a receipt slip from one of the girls at the front? I have a special delivery to make to Mrs. Rittenouer across the street."

"Right away, Ms. Sutter."

Karina watched Janine hustle away. The new employee had come with impeccable letters of recommendation from the sweets division of Royal Foods. The connection to big business had made Karina hesitate, but Janine had professed a wish to learn candy-making at a more intimate scale, where quality was most important. She was always eager to please and had exhibited a strong curiosity about every aspect of the business. One day, she might make a good assistant manager.

Karina brushed the thought aside, for a time when she would want to spend less hours at work, like when she had a husband and children to keep her occupied. That was suddenly a more distant prospect than it had been.

There was room for only one man in her head. And it was a shock to remember that she didn't even know his name. She really was crazy for doing this.

But, wow, the risk was giving her quite a rush. Maybe she should have jumped out of the box years ago.

Debby and Janine both arrived at once, bumping into

each other at the office door. "Got your truffles," Debby said, holding the signature copper-metallic box high.

Janine gave her shoulders a twist. "Here's the receipt." She surveyed the box with skepticism. "Doesn't Mrs. Rittenouer always buy peanut clusters?"

Debby's smile was acid. She thought Janine was a suck-up and had no compunction about telling Karina so. "Thanks, but you can go now. I've got this handled. The girls are preparing an order of peanut clusters as we speak."

"Of course." Janine returned to her desk, properly chastised even though the tic near her eyes said otherwise. She'd sworn the twitch came from her new contact lenses, but it only showed up when she was irritated or nervous.

Debby shut the door with an emphatic clap.

"You have to stop the squabbling with Janine," Karina said absently, busy filling out the receipt. "It doesn't make for a happy work environment."

"Never mind that. This is for you."

A dark chocolate espresso truffle appeared on the desk blotter. Karina looked up at Debby with surprise. "I don't need that…yet."

"I think you do. For courage."

Karina poked at the luscious candy with her pen. "It's not courage I'll be feeling after a double-strength Black Magic truffle." The sinfully rich treats were another of Debby's inventions. The dense chocolate centers were infused with a variety of flavors from champagne to mandarin orange, but it was the unique cocoa beans that gave the hefty tidbit its incredible *oomph*. Word was, one truffle could result in an entire evening of passion.

Or several hours of intense frustration.

"Eat it," Debby said.

Karina took a deep breath. "I don't want to waste the effect. We have to give mystery man time to eat a few of the truffles I deliver. Once he's good and worked up, then I'll—" She swallowed reflexively. "I'll take my medicine."

A hoot of laughter came from Debby. "Medicine! Gawd, Kare—I know women who'd kill for these truffles."

Karina caught her lower lip between her teeth, hesitating. She shook her head. "I realize that, but I'm afraid of what will happen if I go over there all hyped up. I might become too aggressive and that's not me."

"You keep forgetting, that's the whole idea." Debby pushed the truffle closer, leaving a trail of cocoa powder on the blotter. "You have this great power at your disposal. Use it, woman."

"It's too soon. I could end up, you know, jumping his bones."

"Exactly. But I don't think so. If it was me, yeah. But you're resistant to the effects because of your inhib— um, your discipline. One truffle should give you just the right amount of daring to see this plan through."

"That makes sense," admitted Karina. She didn't consider herself inhibited. Particularly not in light of the past several weeks and the provocative game she'd been playing with her new neighbor. There were just some things that should be private, a concept Debby didn't always understand.

At the same time, she needed every impetus she could get if she really, truly wanted to go through with this crazy ploy.

And *that* was the real question. *Did she?*

Something inside her answered without hesitation. A newly brazen part of herself that she'd always contained. *I do.*

"Go on," Debby urged. "Call it chocolate courage."

In what seemed like slow motion, Karina reached for the round truffle. Temptation exemplified. Beneath the liberal dusting of cocoa powder and cinnamon, the glossy chocolate was so dark it was almost black, swirled into a curlicue on top. Her mouth watered with anticipation.

The generous mound was weighty as she lifted it to her lips. She parted them, her tongue seeking the first silken taste. The heady aroma filled her nostrils as she gave the truffle a lick, then bit into it. Her teeth pierced the shell, sinking into the dense espresso filling that was so rich and flavorful she almost swooned as it coated her taste buds.

"'S goooood," she said through the sweet mouthful. Her eyes closed as she savored the candy to the fullest before swallowing and taking another bite. The Black Magic truffle was the shop's most intense treat and was sold for a hefty price, singly or in various sized boxes. Not to gouge the customers, but to keep them from overindulging.

Karina popped the last bite into her mouth. Already, she was dizzy with a chocolate buzz. Soon, magnified by the secret recipe, the wondrous side effects would begin—the rush of euphoria, the flush of warmth, the growing, spreading hunger that would seep beneath her skin until she was itchy with the desire to rub herself against a hard male body, her supersensitized nerve endings producing a rosy glow that would signal an open invitation to her chosen mate.

Under normal circumstances, Debby would have been correct about Karina's resistance to the chocolate aphrodisiac. But this time, when she was already ripe with teasing and flirtation, Karina knew that the truffle would take her to an unexplored fever pitch of longing.

She licked the last smears of chocolate and cocoa powder from her fingers.

Get ready, stranger. I'm coming over to screw your brains out.

Yikes. That simply wasn't like her. Had to be the cocoa beans talking.

2

MUFFLED IN A WOOLEN COAT, gloves and a knit hat with ear flaps, Karina went to the corner to cross the street at the traffic light. Obeying the jaywalking rules gave her a few extra minutes to pull herself together, but the rolling warmth inside said that wasn't going to happen, no matter how much time she took. Her stomach felt like a dryer on high, going round and round and getting hotter and hotter.

Nervousness. But also the hunger. The *lust*.

She shouldn't have eaten that truffle.

The pedestrian light switched on and the small group surged off the snowy curb, carrying Karina in their momentum. She kept her gaze fixed on the fur trim on the hat of a squat woman in front of her, avoiding eye contact with nearby males, should she become attracted to one of them, or vice versa. Maybe she was overreacting. The Sutter recipe wasn't supposed to be *that* potent. Their chocolate was a sexual booster, not a skyrocket.

Even so, Karina wasn't taking any chances.

Except this one, she silently added, stopping in front of the mystery man's narrow stone-block building. Stamping her boots, she looked it over. A men's clothing store occupied the ground floor, but above it were six stories of residential units. She knew that her guy lived in a third-floor apartment that overlooked the street, so that would narrow the search a lot. Going to him was risk enough; it would be disaster to end up at the wrong place.

She glanced at the Sutter Chocolat storefront, decorated for the winter with a garland of cedar entwined with a string of red lights. Debby stood watch at the window, poised behind the holiday display in her white apron, urging Karina on.

She shooed Debby away. This was getting too much like school, when she and her girlfriends had schemed over how to attract boys' attention but rarely followed through with their plans. She hoped mystery man wasn't looking out his windows again and observing the entire procedure.

The door to the lobby was open. Karina peered through the iron grate over the glass before entering. The space was no more than eight feet square—just big enough for two bodies, a bank of mailboxes and an intercom system. She studied the name labels, looking for ones that appeared newly applied. Apartment 302B had no label at all. Right floor. Had to be him.

Karina juggled the two small Sutter gift bags she'd brought along, then reached up to press the buzzer for apartment 206D. Annie Rittenouer answered with a "Yeah?"

"Karina Sutter, with your delivery."

"Hot damn. C'mon up."

The inner door buzzed. Karina grabbed it with a gloved hand and quickly jogged up the steps, concentrating on breathing evenly despite the tumbling excitement inside her.

Mrs. Rittenouer lived on the backside of the second

floor. She was waiting with the door open and eagerly snatched the bag Karina offered. "Thank God you had a sale because I'm addicted to these darn things and I've already run out of my week's supply," the peroxide blonde said in a gravelly smoker's voice, looking as if she'd be shoving the candy in her mouth before the door was closed. She signed the receipt without double-checking the total. "My Jackie complains about the cost, but I know how to shut him up." Tittering, she backed into the apartment and swung the door shut.

"Enjoy your chocolates," Karina said.

The door opened and Mrs. Rittenouer stuck her head out. "I don't know what you put in these, but don't ever stop."

Karina nodded. "Thank you for your business, ma'am. Happy holidays."

The woman had her nose stuck in the gift bag, inhaling the chocolate fumes. "They will be now."

Certain that Mrs. Rittenouer would run out of the peanut clusters long before Christmas arrived in several weeks, Karina turned and headed for the stairs. Music blasted from one of the second-floor apartments, but no one appeared to ask about her business in the building. She climbed to the next floor, growing moist inside her winter coat. Her skin felt feverish. The truffle packed quite a punch.

At the third-floor landing, she stopped to unbutton the coat and remove her gloves. Merely the chance that she'd get to touch the object of her desire with a bare fingertip set off a new round of tingling excitement.

"These truffles had better work on *him*," she muttered, searching the doors for 302B, "or I'll be hurting for sure."

The hall cricked to the left, forming a nook where she found the correctly numbered door. She put her ear near it, hoping for a clue about the occupant.

Nothing. Mr. Anonymous *would* be the silent type.

Karina aimed a finger at the doorbell. *I can't do this,* her mind said, but her thrumming body had another idea. When she closed her eyes to summon her daring, an image of the mystery man rose up, accompanied by a fresh surge of lust. She remembered the one scorching instant when the attractive stranger's eyes had connected with hers, the very moment when his interest had seemed reciprocated.

She blinked. Of course, that had been before she knew that her blouse was open, before she'd consumed the intoxicating truffle.

Even so, she wanted to feel that way again.

Do it.

A RUSH OF FEAR streaked through Alex Anderson when the doorbell rang, simultaneous with a shot of adrenaline that had him out of his chair and on his feet before the *dong* after the *ding* had died. He despised the fear, as familiar as it was. The adrenaline was okay. He'd learned how to channel it for his benefit. Self-defense and split-second reactions were all about adrenaline.

He stood in the middle of the living room, waiting, telling himself that he wasn't overreacting. The excessive caution could one day save his life, just as a moment of inattention had almost lost it.

Several seconds later, the bell rang again. He hadn't buzzed anyone up, so he had no intentions of answering.

He went to the window, sliding a finger between the tattered blind and the window casing so he could see the street below. Nothing suspicious at first glance, but he searched the faces carefully while keeping himself hidden. Even the most innocuous pedestrian could be lethal.

His gaze went to the buildings across the street, looking for a sniper, a lookout, anything out of the ordinary at all. There was no sign of trouble, but that meant nothing. It was too soon after the attempt on his life in the Florida Keys to allow himself to believe that he was safe.

Briefly, his glance landed on the row of windows that had been his worst distraction of late. The woman who lived there…

He shook his head, dislodging the alluring images. He couldn't afford to let his guard down.

The doorbell rang a third time, followed by a sharp *knock, knock, knock.* His visitor wasn't giving up.

Alex moved silently into the small foyer. When the knocking started again he put his eye to the peephole.

What the hell? It was *her.*

The woman from the windows, from the sweetshop. The untouchable blonde princess who'd become, with one inadvertent flash of her breasts, the woman he most wanted to touch.

She was harmless, but a very wicked distraction. He'd have to get rid of her, fast. And irrevocably.

He slipped off the chain and flicked the dead bolt, throwing the door open with a snarl that could have peeled paint. "What do you want?"

Surprise flashed across her face. She stepped back. "I'm sorry to bother you."

Alex scaled back the attitude. What had he become? A miserable heel who frightened pretty women with roses in their cheeks.

"Sorry," he said. "I wasn't expecting company."

She gave him a wary look, hesitating for a couple of seconds before she responded. He almost caved when she licked her lips, leaving them shiny pink and looking impossibly tender. "Uh, I was making a delivery in the building, so I thought it would be neighborly to—give you—" She faltered, couldn't seem to find any words, and held out a small gift bag instead of explaining.

He stared as if a rattlesnake dangled from her fingers. "What is it?"

"Chocolates."

"I don't eat chocolates."

"You'll like these."

He peered into the bag. A fluff of green tissue paper concealed the contents. He wasn't all that suspicious of the offering. He'd been observing Sutter Chocolat since he'd moved in and had no doubts about its legitimacy, but the defenses he'd developed in the past couple of years weren't easily cracked. Even by a spun-sugar confection of a woman who couldn't possibly be any danger to him, except as an attractive nuisance.

Which could be as big a mistake as any other, considering the death threat hanging over his head.

"Truffles," she said. Ignoring his scowl, she smiled. "The best you'll ever taste."

He studied her face, rattled by the experience of seeing her up close. She was a classic beauty with large toffee-colored eyes that tilted up at the corners, a long, narrow nose and those incredible edible lips.

On the other hand, one of her eyebrows arched higher than the other, unbalancing the perfect face. She wore a goofy striped hat that covered the hair he knew to be blond. Two fuzzy pom-poms dangled at the end of yarn strings tied in a bow at the top of her head.

The pom-poms brushed her flushed cheek when she tilted her head and shoved the bag at him. "You have to try them."

He pulled back. Why did she sound so urgent?

She blinked. "Excuse me. I didn't introduce myself. I'm Karina Sutter. I own the chocolate shop across the—"

"I know who you are." His gaze went to her breasts. He forced it back up.

The becoming pink glow turned into ruddy splotches of embarrassment. She gave an awkward laugh, clearly appalled by the incident regardless of her surprise appearance on his doorstep. "Yes. Ahem. About that—"

Alex shrugged. "It was nothing."

Her eyes narrowed. "Nothing?"

"I mean—I didn't see…" Of their own volition, his eyes dropped again to the front of the blouse that showed beneath her open coat. The same blue blouse that he'd last seen gaping open over a tantalizingly sheer bra. Until the moment when she'd mistakenly flashed him, he hadn't understood why women spent ridiculous amounts on sexy undergarments, but one look at the pink tips of her breasts set off by lace and, well, he'd suddenly become a believer.

"I didn't see much," he said. Only enough to make him want to worship at her feet.

Her smile wavered. "My buttons got stuck on my apron and as I was pulling it off—" She stopped, seeing that his face remained impassive, as if he didn't care one way or the other. She'd never know the effort that took.

She let out a little sigh. "Let's pretend that didn't happen, okay? We can start again." She switched the bag to her left hand and held out the other for a shake. "Karina Sutter. And you?"

"Alex." The lie came easily, so similar to Lex, the nickname he'd grown up with, that he could react without having to stop and think *Oh, yeah, that's my false name.* Then again, he'd gone by Chris in Big Pine Key and that hadn't stopped them from finding him.

Karina's hand hung in the air. Her left eyebrow inched even higher.

"Anderson," he said, reluctantly taking her hand. "Alex Anderson."

He would have let go immediately, but she clung, her slender fingers curling toward his palm, moving in a subtle, sensuous dance that made him prickle with awareness.

His jaw clenched. *Sonovabitch.* The princess wasn't so untouchable after all. She was coming on to him.

He stared, trying to read her again because apparently his first impressions had been way off if she was really asking for what he thought she wanted with those flirtatious fingers of hers.

After three weeks of observation, he'd believed that she was a rather normal single woman who put in long hours at her store and kept her personal life in neat order. She was prettier than average, but possibly lonely nevertheless, considering the restless way she moved around her apartment at night. There was a unique aura about her—serene, gentle, gracious—but she'd also seemed distant, like the golden-haired angel atop a Christmas tree. Now and then he'd wondered if she knew he was watching since she seemed to lurk near the windows almost as often as he did, yearningly alone, waiting for something to happen.

Looked like her idea of *something* was far different than his. He prided himself on his ability to read people and would have bet a thousand bucks of his dwindling life savings that she wasn't the type to arrive on his doorstep with a come-on. The error in judgment bothered him.

The contact of their handshake had lingered too long. Her eyes flickered uncertainly before her lids dropped, veiling her thoughts as she withdrew her hand from his grasp. "You don't have a label on the board downstairs," she said in a husky voice. She looked at him through her lashes, resuming the flirtation with a provocative curve of her lips. "For your name."

"I'm a private person." *Hunted like a dog.*

She held out the bag again, squirming a little as she rubbed her thighs together. He wondered if she had to go to the bathroom. "A gift, to welcome you to the neighborhood," she said.

This time he took the offering. "Yeah. Thanks."

Suddenly she swept off her knit hat, straightening up and throwing her head back. "Black Magic truffles," she said with an air of command, leaning toward him with an intense focus. "One of my shop's specialties. I *insist* you try one."

He reached into the bag and pulled out a small copper box, the lid embossed with a complicated design centered around an ornate letter *S*. "I'll be sure to do that."

She pressed forward to lift the lid, forcing him to back up a step into his apartment. "Delicious," she said. But her eyes weren't on the contents of the box, an assortment of a half dozen round truffles nestled in pleated cups.

She was looking at *him*—with a noticeable hunger showing in luminous eyes framed by dark gold lashes.

She even licked her lips, sliding the tip of her tongue between them in a deliberately sexual way.

He had the distinct feeling that if he invited her inside, they'd be tumbling naked onto his bed within minutes. For one fantasy-filled moment, he considered letting that happen. It was months since he'd been with a woman. The last time had been unsatisfying—a brief, meaningless relationship in Florida that he'd known from the start could never go anywhere even though he'd been trying to build a regular life. He'd pegged Karina as the serious-relationship type.

Evidently his impression had been wrong. She wasn't so distant after all.

"Invite me in and I'll share them with you," she said, her color deepening again. She brushed a restless hand over the front of her blouse, slipping her fingers into her open collar and caressing the hollow of her throat.

No mistaking that body language.

"Uh…" Alex stood his ground, even when she advanced to within a couple of inches of him. He was *not* letting her into his apartment.

But he wanted her. With a swift, strong passion that was matched only by his instinct for self-preservation.

He'd let go of so much that he'd mistakenly believed there was nothing left to lose. This woman, though…she was offering him the world. Contact, closeness, comfort. He ached for all of that. And the prospect of an hour or two of hot lovin' with a needy blonde wasn't bad, either.

Maybe *too* needy?

She'd lifted her gold chain necklace to her mouth and

was absently running the chunky links against her teeth. With a rising temperature, he watched the links disappear between her lips, then slip out from the side of her mouth. When she saw his interest, she dropped the chain and purred, "I need something to nibble on. Are you willing…"

Ready, willing and able. More than she'd ever know.

"…to share?" She plucked a truffle from the box and bit into it, closing her eyes in ecstasy. "Mmm. Raspberry vodka. You don't know what you're missing."

Oh, yes, I do.

He stood silently, watching with a melting resistance while she finished the chocolate, making little moaning sounds of enjoyment that could easily have been mistaken for sexual pleasure. She was close enough that he could feel her body heat. The warmth mingled with the scents of rich chocolate and her light perfume to further weaken his resolve.

He couldn't take much more of this. He had to get her out of here.

She popped her thumb into her mouth to lick it clean, then looked up at him again. "Take just one taste," she coaxed. Her lips puckered. "I brought them over for you, special."

She reached for the box to select another candy and he pulled it away. "I can't—"

"Why not?"

He could have explained that he was mildly allergic to chocolate. The last time he'd had some his lips had swelled like a blowfish and he'd been hit with a short but fierce headache. Except that getting into a real conversation, especially one that revealed personal information, would only encourage her. And, of course, prolong his torment.

He had to get rid of her *now.* Being rude was the only way to do it.

"Thanks for the candy," he said, clapping the lid back on the box and nudging her over the threshold, "but I'm not buying the rest of it." He laid a hand on her shoulder to turn her, then dropped it to her behind and boosted her away from the door.

"Hey." She whirled, resisting. "What do you—"

He shut the door in her face.

A sound of outrage came from the other side, followed by a thud. Then nothing.

Alex put his eye to the peephole. A microscopic Karina was standing where he'd left her, staring dumbly at his door. She pressed both hands to her cheeks, briefly covering her eyes, then gave the end of her nose a hard pinch.

"Well, that was embarrassing," she said in a conversational tone, then jammed her hat on her head and stomped off.

He let out a breath of relief that she'd given up so easily. Safe again.

Lonely, too, he realized as he returned to the sparse living room of the sublet apartment. He tossed the box of truffles on a scratched desk, one of the few furnishings the leaseholder had left behind, and went to the window. With a snap of the blind, he had a clear view of Karina as she emerged from the building a minute later, moving briskly along the street, the silly little pom-poms swinging at the back of her head.

Regret gnawed at him. If he'd been another man…

Hell, he'd be getting on her if he'd been the man he

once was—Mark Lexmond, firebrand defense attorney at an up-and-coming firm, known as Lex to most acquaintances and all his friends, an idealistic fighter for justice who drove a red convertible with a surfboard sticking out the back, "owned" a corner booth at La Caridad and played drums in a weekend band called The Curl.

But Mark Lexmond was dead.

So were his other identities—Pete Rogers and Chris McGraw—assigned by California's Witness Protection Program as administered by the U.S. Marshals.

Pete had been a stopgap identity while he waited for the justice system to investigate the tangled mess of threats and murder instigated by a notorious crime kingpin named Rafael Norris. A year earlier, Norris's son had been killed in a drug deal gone bad. Lex had been assigned as the defendant's lawyer. He'd helped broker a deal with the federal authorities to reduce his client's charge from second-degree murder to manslaughter. The deal and the reduced charge had enraged Norris, who had sworn vengeance in the name of his son. Soon afterwards, the defendant had turned up dead. Since Lex was next on the list, the Marshals swooped in.

Chris McGraw was supposed to be his permanent name. Strange at first, but after a while he'd settled into his new identity in Florida as a loner with no family ties. He'd found a job as a bartender at a waterfront dive that reminded him of home, rented a bungalow hidden by palmettos. He'd begun to lead a seminormal life. Eventually he'd let his guard down, allowed a few simple pleasures back into his life. And then...

His mind skipped over those last bloody, terrifying hours in Florida.

Maybe it was only paranoia, but the attempt on his life in Big Pine Key had led him to suspect corruption in the Witness Protection Program. Unwilling to trust the system, he'd dumped all contact with the U.S. Marshals and had gone out on his own.

Even so, there was no telling how long Alex Anderson would survive. The huge population of New York City made him feel anonymous and safe, but all it would take to have him moving on was one slipup, one small sign that he'd been tracked down. A loitering pedestrian, an unexpected knock at the door, a stranger showing too much interest in his past...

A stranger showing too much interest, period.

Not that he suspected Karina Sutter of devious intent. Still, welcoming her into his bed would be a monumental mistake.

Lex—*Alex,* he reminded himself—jammed his hands into his jeans pockets, too aware of the thickening at his groin. She'd invade his dreams tonight, as she had most other nights, all golden and pink and cream and heated whispers of enticement, but that was good. Frustrating, but good. Anything was better than the nightmare images he usually suffered.

Cold comfort, he thought, following Karina's progress as a scattering of snowflakes drifted from the sky. At the door to Sutter Chocolat, she turned to glance up at his building before going inside.

He couldn't see the expression in her eyes, but he knew that she'd glimpsed him at the window. Her stance stiffened, as if she were taking a deep breath to control her emotions. Longing clutched at his gut.

He yanked the blind back over the window before she could sense his reaction and decide to try again. Saying no the first time had been extremely difficult. Turning down a second offer might be impossible.

And deadly.

"WHAT HAPPENED?" Debby said.

Karina walked by, jerking her gloves off finger by finger. She looked at her bare hands for a moment—they were shaking—and wished that she could wrap them around Alex Anderson's neck…or cock.

His *cock?* Another surge of hot blood rose toward her face. What was going on with her? She did *not* think that way!

Blame the truffles, she decided. But a voice inside her head said, *That man. His fault.*

She moaned. "I'm in trouble."

"What? How?" Debby was flustered. "Did you meet the mystery man? Did you make a date?"

They went into Karina's office and closed the door. Karina ripped off her coat, hoping to satisfy herself by removing only one layer. Her clothing felt unbearably heavy and itchy on her skin.

She took a deep breath to quiet her drumming heart, but the air caught in her chest. She was all out-of-sorts inside. Nothing working right. "His name is Alex Anderson and he shut his door in my face."

"No," Debby breathed.

"Yes."

"What did he say?"

"Almost nothing. I gave him the chocolates, he gave me his name, we shook hands. Then I threw myself at him—"

"No."

In spite of Karina's own disbelief over her rash actions, she was annoyed. Did Debby have to sound so totally shocked? Sure, she wasn't a femme fatale, but she wasn't a vanilla pudding, either. She had sex appeal. Just not the *obvious* kind.

Hah. That was ironic when she remembered how she'd stroked Alex's hand, her orgasmic consumption of the truffle....

"I ate one of his truffles."

Debby's mouth squared into a visual *uh-oh*. "Why did you do that?"

"He wasn't responsive. I was trying to get him to take a bite, and before I knew it I'd eaten an entire truffle by myself." Karina ran her hands over her hips and thighs. Her skin felt so aroused, as if she were a cat and Alex had caused all her hackles to rise.

"You shouldn't have done that. They were double strength."

"I know." *I can feel it.*

Although part of her wondered if her reaction to Alex was due to more than just the chocolate.

Debby arched a wary look at Karina as she fretfully undid another button on her blouse and opened the collar wide, sliding her fingers beneath a bra strap and pushing it over her shoulder. "What are you doing?"

"Nothing. I'm just so...constricted."

Debby grimaced. "Do you have a vibrator?"

"A what?"

"A vi-ber-ate-her."

"Debby!" Karina fanned her hot face. "No, I don't."

"Cripes. Why not? Do you have an electric toothbrush?"

"Oh please."

"Well, it's either that or get kinky with a clothes washer."

"I'm not interested in dating my appliances. I'll just—" Karina slumped into her desk chair, but she couldn't sit still for long before she had to squirm again. "I'll ride it out. The effects can't last that long."

"Uh," Debby said.

"What?"

"Do you remember Rog Horowitz?"

"No."

"The one who dumped me because he was embarrassed about the broken nose."

"Oh, yeah." Karina's eyes widened. "You're telling me you used the chocolate on him?"

"Rog didn't have much staying power. I fed him a double dose of the Black Magic truffles after dinner one night. We were at my place, so I thought we'd be safe. Well, Rog was so impressed with the surge of energy that he wanted to try a gymnastic maneuver, which was not a good idea for a man of two hundred and fifty pounds with no discernible athletic ability. You know those shelves I used to have behind the futon? Imagine Rog, naked, sweaty and red-faced, humping away—"

"He banged the shelves instead of you? Ouch."

"Sort of. We were doing this odd position and I lost my balance. Rog fell off me, nose first."

"Why did that make him dump you? Wouldn't he want more?" More, Karina thought. God, yes, *more*.

"The doctors assumed Rog had taken Viagra without a prescription, and they warned him that the strenuous activity could be too much for his heart. Since he was a bit of a hypochondriac anyway…" Debby flipped a hand. "Whatever. There are more fish in the sea and I'd rather hook a swordfish than a flounder."

Karina shot her employee a suspicious look. "Why *did* you have that batch of truffles ready to go?" She had a loose agreement with the staff that because the business had to be careful with the limited supply of the unique cocoa beans, personal consumption was to be kept to a minimum. She didn't need a store full of randy workers inventing new uses for the kitchen appliances. Traditionally, her family had always used the precious beans sparingly. In fact, if her Swiss grandmother had been alive, Karina would never have been allowed to go commercial.

"I saw how interested you were in the guy across the street," Debby said. "Figured you'd be needing the truffles sooner or later."

"You thought I couldn't interest him on my own?"

"Of course you could. But a little extra help never hurts. That's what keeps Victoria's Secret in business, and us, too."

"Whatever." Karina sighed, thinking of her new matching underwear. "Looks like I won't be launching myself at any headboards." *No thanks to Alex Anderson.*

Debby shrugged. "I'm just saying…"

"It's not that bad. I'll survive." Karina squirmed.

"I don't get it. How could mystery man turn you down?"

"He was *very* unfriendly."

"Wait till he eats the truffles. He'll be sorry he got rid of you so fast."

Bingo. Karina's head snapped up. "You're right. Except he said that he doesn't like chocolate."

"But he still has them?"

"Yes."

"No one resists my chocolates for long. He'll eat one. Be ready for when he does."

Karina shook her head. "I told you. He was not nice. The chocolate's not strong enough to overcome that. I didn't even get inside his apartment. From what little I could see, the place was nice enough, but practically empty."

"But he just moved in."

"Three weeks ago. Most people get a couch, or at least a futon. They keep food, they smile at neighbors."

"As long as he has condoms, what do you care?"

"No, I won't be back there. Something wasn't right with him." Karina wanted to say more about how uneasy he made her, watching her from a dark, empty apartment, but she bit her tongue. After all, she was partly to blame. She'd been trying to attract his attention, which was vaguely hurtful to her pride now that she knew he had no real interest in her.

"How did he look up close?"

Karina swallowed. "Wary. Hard. Haunted. Sexy."

"Still a mystery then," Debby mused, looking as if she wanted to come up with another plan.

"Don't even," Karina said.

"You'd rather suffer?"

"I'll buy a damned vibrator if it gets too bad."

Debby laughed. "I hear The Pink Pussycat delivers."

3

KARINA DIDN'T LAST LONG at work. Debby claimed that even the double-strength effects would wane after several hours, but by midafternoon Karina was still unable to settle down, what with the cravings and the pictures in her head and the empty, aching heat between her thighs. After snapping at Janine for failing to keep the carafe of ice water filled, she knew she had to either go home or go pound down Alex's door.

Janine's head picked up when Karina sailed through the outer office with her coat over her arm. She blinked beneath the razor-cut spikes of her dishwater-blond bangs. "You're leaving again?"

"Going home early."

"All right. What should I do for the rest of the day?"

"Just, you know—" Karina couldn't focus. "The usual."

"I finished the shipments. I'll organize files."

Karina made an agreeable sound, even though her files were already organized, alphabetized and cross-referenced, both hard and soft copies.

Hard and soft…ooh.

She put her head down and squeezed the end of her nose all the way out of the store, determined not to linger over the displays of Bellini truffles or the mocha-mint mousse cups or the tins of hot-chocolate mix that would taste so good on the kind of long, lonely night she had in front of her....

The trip from the front door of Sutter Chocolat to the vestibule of the apartments upstairs was ten steps long. She counted each one, exerting tremendous willpower to keep herself from looking up at Alex's windows. Perhaps she should have been equally concerned with random male pedestrians—in case the chocolate aphrodisiac was indiscriminate—but the possibility of other men didn't really enter her mind. Alex filled her thoughts, all on his own.

Fill me.

"Stop it," Karina said as she unlocked the door and just about threw herself inside.

Fill me. Hard and deep and fast.

Frederick Alonzo, who lived in the second-floor apartment across from her own, was getting his mail. "Miss Sutter," he said, bobbing his head. He was in his early fifties with salt-and-pepper hair and a shy smile. As her tenant for less than a year, he'd proved to be clean and quiet, always a gentleman. "Good day."

Karina closed her eyes, feeling for the wall so she wouldn't lose her balance. "Hi, Mr. Alonzo."

There was a moment's silence while he shuffled through his mail. Karina cracked a lid and saw that he was looking at her with concern. "Dizzy, Miss Sutter?" He took a step closer. "Are you ill?"

She held up a hand to stop him, then waved it at her face. "I'm, er, a little hot."

"Fever. *Tch, tch.* You ought to get upstairs and crawl into bed. Take care of yourself."

Karina almost choked at the image that brought to

mind. Did she have The Pink Pussycat's number? Did they really deliver? Of course they did. One of the ben- efits of living in New York was having all your needs met via telephone and courier service. Even *this* kind.

"Yes, thanks," she said to the tenant. "I will be sure to do that."

"You don't want the flu."

"No."

Mr. Alonzo offered his arm. "I'll help you up."

"Thank you, but no." Although she had only neigh- borly feelings for the guy, she wasn't taking any chances. He wore tweed jackets, wrote bad poetry and wasn't altogether unattractive. She'd always thought that his kind nature gave his mild blue eyes, lop ears and round tummy a certain cuddly stuffed-animal appeal—

Karina slammed her eyes shut again. Alex Anderson had unadulterated animal appeal. *Rrrowr.* She'd stick with him for the time being.

Mr. Alonzo edged toward the stairs. "If you're sure, then."

"I've got to pick up my mail," she said brightly, wip- ing her forehead with the back of a hand. "I'll be along in a minute."

"Take care, Miss Sutter. Give me a ring if you need anything."

She'd flag an SOS at Alex if it got to that. No doubt he would be sneaking peeks at her again, especially after the fool she'd made of herself.

Karina's whirring mind snapped to a stop. If Debby was right and Alex *did* eat one of the truffles—well, there was still a chance of there being a seduction to- night. Or at least of getting some of her own back.

Resolutely, she climbed the stairs, each step an escalating degree in torment as her thighs swished back and forth, rubbing until she was so sensitive she swore she'd go off at a touch. If she'd lived any higher than the second floor, she'd have had to stop for a cigarette.

Finally home. She let herself inside with a relieved exhale and locked the door behind her. The apartment was her haven, even on days when she wasn't desperate for privacy. After the business had proved such a success, she had consulted with her accountants and bought the entire building as an investment instead of continuing to pay exorbitant rent. She'd indulged herself by combining two small apartments into one, taking down a section of the ceiling and having a spiral metal staircase installed to give herself access to the loft and bedrooms above. The rooms were now generously sized, the decor simple, modern and elegant. There were blond wood floors and shelves, lots of cream and ivory, with clean-lined furnishings upholstered in ice blue and palest green. Tasteful was the word, except for a few funky touches from her carnival collection. There was even a fortune-telling machine near the archway to the living room.

Esmeralda the Gypsy Queen. She was a gaudy creature boxed in Plexiglas, the top half of the life-size mannequin done up in a glitzy costume with fringe and hoop earrings. Karina kept a bowl of quarters on top of the case for the guests who invariably wanted their fortunes read.

She reached for the coins. "I need answers, Esme," she said, feeding fifty cents into the slot. "Will I be lonesome tonight?"

The colored lightbulbs outlining Esme's booth flickered on and off in an alternating pattern of red and purple and gold. A crystal ball had been affixed to a platform draped in velvet to disguise Esme's missing lower half. The fortune-telling prop lit up with a twinkle of lights concealed inside the frosted globe. Next, the mannequin whirred to life. Her eyes opened and one arm came up, raising an open palm near the glass. "Give me your hand," the automated voice said. "I will tell your fortune."

Karina placed her palm on the touch pad, which shone green, warming her skin. For fun, she told her friends that Esme was never wrong, but of course that was pure bunk.

After a few tinkling bars of carnival music, Esme's black marble eyes blinked and a card dropped into the receptacle near the coin slot. "Fortune foretold."

That was what Esme always said—she was a very limited conversationalist. Only the cards differed. Karina had entertained the thought it would be amusing to refill the machine with more unique hand-printed cards, but she'd never gotten around to it. With little expectation, she reached for her fortune.

"A dark stranger will enter your life," she read.

Wow. What were the odds?

With a short laugh, she gave Esme's cubicle a pat. Maybe one in twenty. Karina had never kept track of how often the cards were repeated. She couldn't actually remember a specific instance of a person getting the "dark stranger" card, but she was almost certain that it had happened.

"Pure coincidence," she said, thinking of the man who was no longer a complete stranger as she crossed to the windows. The afternoon light was already beginning to fade. These December days were so short. But she didn't turn on the lamps. Not yet.

The sheer curtains were open and the linen shades up. She clung to the exposed brick framing the tall windows that overlooked the street, the fortune card clasped between her fingers. One peek. Just to see if he was there.

The dark stranger.

"Nonsense." Karina tilted her head to look out the window, quickly scanning for Alex's window. His tattered blind was down. If he was watching for her, she couldn't tell.

She withdrew and pressed her forehead to the brick. The fortune, meaningless though it was, had only served to ratchet up her tension. Her body was strung taut, vibrating even at the marrow. She needed relief so badly that every fiber of her being was screaming for it. And there were a lot of them. She ate her muesli religiously, to combat the high fat content of the shop's sweets.

Another peep out the window. *Go for the truffles, Alex. Please. I need you to want me as badly as I want you.*

Still clinging to the brick, she put the card between her lips, then brushed her palm across her front. Yes, her nipples were hard and rubbing against the lace edges of the bra. She slipped a couple of fingers inside her blouse to free them, stopping to flick the sensitive nubs a couple of times as the heat inside leapt higher, making her soften and swell with wanting. She rocked her hips, chafed her thighs. *I could call someone else.* Bradley or Quinn, any of the men she'd dated in the past. They might be willing to engage in a quickie without expecting more.

But…that wouldn't be the same. For some reason, she was obsessed with Alex.

Some reason? She laughed silently. *You* know the *reason*.

The game had begun a week after he'd moved in, when she'd first begun to notice him on the street. Having no previous interest in exhibitionism, she hadn't consciously decided to tease him. That had crept up on her.

First she'd seen him a couple of times standing near his window during the day, looking out. Nothing strange about that, except that he'd always ducked out of view whenever a pedestrian glanced up. She'd even waved to him once while she was washing her windows on a Saturday morning. He'd seen her, but he'd turned away without returning the friendly gesture. She'd shrugged that off.

Next she'd become aware of him in the evening, when his blind was halfway up more frequently. That had seemed odd, so she'd paid attention and eventually realized that he rarely turned the lights on in his apartment. He sat in the dark, a shadowed figure near the window. Barely visible. Just watching.

Watching what? Who? *Her?*

Karina's initial response had been outrage at the violation of her privacy. She'd been more scrupulous about keeping her windows covered. But the dark stranger had become a part of her life, even her dreams, and she'd found herself thinking about him all the time. Wondering, imagining, supposing.

Supposing she was the kind of woman who liked to be watched.

She'd begun leaving her windows uncovered a while longer than usual. When the lights were on, she knew he'd have a perfect view into her place from his third-floor apartment. The living and dining room, the master suite upstairs—all faced the street with eight-foot-tall windows that offered an equally good view inside as out. She wasn't ready to go as far as a true exhibitionist, but she was always aware that he might be watching, so she began to move with more grace, almost posing herself when she lay on her couch, swinging her hips as she walked about the rooms, lingering near the window while she took her hair down and brushed it out, or buttoned her shirt.

Her modesty had prevailed and drawn the line at nudity. But that line had become smudged after she'd taken to wearing a robe with only underwear—occasionally nothing—on underneath. He might have caught glimpses if he was a dedicated watcher: the curve of a breast, the flash of a thigh. Nothing more explicit. Harmless titillation, she'd assured herself.

"Until today," she whispered, mortified all over again. After the show she'd been giving him for the past two weeks, Alex had reason to believe that she'd flashed him on purpose, regardless of his denial. Her only saving grace might be that he still believed she was an innocent player in their voyeuristic little game.

In all of her previous posturing, she'd tried not to be obvious about staring his way, even though she *knew* he was watching. The angle of his head in the darkness, the prickling tension of her reaction. Some evenings she swore she could feel his gaze roving across her body. And she knew that he wanted her.

Hah. Delusional.

But was she? Hadn't there been a hint of desire in his eyes when he'd watched her moan over the truffle? His jaw had clenched so hard he might have cracked a tooth. If it hadn't been desire, he'd been withholding a strong emotion of some sort.

Maybe disgust. She slipped the fortune card from her

mouth, letting the edge drag across her lower lip. But then why did he watch her?

Karina took a breath and pushed away from the brick wall. Let him stare all he wanted!

Tonight, she was reckless. Tonight, she'd really give him something to see.

ALEX SAT DRUMMING his fingers on his knee. There wasn't much for a man to do, isolated in a small apartment, night after night. Television didn't interest him, though occasionally he turned on the small portable set for the company. He liked movies, but had no DVD player and not much desire to get one when it was only another item to leave behind the next time he moved. His laptop computer sat on the desk and he amused himself there at times. An hour or two of inaction was all he could take before he was pacing the studio space like a cat in a cage.

Mark Lexmond had been a get-up-and-go kind of guy. Running, surfing, playing in a volleyball league, meeting up with friends at the various dive bars and colorful cafés that populated his Venice Beach neighborhood. He worked long hours at his law firm, so when he played, he played hard.

There were always single women around, and his guy pals were a varied lot. He tended to accumulate people as well as possessions, rarely discarding either. His ocean-view apartment was a cheerful hodgepodge of saggy chairs, beach gear and guy toys like an expensive stereo system and his precious drum set. Frequent guests dropped by to jam or watch a game and wound up sacked out on the couch or even the floor. The spare bedroom was occupied by a stream of roommates who came and went like the tide, knowing that Lex was easy about the rent check being late or girlfriends who staged minidramas in the middle of a Lakers play-off game.

Once every month or so, Lex rounded up the available bodies and held a free-for-all housecleaning event, where they pitched the accumulation of beer cans and take-out cartons, swept the sand off the floor, scrubbed the grunge from the bathroom and decrusted the oven and microwave. Most of his girlfriends had at one time or another tried to inject some design into the rooms, but they usually gave up after buying a few floor pillows, alphabetizing his CDs or separating his suits from his Hawaiian-print shirts.

He propped his arms behind his head. Yep, he'd been a happy-go-lucky guy who wished for nothing more than a satisfying sense of accomplishment from his work and an equally satisfying tumble from the closest available babe. Troubles had rolled off his back.

Sure, there'd been days when the realities of his job got him down. Along with the repeat offenders who always swore that this time they were innocent, he'd seen a lot of hard-luck cases who deserved a break that he couldn't always deliver. But his natural optimism was a strong force and when his mood had threatened to turn blue, he'd beat the hell out of the snare drum or head out to the beach to let the surf toss him around. The powerlessness of man versus nature had always adjusted his perspective.

What he hadn't been prepared for was being powerless against Rafael Norris, a truly amoral man who'd do anything to avenge the death of his son.

But Lex—*Alex,* he reminded himself again with a soft oath. He had to think of himself as Alex now, even to himself.

Alex Anderson was not Mark Lexmond.

Alex was solitary. Abrupt. Defensive. Closed. He avoided eye contact. He made no small talk. He had no friends. Needless to say, no lovers of any duration.

Thoughts of Karina Sutter immediately filled his head. When a man was a virtual prisoner, even the smallest connection, especially one that included the touch of skin on skin, became hugely important. He'd replayed her visit in his mind all afternoon until the minor episode was magnified to outrageous proportions.

He got up and stalked around the studio, from the bedroom nook to the living room, past the galley kitchen and the bathroom door, following the route he'd taken a hundred times today. Soon a path would be worn in the floorboards.

Karina had been expressing a bit of interest, that was all. She'd run if she knew what she'd be getting herself into with him.

Lights went on across the street. Alex moved closer to the window, cautiously keeping away from the glass as he pulled the blind down. The sky was the color of steel. It was early for Karina to be home from work.

Peering from the side of the blind, he did his usual scan of the street, then the nearby windows. Normal activity, picking up as the day grew short and people either returned home or prepared to go out. Karina's apartment was dark downstairs, but the lights upstairs were on. He wondered if she had a date with another of the smooth operators he'd seen arriving at her door over the past three weeks. There'd been two or three of them—interchangeable in their handsome, clean-cut looks. Even in his incarnation as Mark Lexmond, he hadn't been her type. He'd worn goofy ties and had used his briefcase as a basketball hoop, dartboard and waste can combined.

Still, envy slipped past Alex's defenses. He'd begun to think of Karina as *his*. Which was both stupid and dangerous, not to mention delusional.

Shiny glass flashed across the way. Karina's bathroom. He saw movement—a pale body indistinct in the steam of a shower. Excitement stirred in the pit of his stomach. The bathroom window was completely uncovered. Bedroom, too. She had to know that he could see inside.

Had to. Which meant that all along she had known he was watching and she'd liked it that way.

Maybe he'd been slow on the uptake, but he was beginning to get it now. Her move this afternoon had been the next step in their game. Now that he'd rebuffed her, she was going to get to him in another way.

He groaned and reached for his binoculars. The steam had risen, but he could see that she was in the shower, spectacularly nude behind the glass door. Rows of brick sprang into sharp relief when he brought the glasses up, but he quickly adjusted the angle, finding Karina's apartment with a learned skill.

There she was. Showering with the shades up. A first.

She raised her arms, soaping her hair. The curves of her body wavered behind the steamy glass. Alex thought briefly of playing the gentleman and putting the binoculars away, but if ever a woman wanted to be watched…

Her head went under the stream of water. He dropped the binoculars and gave the lenses a quick polish with the hem of his T-shirt, returning in time to see the shower door swing open. Was she actually—

Holy shit. She was. She did.

She stepped naked from the shower. He sharpened the lens focus and saw breasts. Poached pink skin beaded with droplets. A narrow strip of golden pubic hair…

Situated directly across from the shower, the bathroom window extended almost from floor to ceiling, giving him a nearly full-length view as she reached for a towel. *Oh, hot mama, don't cover up yet,* he thought, his pulse jackhammering while he scanned down her sexy body. *I want it all.* He already knew her breasts were perfect—round and firm, big enough to fill a man's hand, but not so large they swung past her ribs like heavy grapefruits. She had a narrow waist, a flat stomach, nicely flared hips. And the sweetest spot of all…

She turned sideways, wrapping the towel around herself. For a moment she froze, gripping the towel to her breasts, slightly hunched over—almost as if she were in pain. A cringe? He lowered the glasses, abashed by his lascivious interest. Of course he had to look. Any guy would look. But he'd feel more at ease if he knew for sure, one hundred percent positive, that she was a willing participant.

Invite me in.…

She'd said it, but he'd declined. What she was doing now was only another offer. *Had* to be intentional.

Karina had disappeared from view. He scanned her apartment through the binoculars, suddenly finding her when she came out of the bathroom, combing her wet hair as she walked into the adjoining bedroom. She still wore the towel, so he trained the glasses on her face, catching the furtive glance she shot at the windows before turning on a bedside lamp.

Expecting her to hurry over to close her curtains, he straightened and eased away from the crinkled blind.

The window covering suddenly shot up on its roller with a *whir* and a *snap,* exposing him to the street.

And to Karina.

He didn't need the binoculars to know that she saw him. Their eyes connected over the distance—he was one hundred percent certain of *that.* He might have quickly moved out of the window or at least looked away, but for once he chose not to. He wanted her to know, without a doubt, that he was watching.

Then he'd see what happened.

After a couple of seconds, she lifted her hands to her hair, skimming the wet strands back from her face. The motion did interesting things to her towel sarong, making it gap over one thigh. He imagined ripping it off and throwing her on the bed. Or kneeling at her feet, running his hands along her clean silky body, burying his face in the heat between her thighs....

Instead of going for the curtains, she turned and opened the closet. Hardly believing it, he leaned forward, bracing one hand on the window ledge. Panting like a runner.

With a casual flick, she discarded the towel.

Alex let out a moan, his fingers tightening around the binoculars. No surprise, she had a gorgeous ass. The kind a man wanted to bite into like a ripe fruit. Pert and round, made for cupping. For riding.

He straightened and unsnapped his jeans, slid his fingers inside a few inches, nudging down the zipper. Lex Junior wanted to come out to play, but the idea of jerking off at the window like the neighborhood pervert was just nasty. Painfully, he withdrew. A few more minutes of this torture and he'd be shooting in his pants without having to touch himself.

He was almost glad when Karina slid into a silky blue robe. She wrapped the belt around her waist and left the room, momentarily moving out of his sight. He dropped into the secondhand armchair he'd hauled home from a junk shop, cradling the fullness at his crotch. *Enough.*

But the show wasn't over. Though the light was fading, he was able to see into the first level of Karina's place even without the lights on. She descended the spiral staircase, completely oblivious to the way her robe slid open to flash her long bare legs.

Unless she knew exactly what she was doing, he considered. The visit to his apartment had been engineered. Why not this?

Alex gripped the arms of the chair. "You're trying to seduce me, Mrs. Robinson."

Lights went on downstairs. The shades stayed up. He retrieved the binoculars and followed Karina's progress through the apartment as she went to the inner area he'd deduced was her kitchen. She emerged with a glass of red wine.

"C'mon, darling. What's the plan?" he breathed. She moved out of sight again, but only for a few seconds before she was back, swaying her hips and shoulders, holding the glass aloft as she twirled. Music, he thought, as the robe flared out around her slender legs.

She danced for a few minutes, then gracefully draped herself across the armless couch that faced the windows, making a pretty picture in the golden lamplight with her blond hair loose around her face and her pale limbs and the robin's egg blue of her robe against the ice-blue upholstery. She sipped the wine, staring across at him with one shoulder bare where the robe had slipped off it. He moved the binoculars one degree lower to the silk lying open across her chest, one side of the drooping lapel held up only by the hardened pink tip of her breast. A slight shrug and it would drop....

Alex put the glasses aside and settled himself deeper in the bowed cushion. Karina was showing no intention of getting dressed to go out, and there was no way he could make himself stop watching. It was going to be a very long night.

WAS HE WATCHING?

Yes—he wasn't hiding that. She could see him sitting near his window.

Was he touching himself?

Yes—unless his willpower was made of iron.

Karina's clearly wasn't. She let her hand drift along her thigh. Her skin seemed to reach toward the touch. She could only imagine how sensitive she'd be if it were Alex's hands on her, roaming freely. The pure pleasure of that would be stupendous.

Pure? Not exactly. She'd cheated on Alex with a truffle, though she doubted that he'd mind if he knew.

Several hours had passed since she'd eaten the candies and she was still aroused, even after the long shower. The effects should have worn off by now, and instead she remained hot and primed for action. She told herself that only a powerful force beyond her control could have made her show off for Alex the way she had, parading naked for him—and anyone else with a view. She'd be dying of embarrassment tomorrow, but for now, the ache was too sharp, the need too great. She could only think about getting satisfaction. And she was becoming reckless enough to accept any kind at all.

Unfortunately, Alex didn't appear to be as driven.

She'd hoped that the sight of her would make him so crazy with lust that he'd have to charge over and bust her door down to have her.

Oh, yesss. Nice fantasy. Her eyes closed as her fingers glided along the seam of her robe, parting it just enough for her nails to trace tingling paths on the surface of her skin. She slid lower on the sofa, raising one leg along the back.

Alex, touching me. She slipped a hand beneath the silk, stroking over her ribs, up to one breast. The weight of it was nice, but not enough. She wanted Alex's hand, his mouth on her nipple, his body covering hers, conquering and dividing as he parted her with a hugely engorged erection....

What the—?

Karina sat up, shocked to find her robe gaping open and her hand between her legs. Heat flared—at her sex, in her cheeks. She didn't dare look out to see Alex's reaction. Head down, she clenched a hand on the front of the robe and ran over to the light switch, then the curtains. She wrenched them shut, but they were too sheer to offer much privacy. She reached for the dangling cords that controlled the shades, trying to keep herself out of the window.

As if it mattered. She'd already gone too far.

She abandoned the cords and peeped out between the curtains. Alex was still there, standing now with his nose practically pressed to the glass. Trying for a better view, she assumed, gritting her teeth against the impulse to give it to him.

The other windows in his building appeared empty, but she couldn't be sure that there'd only been an audience of one. This couldn't all be blamed on the chocolate. She must have been out of her mind.

But so into her body.

"I will never eat one of those truffles again," she vowed. A rash promise. Damn Alex, anyway! *He* was supposed to be the one who couldn't control himself.

Instead he was the safe detached observer while *she* put on a wanton sex show. The worst part was that she was still turned on.

Which was also the best part.

A river of emotion ran through her. Audacity, humiliation. Passion, frustration. *It was the best of times, it was the worst of times,* she said in her head, pressing herself up against the brick wall. She wriggled a little, letting the robe fall open again. The rough texture abraded her nipples and she moved over a few inches to touch them to the glass of the windowpane. The icy cold was a shock against her fevered flesh and yet she liked it. She wanted to be startled. Blown away. Scandalized.

"Alex," she pleaded. He saw her.

He was watching.

After a few seconds she deliberately put her hand over her pubic mound so that he would know what she was about to do. Fading back a few steps, she let the curtains that she'd brushed aside drop between them again. Her figure would show through the sheer fabric, but the view wouldn't be as explicit.

She stroked two fingers between her labia. *Let him see. Let him know.*

As she fingered the hard bump of her clit, a little smile found its way to her mouth—a teasing pout. Her head lolled, weaving from side to side as she pleasured herself. Alex was watching, frustrated, knowing that he could have been inside her, but also that she was perfectly capable of coming without him. Her hand moved faster, rubbed harder. Jolts of sensation shot through her and when her knees started to go out, she lurched forward, barely keeping herself upright with one palm pressed to the window as a sharp, short climax burst beneath her fingertips.

"Aghhh." She flopped around so that she was leaning up against the brick again, limp and quivering from the vaguely disappointing orgasm.

Never mind. At least she'd taken the edge off. Although she couldn't see Alex, she was sure that he was riveted. Eventually he would eat one of the truffles and know the hunger and the longing that had built up inside her for the past few weeks and ultimately driven her to such incredible lengths.

Then *she* would be the one in control. She could say yes or even *no*…if she wanted him to know exactly what it was like to suffer.

4

During a long, sleepless night, Alex had decided that it was time to try to be a normal person again. He would bank the memories of his life as Mark Lexmond, banish memories of Florida and the horror and guilt of seeing an innocent person killed one foot away from him, rein in the paranoia, and start fresh.

He had to believe that he was safe. Especially if he wanted to approach Karina.

Which he did. No denying that.

He showered and shaved, ran a comb through his hair and made a mental note to find a barber, put on his least wrinkled clothes, and headed out with only a brief detour to the window to check for loiterers—and Karina. There'd been no sign of her since the previous evening's awe-inspiring performance.

On his way to the door, he noticed the abandoned box of chocolates. Cockroaches would swarm if he left them out. He fitted the lid and tucked the box into the roomy pocket of his long coat. Maybe he could find someone who'd enjoy them—a neighbor, a street person.

Outside, a delivery truck blocked his view of Sutter Chocolat. The back doors were hanging open. Alex stepped off the curb between the truck and a car with its nose nudged into the loading zone, giving the door a shove so he could get by.

Thunk. "Hey!" barked the driver, backing out with a loaded dolly. He rubbed his nose. "Watch what you're doing, man."

"Sorry." Alex held the door. "Let me give you a hand."

The driver pushed the dolly over a few feet to give them room to swing the doors shut.

Alex eyed the boxes, prominently marked with perishable contents labels. "Sutter Chocolat?"

"That's right." The driver shoved his hands into his jacket pockets. "That store—" He shook his head. "Uses one helluva lot of chocolate for a small business. Seems like I'm here every other day."

"It is a busy place."

Wheeling the dolly before him, the deliveryman looked for an opening in traffic. "You ever been there?"

Alex shook his head.

"They've got great chocolate. The girls slip me free samples every time I come by." The man winked. He was young, muscular and full of jaunty bravado. "Can't afford the stuff on my salary."

Alex remembered the truffles in his pocket. "Maybe you'd like these." He offered the box. "As an apology for your nose."

"Hey, thanks." The delivery driver popped the lid. "One's missing."

"They're leftovers, if that's okay."

"Doesn't bother me." The guy tossed an entire truffle into his mouth. "Thought you've never been to the shop," he said thickly.

"The candy was a gift." Alex raised a hand to signal for an empty cab that was crawling by in the bumper-to-bumper traffic that was apparently a constant during the holiday season. He usually walked, for the exercise and for the illusion that he was getting somewhere fast when his life was stuck in a holding pattern. "I'm allergic."

"Your loss, my gain."

"Happy holidays." Alex jumped into the cab, giving the deliveryman a casual wave goodbye. He wanted a hearty breakfast for a change, then a haircut. Maybe a little shopping. He'd left Florida with nothing but his life.

KYLE MURPHY GAVE UP on cutting across the street and wheeled the dolly to the crosswalk, licking chocolate off his teeth as he went. He patted the foil candy box he'd stuffed into his jacket pocket. Good stuff. Nice of the guy to share.

By the time Kyle reached the chocolate shop, he was feeling unusually warm despite the chill wind. He set the dolly out of the way of pedestrians and paused to unzip his jacket. The sweetness of the chocolate lingered on his tongue, and he would have sworn he felt it moving through his bloodstream if that hadn't been dippy enough to sound like something his psychic-healer sister would say. The warmth rising from his skin was just good old-fashioned sweat. Those bricks of bulk chocolate weighed a ton and he'd had to lift out three boxes of them.

The store was still closed—didn't open till eleven. He knocked at the heavy oak door, peering through the small square panes of the inset window. From previous visits, he knew the kitchen staff was operating in the back. A worker he didn't recognize came to let him in.

"I know the way," Kyle said when the man started to show him toward the back. "Thanks."

He wheeled the dolly through the swinging doors that led to the working side of the store. The new office assistant gave a start when he arrived, pulling out of a file drawer like a kid caught with her hands in the cookie jar. She was a flighty one.

"Delivery," Kyle said. He pulled the signature board out from its holster at his waist. "Sign here, please."

"I've seen you before," the girl said. She scribbled her name on the electronic pad. "I'm Janine Gardner."

"The new girl," Kyle said, giving her a friendly smile. She wasn't bad. Actually sort of cute, he decided, tugging at a too-tight uniform collar as the unusual warmth crawled up his throat. Women flocked to him like gulls to a fish; he didn't usually get nervous around one unless he seriously liked her. The strange thing was that on previous visits, Janine hadn't struck him as particularly special. Kind of prissy and stuck-up, even.

"Can you take the boxes to the storage area?" she asked.

"Sure." Reluctantly, Kyle left Janine behind and pushed the dolly toward the porthole door that led to storage shelves lining a wide corridor adjacent to the kitchen. With what he hoped was a debonair flair, he executed a neat swivel and backed through it, raising his brows at Janine. He even flashed a dimple. She leaned across her desk, watching him with suspicious eyes until the door swung shut.

"Slow down, Fred Astaire," said a female voice from above. Sharply.

"Huh?" Kyle looked up at the same moment that he backed into a sliding ladder positioned to reach the highest bank of metal shelves. It was a heavy ladder, set in place, but he was a big guy and he must have given it a good jolt because suddenly the woman perched half-way up it was flailing her arms and falling backward.

Kyle put out his hands and caught her. She landed squarely in his arms with a solid *whump*. "Whoa," he said, knocked off his game but not off his feet, even though she was a plentiful armful.

He looked into her surprised face—bright blue eyes, a snub nose, pinkened cheeks—then hefted her higher against his chest. "Don't worry, missus. I've got you."

Her eyes widened. "You certainly do."

"I know you," he said. "You're the cook."

"The *confectioner.*" She wriggled, wanting to get down.

Instinct made him tighten his arms to keep her close. "I'm Kyle Murphy."

"Yes, I know. You're the delivery guy."

How come he'd never noticed her before, either? She was *much* cuter than Janine. Curly hair the color of a Hershey's bar and a fantastic rack judging by the cleavage showing above her apron. The full curves below were pillowed against his chest. There was a sauciness in the way she met his eyes without blinking. And she smelled like chocolate. A big plus in his book.

His temperature soared even higher. Damn if he wasn't getting hard. "What's your name?"

"Debby Caruso."

"Oh, yeah." The girls out front invoked the name when they gave him extra freebies: *Don't let Debby see. She'll scorch our hides.*

Kyle wasn't scorched—not yet. But he had a very nice sizzle happening.

"You might want to put me down," said Debby. She patted his bunched shoulder. "Although I really do appreciate the display of manly strength."

Before setting her down, he showed off by levering her like a barbell. She whooped, then tottered a bit on her heels when she touched ground. He kept a hand on her waist to steady her. Well, technically on her hip. Maybe her backside. The firm curve of it under his palm was lust-inducing.

"Careful," he said, with an unusual constriction of his throat.

"Kyle," she said, and he found himself mesmerized by the sound of his own name. "Kyle," she repeated, looking as if she were almost as dazzled as he, "would it be too cheesy of me to say that I think I've fallen for you?" She laughed, her eyes bright with a catchy sparkle. "Oh, my. I'm just kidding of course."

Kyle didn't answer. He only smiled and put his free hand on her other hip—okay, backside—and gave her a lusty squeeze.

She widened her eyes again, but didn't seem at all offended. In fact, she planted her hands on his chest, rocked forward on her teeter-totter shoes and gave him a short but exceptionally tasty kiss in return. "Thank you for rescuing me."

The thickening sense of pleasure that had started outside on the sidewalk had completely enveloped him now, as if he'd been dunked into a vat of the richest, warmest fudge sauce in the Willy Wonka factory. There was only one word to define Debby Caruso's kiss, and he said it out loud with an exhilarating, almost triumphant emphasis: *"Sweet!"*

DEBBY BARGED INTO Karina's office without knocking. "He's here," she hissed, holding the door.

"Who's here?" Karina said automatically, her eyes

going to the clock on her desk. Quarter past eleven. The store had barely opened. Alex usually didn't go out for at least another hour or two. Not that she was going to be watching for him today. After the way she'd behaved, she'd prefer never seeing him again.

And what a big fat liar we are.

"Alex, of course," Debby said. "He's *inside* the store!"

"Inside?" Suddenly Karina felt unhinged.

She'd risen that morning, wincing at the memories of the night before, and had only managed to come to work because the thought of staying cooped up in her apartment—the scene of the crime, so to speak—was even worse. She'd kept to her office all morning, telling herself that she must feel ashamed even when, strangely, she wasn't. Not completely. The effects of the chocolate had eventually lessened, but she still didn't feel quite like herself. Masturbating in front of a virtual stranger, even behind a curtain, would normally have made her want to curl up and die.

"He must be looking for you." Debby didn't know what Karina had done to ensure that Alex had seen plenty of her already.

Karina considered. "Maybe he already ate the truffles and wants to buy more." That would be huge. If Alex was jonesing for chocolate, and therefore sex, didn't she want to be there?

"If he ate *all* the truffles he wouldn't be decent to make a public appearance for some time," Debby said with a knowing chuckle.

Karina stood and straightened the white cashmere sweater she'd worn over a black turtleneck and pants. "Do I look okay?"

"Perfect as ever."

"Except when I'm inadvertently flashing my boobs," Karina said, trying not to think of her advertent full-body exposure.

Debby grabbed her by the arm and hustled her from the office. "Hurry up. Either he's going to leave before you get there or end up being molested by one of the customers."

"Hold my calls, Janine," Karina said over her shoulder as she allowed herself to be escorted to the front of the store.

Once they were through the door, Debby gave her a little shove. "Go get him."

When Alex saw her and his expression changed from slightly bored to intense, the embarrassment that Karina had been waiting for hit her all at once like a tidal wave. She put a hand over her face. Good God. She'd done things in front of this man that had never happened with anyone else, and yet the amazing truth was that they'd barely spoken—or touched. How was she supposed to carry on a conversation with him when she knew what images were running through his mind?

Karina forced herself forward, bypassing the clerks shoveling up candies and serving take-out cups of the store's popular hot chocolate. She halted at the corner of the long display cabinet, away from the registers, and threaded her fingers until they were interlocked, a physical reminder to get a grip.

"Hello." *Alex.* "May I help you?" Her voice was as stiff as…well, she didn't want to think about what that comparison brought to mind.

Alex had followed her on the other side of the case, sliding one hand along the top of the glass. His hair had been cut, making it look darker without the shaggy bleached ends. At first she wasn't sure she liked the new style because most of the men she dated were well shorn, but one look into Alex's eyes and she knew that nothing so superficial could make him like the others.

But it was impossible to define why. He was an enigma.

She raised her brows, a light flush creeping into her cheeks. He didn't speak.

"Did you want more of the truffles?"

"No." Another long pause before he made a motion with his head toward the display window. "Can we talk?"

"Outside?"

He moved over a step. "Right here."

Without the counter between them. She didn't know if she liked that idea, but it certainly made her flutter inside. She couldn't blame the chocolate either, unless she'd become sensitive to fumes. She didn't think so. Her most potent stimulant was Alex.

"All right." She nodded, shooting a wary look at his serious face. *Please don't mention last night. I will die.*

She met him near the windows and plunged right in, keeping to an I'm-just-a-happy-shopkeeper expression. "Did you try one of the truffles the way you promised?"

"Did I promise? I don't remember."

"I think you did."

He looked past the top of her head. "The truffles were delicious."

"Don't eat too many at once," she warned. *Blink.* "Um, they're too rich for that."

"Not a problem."

She determinedly held her bland smile. "Well, good."

"I, uh…" Alex rubbed a couple of fingers across his

clean chin. No more stubble either. "I wanted to apologize for being rude yesterday, at my door. I'm not usually—" He stopped, a deep groove etched between his eyebrows.

"But I interrupted you." Karina glanced across the street at his building. "You work at home?"

"Sort of."

"On the computer, I suppose."

"Yeah. I'm a writer."

He said that with no hesitation, but for some reason she didn't believe him. Possibly because she'd seen him sitting near the window with a laptop computer but he'd never seemed particularly absorbed. Weren't writers supposed to lose themselves in their work?

Unless he had writer's block. That might explain his irritability. She gave him a warm look to show that she could be sympathetic. "Published?"

"A *frustrated* writer," he said.

"I see. Then you've found the right city. New York is filled with frustrated writers. You can see them on the street, staring bitterly at stacks of bestsellers in the window of any Barnes and Noble superstore."

Alex almost smiled. "Do you want to go for coffee?" he blurted.

She didn't know why she was surprised. Had she expected him to waltz over and service her on the closest available surface?

Or maybe she was supposed to substitute the word *nooner* for *coffee*. That would be bold of him, but then she'd given him good reason to believe she might say yes.

"I guess you can't leave work," Alex said.

"That's not a problem. I'm the boss."

"Right. Sutter Chocolat."

"The thing is…" How to put this? Unless it was a euphemism, coffee sounded like a date to her, and that meant becoming acquaintances, friends, boyfriend and girlfriend, la la la, the whole enchilada. She had that with other men.

Granted, part of her wanted to get to know Alex, peel away a few of his layers. The good girl that up until yesterday had been prominent in her was loudly demanding it, bolstered by the notion that only tramps had emotionless one-night stands.

And sexually confident women, Karina told herself. Women who knew what they wanted and went for it. She could be one of those women, especially with another dose of chocolate courage.

She took a deep breath, preparing to suggest that they skip coffee and get straight to business, and then copped out as soon as she opened her mouth.

"Sorry. Now's not a good time." She couldn't be positive that coffee didn't mean coffee. As hard as it sounded, not to mention unlike her, getting into a relationship with him wasn't her goal.

Alex's eyes were the color of blue-gray slate, and suddenly just as flat and cool. "Oh."

"We're so busy…"

"I understand." He thrust his hands into his coat pockets and began edging away. "This wasn't one of my better ideas anyway."

She wanted to put out a hand to stop his retreat, but she didn't know how to explain what she wanted from him. She'd already given him a gigantic in-your-face clue.

With a jingle of the old-fashioned bell over the door, he left the shop.

Debby rushed up, wailing. "Oh, crap, Kare. What didja do wrong?"

"He invited me out for coffee." Karina's eyes were on the window. Alex had paused outside to turn up the collar of his coat. He flicked a sidelong glance at her, then hunched his head onto his shoulders and strode away.

Debby was asking why she hadn't gone.

"I couldn't, that would be…" Karina brushed Debby aside, losing her train of thought as she impulsively raced for the door. The brisk air hit her like a slap, but she gulped the cold into her lungs and charged off, waving a hand. "Alex! Wait up!"

He was already at the corner, but he'd heard her. The light changed and the crowd surged into the crosswalk. Karina's stomach dropped, until she realized that they were parting around Alex like a rock in the river. She crossed her arms, hugging herself as she jogged to catch up.

"Alex." Her breath puffed vapor into the air. "I— umm…"

For a moment he looked at her with the same hard eyes, but then he relented and said, "What are you doing?" while he pulled off the gray scarf that had been hanging inside his jacket collar. He wound it around her head with a certain carefulness that made her chin lift and her cheek turn toward his touch.

Abruptly he removed his hands. "Go back inside."

"I came to say…"

"You didn't change your mind." He was certain.

"Not about coffee," she admitted. "But…"

She bit her lip. Why was she having such trouble finishing sentences around him?

"You're shivering." He put his arms around her, but not as if he relished the chance to hold her. A purely gentlemanly action. "Go back to your store."

"Tonight," she said, into the buttons of his shirt. He was *warm*. And solid. She wanted to melt all over him.

He gave her a quizzical "Huh?"

"Eat one of the truffles tonight," she whispered in a husky voice.

Alex frowned, setting her back a little to study her face. "Why?"

"Just do it." She held his scarf under her chin with one hand while she reluctantly backed away into the stream of pedestrian traffic. Impatient shoppers jostled her this way and that, but she didn't take her eyes off Alex. If he could only look into her and read the desire that had taken over, he would know how good they could be together.

This once. Only once, to last a lifetime.

"Eat one of the truffles," she said, having to raise her voice as the crowd pushed against her, bumping her with shopping bags, "and I'll meet you. Tonight." Her knuckles pressed beneath her chin. "At the windows."

"The windows?" she saw him mouth, before she was caught up in the crowd and had to turn to make her way to the door of her shop. If she hadn't started out in search of a fling, if there weren't lingering doubts about Alex's situation, she'd have accepted his invitation in a heartbeat.

But with all that had happened, it was too late for that. He was no more than her one-night-only mystery man.

No regrets. Think of the truffles and how they'll make you feel. She ducked her nose into the folds and scent of Alex's scarf. She hoped that Debby had made extra candies, even though it was possible that she might not need one. She was already aroused...and even daring. All on her own.

KARINA'S LIFE HAD BEEN normal up to now, and after Alex, it would be normal again. This was what she told herself while molding marzipan with Debby in the kitchen an hour later. The rest of the kitchen staff was on lunch break, so Debby had snagged Karina for a private chat. An entire rack of assorted candies ready for boxing sat nearby, scenting the air with the aroma of melted chocolate and fresh vanilla beans.

Karina had expected to get grilled. But Debby seemed distracted. She hadn't picked up on Karina's lie about what she'd said to Alex, and she was not a good liar.

"That's all?" Debby rolled a lump of marzipan into a pear shape. "You ran out of the shop only to tell him that you'd love to go for coffee another day?"

Karina was forming bells. She flattened and molded a ball of the malleable candy to create the curved lip. "I could tell he hadn't tried the truffles yet. He told me he had, to be polite, I suppose, but it was obvious he hadn't. He wasn't all that interested." Certainly not in comparison to how aggressive she'd become.

"Oh, make no mistake—he was interested." Debby nodded encouragement. "You got him to come into the store, for one."

"Yes, wow. What a major step."

"He asked you out." Debby pinched off a tiny bit of the green marzipan to form a leaf and stem, then set her finished pear on a tray covered with waxed paper. "Only a hundred to go."

"This is like Play-Doh."

"I used to always try to eat my Play-Doh."

"Always? One taste didn't teach you?"

Debby flexed her fingers before rolling out the next

pear. "Nope. I'm a gobbler, not a thinker. Not like you."
Her smile was smug. "When I find an interested man, I
make my move right away."

"But I didn't want to go for *coffee*."

"Then why tell him you'd go another time?"

Karina sliced off another chunk of the red marzipan.
"Because sooner or later he will eat one of those truffles, and when that happens I want him to think of me
first." True enough.

Debby chuckled. "Can't let some other woman reap
the benefits."

"I…" The entire story was ready to burst out of Karina, regardless of her usual reserve. She was losing her
inhibitions right and left. No way could that be blamed
entirely on the chocolate. The idea that some of this was
coming from her unadulterated self was a bit alarming.
What happened if, afterward, she discovered that she
was dissatisfied with her normal life?

So what? she answered herself. People evolve.

She would cope. As long as it was a natural process,
and not as the result of an aphrodisiac. She must not forget that this *was not real.*

Alex could not be more than a fling.

"You're mashing that bell into a pancake," Debby
said mildly.

Karina tossed the overworked candy into the trash.
"There's something I haven't told you. I've been flirting with Alex."

"Yeah, if that's what you want to call flashing your
boobs."

"Not that," Karina said, although Debby had no idea
how correct she was. "At night. From my apartment
windows. I've seen him watching me."

"Oh." Debby made a baby-doll face—mouth in a circle, lids blinking up and down. "Like…peeping?"

"Kind of. Except that he knows that I know he's watching."

"Everyone does that in the city." Debby shrugged. "Window-watching is the New Yorker's favorite spectator sport. There's this guy across the air shaft from me who yells over to me to pick out his ties. And of course Whitney and the Strangler."

Their friend Whitney had a telescope in her office on the twenty-ninth floor and swore that one night when she was working late she'd seen a man strangling a woman on his bed. The police had treated Whitney like a crackpot but ever since she'd been obsessive about tracking the Strangler's movements. She even kept a log.

"This isn't like that," Karina said, her voice sounding funny even to her own ears.

Debby noticed and glanced up sharply. "What do you mean?"

"I've, ahh, enticed him."

"Ooh. And…?"

"And last night I took a shower with the shades up. I stepped out naked, no towel. He saw everything."

"Nuh-uh. You *di'n't!*"

Karina buried her face in her sticky hands. "I've become an exhibitionist."

Debby exhaled, flabbergasted. "It was the truffles."

"I'd like to think so, but the truth is that I liked it. I felt—" Karina dropped her hands, smiling a little to herself "—wild."

"Ohmigawd. Look at you." Debby reached across the worktable and playfully slapped Karina's arm. "Hell on wheels."

"You're right. It was the chocolate, not me. Not the real me, anyway."

"The chocolate can't make you do something *that* out of character. You know, like they say a person who's been hypnotized wouldn't commit murder."

"Hmm…you think?"

Debby pushed the tray of marzipan miniatures aside and leaned her elbows on the marble-topped island. "So what happened then?"

"I put on a towel."

They laughed. "But what did Alex do?" Debby insisted.

"Well, nothing. He watched. And after a while…" Karina cleared her throat. "I pulled the curtains and went to bed."

"Disappointing." Debby frowned, then brightened. "Except now we know why he came into the store today. He was here to continue the game."

"By asking me for coffee?"

"He could hardly say he wants to do you dirty two ways from Sunday."

"But that's what I want, in a manner of speaking."

"Kare, only you could be prissy and horny at the same time."

"Am I being prissy?"

"'In a manner of speaking'? What *is* that?" Debby dug her fingers into the brick of marzipan. "Girl, you've got to shed your inhibitions and grab life by the balls. Or grab Alex by 'em, at least."

"That's what I'm trying to do." Karina blushed. "The first thing you said, not the—"

"Ha! Maybe that's why he looked so constipated."

Karina was incredulous. *"Constipated?"*

"Kind of tight and inflexible, like he was scared to—I don't know—to live."

"He says he's a writer."

"That explains it, then. Writers are just one big glob of neuroses and insecurities."

"How would you know?"

"My ex, remember?"

"Oh, right." Debby had been married at twenty-one to a fortysomething writing instructor she'd met at school.

Early on, she and Karina had been a little awkward with each other since they were so different, but they'd eventually bonded over a late night kirsch-infused fudge cake. Debby had confided how everyone thought she was marrying a father figure when it had turned out that it was her ex-husband who'd wanted a mother, nurse-maid, housekeeper and cook all rolled into one. She'd enjoyed only the latter position, so she'd dumped the husband after five years, four of which were spent in couples therapy, and enrolled in cooking school with a vow to live for herself from then on.

In the spirit of sharing confidences, Karina had talked about her background, growing up in exotic locales with an industrialist-turned-diplomat father and a mother so devoted to being the ideal hostess she'd molded Karina into the perfect party accessory. Her father had retired from diplomacy midway through her teen years, and she'd been able to finish out high school in a ritzy New Jersey suburb. Since then, her parents had moved back to Switzerland, the country of her father's birth. She saw them two or three times a year on exchange visits. They thought Sutter Chocolat was an amusing trifle to keep Karina busy until she settled into her *real* life.

"Where's he from?" Debby asked.

"Alex? I don't know. I didn't ask." She hadn't had much chance, but the less she knew about him, the better. Sharing stories would lead to sharing feelings.

Would that be so wrong? she wondered. Maybe the chemistry she had with Alex was there for a reason—the ignition key to falling in love.

Bad idea. Think of his sneaky ways, his isolation. There was something wrong with a man who lived the way that Alex did, even considering that he may have just moved to the city.

"I met someone, too," Debby said, interrupting Karina's inner debate. "This morning."

Karina blinked, surprised her friend had managed to hold out for so long. "You did?"

"His name is Kyle Murphy. You've probably seen him bringing our supplies." Debby named the parcel service and quickly told how she'd fallen into Kyle's arms. "I don't know how big his package is yet, but I'm pretty sure he can deliver the goods."

Karina groaned. "That was really bad."

"There's got to be a million of them. I'll try to think of better puns for the date."

"He asked you out?"

"Dinner," Debby said. "Nothing fancy—he says he knows a little place that serves good food for less than the national debt. I'd offer to split the check, but I don't think he's that kind of guy. We'll see how he feels after I order my usual."

"You don't order more than the average wo—"

"C'mon. You know I don't stop at salad."

"There's nothing wrong with that."

"Yes." Debby sighed. "A healthy appetite for a

healthy girl. Fortunately, Kyle is a big man. Not fat. He's built like a tree trunk with muscles. He lifted me like I was a feather." She sighed again, with appreciation. "Maybe not a feather. But it wasn't like I threw his back out, either."

"Of course you didn't! I'm so excited for you. When do you go out?"

"Saturday night."

"New clothes?"

"Absolutely."

"Shopaholics Anonymous!" Karina and Debby rapped knuckles over the marzipan. There was nothing they liked more than their weekend shopping excursions with Whitney or one of a rotating roster of women friends whose availability was subject to credit card limits.

"We could pick you out a peekaboo bra," said Debby.

Karina laughed. As usual, a girl-to-girl talk had lightened her tendency for serious introspection. She would follow Debby's lead—enjoy the flirtation with Alex for what it was and not worry about the consequences. "Thanks, sweetie, but that's not necessary. I've already mastered the art of revealing myself."

"I just realized that there's a flaw in the plan," Debby said, dropping her voice as two of her assistants came in from their lunch break. "You know the Shopaholics Anonymous rule: new affair, new clothes. That doesn't work if all you want to do with Alex is get naked."

"For one night only," Karina pointed out. "That doesn't even qualify as an affair. Exception to the rule."

"I guess."

"In this case, new sheets would be more appropriate than wardrobe." Karina crossed mental fingers; she was making a lot of assumptions about Alex's willingness.

"Satin sheets?"

"Uh…"

"Covered with rose petals."

"Hell, no! This isn't about romance, Deb."

Karina made herself sound cynical and proud of it. Even though a piece of her fluttery female heart wished for just a little bit of romance.

5

FRANK WHITMAN.

Alex sat on the counter of his galley kitchen eating a ham and Swiss on rye, kicking his foot against the cabinets like an antsy kid on a car trip, and thinking about Frank Whitman. He didn't really *want* to think about the man, particularly after his decision that morning to be a normal person again, but it was the one sure way to get his mind off what Karina was doing to him.

According to the newspaper reports Alex had looked up after the fact, Whitman had been a sixty-three-year-old parks administrator vacationing in the Florida Keys with his wife Joanne. They were planning to buy a condo for their retirement, but on the last day of Whitman's life they'd been merely enjoying their vacation, taking a walk along the harbor after lunch at a sidewalk café. He'd worn sunglasses and a flamingo T-shirt, and had just bought an Italian ice from a street vendor. The ice hadn't even begun to melt when he'd been shot through the neck by a sniper's high-caliber rifle from a boat in the harbor.

For those first frantic moments, nobody but a man going by the name Chris McGraw had known what was happening. There were screams, panicking tourists, spouting blood. Alex aka Chris had thrown Whitman's wife to the ground behind the vendor's cart and covered her with his body even though she'd struggled to rise, to go to her husband and hold him in her arms.

Frank Whitman had died on the spot, clutching his throat, his hands red with blood, two years from retirement and a life in the sun. His only crime had been being in the wrong spot at the wrong time, just as Alex's misstep had been believing that all defendants deserved representation.

His stomach revolted. He threw away his sandwich.

The cabinet door bore a scuff mark. He could sand that off. Make it a project and sandpaper all of the doors, taking away years of grime and the nicks and scratches. Prime and paint, good as new.

Starting over was easy.

Remembering was hard.

Alex swore. He jumped off the counter, drawn to the window like a fly to honey. Steel to magnet. Man to woman. All those clichés that he hadn't experienced for too long now.

The sky had darkened while he'd huddled in the kitchen. Lights went on in the row of brownstones further along the block, where rows of chestnut trees turned the street into an allée. Nice in spring, he imagined, wondering if there were any chance he'd still be in the city by then.

Although the teeming masses were supposed to give him a sense of anonymity, he'd discovered that Manhattan was a series of neighborhoods. Granted, a man could be unknown even in his own neighborhood, but in time that would wane. Stay long enough, and he'd become recognized by the denizens as the grouch, the lone wolf, the watcher in the window. If he weren't already. While he'd been tracking their patterns, they'd been learning his.

Humans were herd animals, filled with the instinct to meet, socialize, mate. They said hello at the fruit market. Waved from adjacent windows. Bumped into each other at the Italian-ice stand, where it was a natural friendly impulse for one guy to bend and retrieve the change the other had dropped, especially when the other guy's colorful shirt had been so familiar in a nostalgic way.

A scooped up handful of nickels and dimes had saved Chris McGraw's life from the assassin's bullet. What would save Alex Anderson's?

Not Karina Sutter. He couldn't ask that much of her. Still, he searched her empty windows. Too early...or had she backed out?

The city had left its grime on him. He went to take another shower. The pounding water felt good, even though it was a weak substitute for the scouring salt water of the ocean he craved.

He'd grown up in the surf, a California native who'd thought he'd always live in the state, where most of his family and friends were located. But his mother had passed away some time ago and after that his dad hadn't wanted to live in the family's rambling redwood house anymore. As the only child, the place was passed to Lex.

When the Norris murder trial had gone so wrong and he'd had to tell his dad that he was disappearing into the Witness Protection Program, he'd given back the keys at their last short meeting.

He didn't know what had become of the old place, but he thought of it now and then. He'd even dreamed of returning, but in the warped visions his subconscious conjured up, the house was empty, offering little comfort or shelter.

He vigorously shook his head as he emerged from behind the yellowing shower curtain, spraying water across the fogged mirror over the sink. Ignoring the stubborn arousal that had kept him semi-erect even though he'd tried everything to *not* think of Karina, he quickly dried himself and wrapped the towel around his waist.

His face was indistinct in the mirror. Like Karina last night, behind the curtains....

"Oh, hell. Can't you stop?" His fingers grazed his chin, wondering if he should shave again.

He snorted. For what? His date with a window?

Karina was impossible to figure out. He'd offered her the normal guy he'd been sure she'd prefer and she'd turned him down flat. For what? A truffle and a promise—an *implied* promise—of further titillation.

At a distance. No touching, no talk. Appropriate, but terribly ironic.

"This is what I've come to," Alex said out loud as he stepped into a pair of dark blue sweatpants. He added a pair of socks and flannel shirt, also new.

Technically, all of his clothing was new. The stuff Chris McGraw had been wearing on the day Frank Whitman had been murdered were spotted with arterial spray. He'd known better than to risk a return to his rented room to gather even a change of clothes, so he'd bought a T-shirt and a pair of cheap cotton drawstring pants from a street vendor, then dumped his stained clothes at the bus station before buying a ticket north.

Although he'd lived in Big Pine Key for five months, he'd moved on in five minutes. He consoled himself with the knowledge that the people he'd met there probably hadn't remembered Chris McGraw past a couple of salty margaritas and gaudy sunsets. The long-haired guy who'd spent his days at the beach and worked off the books as a bartender in a rinky-dink outfit called The Nautilus had had *drifter* stamped all over him.

Maybe that was why Karina didn't want to get involved. She saw that he was no prize.

"But I'm good enough for kicks," Alex said, his interest rising sharply when he saw from across the room that her lights were on.

His blind was already up. He grabbed the binoculars, giving no thought to checking for suspicious characters. His attention was on Karina, and Karina alone. They could shoot him through the heart if they wanted; he wasn't taking his eyes off the apartment across the way.

"Damn." That carelessness was what he'd been afraid of when he'd first laid his eyes on her. But for the moment, he couldn't make himself revert to caution.

Colored lights flashed, illuminating Karina standing before a device of some sort. Alex zeroed in with the binoculars. He'd noticed the figurine before but he hadn't realized exactly what it was. A fortune-teller— a carnival booth. Karina was proving to be more whimsical than he'd assumed.

She walked across her living room, looking at an item in her hand. When she looked up and saw him standing in his window, the item—a card—fluttered from her lax fingers. For a moment, she stared at him with big eyes, then collapsed onto the blue sofa as if she couldn't hold herself upright any longer.

Weak in the knees, Alex thought. *People are always falling for you.*

Not funny.

Karina did nothing for a couple of minutes, except stare at him watching her. He did not back away. This was almost a confrontation. A staring match.

Eventually her lids lowered slightly. Involuntarily, he took one hand off the glasses and put it on himself, following the path of her gaze along the strip of bare chest that showed from his unbuttoned shirt. He stroked himself, widening the gap, then let his hand rest at the drawstring of his sweats, fingers inside the waistband, touching below his navel.

Karina slid her arms out of her coat, then lazily reached up to undo the buttons of her blouse. Slowly, deliberately, one right after the other, without moving from her slumped position on the couch. She pulled the tails out of her waistband when she was done, but stopped there.

Alex studied the inside curves her breasts, molded by a white bra. Tantalizing, but not enough.

"Come on, baby, show me something," he crooned.

She sat forward, making the blouse hang loosely, but did no more except continue to stare at him.

A challenge, huh? Alex whipped his shirt open all the way, to see what she would do.

She followed suit, except her bra was still on. "No fair." He passed his hand up over his bare chest, across his right nipple, then shrugged off the shirt entirely.

Karina's head inclined. She dropped her blouse. Skated a hand upward over her torso as he had, but paused to cover her breast, hesitating, or…

She undid the clasp, sitting with the bra loosely covering her breasts before she straightened with a snap and pushed the straps off her shoulders. Naked from the waist up, she sat on the edge of the sofa with her hands folded in her lap and her hair up in a bun. A proper lady, displaying her breasts. Defiantly?

He looked, burning the sight of her into his brain for the lonely cold days ahead.

Karina didn't move. He dropped the glasses, rubbed his eye-sockets where the binoculars had pressed, then refocused, and still she hadn't moved except to swipe a hand across her eyes.

So that was it. Monkey see, monkey do. He put his hand into his damp hair, ruffling it up.

She raised both arms, lifting her breasts even higher so the primal surge of his blood became thicker, swelling in his groin. She pulled pins from her bun like a secretary in a fifties movie and her hair dropped around her shoulders, shining like white gold in the lamplight. She gave it a shake, then settled with her hands in her lap, motionless once more.

After another minute of simply looking at the provocative picture she made, he put the glasses aside and moved right up next to the window, standing with his legs slightly spread and his hands on his hips.

"That's it," he said when Karina stood. "Come closer."

But she didn't. She stayed back from the window, by the couch, her hands resting on her hips in imitation of him.

He beckoned with a finger and she put up the corresponding hand, palm out, telling him no. He noticed that her curtains were drawn except in the living area, and he supposed that she felt less exposed, keeping away from the one uncovered window.

He moved back. She had a point.

What now? He let his hands decide as they splayed

across his hip bones, pushing the sweats down a few inches. He was fully aroused and that was as far as he could go without exposing that fact.

Karina unzipped and rocked her hips a couple of times, sliding her pants past her hip bones. He took up the glasses and saw the edge of her underwear. White, to match the bra. She would always match, he decided. But did she prefer panties or a thong? Easy enough to find out.

He did a quarter turn and lowered one side of his sweats as if a nurse was coming at him with a needle. Karina's head shook with laughter, but she copied the movement, turning and displaying one smooth cheek to him, cut into a quarter moon by the elastic of her bikini panties.

Was that fair? He had no underwear to drop. Feeling ridiculous, he tapped his ass. Karina's face lit up with another bout of laughter, though she obediently slapped her butt for him, making the flesh jiggle just a little.

"Oh, man, oh, man," he said with a groan, pressing the eyepieces into his sockets again. "You are fan-frick-ing-tastic, lady."

But what now? He'd have to expose himself if he wanted to see more.

He rested a knee on the seat of the armchair that sat beside the window, facing front again. Without lowering the binoculars, he put his other hand down the front of his pants.

Karina did the same, stretching out the elastic of her underwear. He held himself, felt the pulse of desperate need but ignored it to watch her face as her fingers moved inside her panties. Her eyes closed, her head tilted back. She bit her bottom lip.

After a couple of seconds, her eyes opened. She must have forgotten about her worries about others seeing because she only looked at him. The color in her face had risen so that she looked feverish. Bright-eyed and needy, but waiting for his cue.

He dropped the glasses on the chair and jerked at the knot in the drawstring of his sweats. As soon as it loosened, the pants slid down and he cupped both hands over his erection, holding on to his last thread of decency, as if it mattered anymore. He was a goner.

Karina shook her tail so her pants dropped. They caught on her boots, but were loose enough to step out of. A couple of tugs and the panties followed, skimming down her smooth thighs. Her hands pressed flat over her pubic triangle, but she lifted one foot and put it on the couch behind her, raising her knee, separating her thighs.

Alex looked at his own leg, having forgotten it was propped up that way. He smiled to himself. Brilliant. Just brilliant. Now all he had to do was show her his and she would show him hers.

A thought flitted through his mind—how miserable he should be that he'd completely lost contact with humanity and had to find his satisfaction this way—but he dismissed it. He was Alex now, not Lex, who had formed no lasting bonds with women, either, so what did it matter? There were friends who missed Lex, no doubt. They probably raised a glass to him still, although even that would soon die off as the old crowd disintegrated, with different jobs, new addresses, marriage and children to keep them occupied.

He would have none of that, unless he went ahead and built a life based on a lie. That thought was a lot sadder than sharing a mutual sexcapade with a woman who wanted only that.

Take what you can get. Enjoy her.

Karina was waiting. He couldn't see her face because she'd dropped her chin to her chest, her shoulders hunched so her arms pressed into her breasts, making them full and round. She still held one hand flat for cover, but he could see the slight movement beneath it, the strain in her body as she kept to small secret strokes.

He'd clasped a fist around himself and was making movements of his own. What the hell, he thought. Now or never. He took one hand off, then, with a wince, the other, and his erection swung free, so rigid by now that it curved against his belly.

Karina had seen. She stared at him for a moment and he had to clench his hands to keep from touching himself, the need for completion was so great. She seemed to be equally tortured, her face contorting as she raised her hands up, sinking them into her hair and holding her head, her elbows almost meeting in front of her face.

Alex wanted to look at her through the magnifying lenses, see if she was swollen, or open enough to show her glistening wetness, but he was too stricken to move.

Was this the best he could expect from now on? The sadness and frustration of that bleak future rose up to overwhelm him and suddenly his control burst, slicing away the tight bands that had been wound around him, keeping him safe since Whitman's death, but also so cold. So alone.

The hell with caution. He wanted to feel again.

KARINA HAD THOUGHT she was torn between her arousal and her old inhibitions, but when Alex suddenly disappeared from his window she was struck with only one thought.

Come back. I'll do anything—anything….

And it was true. She'd eaten another of the Black Magic truffles and the clawing need inside her was so strong she was ready to plaster herself against the window to lure him over.

And he'd just *stopped?*

"You bastard," she said, sinking onto the couch and covering herself with her blouse. She pressed her thighs together so tightly she could have crushed apples into cider. *How could he leave her like this?*

She'd exposed herself, offered herself, and he'd seemed receptive. Still, his window remained blank.

Never again. With a screech of frustration, she kicked her pants away, then scooped them up, along with her underwear, and went to drop the linen shade with a vicious wrench. *Never. Again.*

The door buzzer went off. She dropped her clothing. Alex?

A chill raced over her skin, drawing a hot flush behind it. She shivered, clutched herself, wiped the back of her hand over her damp forehead. Oh, God…*Alex.*

What did she do now?

Bzzzzz.

She had to answer. Feeling ridiculous, she ran across the living room wearing only the knee-high black leather boots that looked like something out of *The Matrix.* Or a bondage video, she supposed, crossing her arms over her naked breasts. She pressed the button of the intercom without saying a word.

"It's Alex," came the disembodied voice. "Let me in."

Another shiver raced up her spine, but it couldn't

touch the fever burning her up inside. She stabbed the button to release the lock on the downstairs door, then slid open the bolt on her apartment door before backing away.

He'd sounded dead serious. How many truffles had he eaten? She imagined Alex barreling up her stairs with one hand wrapped around his erection like a sword. Her head buzzed. Was that her, giggling? And how had she gotten all the way across the room? Should she grab her clothes?

She couldn't think. She shook herself, tweaked her nose, hoping to regain a few shreds of common sense. When Alex got here, she'd have to say something—an explanation, a come-on, a throwaway line—anything at all to make the situation more acceptable.

Impossible. There was no way to make their game socially acceptable. She was standing naked in an apartment with an unlocked door.

The door crashed open. Alex stood in the opening, six feet of hard-charging male. Panting, intense, bright-eyed and wild. His long coat hung open. The shirt he'd thrown on was misbuttoned. The outline of an erection showed beneath his sweatpants.

Wow. She backed up a step to lean against the brick wall, forgetting that she was nude, except for her boots. Then Alex's eyes swept over her like strobes. Her nipples and fingertips and toes tingled as if she'd been plugged into an electric outlet.

He said nothing. Just reached back and slammed the door, then strode toward her.

She literally quaked in her boots. The old saying rang in her head. *Be careful what you wish for....*

Alex grabbed her face in his hands and kissed her. It was a whirlwind of a kiss, and she was sucked into it, powerless. He filled her mouth with his hot tongue whether or not she wanted it, but she did. She did. She wanted all of him. This would never happen to her again, so she'd better enjoy the hell out of it.

The kiss was unapologetically rapacious, thrilling Karina. Her dates were always so gentlemanly. Who'd have known she wanted a dangerous man like Alex, one who didn't stop to say *please, may I?*

You knew, she thought, even if it was only subconsciously. That was why she'd started on this path.

Alex sucked on her tongue, slowly drawing back until she was left panting. As she stared into his hard, stormy eyes, the knowledge hit her that she was about to have sex with a man she barely knew. They'd exchanged no more than fifty words!

He put a hand over her mouth. "Don't talk."

She made a muffled sound of argument, pushing her arms against him where he'd trapped them against his chest.

"Shh." He exhaled against her neck. "You know it's too late to back out," he said silkily into her ear, just before his mouth opened to kiss and suck at her throat and neck, her collarbone, and—*oh my, oh my, oh my...*

She rose to the tip of her toes, following the drag on her nipples as he drew on them with wicked teeth and a hot suctioning mouth, the pull so strong in her body it was like being lost to the ocean's undertow.

As if he sensed her yielding to the inevitable, he reached around and lifted her high into his arms, right off her feet. After the first instant of disbelief, she let her eyes close and her head fall back, giving herself up to the dark world of pleasure and sensation. She was ready for anything.

ALEX KNEW THE WAY to the bedroom. Surging with a triumphant strength, he swept Karina to the spiral staircase. Heading straight upstairs to the proper door, he opened it with a kick of his boot.

The room was shadowed, but not so dim he couldn't see. There was a carousel horse in one corner. A full-length dressing mirror leaned against an interior wall. Opposite was the bed, a contemporary platform low to the floor. He spied an armless chair, upholstered in pink silk, similarly low to the ground.

He lowered Karina just far enough for her toes to touch the carpet, but kept an arm around her waist so she couldn't quite stand on her own. With his other arm, he dragged the chair to the foot of the bed.

"What are you doing?" A nervous thread ran through her voice.

"I told you not to speak." She wanted nothing but sex games; he would comply. That was better for him, anyway. An ongoing relationship would make him vulnerable and put her at risk.

She flinched beneath his grip. Started to insist, and then took one look at his face and closed her mouth.

He wanted to smile to reassure her, but instead he buried his face into her hair, inhaling the clean citrus smell, drugging himself with the beauty of her lithe naked curves as he ran his hands over her skin. She'd gained her balance, so he reached around and put a hand between her legs. Not to feel her up—though that was a nice benefit—but to urge her to rise an inch or two.

As his fingers sank into her softness, she let out a squeak of alarm, jerking herself taut again. He looked into the mirror, liking to see her that way, pale hair in disarray, body naked and quivering for his touch. Her eyes were wide, the pupils gone so large that only a golden rim showed around them. A hundred questions must have been lined up on the tongue peeping from between her parted lips, but she didn't say a word.

"Good girl." This time, he let her see the smile. It became wicked. "Now bend over the chair."

Even with the sounds of city traffic that drifted up from below, the room was quiet enough that her indrawn breath was obvious. Her buttocks clenched. After a tense pause, she wet her lips to whisper. "I can't."

His fingers moved inside her. "But you like showing yourself to me."

Her shoulders twitched, neither agreement nor denial.

He flicked his thumb over her clitoris and she arched back against him, air hissing between her teeth. His other hand cupped her jaw, elongating her neck to receive his kiss.

"Please…"

"I said that, too." He nipped at her nape. "While I watched you tease me. Do you know what torture you put me through?"

She made a humming sound as he slipped his fingers out from between her legs and dragged them across her belly, leaving a telling sheen of her lubricant. "So wet. I know you want to do what I tell you."

The instant of surrender showed in her eyes. She nodded.

He pressed the small of her back. "Bend over."

She had to stretch forward to grab the back of the chair, putting her body on perfect display. "On your toes," he reminded her, giving her rounded behind a light squeeze. "And put your hands flat on the seat." She strained to reach, sliding her arms down the backrest while keeping her ass elevated.

So tempting. He took a long, relishing look before he stepped closer. With a moan of pleasure, he ran both hands along her taut flesh, up to her back, bending over her so he could catch her head between his hands, her tousled hair like a skein of raw silk. He tilted her face up so she had to look at herself in the mirror. Her breasts were pushed forward, resting on the padded back of the chair. Her soft mouth quivered.

"I could take you this way." His erection was pressed into the intimate crease between her buttocks. He nudged against her and she had to widen her stance to keep her balance, giving him even better access. The juicy heat of her made his balls draw tight. "Hard and fast. Would you like that?"

Her chin jerked higher, resisting as he manipulated her head to nod. "Say yes, Karina."

She refused, forgetting that she'd already surrendered herself to him.

"You're right." He studied her defiant face in the mirror. "That would be too easy."

She blinked, worried now.

"I want you to know exactly what you did to me." He guided her to stand upright, but before she could regain her senses and offer resistance, he boosted her over the back of the chair and pushed down on her shoulders until she sat, still facing the mirror.

Her eyes immediately closed.

"Open them," he said. "And your legs, too."

"I can't."

"Oh yes, you can." He pulled her head all the way back so her nose was aimed at the ceiling. Her mouth opened instead, perhaps to protest, and he covered it with a long deep kiss. She swallowed convulsively, struggling a bit against him when he slipped his tongue between her lips. He stroked her soft cheeks, then her throat. Eventually she relaxed. Slowly he drew away, releasing her. She didn't move, except to gasp for breath, and he wondered if she'd take his cock as easily. But he was as hard as an iron bar, and though she didn't know it, he could never be that forceful. The play-acting could go only so far.

He stripped out of his clothes, flinging them carelessly aside, and when he looked up Karina was watching him in the mirror with her eyes dark and her lips curved into a satisfied smile. She wasn't as reluctant as she put on.

For a second, an idea ran through his mind—that she might have been enlisted to seduce him, to keep him occupied. But that was absurd. No more than his overworked paranoia.

Whatever the risk, she was worth it.

"Think you've got me?" he asked in a gruff voice. He sat on the very edge of the bed, directly behind her chair, spreading his legs wide and circling her with his arms. "We'll see how you feel after I show you what happens to naughty little teases."

Her eyes opened wide. She started to answer, then bit down on her bottom lip.

He grazed his mouth along the slope of her shoulder, breathing in her scent. He felt primal, stripped bare. Circumstances had already robbed him of the conventions that normally would have kept him from being this way with a virtual stranger. There was a grim satisfaction in knowing that he was finally receiving some benefit from his expulsion from society.

In the mirror, he lifted his eyes to Karina's. "Touch yourself."

Quivering, she touched her breast with a delicate finger.

Very nice. He copied her, tracing one finger around her pebbled areola. Her nipple was distended, colored a deep pink. He held it between his thumb and forefinger and squeezed, urging her to follow with her own hand.

"Feel that?" he whispered.

She nodded and let out a throaty sigh, rolling her nipple beneath her fingers.

"Where do you feel it?" He reached to put his free hand on her thigh and felt the ripple of her instinctive reaction. She was all nerve endings, aroused by the slightest touch.

Their heads were together. Restlessly, she moved her cheek against his and whispered, "You know."

"But I want to see." His fingers crept to the inside of her thigh, digging into the soft muscle.

She resisted his pressure for a moment, then suddenly wrenched her legs apart, planting her heels on either side of the chair. Another deep rippling shudder went through her. Her hips tilted, giving him a better view. "Is that what you want," she said, a note of near-hysteria in her voice.

"Also what *you* want," he quietly answered.

She tried to calm herself, but the frantic edge remained. "I didn't know what I was doing. It was the choc—"

"Hush. No excuses."

Her head dropped forward.

"Uh-uh." He took his hand off her leg to tip her chin up again. "I want you to look."

She did, with snapping eyes, chin held high on his fingertips.

Their image in the mirror was one of the most erotic sights he'd ever seen. All that pale skin framed by his brown arms and legs. Their two hands covering her breasts, light and dark, fragility and power. The sinuous grace of her elongated torso, the blatant positioning of her thighs, the tall black boots with steep heels that kept her knees elevated. The gleaming rosy-pink of her vulva, opened like a flower. And especially the look in her eyes as she absorbed the sight of herself, explicitly exposed, so aroused, vulnerable, wanting.

"Beautiful," he said.

She nodded.

He let her chin go and caught the hand she'd placed over her breast, dragging it lower. "Now you'll touch yourself for me," he said, "just like you did before."

Although she squirmed a little, she let him slide her hand beneath his, caressing her flat stomach, the patch of honey-colored fur. Fingers interlaced, he slid them along her swollen lips to dip between the wet folds. She made a sound in her throat and rocked her bottom in the chair, the muscles in her legs clenching and flexing as she fought against the conflicting desires that he easily read in her face. There was still a modicum of modesty in her, even though it was obvious that she also craved a wildly shameless release.

He urged her head around so he could kiss her. "Do you need me inside you?"

"*Yes.*" Her breath was hot and sweet.

"You should come first." Their slippery fingers tangled. "But I can't quite reach. You'll have to do it for me."

She whimpered, lifting her hips off the cushioned seat, offering herself, but he was already pressed as close as possible against the back of the chair, entwining her in his arms.

"No." He grasped her wrist. "I want to see you do it. Give me your hand."

"But I want—"

"You'll get it." She let out a soft grunt as he guided two of her fingers into her tight passage. "That's good, isn't it?" He felt her tremble beneath his arms. Her body strained, bowing upward again, trying to tempt him into losing control. "Don't take them out," he ordered.

"But I want—"

"Impatient little hussy."

A sharp inhale. "I am *not* a—"

"Tell that to the mirror. You're a bad girl and you know it."

She moaned, working her fingers in and out. "Yes."

He brushed his finger across the prominent pearl of her clit. Trapped against the back of the padded chair, his penis jerked in response. "Yes, what?"

She threw her head back. Total abandon, complete submission. "I'm a bad girl. And I want you to watch me. I want you to make me come."

"We'll do it together." And hope that he could contain his own orgasm for a while longer.

He'd been circling the hard knot of exquisitely sensitive nerve endings, flicking it occasionally, but now he touched squarely and rolled the nub beneath his fingertip, making her cry out with pleasure. Several strokes and she was vibrating beneath his palm as a climax ripped through her. Her hair whipped his face as she tossed her head from side to side, little yelping sounds flying from her open mouth. He stretched forward one final millimeter to feel the spasmodic clenching as she rode her own fingers to completion. He cupped her, stroked her, dipping into the moisture seeping out from between her fingers.

Finally, her body gave one last shudder and went lax. After a moment of silent shock, she buried her face against his neck. "I can't believe…"

"Don't get skittish on me now," he said, and with a great heave, dragged her limp nude form backward onto the bed. "I have other plans for you."

6

KARINA WAS TOO WEAK to object when Alex dragged her onto the bed, not that there was any reason to. Every bone in her body had turned to liquid and her mind to mush, but she was cognizant enough to know that she wanted more. The effects from the truffle she'd eaten earlier were still there—a light-headedness that kept the thinking part of her brain disconnected from her base instincts, the itchy warmth of her flesh, the urge to rub up against the closest male body, the hollow ache that cried out to be filled.

Clearly, one orgasm wasn't adequate.

She was lying on top of Alex. His hands were on her breasts, moving in slow circles that kept her nipples trapped beneath his palms. His hot rigid penis pressed between the cheeks of her bottom like a branding iron. A small repositioning and he'd be sliding up into her, giving her what she craved.

Think what you're doing, said a distant part of her brain. *He's a stranger.*

"Too late," she mouthed, resolutely keeping her eyes closed so she wouldn't have to confront the reality of the situation. Tonight was all about fantasy. Sex was always a risk, but at least this time her heart wasn't involved. She could take what she wanted and walk away tomorrow morning without regret, knowing that Alex had done the same.

As long as they stayed away from the truffles, there'd be no future complications.

A perfect scenario for her first—and only—one-night stand.

She moved atop Alex, rubbing her butt into his groin. He sucked air through his teeth. "Watch what you're doing or I'll be doing you," he teased.

She laughed lazily. Her hand drifted along his flank. "What's the holdup?"

"You really are the most impatient—"

"But you must be, too," she interrupted, giving another squirm. "Even more than me."

"I've learned self-discipline in the past few years."

She opened her mouth to ask what he meant, but instantly tamped down the curiosity. For the plan to work, she had to keep him strictly in the dream-lover category. Having him living across the street might be a problem, but as long as he continued to remain remote and uninvolved, they'd be okay.

But how did she tell a guy that she wanted only sex, not talk?

Well, there were ways—ways that had nothing to do with words.

She slid off him, rising to a sitting position so his hands had to drop from her breasts to her waist. Out of the corner of her eye, she saw his freed erection bob up. The size and brazenness of it made her breath catch in her chest.

Other lovers had always been moderate in the bedroom. In response to her own behavior, she supposed. Lights dim, or off altogether, a self-consciousness about the lovemaking being a part of the developing relationship, tissues and a robe at hand. And always, always, consideration for the partner's feelings and preferences.

Not like Alex, with his unapologetic commands. Yet somehow, everything he'd done had been just right. She'd never lost herself in the blatant pleasures and sensations of pure sex, but he'd made that possible. As if he'd known every secret fantasy and had come to sweep in and out of her life and fulfill them.

Of course, there was also the effect of the truffles. She mustn't overlook the truffles.

Alex had propped his head up on his crossed arms. He nodded at the mirror. "You've always liked to watch yourself?"

Karina looked up from unzipping her boot. The room had darkened so that the mirror reflected only vague shapes, shrouded in shadows. "No."

He chuckled.

"I'm being straight. I've never used the mirror…that way." She peered into it, watching her shadow-self slowly draw her leg up. There was a languid grace in the way she extended her arm, a certain eroticism about the contrast between her pale skin and the leather boot she unzipped. Hmm. "It's for dressing."

Alex captured her between his legs. "And now it's also for undressing." He tugged on her arm. "C'mere."

"My boot." She twisted to peel it from her calf.

He tapped her hip. "Now."

"Stop giving me orders," she said, but she gave in, kicking away her boot and stretching out to kiss him, lying side-by-side. After a minute, his hold on her softened, became an embrace, a caress. The sexual energy still hummed, but there was something more building beneath it with every gentle kiss. Something dangerous, in an entirely different way.

Karina pulled back. Alex's eyes were open and watching her. They were no longer slate-hard. Still indecipherable, except that she sensed the secretive longing in him.

She grasped at straws. *It's the truffles. They're making us needy.*

But it was too late. Her emotions had shifted and when she touched his chest it was with a genuine caring. "What do we do now?"

His lower body nudged her. "You have to ask?"

She kissed his chest, licking at the salt and musk of male skin. Springy hair smoothed beneath her hand, darker than the hair on his head. Muscles ridged his flat stomach; she felt his ribs through his skin. He was even leaner than she'd expected, but wiry and taut. She found a few small scars. Everything about him said he was a man who'd lived hard and rough, but there remained her first impression—his casual beach-bum appeal. Confusing. Could have been a false lead.

Did it matter?

He'd remained motionless under her explorations, but it was obvious that he couldn't wait long, regardless of the formidable self-control he'd mentioned. His erection twitched against her stomach, begging for attention. Tentatively she ran her fingers along the swollen length, tracing the pulsing vein, then around the edge of the flared head. She loved the sense of life and power that thrummed beneath her touch.

"Karina…" Almost begging.

Even though they were supposed to be living a forbidden fantasy, she liked hearing him say her name.

She smiled and kissed his shoulder, closing her eyes as she steered him toward the crevasse between her parting thighs. He took her leg by the back of the knee and pulled it up to wrap around his hip. She wormed closer. Open for him.

"Do you have a condom?" he asked in a husky whisper.

"Oh." She was startled out of her daze. She never forgot. She was *always* responsible. But it had been a while since she'd been tempted by any of the men she dated. "There are some in the bathroom."

"Never mind." Alex had reached over the side of the bed and found the sweats he'd tossed aside. He took a strip of condoms from the pocket, keeping his arms wound around her as he busily ripped off a packet and tore it open. "Move up an inch," he said, his fingers gliding through the moisture that had gathered at her entrance.

She was so tender and aroused, even that light touch sent her head spinning. "I want to feel you inside me," she heard herself saying from a distance. "But go slow."

"Anything you want." Sheathed, he pressed against her, teasing her with his fingers first and then the advance and retreat of his swaying erection. She hunched her hips at him, slinging her top leg even higher around his waist. How could he be so cool? The secret-recipe chocolate had made her molten and greedy. She wanted only one thing and—timid words aside—she wanted it now.

Alex took hold of her butt and tilted her to receive his thrust. For a moment the pressure was too much. She almost cried out in relief as finally her tissues gave way, allowing the head of his erection to push inside. He was so big she stretched to accommodate him. Thankfully he allowed her a moment to adjust before giving her another inch.

She sighed at the sense of fullness, ready for more. She wanted him deep. But they weren't in a position to gain full penetration, and another part of herself was savoring the intimacy of lying in his arms, watching furrows carve into his brow as he filled her degree by degree.

When they were joined as deeply as possible, she brushed a hand over his forehead and kissed it, feeling more tender emotion for him than she'd expected. Almost as if he'd opened her heart.

This was trouble, she realized with a frisson of worry, but there were too many pleasurable sensations rolling through her to concentrate on what was only a fleeting thought.

They rocked together like a dinghy riding the waves. A familiar sweet warmth lapped inside her, flushing her face and chest.

He murmured. "Is this good for you?"

"Really good."

He had managed to work one arm beneath her. Both his hands pressed against her backside, urging her closer. They squirmed together, panting, sweating, striving.

"Ungh." He grunted. "I have to—"

"Yes," she said as he hunched his shoulders and pushed her onto her back. Her thighs fell wide open. He dug one knee into the bed and drove into her, desperate now, using every muscle and sinew in his body to thrust repeatedly. The rhythmic motion set off vibrations in her that escalated until she was shaking from head to toe. With one last push, she tipped over into the long, liquid free fall of her climax, losing herself in the whirlpool of sensation.

Alex rose up to his knees. He lifted both her legs and flung them over his shoulders, pulling her hips off the bed too as he plunged even deeper, touching off another orgasm that broke over her. He rode her through it, until she was gasping, and then finally he dug deep and let go of his own climax with a hoarse shout that seemed to echo inside Karina's head. The lashings of pleasure gradually diminished to waves, then soft ripples, leaving them floating again in a gently rocking sea of contentment, their slick bodies entwined.

Karina was sprawled on her back, with Alex collapsed partway on top of her. Instinctively, she reached for him, winding an arm around his heaving shoulders, but he brushed her away, flipping over—and away from her—instead. They lay side by side, panting.

"You ate the truffles," she said after a minute or two.

"Umm."

He couldn't talk yet; she smiled. "Several of them, I'll bet."

"Mmm."

"They're incredible, aren't they?"

"Shh."

She pressed a couple of fingers to her lips. Tasted *him*. Better than chocolate.

After another little while, she said, "I don't normally do this," then cringed at the apology in her voice. She was a sexually confident woman—trying to be, anyway. There was no need for her to make excuses. Not even the chocolate could account for tonight. She'd wanted Alex from the first time she'd seen him, *before* she and Debby had ever thought of using the truffles to snare him.

The aphrodisiac took the edge off her nervousness,

the way some people used alcohol to loosen them up. No difference.

"What I mean is I don't, ahh…flash my neighbors. As a habit. You're the first." She cringed. "And the last. I'm not into kinky sex, is what I'm trying to say."

"Pity."

Oh. Her eyes widened. "Pity?"

"We could have had fun."

"But this is a—" She faltered. It was a fling, at least it was supposed to be. Naturally, because of the way it happened, he'd probably believed she was always this wild. He'd be wrong. She was not ready to get into a weird sex thing with him, even if the very thought produced a throbbing between her legs.

She inched away, rocking her butt on the mattress, then caught herself. "Are you…" She shot a wary look at his profile. "Are you some kind of freak? Whips and chains and leather?"

"No." His laugh was indolent, and not entirely reassuring.

"You're sure?"

He glanced at her. "Do you think that I'm leading a double life I'm not aware of?" There was such an ironic tone to the question that she still wasn't reassured.

"Well, you are mysterious. To me, anyway. I don't know much about you except that you claim to be a writer."

He looked at the ceiling again. "That's right. You don't know anything about me."

Except that you gave me the most powerful orgasms of my life, she said silently, feeling the bottom drop out of her stomach at the mere thought of how much she'd loved having him inside her. Even more—how the first delicious tremors of fear and desire had become a strangely sweet emotion before evolving back into pulse-pounding sexual energy.

She was wrung out, but she hoped he wouldn't go. Not yet. There was something wrong with her. Weren't participants in one-night stands supposed to be eager to leave the scene of the crime? Had to be the residue of chocolate in her system.

Whatever the reason, she wanted him again, and they were still within the boundaries of a fling so there was no reason she couldn't have him. As long as she maintained her detachment. But she had to clean up first before a damp spot formed beneath her. Maybe she could lure him into the bathtub.

That would be too intimate, she instantly decided, picturing them up to the chin in bubbles, all warm and cuddly. Then she had to chide herself. They'd already been more intimate than she'd intended. She didn't seem to be very good at having sex with no prospect of emotional involvement.

Alex was supposed to remain cool, even if she didn't. And he'd started off being all about the sex. But there'd been that moment, when they'd been positioned face-to-face, gently touching…

Karina squeezed the tip of her nose. *You're conjuring up a deeper meaning where there is none, to give yourself "permission." Think straight. It would be best if he leaves now. Don't prolong the situation.*

"Where are you from?" she blurted. Damn!

His upper half jackknifed off the bed. "My last stop was Arizona."

That explained the tan. "Phoenix?"

He shrugged, his back to her as he removed the condom. "Yeah, sure."

She swung her legs over the other side of the bed and found the box of tissues on the low shelf attached to her bird's-eye maple headboard. "If you want to shower…"

Alex didn't answer, just raked a hand through his hair and let out a sigh. He probably wanted to get out as soon as possible.

She glanced at the topography of lean muscles in his shoulders and back, reminding herself that technically she had a stranger in her bedroom. She should know at least a *little* about him, in case…

Her heart squeezed. She was on the pill and they'd used the condom, of course, but there was always a slim chance of pregnancy or STDs. Practical matters, she decided. She was being responsible, just in case. That she could satisfy her curiosity at the same time was a bonus. "What did you do for a job in Phoenix?"

"Wrote…ad copy."

So he was a regular guy after all. No big mystery. "And you quit to become a writer?"

"Yep."

"Fiction?"

"More or less."

"Do you have family in Arizona?"

"No. They're all gone."

"I'm sorry." She paused, but he didn't explain, nor express any curiosity about her.

She volunteered. "My parents live in Switzerland. They're retired. I have an older brother, Ralf, who's an attorney in San Francisco, specializing in international law. He has a wife and two kids, and we all try to get together at least once a year at my parents' summerhouse in the Rhône Valley. I thought I might see them this Christmas, but it turns out that Ralf's involved in a big case—"

She halted her babbling. Even though they were sitting on opposite sides of the bed with their backs to each other, she sensed that Alex was disturbed by something she'd said. About her brother? Could Alex have lost his family? That would explain his air of sadness and desolation. But not his penchant for binoculars.

She licked her lips, suddenly nervous. "Were you…"

Don't ask, don't get involved. Just let him go.

"…ever married?"

She was doing a terrible job of listening to herself.

"No," he said, exhaling so forcefully his shoulders slumped.

Her questions were annoying him. She leaned down and grabbed the pieces of clothing she could reach, dropping them in a pile on the bed.

"I'm a wanderer," he added abruptly. The silent message was: *So don't count on me sticking around.*

How could she respond to that?

She couldn't. "You're not intending to stay in New York, then?"

"Probably not for long."

"Long enough for a lease."

"A sublet." He shrugged. "Any contract can be…"

"Broken," she finished for him. *Like hopes and dreams and hearts.*

Go ahead. Really *finish for him.* She stood. "Well, it's been interesting, but now I really need to take a shower. You know the way out." Her clothes were scattered downstairs and her robe was hanging on the bathroom door. There was always the option of dragging a sheet off the bed, but that was so ungraceful. A fully confident woman would saunter from the room, giving her lover one last look at what he was about to lose.

Karina forced her hands to relax and hang at her sides. With a shake of her head, she tossed her hair over her shoulders. Pinning her gaze on the bathroom door, avoiding both the mirror and Alex, she strolled across the room. All jumpy nerve endings and goose bumps, so aware of his eyes on her that they felt like a laser beam cutting into her skin.

She was about to safely shut herself in the bathroom when Alex appeared in the doorway. His eyes were hot and alert. "Maybe I'll take that shower."

Her heart leaped, but she remained cool. "You can go first then."

Surprise flickered on his face. "I thought we'd do it together."

"That would be so intimate," she purred, giving his body a sloe-eyed perusal. She resisted licking her lips. "You were giving off 'keep-away' vibes out there."

"I've never been good at the post-coital thing—cuddling and calling each other pet names."

A small grin twitched at his mouth, though, and she wondered if he was being completely honest. There were flashes in him of another sort of man, which confounded her at every turn. She couldn't seem to get a firm grip on his personality.

Except that *way,* she thought, glancing at his swelling penis.

"Cuddling?" She made a fake cough. "Any one of the Central Park statues is better at cuddling than you."

He laughed. And stepped close enough to wind his arms around her. His hands went to her breasts, lifting them with gentle fingers as his thumbs took a lazy sweep over her nipples. Back and forth until the flesh had drawn into tight, tingling buds. "See?" he said into her hair. "I can cuddle."

She wanted to resist, but desire was looping and swirling, entwining her like silk ribbons. "That's not cuddling, that's second base."

He began to pepper her with light, ticklish kisses. The back of her neck, her shoulder bone, the inside of her elbow, behind her ear. "And what is this?"

"Seduction," she said, although there was no need for it. She was already thoroughly seduced.

"Not if I stop before it goes farther." His hands skimmed over her backside, one finger tracing the seam. "Do you want me to stop?"

She slid a foot along the tumbled-marble tiles, opening her legs for him just a little bit. "Third base," she said as his finger teasingly stroked her without actually entering.

"What's with this baseball obsession?" he muttered into her neck.

"Don't you like baseball? I became a huge fan when I was twelve and we got satellite TV."

"It's okay. Surfing is my sport."

"In Arizona?"

"*Was* my sport. I've moved around a lot."

His voice was casual. If her hands hadn't been on his shoulders, she wouldn't have realized just how tense her questions were making him.

"I like the feel of water on my skin," he said, pulling away from her to twist the taps on the walk-in shower.

"We could use the bathtub instead." She indicated the claw-foot tub that sat below the tall window overlooking the street. During the apartment renovations, she'd splurged on every deluxe fitting in the book. The friends who considered her so restrained and disciplined were flummoxed when they saw the positively sensual setting of her private bath.

"Have you ever tried sex in a bathtub? It's not easy. The water washes away the natural lubrication."

The insistent pulse between her legs had returned. "I thought this was about cuddling, not sex."

Alex sent her a narrow look.

She raised her eyebrows.

He relented without an argument, shutting off the taps. "All right. Just don't expect me to call you cupcake."

"Please." She got the apothecary jar of bath salts. "I have more dignity than that."

"Pookie."

She chuckled. "Spare me."

"Don't tell me you want to be called cuddle-buns," he said with a low growl as the tub filled.

"God, no." Karina could hardly believe they were laughing and teasing like a regular couple. She'd been prepared to boot him onto the last train to One-Night-Standville, if only to beat him to it before he ran out on her.

When she bent to sprinkle the eucalyptus salts into the stream of water, Alex ran his hand along her derriere and she reminded herself that this was still about sex. They hadn't burned through all of the aphrodisiac yet, and even if they had, well, there was plenty of natural combustion to keep the flame alive.

One-night stands could end in the morning just as well.

THE ROSY-GRAY DAWN was creeping past the curtains before Alex could make himself ease away from Karina. He did it by increments, because—or so he told himself—she was lying on his arm. The numbness of the sleeping appendage was preferable to the guilt and regret gnawing at him for leaving her this way. Men who ducked out were chickenshits in his book. Not that he hadn't had his share of brief affairs over the years, as long as the woman was on the same track. Even then, he almost always had waited to say a cordial goodbye in the morning, and he'd made sure they had his name and number, too.

This time, leaving unannounced was the only way to go.

It was bad enough that he'd given in and come over to ravish her the way he had. Pile on the complications—that he'd put them both at risk, how emotional he'd been for a few minutes in the middle there, the awkward interrogation, the much less awkward but all the more troubling scene in the bathtub...

With Karina warm, naked and wet in his arms, his defenses had splintered like shale. Luckily, she'd been silent more than she talked, with no more of the probing questions. She'd chatted a little about the pleasures of New York at the holiday season and he'd bitten down on his tongue to stop from asking if she'd share some of it with him. She'd mentioned her shop, making comments about the potent product that he hadn't understood, but put down to the female obsession with chocolate. Maybe he should have confessed up front about his allergy, but she'd seemed so damn proud of those truffles. It was not as difficult for him to lie as it had once been.

The bath had stayed fairly innocent. He'd held her, caressed her some, aching with gratitude for the feel of a supple female body nestled against his chest. Her serene voice, soft touch, sweet scent. At one point, tears had even prickled at the back of his eyes, and he'd had to lay his head on the tub, blinking and swallowing until the lump in his throat had gone, hoping like hell that she hadn't noticed.

They'd finally climbed out of the tub, raided her kitchen for crackers and cheese, then got back in bed with the food that went mostly untouched after he'd realized that there were only so many hours until morning. He'd made love to her again, intending to keep it simple and fast, but after a few minutes of kissing she'd started working her way down his body and at that point the only polite thing to do was to reciprocate.

Alex gathered up his clothing and stood in the doorway for another minute, filling his eyes with the sight of Karina, smiling in her sleep. He was certain of only one thing: *normal* guys didn't slip out in secret and leave a woman like her behind.

But he had to do it. He couldn't be absolutely positive that no one had trailed him from Florida. He might *never* be sure.

Karina deserved better.

He moved silently to the loft area that opened off the staircase and slipped into his clothes. The spiral stairs creaked a little as he descended, boots in hand. By the time he got to the bottom, he was halfway expecting Karina to have awakened and be glaring at him from the landing, but when he looked up she wasn't there.

His getaway was clean. *Unfortunately,* he thought, which gave him a blip on his internal radar screen. *You're getting too close, man. Back off before you're drawn in so deep you forget the risk. One moment of inattention is all it'd take.*

The floors were hardwood with seagrass area rugs. Deciding to put his boots on out in the hall, he padded to the door. The fortune-teller in a glass booth caught his eye, and he stopped to stare. What an odd item for Karina to own. Didn't seem to be her style at all. Although there had been that carousel horse in the bedroom, he vaguely recalled.

Aha. The machine lights up, he remembered. He'd seen it from his windows. Karina had taken a card from the device and dropped it…somewhere….

Curiosity got the better of him. He listened for sounds of stirring upstairs, then went to the living room to look for the fortune.

The card was on the floor beside a glass-topped coffee table. Alex picked it up, turned it over in his palm. Beware The Man Bearing Gifts.

His gut clenched, for no reason that he could see. The men he had to look out for came bearing guns. The fortune meant nothing. Nothing at all.

7

"STEP AWAY FROM the low-riders," Karina said in a monotone. "This is a matter of ego security. Please, ma'am, step away from the low-riders."

Debby looked up, guilt splashed across her face. Her fingers were poised near a rack of low-slung leather pants with lacings and nail-head detailing. "I just wanted to look. I wouldn't actually try any on." She gave the soft leather a lingering caress. "Not after the last time."

Karina was relieved. Several months ago, Debby had wiggled into a pair of hip-hugger pants on one of their Saturday retail therapy sessions. One look at her tummy bulge in the merciless dressing-room mirror and she'd plunged into a rigid seeds-and-weeds regimen. The diet had wreaked serious havoc with her culinary inventions for Sutter Chocolat. The line of carob candies had not been a big seller. Armed with chocolate temptation, Karina and the other employees had been forced to stage an intervention for the sake of the business—and Debby's sunny personality, which had taken a nosedive into her edamame salad.

"Don't give the pants another thought," Karina said. "Confectioners aren't meant to wear low-riders."

Debby stuck out her lip. "*You* could wear them."

"I'm management. You're the creative one."

"What does that mean?" asked Whitney Smythe, the third participant in the day's Shopaholics Anonymous outing, who was frequently oblivious. A natural brunette with curls, her hair was so straight and blond she had a standing appointment with her stylist to maintain the look. She spent more on its upkeep than rent, but then she shared a studio apartment with Japanese twin sisters and slept on a single-bed mattress in a room so small there was only room for her and an overstuffed clothes rack.

Karina steered Debby away from the leathers and toward the feathers. Deb was a boa type of girl. "It means that she's free—"

"Fat," Debby said cheerfully.

"Free," Karina emphasized with a push at her friend's back. "Arty and original. Unfazed by sizes and rules."

"So then you're the opposite?" Debby looked skeptical and Karina hoped she wouldn't bring up the contradicting proof with Whitney around.

Instead Debby reached back and snatched up a pair of the leather belly-pants. "Let's see *you* try these on."

Karina sailed ahead. "Not my style."

Debby handed the pants off to Whitney, who gave them an interested examination, being both arty and managerial in her job as a features editor at *Hard Candy,* a racy lifestyle magazine for men. She'd been trying to talk Karina into an article about her chocolate shop, but the publicity was the last thing they needed.

Debby caught up to Karina and gave her a nudge. "Are you sure about that—your style? Seems to me you've been undergoing a radical shift in philosophy. Depending on what happened last night, that is."

"Last night…" There were no words to explain. Fortunately, Whitney interrupted before Karina had to think some up.

"*I* will try them on," she said, waving the pants. "I have an invitation to an MTV bash next weekend and I need to look hip and funky."

"Will Funkmaster Z-Row be there?" Debby handed Whitney a burgundy velvet top. The bodice was criss-crossed with ribbon and buckled leather bands, the price slashed by fifty percent.

"Who?" Whitney frowned. "The rapper? He's so a hundred-and-five minutes ago."

"Z-Row's a classic," Debby said. "He's big and cuddly. I just want to squeeze him."

Cuddly? The coil of restraint in Karina loosened at the reminder of her conversation with Alex. It was hard to act like she was normal when she began feeling so loose and loopy inside.

Loopy about Alex, even though she'd awakened to an empty bed and all the shades drawn in his apartment. She'd told herself that his early departure was convenient, not disappointing. They'd avoided all the fumbling weirdness of acting like they were cool with each other, that engaging in a night of illicit sex meant no more than changing clothes.

She had no business feeling abandoned. Imagining they'd shared something special, wishing to see him again—that was so predictable, so female. The chocolate courage was supposed to have carried her past those conventions.

"But I am not the unconventional type," she muttered, and Debby's head came up from her tussle with a pile of feathery sweaters.

"The leather," Karina explained. Whitney was still lurking nearby. "All wrong for me."

"Sounds like you're trying awfully hard to convince yourself of that."

"Maybe so." The warm throbbing she felt between her legs whenever she thought of Alex was merely the aftermath of being very well laid.

"Oh?" Debby's curiosity was engaged, but Whitney hailed them from the doorway to the dressing rooms. Debby waved her off, calling, "Give me a couple of minutes to find my size." She hooked her hand around Karina's elbow and hauled her toward the Lady Bountiful section of the boutique, where they'd be assured of privacy. Not many fashionistas would be caught dead lurking past size eight.

Debby squinted an eye and looked Karina up and down. "Did you hook up with Alex last night?"

"I can't say anything around Whitney."

"How come?"

"You know she'd tell everyone we know. I don't want to get a bad reputation."

"Hah! That's about as likely as Santa delivering crack door to door."

"That happened. The police arrested a ring of street-corner Santas on drug charges." Karina straightened a cuff on her suede jacket. "Prepare to be astonished."

Debby rubbed her hands together. "Now we're getting to the good stuff."

"We're not getting anywhere because I can't go into it here. Wait until lunch, Whitney's got her hair appointment and can't come with us."

"No fair keeping me on pins and needles." Debby eyed Karina with dawning suspicion. "The truffles. You tried the truffles again. Damn! I should have recognized the post-cocoa-bean glow."

"I'm not glowing." Karina pointed to her face. "That's good old-fashioned embarrassment."

"You're so Victorian. It's adorable. Just tell me—was it the truffles?"

Karina nodded. "I told Alex to eat one and then I—" She felt her cheeks heat at the memory of their window assignation. Okay, so Debby was right; she was glowing like the Rockefeller Plaza Christmas tree. "Let's just say I invited him over."

Debby's voice rose to a peak. "A-a-and?"

"The truffles really are magic."

Debby did a cha-cha in a little circle, pumping her fists like maracas. "Karina got some, Karina got some," she sang in tune to "La Cucaracha."

Karina gave in to her giddiness and joined the dance. "And it was hot stuff, it was hot stuff," she sang. Silly, but she loved it. The last time she'd been ga-ga over a guy had been…never. Maybe when she was thirteen and so in love with Patrick Swayze she'd watched *Dirty Dancing* on video every day after school.

"Hot stuff?" Debby halted. "This I've got to hear. Is it time for lunch yet?"

"We've barely begun to shop. We have to find you an outfit for your date with Kyle, and Whitney has the MTV thing—"

On cue, Whitney wailed from the dressing area. "Kare, Deb—emergency consult. I look like a velour pirate!"

"Coming." At random, Debby grabbed a few garments off the racks and they made their way to the curtained cubicles, where they squeezed in with Whitney and gave the holidays-in-bondage top a quick thumbs-down, while the decision on the pants remained pending, per their pairing with the right top.

The holiday shopping season was at its zenith. Chatter rose all around them, in various accents and languages. Next door, a Korean mother-daughter team were in a hissing debate over the girl's wish to wear a dress with cutouts. Farther down, a snappish woman with a surgically chopped Pekingese nose threw garments over the curtain of her stall, screeching that the size fours had been altered in the past month.

Whitney shimmied into a spangled tank. "Not buying anything, Karina?"

"She's only into taking clothes off, not putting them on," Debby said, making a face while Whitney wasn't looking.

Whitney blew strands of bleached hair out of her eyes. "Huh?"

"I'm here as your advisor," Karina said from her position on a ledge seat in the corner, out of the way. "That top would be better in red." She swept the feathered sweater out of Debby's hands, leaving her in a gray wool skirt and a bra. "Yellow, Deb? Are you planning to audition for *Sesame Street?*" She gathered the rest of the rejected garments off the floor. "Your delivery guy sounds like a good prospect. I'll go find you something slinky and sexy so you can really wow him."

"God, I wish I had your breasts," Whitney was saying as Karina picked her way toward the curtain.

"You can have them in return for your butt. That thing is teeny-tiny, even in a thong."

"Pilates classes," Whitney said, a smug sylph. "Karina comes, why don't you?"

Debby giggled. "I'll try to—tonight."

Karina made a choking sound and was just barely able to exit the changing room before she blew a gasket.

"There are no classes tonight," a befuddled Whitney was saying as Karina trotted away, snorting into her hand. She dropped the clothes on the sales counter and went off to find Debby a dress that would set her up for a magical evening. No one deserved it more.

"I'M ALWAYS SHOPPING with you." Debby tucked her shopping bag under the table. They'd dubbed her new dress Black Magic. "For richer, for maxed-out credit, in sickness or in health, till sample sales us do part."

Karina gave a modest shrug. She'd found Debby a little black dress that hugged her curves without turning them into bulges, dipped in low *V*s front and back to show off her friend's flawless skin, and yet had wide crisscrossed straps that concealed her upper-arm trouble spot. "'Twas nothing. The gods blessed us."

"Serendipity," Debby said with a dimple, which was why they'd chosen the popular restaurant despite it being packed with screaming kids. That, and to sample their competitor's hot chocolate.

"But now that Whitney's gone…" Debby sipped her chocolate, then leaned toward Karina with a foam mustache above her salacious grin. "Tell me about Alex."

Karina touched her upper lip. "He was…I mean, *it* was…" She sighed. "Just fabulous. He swept me off my feet."

Debby licked the mustache. "Details, please."

"There aren't a lot to tell. We hardly talked. He was smoldering."

"Smoldering?"

"That sounds over the top, I know. But he was. He, um, kind of took charge and…you know. It was just overwhelming. I had no control over myself and the sex was shockingly good."

Debby nodded as she dabbed with a napkin. "Why am I not surprised? It figures you'd like having the decision taken out of your hands."

"How do you mean?"

"Put him in charge and you can have the hot, sweaty jungle sex experience while still maintaining your good-girl standing. Otherwise known as having your cake and eating it, too."

Karina frowned. She wasn't sure that she liked the sound of that. "Don't forget—*I* instigated the affair."

"True. Baby steps."

"But I'm not stepping out again. This was a one-time thing, remember?"

Debby smirked. "I always figured you'd change your mind if the sex was really good."

"Well…" Karina dunked her spoon into her cup of hot chocolate, stirring the disintegrating whipped cream. "The thought has crossed my mind."

"Do tell!"

"I'm tempted," she admitted. "He's right across the street, and it's not as if I have to worry about us developing a relationship. He was clear about not wanting that. He even pulled out the standard 'I'll be moving on soon' line that guys use to keep marriage-minded chicks at bay. So I have no expectations in that area."

Debby grinned. "But an endless supply of truffles."

Which all sounded good, if not reasonable, but Karina knew that continuing the affair would be asking for trouble. Common sense prevailed and she shook her head. "No. It's smartest to stop now."

"Aw, that's no fun. How about when the truffles run out?"

Karina considered. "I gave him a half dozen, but I ate one on the day I delivered them. And he ate at least one last night, if not two. That leaves four truffles at most."

"And four fu—"

"Four's too many. I might get feelings after four times." Pffft. She had feelings after just *one*. It was bothersome, having to tamp them down all the time. Four more nights with Alex and she'd be thinking about ways to turn him into a proper boyfriend, which he clearly did not want to be.

And the truth was that she didn't consider him a very promising prospect anyway. His actions were mystifying. His personality was mercurial. He was a wanderer. He didn't even have a job, aside from being a wannabe writer—if that was even legitimate. There wasn't much to recommend him.

Except the sex.

And…yet some small, impractical part of herself still believed in fate.

She swallowed a large gulp of the hot chocolate. "He left me. I woke up this morning and he was gone."

"Yeah, I hate when guys do that." Debby flashed an irreverent smile. "The only thing worse is if they leave cash on the nightstand."

Karina laughed; Debby could always get her to do that. "Okay, so it wasn't that bad. I'd given him no reason to believe I wanted him to stay."

"And it's not as if you don't know his name and where he lives. He didn't *vanish*."

"Somehow, though, I got the feeling that he might do exactly that." Karina flicked her fingers in the air. "Poof."

"Use your powers of persuasion, along with the truffles. Trust me, he won't leave."

"I don't want to keep him by artificial means."

"You're so naive, Kare. Women have been using their wiles to keep men since Adam and Eve. The lugs don't know what they want. We have to tell them. That's why biology made it so they think with the little head—for our convenience. The little head is easy to control."

Karina shuddered. "Ugh. I can't do that. When I get serious—and it won't be with Alex—I won't play games. It will be an equal partnership of love and respect."

"What a bore. You've turned marriage into a social studies exam." Debby grinned. "No wonder you needed a little fun first."

Karina felt sheepish. Trust Debby to be blunt while pointing out a few hard truths. "I never said the relationship couldn't be fun, too."

Except the model that came to mind was her parents, who'd been a partnership first, always working to put forward her father's career in industry and then diplomacy. They weren't the kind to show each other much public affection, but at least they were still together and seemed content enough. Many of the lovey-dovey couples she knew were either divorced or in the throes of marital disharmony. Being practical-minded had worked for her up to now.

Karina moved her cup aside as the waiter arrived with their food. According to the Shopaholics Anonymous code, they must always order substantial lunches to keep their strength up for the fray. "Enough about me. What about you and Kyle?"

"Is there even a question?" Debby picked up her cheddarburger, momentarily confounded by how to get her jaws around it. "We're *all* about having fun."

"Why not more?"

"I'm not getting remarried anytime soon." Debby mashed the burger together, with oozing results.

"Yes, but what about a long-term relationship? It would be nice to have a guy around for the holidays at least." Karina became wistful as she rearranged the filling in her Ultimate BLT. "Someone to help decorate a tree and exchange gifts with, take to Christmas parties, sip mulled wine by the fire. You know."

Debby nodded with her mouth full. "Even though the only fire I have is the pilot light that's always going out on my stove," she said after she'd swallowed.

"You could give Kyle a truffle." Karina winked. "He'd light your fire."

Debby got a happy look on her face. "The man seems to have arrived already ignited."

"Lucky you." Karina's ego winced over the lengths she'd gone to with Alex. "Imagine when he sees your new dress."

Debby gurgled around her burger. "Oh, yeah, baby. I'm *really* looking forward to that."

"You said he's a bodybuilder. What if he's all into himself, going on about how his body is a temple, blah, blah, blah?"

"I'll ask to worship at the shrine." Debby shrugged. "But I don't think he'll be like that. For sure there were a lot of muscles when I was in his arms, but he didn't have that arrogant way about him. No preening. And I might have even felt a tiny hint of a love handle." She smacked her lips. "'Course, most of my attention was on other areas of his anatomy."

Debby's eyes were shining beneath the curly fluff of her bangs. "How come it's so easy for you?" Karina asked.

"I don't expect perfection from the men I date," came the quick answer. Debby smiled to soften the implied criticism. "After all, I'm not perfect, either, and I wouldn't even want to try to be." She flipped her hair, acting cavalier when Karina knew that there was a real hurt lingering there. "Call it low expectations. Failing at marriage the first time out tends to revise your standards about what men are capable of providing."

"Aw, Deb. Someday you'll meet the guy who'll give you everything you want."

"Maybe, but for now all I expect from Kyle is a hot meal and a good time. Or vice versa." Debby lifted her burger high. "Here's to getting what we want."

Karina did the same. "And wanting what we get."

She neatly bit into her BLT, mentally castigating herself. Why couldn't she be as easy and uncomplicated about Alex? *Carpe diem,* grab for the gusto, put off her concerns until tomorrow. With another of the mindless throbs pumping endorphins into her veins, she thought of the remaining truffles.

Chocolate was a terrible thing to waste.

"HERE WE ARE. Welcome to the little place I like to call my humble abode à la mode." Debby tossed her and Kyle's coats on the back of a chair. Luckily, she'd remembered to fold the futon into a couch, in between tugging a pair of tights past her hips and cooking homemade chocolate pudding so she could lure Kyle to her apartment with the offer of dessert. Not that he needed much convincing. He'd been more than agreeable.

"It's big," he said about the two-room space, which only a New Yorker would understand. One room opened onto the other without doors, so she'd turned the first into her lounge and the second into her kitchen and dining area.

"Big enough for me. Make yourself at home. I'll get our dessert." Feeling very Donna Reed, minus the apron, Debby click-clacked in her high heels to the bare-bones kitchen that she'd dressed up with tangerine paint and a row of old wedding-gift appliances. She took the pudding out of the fridge and at the last minute decided to add chocolate shavings as a garnish. Only a few, from her personal stash of the special chocolate.

She popped one of the dark curls into her mouth. Kyle had been extremely attentive all evening, looking across the table at her as if he couldn't wait to eat her up. But a little insurance never hurt. Karina would be proud that Debby was thinking so pragmatically.

She took two spoons from the utensil drawer and arranged a tray, stopped to make a quick adjustment of her breasts inside the strapless bra that was the only style that worked with the new dress, then returned to the lounge. Eyes avid, Kyle stood as she entered and took the tray from her so she could sit. She was pleased with his continued display of gentlemanly manners. Call her narrow-minded, but she'd expected a blue-collar deliveryman to be the kind to get marinara sauce on his chin and burp after dinner. Kyle *had* dunked a shirt cuff in the wine carafe, but only because he was passing her the bread basket, with the most adoring look on his face.

Not once had there been a hint that he thought she should cut down on carbs or order the salad instead of the baked ziti. After her husband, who'd memorized nutritional labels like some men did baseball statistics, there was no quicker way to win Debby's heart than to enjoy good food and encourage others to do the same. For a time, she'd wondered if she could possibly be friends with a woman like Karina, who ate chocolate only for dessert. Eventually she'd understood that it wasn't about calories with Kare, it was about moderation and self-control. Some people were just wound too tight.

Debby kicked off her shoes and curled up on the futon. She held her hand out to Kyle. Nothing tight about him. He was big and solid, but as huggable as a stuffed animal. "Come cuddle with me, teddy bear."

Kyle put the tray on the coffee table and eagerly dropped down beside her, at least two hundred pounds of luscious male. With a blissful sigh, she put her arms around him and squeezed.

Aha. She'd been right—he had love handles. And, boy oh boy, did she love to handle them. A nice, warm feeling spread through her, almost as if she'd gorged on the aphrodisiac chocolate instead of only a single curl. There were times the extra help wasn't necessary.

"Thanks for a lovely evening," she said, leaning into his massive chest.

He let out a soft grunt, like a contented grizzly. "Thanks for going out with me. Want to do it again sometime?"

"Anytime." Time after time, if they were as good together as she suspected they would be.

"I never thought I'd meet a girl like you."

She blinked. "Me? I'm nothing special."

"Yes, you are."

"How so?" she asked, not intending to fish for compliments. She wanted to know, considering her ex had said she'd never find another man willing to overlook her many flaws.

"Your smile," Kyle said. "And your eyes." He grinned. "You make me laugh, and you feel—" he ran his hands along her arm, down to her hip "—real soft."

Debby moved closer.

"You smell good, too," he added before he began nuzzling her ear. His lips moved toward her mouth. "Like a chocolate cake."

They kissed for a while, until Debby was so out of breath she had to suck air like a racehorse. This made her boobs heave, drawing Kyle's entranced gaze. Oh boy. She shimmied against his chest. "Two scoops. Want a bite?"

"Yum. Looks delicious." One hand moved up and clasped her breast. She closed her eyes, letting herself sink into the caress, willing to overlook the fact that Kyle was not a sparkling conversationalist because what he did say was completely genuine. He had marvelous hands, so large and strong. When he held her, she believed that she'd finally found the man with whom she was the perfect size.

And so is he. Impressed by the wood pressing against her thigh, she reached behind her back for her zipper.

"Oh, wow," Kyle said in a shaky voice as he watched the fitted bodice of her dress peel away to reveal her breasts bursting out of the skimpy strapless bra. He put a thumb to one nipple and stroked until it popped past the elastic. Debby went for his mouth, throwing her arms around his shoulders as he tilted her back onto the futon, burrowing into her.

"You haven't tried the dessert," she said as he clambered between her open thighs, kissing and squeezing every inch of her at once.

He hadn't eaten any of the special chocolate, either, she realized as Kyle worked his hand inside her tights. After that, she stopped caring.

THE TRAIN THRUMMED beneath Alex, returning him to the city, filled with both anticipation and his constant low-grade dread. He knew he was making a mistake, coming back when it would have been easiest to keep on going. But there was no reasoning with his heart.

After leaving Karina, he couldn't bear the idea of returning to the comfortless cage of his studio apartment, so instead he'd walked. And walked. Block after block. Thinking of Karina with such intensity that he'd lost track of his surroundings, startled to find himself at the East River near the Williamsburg Bridge.

Struck by the realization that he'd forgotten to watch for trouble, he'd looked wildly around him. One of Rafael Norris's hired guns could have picked up his trail and followed two steps behind.

The wind had been so bitter off the river that not many people were out. A burly man bundled in a thick jacket with a fur collar had been walking a puffball dog across the frosty ground of the riverside park. A couple of guys huddled together, smoking.

Cursing his lapse of attention, Alex had quickly headed into the shelter of a large brick warehouse. After making sure—as sure as he could be these days—that he hadn't been followed, he'd strode briskly to the nearest subway station. Reaching Penn Station, he'd taken the first train departing, without caring about his destination. All he'd known was that he had to get away.

Not from the danger of being found.

From Karina. His feelings for her were dangerous—for both of them.

And yet, twelve hours later, he was returning, unable to convince himself to leave her. In fact, the day apart had made him want her even more.

He was losing it. Being stupid. Rash.

Letting his guard down and making the kind of mistakes he'd feared.

His one comfort was that there'd been no sign of surveillance during the train journey, which there would have been if Norris's men had picked up his trail from Florida and thought he was trying to escape again. He didn't quite dare to believe, but it was beginning to look like he might be free. Really free, this time. Three weeks and counting, ever since he'd arrived in New York. That hope, that one slender hope of a fresh start, was all he had.

It was enough to send him back to Karina.

For now.

ABOUT NOW, KARINA DECIDED, lurking near the windows of her darkened living room, Debby was probably rolling around on her futon with Kyle Murphy, without a qualm. While *she* was driving herself crazy, waffling back and forth in her mind over what to do, what to do.

The hell with that. She grabbed the weighted cords of the linen shades and yanked them open, one by one. She went around the rooms, turning on every light so the place was lit up like a Broadway stage. Then she stopped in the center, hands on hips, breathing hard, glaring at Alex's dark apartment. She'd checked frequently since getting home from her shopping excursion and there hadn't been a single sign of him. But where else could he be? He had no friends. Nowhere to go.

She stalked to the windows. "Hey, Alex—here I am! Come and get me!"

Nothing.

He must not have eaten another truffle. She had, on impulse, after stopping in at the store to carry a couple of them home for emergency use.

Why she'd done it, she didn't know. She'd been plenty aroused, just from thinking about Alex.

So, okay. It was obvious that her physical needs were real, not manufactured. Alex's, too, she supposed.

Maybe he had this type of affair all the time, but for her, this first taste of wild, ravenous sex had given her a surprising need for it. A craving. Even without the chocolate, she was constantly feverish with the desire to have Alex's hands on her, his mouth, his tongue…she wanted his tongue licking inside her, tasting her….

Frustrated, she rapped her fist on the cold glass. For a couple of seconds, she didn't realize that the resultant knocking was coming from the door.

"Karina." Alex's voice. "Let me in."

With her heart in her mouth, she went to open the door. He stood with one hand on the jamb, out of breath, a light dusting of snow melting into his hair. His cheeks were ruddy and he seemed weary and spent, yet filled with a raging energy that crackled in the cold air that clung to him.

"What are you doing here?" she demanded, forgetting that she'd been begging him—challenging him—to come.

"I don't know. But I couldn't stay away."

She glanced toward his apartment, still undisturbed. "Where have you been?"

"All over. I left here around 5:00 a.m. and I walked out to the river. Then I took a train out to Long Island, all the way to Montauk. End of the line. I've been walking on the beach. The waves were wild. I found a coffee shop…."

He seemed broken up. As if he didn't want to be there, with her, but had come anyway.

A nameless fear nipped at her already crumbling composure. She fingered the lapels of his coat. "Alex. What's going on with you?"

He didn't answer, just took her face in his cold hands and kissed her with a sudden hot, pounding hunger that was almost too much for her to bear. Yes, too much. She'd always thought she was strong, but one wrenching kiss from Alex and she felt herself entering a dark maelstrom where there was no restraint, only the driving need to be consumed.

They staggered together, getting Alex inside, tearing off his coat, slamming the door, all without breaking the contact of their mouths. She fumbled with his shirt, the same one from yesterday, but gave up halfway through, leaving it hanging open, partially unbuttoned. Getting naked took too much time when she had to have him right now, right here.

Right or wrong.

They continued kissing, locked together with their arms and legs as they twisted and rubbed and clung. Alex's hands were everywhere at once—tangled in her hair, diving under her sweater, tugging at her jeans. He got them open, pushed them down her legs, stripped off her panties, and with each brush of his fingers she felt deep throbbing as her desperate craving built to a fever pitch.

Alex lifted her up, pushing her back to the wall. She shivered uncontrollably as he reached down to drop his pants and release himself. His thick penis sprang up, nudging between her open thighs. Reluctant to break contact, but too frantic not to, she unwound her legs from his waist and found her balance. "Condom?"

He made a sound of frustration. "I left them in your bedroom. From now on, we keep them always at hand. On a string around your neck, if we have to."

"It's okay. I stuck one in the pocket of my jeans…." Karina sank to her knees in front of him, searching through the tangle of her discarded clothes. "Here." She held up the packet, then changed her mind and snatched it away. "Let me," she said, another wave of passion surging through her as she saw his hard-on rising proudly from his open zipper.

"Fast." His panting breaths rattled in his chest.

She worked his pants down a little. When she touched him, scooping her palm beneath his testicles, he moaned and hunched forward, keeping upright by slamming his hands against the fortune-telling booth. The mechanism whirred to life, flicking on the bulbs. They were bathed in garish blinking colors as she licked her tongue around the head of his penis until it glistened.

He banged a fist against the booth. The carnival music started up, followed by the monotone voice: "Give me your hand."

Both hands. Karina skimmed the condom down the length of Alex's shaft, rolling him between her palms.

"I will tell your fortune," said Esmeralda.

A sharp cry tore loose from Alex's throat and he

dropped to the floor, giving Karina no time to react before his hands were on her hips, dragging her bare bottom across the floor toward him. He plunged directly into her. She grabbed onto his shoulders, taking him with her as he tipped her over onto her back and began to thrust, pushing a little deeper each time, each lunge edging their bodies along the floor until they were butted up against the fortune-telling machine.

Esme repeated. "Give me your hand."

Oh, yes, give it to me! Karina flexed against Alex's hard body, holding herself taut for a moment of incredible, transfixed sensation as he pulled almost all the way out, then drove deep again, his hands locked on her hips, holding her steady even as she shattered under the impact, lost again to the wild pulsing rhythm of their mutual release.

"I will tell your fortune."

But I know exactly what's coming, Karina thought, flowing inside as the pleasure swept through her over and over again in slowly diminishing waves.

Heartbreak.

No matter what she told herself about chocolate-induced flings, she knew in her heart that she was involved. And that Alex was too tortured for this to be an easy ride.

8

A SMALL WHITE CARD emerged from the fortune-telling booth and fluttered to the floor. The bulbs shut down and the mechanism hummed to a stop.

"What's with this thing?" Alex asked, twisting to look at it.

Karina stirred against him. "That's Esmeralda, the fortune-telling Gypsy Queen. I got her at an auction."

"Why?"

"For fun." She lifted her head and looked levelly at him. "You don't like fun?"

"Depends what kind of fun." He moved his fingers against her bare backside.

"Hmm. Yes, I see. There's that kind, and then there's the other kind. You don't seem like a guy who'd enjoy a carnival."

She was wrong, he thought. Lex would have been shooting down rubber ducks with a water gun, whirling upside down on the roller coaster, gorging on greasy hamburgers and popcorn. But not Alex. Sunny days and happy crowds only made him think of Frank Whitman and the thin line between life and death.

"Except…" She splayed her hand over his chest and rested her chin on it. "Didn't you say you surfed? I'm trying to picture that." She grinned. "Say, 'Yo, dude,' for me, and maybe that'll help."

He wanted to joke with her, but instead he shut down. "I'm not that guy anymore."

She hesitated, then pushed up to sit with her legs pulled in tight. Disconnecting. She pulled her sweater down, modestly covering up as much of her bottom half as she could. "What happened to him?"

He was blindsided by his idealism and belief in the system. "He grew up."

"Of course."

Alex was not ready to move, although he did yank his pants up over his hip bones. His knees were abraded from skidding on the wood floor, and the hard surface wasn't exactly comfortable to lie on either, but for some reason he liked being here with Karina, their bodies relaxed and loose from the sex, no worries on his mind because they were inside and safe.

Another ten minutes. He could give himself that.

She made a move to get up, and he put his hand on her leg to stop her. "You don't seem like the kind of woman who'd enjoy a carnival, either."

"I don't?" She straightened her hair. "How come?"

He shrugged. "Too restrained. Demure. More the type to go to the opera or the theater." He pronounced it *thee-uh-tuh* to egg her on.

"I like those, too, but…" Her eyes shone with umbrage. "Restrained? Demure? I can't believe *you* would say that. I've never been *less* restrained—"

"Outside of—" he flipped a finger back and forth between them "—this."

Suddenly she was crestfallen. "So you think that, um, *this* is…out of character?"

"That'd be my guess." He shrugged. "I don't know you well enough to say for sure."

Her chin went up. "You know me. You've been watching me for weeks now."

If she was going to call him on that...

"You're a beautiful woman," he said quickly. "Any man would watch you."

"Through binoculars?"

"Any way possible."

"Seriously, Alex. What are you doing with them? I know you're not only looking at me. You're sneaky about it, but I've seen you studying the street. Even the rooftops."

Damn. He'd allowed the distraction of her to make him overlook one of the cardinal rules of staying safe: keeping himself nondescript, avoiding notice, blending in. He'd been beyond obvious with Karina.

"Just keeping track of my surroundings," he bluffed.

Her eyes narrowed, but she didn't continue the questioning even though he was sure he hadn't convinced her of his harmlessness.

"I just can't believe—" She shook back her hair. "You think I'm demure. What's a girl got to do?"

He grinned. "When's the last time you went to a carnival?"

Her lips compressed, twitching to one side while she thought. "Not in ages," she conceded.

"Then why the fortune-telling machine?" He patted the booth looming over him. "And the carousel horse in the bedroom?"

"Only a collection. There's also a genuine Ringling Brothers Circus poster in my dining room, and a popcorn maker in the loft."

"They don't fit in."

She gave him a narrow look. "Maybe there's more to me than you can see through your binoculars."

"I suppose that's true." A pang pinched his gut at the knowledge that he'd probably never get to really know her. He'd never had one, but a lasting relationship was built up over time, made up of fun and fights and the quiet times in between. It wasn't only about hot sex.

Though that was always a good starting point.

"I don't know what it is," she said, "but I'm drawn to carnival pieces. There's no psychological significance. It's not that my only happy childhood memory was going to the carnival, or that I was abandoned by my mother when she ran off to join the circus…." Karina laughed. "Maybe I just like the surprise of it, and how my guests react. I don't want to be pigeonholed as easily as you just did." She threw him a look. "Restrained and demure. Huh."

"Says the woman who sets her alarm at the same time every day, even on weekends, and follows the same routine every morning and night—" He stopped. Too late.

Her eyes had gone wide. "You really have been watching me."

"You should close your curtains more often."

A pink blush inched into her face. "I usually do."

"But not lately."

She swallowed. "Okay. Yes. I knew you were watching all along."

He went up on one elbow. "I could tell."

"Alex." Her voice had dropped to a whisper; she avoided his eyes. "What are we doing?"

"Having a little fun with each other, that's all."

"Yes, of course." Then she shook her head, contradicting her words.

"What do *you* think we're doing?"

"I don't know. It started as—" She stopped abruptly. "You said you were gone all day."

"Yes. After last night, I was too restless to stay cooped up in a small ap—"

She interrupted. "You didn't go back at all, you didn't eat anymore of the chocolate."

That again? "Uh, I'm not crazy about chocolate. I'm sorry if that hurts your feelings. I'm sure it's very good."

"Oh, that's okay." She was smiling. "Very okay. I kind of like it that we're doing this the natural way."

"Natural? What do you mean?"

"Never mind," she said quickly. "You must be hungry. I haven't had dinner, either. There's leftover ravioli, if you like. It's not homemade, but I only order in from the best." She'd started to get up, but stopped again and sank back to her knees, giving him a lofty look. "That is, unless you have to cut out on me. Or do you prefer to do that when I'm not awake?"

So. She was not pleased with his silent escape. There was a slight tremor of uncertainty in the way she bit down on her bottom lip, waiting for his explanation. He couldn't tell her the reasons behind his hesitation. But he wanted to stay, holding on to his last hope of a normal life.

He stood and gave her his hand. "I'm not going anywhere." *Tonight.* "Leftover ravioli sounds good."

"I shouldn't forgive you so easily."

"Oh?" He lifted his brows. "I'm forgiven?"

A wry smile flitted across her mouth. "I guess so— against my better judgment. This is a very weird re-ro-rendezvous."

Relationship? Romance? *Hey, now,* he wanted to say. *Hold on.*

"Oh, look!" Karina said, seemingly as glad as he to seize on a change of subject. "You have a fortune." She swooped down to retrieve the little card that had been spat out by the fortune-teller.

He held up his hands. "Oh, no. Not me. It must be for you."

She glanced at their scattered clothing and tugged self-consciously at the hem of her sweater. "I'd say it was for both of us, considering…"

He remembered the card she'd received the previous evening. "I don't believe in that stuff."

"I'll keep it to myself then." But her demeanor changed when she read the fortune. Rolling her eyes, she crumpled the card in her palm. "Pretty silly."

Alex couldn't help himself, which was beginning to be a familiar state when he got near Karina. "What did it say?"

She shrugged and moved past him. "You don't believe in it, so what do you care?"

"I don't." He buttoned his shirt as he followed her, admiring the sway of her hips and the way her sweater cupped her sweet ass. He was hoping she'd drop the card into a wastebasket, but she kept it.

When he got to the kitchen, she was already dumping a Tupperware container of ravioli into a saucepan. The small slip of cardboard was tucked under the edge of an Emmett Kelly cookie jar that sat on the corner of the countertop. He caught himself drumming his fingers on the granite and quickly slid both hands into his pockets, avoiding the temptation to take a look at the card. His fortunes were unpredictable, at best.

"You can set the table."

He glanced up and saw that Karina had been watching him eye the cheesy card of fortune as if it were a scorpion. She wore a smug little smile that he wanted to kiss away until they were back to the chemistry that he found easier to accept.

Relationship?

Romance?

They had their dinner on china plates, with real silver. Wine in goblets. Cloth napkins.

Alex offered to clear and she let him, even though she must have known he only wanted a few seconds alone in her kitchen. When he came out, she had Diana Krall on the CD player, a couple of candles lit, the curtains closed. She was stretched out on the couch with her legs bare and a bemused smile of invitation on her face.

He was torn. The day spent being all tormented and dramatic in Montauk had done him no good at all because he was right back where he'd started. Endangered if he did, damned if he didn't.

"I'm making no promises," he said, and bent over the back of the sleek sofa to slide his arms around Karina and bury his face in her silky hair.

"I don't expect any," she said.

But the fortune card had read After The Darkness, Comes The Dawn. A Brighter Future Awaits.

MONDAY AT WORK, Karina had trouble concentrating on her tasks. She was irritable with Janine, whose eagerness to know every aspect of the business seemed more like butting in. When the girl had hovered over Karina's shoulder at the computer for the third time, she'd finally sent Janine out of the office on a make-work errand, just to get rid of her for a while.

But even then she couldn't seem to get her head straight. Coming down off a sex-and-candy high with Alex was like dealing with a hangover. They'd separated first thing Sunday morning, but had been back together that night, when he'd come knocking on her door once more despite having said nothing about continuing their affair.

Although they weren't exactly having a meeting of the minds—or hearts—there was also no way to pretend that the one-night fling hadn't become a lot more. She couldn't even claim they were turned on by the truffles. He seemed to have no particular taste for them, and she only popped one when she was feeling unsure and wanted the boost of sexual confidence.

Which left them…where?

Karina threw down her pen. All she knew was that she'd never been so engrossed by a man. If only he'd open up just a tad, give her a little something to work with, a hint of his feelings for her.

Then what? Was she ready to accept a stranger in her orderly life on the basis of little more than their combustible chemistry?

Deciding she needed to work with her hands and give her buzzing brain a rest, Karina went to check activity in the kitchen. The scent of melted chocolate had permeated even her office, making her queasy. Too much chocolate lately…or maybe it was the emotional push and pull that she'd intended to avoid.

Karina glimpsed Debby through the porthole window and pushed open the swinging door to the corridor. "Deb, I've had either too many sweets or too much sex—"

Debby whipped around, tugging at her skewed apron. A large, muscular man with thick blond hair and a goofy hound-dog grin stood behind her. Beneath an open, quilted vest, he wore the khaki uniform of their delivery service.

Karina blinked. "Excuse me."

Debby slid a finger beneath her smile to rub away lip gloss smears. "Oops. You caught us. Kyle was just leaving."

"Yes, of course, Kyle," Karina said, giving the guy a nod hello. Not that there'd been any doubt this was *the* Kyle. Debby had phoned in that morning to say she'd be an hour late to work as Kyle had just left her house.

Karina looked at her watch. Apparently a measly four hours was too long for Kyle and Debby to be apart. They had her and Alex beat by a full working day. She wondered how many truffles Debby was using.

"I know, I know. Time to get back to work." Debby shot Kyle a double-smacking air kiss. "See you tonight, huggy bear?"

"As soon as I clock out, creamcake." He lumbered past Karina, doffing the bill of his uniform cap.

"Nice to see you again, Kyle." As soon as the door swung shut, she rounded on Debby, comically shaking a finger at her. "Kissing in the corridor. What are you, teenagers?"

Debby dimpled. "Ohmigawd, yes. I could make out with him for, like, hours."

"If he can keep it up for hours, you must be feeding him truffles around the clock."

"Nope." Debby reached under her apron to retuck her blouse. "It's really amazing. I haven't fed him *any* of the chocolate. We're falling for each other the old-fashioned way. No cocoa beans necessary."

"Oh." Karina blinked in consternation, contrasting them with her and Alex. They would have never got together had it not been for the truffles. Perhaps that meant they weren't meant to be.

"Congratulations. I guess it's the real thing," she said,

trying to beam, and failing. Not wanting to bring her friend down, she turned and fled the corridor, almost bumping into Janine, who hadn't even taken off her coat.

"I got the new candy thermometers you wanted," she said, but Karina rushed past without stopping, one hand lifted to block her face from view as she gave her nose a wicked pinch.

She burst into the front room of the shop and stopped there, while she rubbed at her stinging nose and prickling eyes. It was ridiculous to be jealous of Debby and Kyle when she'd got exactly what she'd bargained for from Alex: a strictly sexual affair without attachment.

Several customers waited in line at each of the cash registers. Karina glanced over the operations, then moved to the hot-chocolate machine as one of the workers reached for the take-out cups they kept stacked nearby. "I'll take charge here for a while. You see to the customers."

The employee gave her a grateful nod. "One French hot chocolate, double on the chocolate, please."

The shop had several signature hot-chocolate drinks, including Aztec made with a dash of chili pepper, and the rich chocolate cream of the French style. Karina got the container of heavy cream from the fridge and dropped in two healthy dollops. She set the cup and pushed the lever on the machine, releasing a hot stream of pure dark chocolate.

The sweet smell went straight to her head, evoking memories of the past three nights with Alex. She flicked the lever, trying to shut off her thoughts as well, but that was not easy. Being with him had changed her in a fundamental way. She'd become so tuned in to her surroundings—inhaling the sweet smells, caressing the embossed copper of their logo, relishing the warmth of the cup in her hand.

That was all real, wasn't it? Then why not Alex?

She passed the hot chocolate to the waiting customer, jolted from her own thoughts by the middle-aged man's familiarity. The shape of his face reminded her of someone she knew.

Perhaps he was a regular. She said hello. "You look familiar, sir. Are you a frequent customer?"

The man's eyes sharpened behind a pair of thick glasses. "Of course not," he huffed, before grabbing the cup and scurrying away.

Karina shrugged. The city was filled with oddballs.

Needing the mindless work, she continued making drinks and boxing small orders for the next hour, until the next shift of part-time employees reported to work. Karina drifted off to her favorite spot near the windows, where she could check Alex's apartment.

He was there, but the casual observer would have missed him. A narrow opening along the side of the blind was the only sign of his presence. This time, he wasn't looking for Karina. The binoculars appeared to be trained on her customers.

She looked them over. A young woman with a lustrous mane of shiny sable hair sat at the table nearest the front window, writing in a notebook with an array of chocolates on a plate in front of her. Pen poised, she picked one up and nibbled at the edge, stopping briefly to swoon with appreciation before she resumed her note-taking.

Karina scoffed to herself. Probably another rival, hoping to duplicate the Sutter family recipe. Except they usually weren't so blatant that they'd plunk themselves at one of the shop's own tables to attempt their research. Nevertheless, the young woman was a beauty and certainly worthy of Alex's attention.

There seemed to be nothing of note about the other customers. At the farthest table, the man she'd thought she recognized sat with his face buried in a newspaper. Occasionally the aphrodisiac effect prompted a male customer to become enamored with one of the clerks. Store policy was that they must urge amorous customers to direct their attentions elsewhere.

Although Karina made a mental note to ask her employees about the lurker, she couldn't see any reason for the man to catch Alex's attention. No, it had to be the stylish young woman he was studying so closely.

I'm not ready to lose him. Karina slid a finger along the glass doors of the display cabinet, searching the contents.

"What are you looking for?" Debby asked, coming up from behind. She put a hand on Karina's upper arm and gave her a squeeze.

"We're out of the truffles?"

"Black Magics? You know we don't stock many of them up front."

Karina's voice rose. "But you have some in the back?"

"We may be sold out. There were a couple left over from the last batch. They seem to have disappeared from the refrigerator." Debby winked.

Karina flushed. "Yes, I took them. But my spectacular weekend of wall-to-wall sex was worth it."

"I'll say." Obviously, Debby was eager to hear more. "Come in the back and help me make another batch."

"Yeah, I could." Karina bunched her fists on top of the display and took a deep breath. "Except I'm falling into a trap here. Kind of a damned-if-you-do situation, exactly the one I meant to avoid from the beginning. But now…" Her shoulders dropped. "How will I ever know what Alex really feels for me if I rely on the double-strength chocolates to ease us along the way?"

"Why do you have to know?" Debby asked. "Enjoy the sex for what it is." Karina looked at her with a bleak expression and she added, "Uh-oh. You're getting serious."

Karina nodded.

"What happened to the short-term fling?"

"I should have realized that wouldn't work for me, but I wanted Alex so much I persuaded myself I could pull it off."

"I know what you mean." Debby nodded. "Sex is never only sex, at least for women. Some women." Debby paused, considering. "Exactly how close are you two?"

"Aside from the physical, not so very. I still don't know much more about him than I did at the beginning. But that just doesn't matter. There's something between us. It's small, barely a beginning." Karina smiled to herself. "As hokey as it sounds, we transcend words."

"Uh-oh," Debby said again.

"I know. Ridiculous, huh?"

"Maybe…maybe not."

"I'm fooling myself." A starker version of the truth hit Karina when she looked at the lovely young woman who'd so easily captured Alex's attention. "I can dress this up all I want, but the reality is that he can't get away fast enough, come morning."

Or even before morning, she added silently, since

Alex continued to disappear while she was sleeping. Not once, but twice.

Debby slung her arms around Karina's shoulders and made a consoling sound.

"After the aphrodisiac and the lust has worn off, we're so awkward with each other," she confessed in a low voice. "Transcending words? Who'm I kidding? Alex doesn't talk to me because he's not interested in getting to know me. This isn't a great love affair. It's a booty call."

A booty call, Karina repeated ruthlessly to herself, trying to crush the romantic notions she'd acquired to keep herself from seeing the blunt, naked truth of it.

As always, Debby was quick with reassurances. "Aw, no, Kare—it's more than that. Has to be! Even the Black Magic truffles aren't *that* strong—"

"Excuse me." The dark-haired girl at the table near the window tentatively waved a hand. "I didn't mean to eavesdrop, but…" She rose, skidding the lightweight wire bistro chair across the floor. "I'm Nikki Silk."

Karina was too startled to respond.

"Nikki Silk," Debby mulled. "I know that name from somewhere."

"Hard Candy," Karina said, remembering. Oh, damn.

"That's right." Nikki approached, her expression hopeful. "I'm a staff writer there. Whitney Smythe said she'd mentioned my name to you? I'm looking for a good story for my next feature in the magazine, and I think Sutter Chocolat is it!"

Karina greeted the announcement with less enthusiasm than Nikki obviously expected. "Thanks, but we don't need the publicity. I've told Whitney that several times." Unfortunately, Whitney was known for missing a lot and forgetting the rest.

"She said I might have to persuade you." Nikki smiled a winning smile.

Karina remained wary. "What were you thinking of?"

"Aside from the story about the most fantastic chocolates I've ever tasted, I was interested in, well…" Nikki pressed closer to the display cabinet, leaning an arm on the green marble top. "What's this about them being aphrodisiacs?"

Debby and Karina exchanged a look.

Karina winced. "You heard that."

Nikki wagged a finger. "Off the record, until you agree otherwise."

"How do we know we can trust you on that?" Debby asked.

Nikki blinked blue eyes. "Because I'm so charming and guileless?" She grinned. "For a reporter, at least."

Almost involuntarily, Karina returned the grin, then introduced herself and Debby. Nikki Silk was tall, thin, gorgeous and outfitted in designer labels, but there was something eminently likable about her. Which didn't mean she would trust the girl with her darkest chocolate secrets. "Sorry. That was a private conversation you overheard. I'll consider the story on the shop, but I won't share personal information."

"But that's where the real story lies. Chocolate aphrodisiacs! I'm dying to know more."

Karina wanted to disappear. "You know enough already."

"How about a bargain?" Nikki said. "I won't ask you questions about your, um, personal experiences, but in return you do let me explore the possibilities regarding the chocolate. And just so you know, I didn't get that from your conversation alone. People are talking about your store. At first I thought this was just about good chocolate, but I've been sitting here for an hour now, listening to the customers. Quite a few of them seem to be well satisfied by more than the chocolate." Nikki arched her pencil-thin brows. "I know you know what I mean."

"We sure do," Debby said, making Karina drag her away.

They put their heads together, consulting in whispers. "What do you think?" Karina asked. "My instinct is not to do this. We certainly don't need an influx of customers."

"Why not? You could make out like a bandit when the story hits the stands. Customers would be lined up all the way down the street, begging you to take their credit cards."

"But we're already at our production limit."

"So we carry our regular recipe chocolates and keep the special recipe to limited availability."

"Wouldn't work," Karina said stubbornly. She'd always worried about how to keep the shop small and personal. The potential profits weren't a prime concern when she already had made more than she needed, with a family trust fund untouched except for the capital she'd used to fund her start-up costs and make the down payment on the building.

"Nikki can write a story even without your approval."

Another worry. "Yes, but what if…"

"She exposes you?" Debby shook her head. "Whitney won't let the article get out of hand."

"It's too risky."

"But participating is the only way you can keep some control." Debby turned to Nikki. "Can Karina make it a condition that you don't identify the store?"

Nikki frowned. "The *Hard Candy* readers would demand to know."

"Tough marshmallows." Debby put her hands on her hips. "The publicity would deluge Sutter Chocolat and possibly force us out of business—"

"Ha!" Nikki tossed her hair. "You could expand into a million-dollar success story."

"Not interested," said Karina. "We want to keep the place as a storefront operation."

"Look at it this way," Debby coaxed. "New Yorkers love to be in the know about an exclusive source for their goodies. There are all those restaurants with unpublished numbers and the underground clubs and the invitation-only guest lists."

"Hmm." Nikki's head tilted to one side. "I suppose I can try to come up with an interesting angle that doesn't include your store by name, but it'd have to be provocative to sell to my editors."

"Whitney's our friend. We'll put in a good word and she'll support you."

"All right." Nikki returned to her table and got a couple of business cards out of a quilted leather pocketbook. "Here's my number. I'll be calling you. But in the meantime—" With a sassy wink, she hurriedly stuffed the remainder of her candy selection into a copper take-out bag. "I'll be calling one of my boyfriends, if you know what I mean."

Karina watched her go, then walked around the counter to clean off the table. Most of the customers had cleared out, including the familiar-looking man. Alex had disappeared from his hiding place near the window. No coincidence, with Nikki's departure.

Karina shook her head at Debby. "I don't know about this article. Seems to me we're asking for trouble."

"Yeah!" Debby clapped. The confectioner was almost as gleeful as when she had a new shipment of bulk chocolate from Brazil. "Isn't it fun?"

9

A BITTER WINTER WIND whistled along the street, making banners flap and rattling the bare-branched trees against their cages. Pedestrians kept close to the shelter of the buildings as they hurried for home in the growing dusk. The sky was heavy with leaden clouds.

A good evening to be home in bed, Karina said to herself as she locked up the shop. A week ago, she would have finished that thought by adding *with a good book.* Now, she had Alex. Sort of.

No more sort of *about it,* she decided. *I've had just about enough.*

A vehicle double-parked outside of the store. The horn blatted three short, seemingly exuberant blasts. Debby waved from the curb. "See you tomorrow," she called to Karina as she climbed into Kyle's delivery van.

Karina smiled, watching as Debby leaned toward Kyle with puckered lips despite the honking horns and irate drivers stuck behind them. After a thorough kiss, he put the truck into drive and the stalled traffic got moving again.

Karina shivered. The warmth inside her door was only steps away, but her eyes went to Alex's windows instead. Chances were he'd come over tonight. She could go home and wait. But…

"Screw that," she said.

Gathering up the proverbial head of steam, she jerked her Peruvian-knit hat down over her ears and marched straight across the street, paying no mind to the horn blasts and colorful variations of the F-word that erupted. It was time she set things straight with Alex.

He buzzed her in with only a moment's hesitation. Climbing the two flights of stairs, she readied her case. She would say that she didn't expect a lot from him, but that it might be nice to say hello before they had sex, or even go out for dinner. She'd have to make it clear that he wasn't being turned into, God forbid, an actual *boy-friend,* but just a…a…

Was there a word for this? They weren't friends with benefits, because she couldn't rightly say they were friends.

Strangers with benefits. Ugh.

She rang his doorbell, having reached no conclusion. Alex, and the way she felt about him, were indefinable.

The door opened. "Hi," he said, looking far too good in jeans and a red sweatshirt that had faded almost pink.

"Hi." She pointed at the Syracuse logo. "Did you go?"

"I've been—" He looked down. "Oh. The shirt. Uh, no."

"Where did you go?"

"To college?"

"No, last night." She had intended to be sarcastic, but the instant the words slipped out she realized how true they were. "Of course I meant college," she corrected hastily.

Alex frowned. "Does it matter?"

"I'm not asking for your PIN number."

He rested his hands on his narrow hips, dragging the

unbelted waistband of his jeans down just far enough so a strip of flat, tanned belly was revealed. She wanted to slip her fingers inside the snap, popping it as she pulled him to her for a kiss. But that would be a very distracting direction to go.

"I went…" He closed his eyes for an instant. "I went home because staying would make this too complicated."

"This? What's *this?*" Karina blurted, making the awkward jump from his mystery past to their mystery future.

"Us."

"Is there an us?"

"Not in the conventional way."

She sighed. "Yes. Indeed. Don't you think it's time we figured out what we're doing?"

A wry grin. "I knew you weren't really the spontaneous type."

"Despite evidence to the contrary, you're correct," she said, keeping her gaze low and her hands jammed into her pockets.

He raised an arm and she thought for one moment that he would caress her cheek, but instead he plucked off her hat. "Come on in, I guess."

Not much of an invitation, but she grabbed it, curious to inspect the inside of the apartment she'd only caught glimpses of.

There was little to see. She ducked a head into a narrow slice of a galley kitchen, where all the doors were off the short bank of cupboards and stacked against the wall, revealing meager rations. A round cardboard canister of oatmeal, a jar of peanut butter, packets of single-serving soup. No sign of the truffles, but he might keep them in the fridge.

She followed Alex to the living space. It wasn't two rooms as she'd expected, but only one, L-shaped, with his mattress and box spring on the floor in the nook. Neatly made, with one lone pillow.

One was his motif. One catch-all desk, with a laptop computer and printer, a short stack of papers, one pen, one cup and the carafe from his coffeemaker with a half-inch of coffee so old the sediment had settled. One folding chair. One lamp. One TV, on the floor near the bed, the cord snaking to an outlet that was pulled half-way off the wall.

One window, with a grungy armchair nearby and the binoculars resting on the sill.

Alex had slid his hands into his pockets. He gazed into the space above Karina's head, detached from her survey.

She walked to the window to see her apartment from his viewpoint. In the growing darkness, not much was revealed, but she could imagine the difference once the lights came on. And the show began, she thought with a residual shiver of disbelief.

She cleared her throat. "So…what do you do in here, all day?"

He shrugged. "Not much."

"What about the writing? How's that coming along?"

"Actually, I, uh—" Suddenly, he looked almost bash-ful, and was avoiding her eyes out of too much emotion, not lack of it. "I have a chapter."

"Oh! That's great."

"Not really. I'm sure it's garbage."

She pressed before he could withdraw again. "May I read it?"

He appeared to think that over. When he came up

with no immediate reason not to, she decided to get even pushier and stepped over to swoop up the stack of printed paper.

He made no move to snatch them back. She ruffled the pages under his nose. "Please?"

"Go ahead."

Surprise. "Right now?"

"You might as well, before I trash them."

"Oh, you creative types. Such drama and angst." Chuckling to herself at how decidedly *un*dramatic he was, she pulled off her coat and dropped it on the armchair before collapsing there herself. She laid the pages on her lap and pushed up her sleeves. "You know, I almost thought you were misleading me, about being a writer. It's one of those things that people say—" She mimicked, *"I'm an artist, I'm an actor, I'm a writer...."*

He went to the card table and snapped shut the laptop. "About this, if I'm misleading anyone, it's myself."

"I'm sure your work's not that bad." She rattled the pages. "Chapter one."

Alex put up a hand to silence her. "I'll go make coffee."

Karina nodded. "I could use a cup."

"Yell when you're finished."

She followed him with her eyes. How cute. He was neurotic about her reading his work in front of him. She'd dated a writer once in college, but he'd been the type to make ten photocopies of his work in progress and try to fob them off an anyone with a sniffle of interest or a connection to publishing, however remote. The fledgling relationship had crashed and burned when she'd mildly suggested that using eight adjectives in every sentence was at least a half-dozen too many.

Sixteen pages of double-spaced type didn't take long

to read. At one point, Alex brought her a cup of black coffee and she held it in one hand, balanced on the arm of the chair. As she turned the final pages, she was aware that he'd wandered into the room again, but he didn't sit until she'd finished.

He perched on the folding chair, his elbows on his knees, looking a question at her.

"Wow," she said, then took a sip of the coffee, which had been sweetened with so much sugar she almost choked. She swiped a knuckle over her lips. "I didn't expect a thriller."

"No?"

"I thought maybe a brooding intense character study…"

"We're always wrong about each other."

She looked up from fingering his pages. "Do you think so? Why, because you couldn't understand my carnival collection?" Alex's writing was swirling in her head. "The first chapter was intense. But the violence, coming so quickly—" She shuddered.

In the story, a young criminal lawyer narrowly escapes death when masked killers burst into his office and take out his client, a Mob figure. The chapter ended with the lawyer out on the streets of New York running for his life.

"You didn't like it," Alex said.

"No, it's that I'm surprised. The story was very involving."

"The writing's rough. It's just a first draft."

"Yes, but so visceral. My God. I could *feel* the lawyer's—Mack's—fear. And the description of the shooting. I don't know how you could imagine all of that out of the blue. But then I'm not the creative type."

She took another sip of the awful coffee. "Have you experienced violence like that firsthand?"

Alex straightened. "Of course not." Each word clipped.

"You should get a package together and find an agent. Maybe you'll be the next John Grisham or Scott Turow—"

"Don't jump the gun."

"That would be a great title. *Jump the Gun,* by Alex Anderson." She laughed. "How does that sound?"

"Like you're jumping the gun," he said, but he looked pleased.

"You'll need a female protagonist."

"A blond confectioner?"

"Nah. A blond assassin with a heart of gold and a mean karate kick." She leaned over to put her coffee cup on the floor. A reasonable guess occurred. She slanted a glance at him. "Unless this story is autobiographical…?"

His eyes, previously alight with his involvement, quickly shuttered. "Why would you think that?"

She shrugged, acting nonchalant because she instinctively felt that she'd hit the nail on the head. "Because it's so real."

"Fiction," he said.

She attempted to tease him. "Then your real name isn't Mack Chessler?"

Alex answered so ultra-casually she believed he was covering. If not his name, then *something.* "Nope, 'fraid not."

"Do you have any more written?"

"Not yet."

"Keep going. It's very good." Perhaps he wasn't actually relating his own story verbatim, but she suspected that each chapter would give her further insights into the enigma that was Alex Anderson. Eventually, she hoped, he'd be able to trust her with his real past.

"More coffee?" he asked.

She wrinkled her nose. "How many sugars did you put in it?"

"Three." His mouth twitched. "Another wrong guess?"

"Uh-huh. Despite my business, I don't have a strong sweet tooth. I like my coffee with one Splenda and a touch of cream."

"I had milk, but it was chunky so I dumped it down the drain."

"You don't keep food at home? No wonder you're so thin." Rangy was more like it. She'd felt the muscles and sinew of his body rippling under her hands, honed to a fine whipcord athleticism. Like the character Mack, he could flee, if he needed to.

"When do you eat?" she asked, glancing over her shoulder at the bed on the floor. They'd made progress this evening, but the possibility of sex loomed in her mind. How easy it would be to walk into Alex's arms and lean down to kiss him, and within minutes they'd be shedding clothes and tumbling onto the bed....

But I didn't come here for that.

He hadn't answered. "Do you have any of the chocolate left?" she asked idly.

"What was that about your lack of sweet tooth?"

Was he evading the question or only teasing? She couldn't tell, just as she couldn't tell about a lot of things with Alex.

She rested her head against the back of the chair, narrowing her eyes at him. "Gosh, you're dense. I'm hinting for sustenance, here."

"I'll go grab us some takeout."

"We could call for delivery," she said. "Or even go out."

"Out?" he repeated, as if he'd never heard the word.

"Yes, *out.* Putting on coats, walking to a restaurant, sitting at a table and ordering off menus like normal people. Thousands and thousands are doing it all around the city at this very moment. We don't have to call it a date. Just dinner."

There was a long silence. She watched him silently debate with himself before he quirked one corner of his mouth, attempting to charm her into doing this his way. "Seems like a lot of bother."

"So is picking up takeout."

"All right. We'll do delivery then. You have a cell phone, right?"

She rolled the sheaf of pages into one hand. "Yes, but this is ridiculous. Is there some reason you don't want to be seen in public with me? Are we supposed to conduct this affair strictly out of our apartments?"

"I told you not to expect much from me."

"Uh-huh. I seem to remember that." She sat forward. "Are you agoraphobic?"

"No."

"A werewolf?"

"Karina." He narrowed his eyes. "Don't do this."

"It's not a full moon, you know." Her laughter had a hard edge. "It's safe to go out tonight."

"I'm not a werewolf," he said with a clenched jaw.

"Are you—oh, I don't know—*famous?*" She gestured carelessly, sending the pages flying. They spilled across the floor. "I'm sorry," she said, immediately getting down on her knees to gather them up.

"Leave them." Alex pulled her up. "I'm not famous."

She rested her forehead against his chest. "I know that. But I'm trying to understand you."

"No, you're asking for more from me. And I can't give it."

"Why not?" she whispered, spasmodically closing her fingers over bunched folds of his sweatshirt.

"I told you. I'll be moving on soon. There's no use in getting involved."

"I'm not looking for a functioning—"

"Yes, you are." His palm brushed across her back, soothing her.

"Only going out to dinner," she continued blindly. "Is that too much to ask for?"

"Maybe not," he conceded, "but what happens after that? We spend more time together, and soon we have a standing arrangement. Then you introduce me to your friends. We fall in love…."

She couldn't believe he'd said that. And although her first impulse was to cling to her mistaken notion that she could have a fling without becoming involved, that would be simply stupid. The sex was getting all mixed up with emotion, and if she was totally honest she'd admit to being halfway in love with him already. Foolish, when she knew so little about him. She'd pinned a lot of her hopes on the way he seemed to be struggling over their relationship, but maybe that was part of his tortured-artist act and in reality all he'd wanted was a piece of her ass. After all, she was making assumptions about his character based on very limited evidence.

"We fall in love," he repeated. She felt his mouth moving against her hair. "And then I have to go. And then your heart is broken. I don't want to hurt you that way."

He cares for me.

"But you don't have to go. You could stay."

"No, it's possible—likely—that I'll leave at a moment's notice."

"Called back to the mother planet," she quipped, although she was in no mood to joke.

Alex kissed her temple.

"You're a spymaster."

His hands moved from her elbows to her shoulders, then around to her back, stroking warmth into her chilled bones. He kissed one eyelid, touching his tongue to her closed lid in a way that made her suck in a breath and go very quiet.

"You're on an undercover assignment," she whispered.

Ignoring her, he kissed the other eyelid. She held still, playing meek while plotting her first move. Except every move she thought of required staying in and getting physically intimate, not going out and coaxing him to reveal his well-hidden thoughts.

"My competitor has sent you to steal the secret recipe," she guessed.

"Yeah, that's why I need to taste you." He licked his tongue between her lips, parting them with delicate precision. She rose up to her toes to return the kiss, squeezing and bunching his shirt in her fists until she'd pulled it taut across his back.

Suddenly his head lifted. "What secret recipe?"

"Family recipe," she said, then cocked her head back. "You haven't noticed that my chocolates are extra good?"

"Of course," he said, kissing her again.

"You don't have to—" She put her hand over his mouth to push him away. "I'm fine with you not eating them. Really. Guys don't seem to have the same appre-

ciation for the chocolate as women. But they learn to."
She raised her eyebrows.

"Well, for me, it's not a matter of acquiring a taste—"

"You're already a connoisseur. That's obvious every time we kiss."

Alex looked confused, until she kissed him, and then he knew exactly what to do. He felt very good, very right, in her arms—though there was less urgency, there was also a sweeter tone to their intimacy.

"So let's do it," he said, breaking off a kiss.

Thud. Had she been thinking he was sweet?

"Let's go out to dinner like normal people."

Oh! "Why the sudden change?" she asked.

He wasn't quite meeting her gaze. "It's only dinner, right?"

"Absolutely."

"I don't know why I was opposed." His eyes skimmed her face. "As long as you understand…"

She nodded emphatically. "Yes, of course. It's only dinner."

LATE THE NEXT AFTERNOON, Alex was back at the window. Perhaps he'd been overly paranoid these past several weeks, but nearly being killed did that to a guy.

The previous evening with Karina had been like balancing on his board at the edge of a monstrous wave, racing toward the protection of a distant shore but fearing he'd never reach it in time. Given his situation, his life would always be unstable. Safety could be snatched away at any second.

He'd told Karina good-night at her door. Her bewilderment had pulled his heartstrings, but he'd remained firm. After going over the decision endlessly in his mind for the past few days, he'd convinced himself that leaving her was the courageous thing to do.

Except that leaving is for cowards, he thought, lifting the binoculars. The real test would have been taking up her challenge for more than a dinner out in public. But he was still too wary to open himself up that way.

Early on, in L.A. after Rafael Norris had followed through on the first of his death threats by arranging the execution of the defendant who'd killed his son, Alex had made it his business to learn how to create his own false identity and leave no tracks, independent of the Feds, never imagining how soon he'd use the skills.

Following the attempt on his life in Florida, he'd faced the stark reality of a lifetime of being completely on his own.

His life savings were in a numbered account, but were dwindling rapidly. The original plan for his life as Alex Anderson had been to find a job in the city as soon as he was comfortable that he was safe, keep his head down and hope like hell that he wouldn't be found again.

Karina had changed all that. Like it or not, he was involved with her.

He had two options: kiss her goodbye, and get out while the getting was good, or make the leap of faith that he'd been clever enough about creating his new identity that no one would find him.

It happened. Wanted persons could live for years, happy and unharmed. They held down everyday average jobs, they married, they had families, with no one ever suspecting the truth.

That prospect was tempting. Each minute with Karina made him want it more. The problem was that he'd be risking her to please himself.

No way.

Back to option one.

Alex watched the street, paying particular attention to Karina's shop. Sure enough, here came the man in question, short and slightly round, garbed in a trench coat and muffler, with the lenses in his glasses fogging up as he stepped from a warm cab into the cold air. In the course of Alex's daily observations, he'd begun to notice the frequent customer and wonder about him.

The man always ordered a hot drink, sat and read the newspaper. Nothing particularly suspicious in that, except for the frequency. And, as Alex had noted, the man's preoccupation from behind his newspaper with the goings-on in the shop.

A henchman hired by Rafael Norris—well-funded by his "career" as a Southern California drug trafficker—would be slick and professional. This guy seemed like an amateur. Still, the chocolate shop was a perfect observation point, so Alex had continued to keep track of the bespectacled customer in case the guy was keeping track of *him.*

Even Karina had noticed the man. She thought he was hooked on her chocolates, or interested in one of her clerks. Throughout dinner, she'd chatted in nervous stops and starts about everything that was happening in her life, filling in the blank spots in their conversation whenever Alex managed to dodge another of her questions about his past, his family, his likes and dislikes and on and on. He'd fished for more information on the customer, but she'd had nothing to tell.

Alex focused on the suspicious guy as he entered Sutter Chocolat. As usual, the man waited patiently in line, placed an order, went to sit at one of the tables. He sipped the drink while surreptitiously studying the store. At most, he'd exchange a few words with the employees—the clerks in their aprons, the girl who greeted the deliveryman when he came to pick up an outgoing shipment.

Not once had he revealed an interest in the building across the street. Alex had begun to accept that his suspicions were baseless.

Karina must be right. Still, it didn't hurt to keep an eye on the lurker anyway. Alex lowered the binoculars and got more comfortable in the armchair, settling in to be patient.

HE AWOKE WITH A START a long while later. Bewildered for a moment about where he was, even confused that there was no sea salt in the air. Until he looked out the window and his hellish situation snapped back to him.

Except that it was night. By the looks of the neighborhood, late night. The businesses were closed and gated. He'd managed to sleep for hours, when usually he woke frequently, attuned to every suspect noise.

He stood, stretching to relieve his stiff muscles. Karina's windows were closed and dark. Had she waited for him? Seen his silhouette in the chair and tried to get his attention?

Alex grunted and went to check the time on the clock on the stove. He'd always been a slacker about being on time, and had raced through the L.A. courthouse corridors on countless occasions, tucking in his shirt or knotting a tie. But at least he'd owned a watch in those days, and a clock. Now he'd given up caring, because he'd sunk so low that he'd believed there was nothing left to care about.

Karina might be his last chance at happiness. But only if he were willing to risk her.

"Stop," he said out loud. Why go over it again? The pipes rattled when he turned the faucet on. He splashed cold water on his face and returned to the window, drying himself on the sleeve of his T-shirt.

He'd never be able to go back to sleep. But what was he going to do—sit by the window and stare out at her place like a lovesick puppy dog?

A cab stopped a short way down from Karina's door. A passenger moved in the back seat and for a moment he thought it might be her, until the figure emerged, bundled in a puffy ski jacket with the hood up, a deep ruff of fur trim obscuring the person's face.

Were the passenger's movements fervent? Suspicious?

Alex let out a huff of air. Face it, he was obsessed.

But he continued watching as the passenger sidled along the sidewalk until the cab drove away, then walked briskly to the door of Sutter Chocolat. Alex estimated that it was a man of average build, but he wasn't even certain of that.

The door opened before the person knocked and he slipped inside.

Karina had a visitor, Alex thought.

To her store.

After 1:00 a.m.

With the lights out?

Every instinct that he'd developed in the past year was screaming on red alert. He damned himself for not keeping a cell phone, for not even getting her number.

He wanted to run to her rescue, but he delayed, waiting to see if lights would go on in the store and if somehow the late-night visit would make sense.

When that didn't happen, he yanked his gun out from beneath the mattress, grabbed his keys off the table and left the apartment. He took the stairs at a gallop, slowing only when he paused to tuck the gun into his waistband before stepping out the street door into the frozen air.

Shit. No jacket. That would look odd, if he was being watched. He curled his hands up into his sleeves, hunched his shoulders and took off at a brisk walk, risking no glance at Karina's shop.

Once he was far enough away, he cut across the street and sped to the door that led to the living quarters above the shop. Locked, dammit. Of course. Alex leaned on the button for Karina's apartment, wasting precious minutes trying to raise a response.

No answer. Not home? Or…

There were too many variables. Before he made a move, he had to be sure she wasn't in her apartment. He jammed his fingers down on every other apartment's buzzer until finally a shambling male figure wrapped in a robe appeared on the other side of the glass. Instead of pajamas, a regular shirt and pants showed underneath. The tenant rubbed his eyes and peered out. "Door's locked."

Obviously. Alex's attempt at a smile was pathetic. "I'm a visitor." Discreetly, he pulled out the tail of his shirt to cover the gun at the small of his back.

"Not mine, you're not. Buzz the apartment you want or go away."

"I tried that. No answer."

The tenant's face pressed against the glass, looking him over. "Can't help you."

"Please, just go and knock on Karina's door," he said, straining to keep his voice low. "She should be home, but she's not answering. I'm worried about her. Tell her Alex is downstairs. She'll let me in."

After an agonizing minute, the man nodded and returned to the stairs, climbing so slowly in his flapping slippers that Alex was ready to go ahead and just shoot out the glass. He jogged in place, although the adrenaline in his system was doing a good job of zapping away the cold.

When no response came, he pressed Karina's buzzer again and again. *Please be asleep. Just asleep.*

Finally the intercom crackled. "Who is it?" Karina said, in a sleepy voice. "Do you know how late it is?"

"I know. But this is—" He caught himself, aware that the neighbor could be listening in. Strangely, the man apparently hadn't given Karina Alex's name. "It's important. I have to see you right now."

She inhaled. "All right." She buzzed him through.

Alex ran up the stairs, arriving as she shooed the robed neighbor back inside his apartment. "Sorry to disturb you, Mr. Alonzo. I don't normally have visitors at this time...."

Alex hustled her inside, not caring that Alonzo was watching with some suspicion, holding a cell phone in his hand.

He slammed the door. "Quick, tell me if—"

"Alex!" She went to throw her arms around him. "You came."

"Stop, Karina." He clasped her shoulders, holding her away. "Listen to me. There's someone in your shop."

"Someone in my shop? Oh, come on." It took a couple of seconds for her to process that he hadn't arrived at her apartment for his nightly visit. "What do you mean? Burglars?"

"Maybe not." He stepped back, trying to think of rational reasons for what he'd seen. "Who has the key?"

"Only me and Debby."

"Would she have any reason to be down there right now?"

"Well, no, unless…" Karina looked bemused. "Unless she ran out of chocolate."

"You're not serious." He'd heard of chocoholics, but this was ridiculous. "Hold on, let me explain. I saw a man arrive in a cab, and someone let him into your store. Do you see? Someone was already inside. I couldn't tell who, but it's safe to assume the person had either a key or the alarm code."

"Was it Kyle in the cab? The buff delivery guy," she elaborated when she saw Alex's confusion. "He's Debby's boyfriend, so if it's her downstairs, we'd better not disturb them. They might have stopped by for, ah, dessert."

"What? Wait a minute. This man wasn't built—he was on the short side. I didn't get a good look at him, but he *might* have been the lurker you mentioned."

"How can that be?" Karina let out a yelp, finally realizing that the situation was serious.

"It's no ordinary break-in. The alarm didn't go off." Alex paused. "I think it's an inside job. Maybe one of your employees?"

Unless Norris had managed to track him down again, Alex thought, with a stone-cold horror. But if that had been the case, holing up in Karina's shop made no sense. Even for a sniper.

Karina gasped. "Industrial espionage! They might be after my secret recipe. Alex, we've got to call the police."

He'd rather not have the cops involved lest they ask too many questions, but there was no way out of it. "All right. You do that, and I'll go downstairs. Lock the door behind me and don't come out no matter what until the cops are here."

She grabbed at his arm. "No, Alex. That's too dangerous—"

"It's okay." He reached behind him. "I have a gun."

Karina stared at the illegal firearm he slipped out of his waistband. "Alex—my God. Where did you get that?"

10

"DON'T FREAK. This is my protection, just in case." Alex palmed the small silver gun before reaching for her door. "We don't know what's going on downstairs."

Karina grabbed at his arm. "All the more reason for you to stay here." Let them have her recipe, as long as Alex stayed safe. "You can't run around with a gun. That's crazy. You'll shoot somebody. You'll shoot *yourself.*"

He managed a grim smile. "The safety's on."

An explanation hit her like a hammer. "Were you a cop?" Shock froze her blood. "Are you *still* a cop? L-like on a stakeout?"

"No," he said, swinging past the door. "Stay inside. But give me your keys so I can get in without them hearing me. I'll need the alarm code, in case they've turned it back on."

She'd handed over the keys and repeated the pass code before she had a chance to think it over. He was no longer a stranger, but…

"Alex. Wait."

He looked at her, his blank face showing nothing.

She stalled at his cold efficiency. If he wasn't a professional of some sort—NYPD, P.I., FBI—what was he?

"This is too dangerous," she blurted. "I can't let you go."

"You are not coming with me."

"Then please stay here with me." Good idea. She was determined not to be one of those brainless girls in movies and books who insist on going along, only to end up getting in the way or becoming a hostage of the bad guys. She had more sense than that. But then she never expected her life to feature such drama either.

"We're wasting time." Alex reached for her. In the movies, he would have pulled her into his arms for a brief hard kiss and said he loved her. Instead he pushed on her shoulder, urging her back inside. "Go call the police."

"All right." She gulped. "Promise me you'll be careful."

"Don't worry. It's probably Debby."

"Then don't you dare shoot her!" Karina called after him, even though she knew he was only reassuring her. At first she hadn't believed he was serious about a break-in. But an attempt to steal her recipe made sense. She'd turned down many lucrative offers.

She ran to call 9-1-1, was put on hold for an agonizing minute, then reported her address and wasted more valuable time trying to explain why the shop's security alarm hadn't gone off. "It's got to be an inside job," she said, repeating Alex's assertion, and was poleaxed by the likelihood. How? Who?

She hung up the phone, put a robe on over her pajamas and went to hover in the hallway, listening for sounds of a chase—or gunshots.

Mr. Alonzo appeared, creased with worry. "What's happening?" he whispered.

"There's been a break-in at my shop…we think."

Her neighbor reached inside his open door. "I have a baseball bat. I can go downstairs to aid your young man with apprehending the burglars."

"Oh…no. Please don't do that. I'm sure—" She exhaled in relief as the sound of sirens grew closer. "Thank goodness. The police are coming."

But the sirens faded as the vehicle veered off onto another street. "Any minute now," she added, then it hit her that it could be awhile yet. Meanwhile, Alex was alone downstairs, playing the hero.

"Give me that bat," she said to Mr. Alonzo.

He wouldn't release it. "We'll go together."

Karina shoved her feet into boots and grabbed a ski pole from the back of her hall closet. Some backups they made. But she wasn't willing to wait forever, whether or not her common sense was screaming to leave the thieves to Alex. He'd seemed strangely cool and competent. Why was a question for later.

She and Mr. Alonzo hurried downstairs. "We'll just take a peek," Karina said as they crossed the frosty sidewalk from the apartment door to the shop. The door was open, the alarm shut down, the shop dark and quiet. If there had been a burglary, no damage was visible.

They stood just inside the entrance, listening. "I don't hear a thing," Mr. Alonzo said, lowering the bat.

"But what if—" Karina swallowed. She imagined Alex bludgeoned, bleeding, unable to call for help.

"Stay here. I'll go look in back."

"We'll both go." She remembered her resolution not to be the blundering fool. "But carefully."

They tiptoed across the shop and peeked through the porthole window in the swinging door that opened to the short hallway of the reception area. Nothing to see, except the glow of a light.

Karina put a finger to her lips. Mr. Alonzo nodded and they quietly moved inside, the door making a small sound as it swung shut behind them. She peeped around the corner. The desk lamp on Janine's desk was on. The door to her own office stood open.

Mr. Alonzo hefted the bat as they looked inside. Again, nothing seemed to have been disturbed, but all the lights were on in the windowless office.

"They've been here," Karina whispered, glancing behind the desk to be sure there wasn't a body lying on the floor.

"Don't touch anything," Mr. Alonzo said when she tucked the ski pole under her arm and went to open the narrow coat closet. "Fingerprints."

She stopped. Her eyes went to the wood panel that fronted the wall safe. If the intruders knew the layout of the office, they'd start there in a search for her secret recipe.

Suppose Alex had been wrong? Or led her wrong?

No, that was ridiculous.

But he's been watching you—and the shop—through binoculars.

Only to plan such an elaborate ruse? "Forget it," she muttered.

Mr. Alonzo looked at her, silently questioning.

"The kitchen," she said. "This way."

They passed through the second corridor lined with shelves—at a glance, untouched—and were about to step into the dark kitchen when a hand touched Karina's shoulder.

She let out a yell and whirled with the ski pole raised, but Alex caught it in midair. "You'll put an eye out," he said.

"Alex!" Relief washed through her, pushing out the moment's fear. "How did you get behind us?"

"I went out the back door, looking for the burglars, then I couldn't get back in again and I had to come around." The back exit was a self-locking safety door that opened to a narrow walkway between buildings.

"You didn't catch them." Karina was just as glad, especially when she thought of his gun. It had disappeared again. Her gaze went to his face. He appeared very contained, though breathing hard.

He took the ski pole. "Didn't even see them, I'm afraid, except for hearing the back door close. They must have heard me coming in the front and were able to leave in time."

"Oh, no—the grate." Karina led the two men back to the office and pointed to a decorative grate in the ceiling. "I forgot. My hallway is right above, and voices carry through the grate. It's never mattered because I'm usually here during work hours."

Alex stared at the ceiling. "Damn."

"Seems lucky to me," Mr. Alonzo said, looking greatly relieved. "The burglary was stopped before it started."

If there even were a burglary to begin, Karina thought, in spite of herself. The story seemed absurd, except that Alex had no knowledge of her valuable recipe. And she trusted him, the same way she was drawn to him—instinctively.

He studied her and Mr. Alonzo with eyes as flat as dull silver coins. "Do you see anything out of place?"

"Aside from the lights…" She shrugged. "Give me a minute. I'll check the office."

"Fingerprints," Mr. Alonzo said again.

Alex shook his head. "It's doubtful the police will dust for prints, especially since there's no evidence that anything was touched. And this being—" He looked at Karina again, with a shrug. "An inside job."

Mr. Alonzo was curious. "An inside job?"

"We don't know that." Karina was dismayed at the prospect since she'd been so careful about hiring, especially after a problem with an earlier employee who'd been caught filching from the cash registers. She went to sit behind her desk. "Someone's been on my computer."

Alex appeared to look over her shoulder. "How do you know?"

"The keyboard's been moved. Only a couple of inches, but I can tell." She tapped the key to remove the screensaver. "I don't know if it's possible to tell if they tried to access my files, but they couldn't get in because I have a special password-protected program for documents like my customer addresses and our recipes and suppliers."

"Our voices must have scared them off." Alex didn't sound entirely convinced. "Is my name on your customer list?"

"You're not a customer. Yet. The truffles were a gift." She closed down the computer. "I didn't even know your name at the time."

"The police are here," Mr. Alonzo called from the doorway. "I'll go let them in."

Alex moved away. "Listen…" He paused, shifting nervously from foot to foot. "Don't tell them about my gun, okay?"

She stood with a snap, shooting her desk chair back. "Why not?"

"Just don't."

"I want to know why."

"Later," he said, looking toward the noise at the front of the shop.

"Promise me an explanation," Karina insisted.

Alex seemed reluctant, but he gave her a quick nod before leaving to greet the law. Karina grimaced, not at all sure that she was doing the right thing. Once more, she listened to her heart instead of her head and decided to believe in him.

"YOU'RE VERY CALM," Alex said, some time later after the police had departed. Karina had relentlessly combed her office looking for clues until finally he'd taken her by the hand and led her upstairs to her apartment. He'd sat her on the sofa, wrapped her in a white-fur throw, and gone to make her a cup of coffee with a shot of cognac. He'd taken one swig himself. For the Dutch courage to keep on lying.

"Thinking," she said, holding the mug under her chin.

"About?"

"How a person on my staff could have done this."

"Literally?" he asked, to stall. She'd resisted the idea that she might have been betrayed and had sworn up and down that there was no one who'd do that to her.

"Yes. How would a person get into the shop?" She sighed before answering herself. "They would have had to get a key and the security code, but I suppose that wouldn't be too difficult. I've punched it in with employees standing right there beside me."

Alex sat beside her and she pulled her elbow in, keeping her face turned away from him. He'd had her change the code when they locked up after he'd negotiated the tricky dealings with the cops. "Where do you keep the keys?"

"In my purse. Sometimes in a desk drawer." She sighed again. "Or even on the desk."

"What's so valuable about this recipe?" When she'd mentioned the various files, he'd considered the possibility that the intruders had been after his address. Which only showed that his paranoia was way out of bounds since he was right across the street, in plain view. Particularly if the constant lurker and the night's second burglar were one and the same.

"My chocolate's unique." Karina stirred beneath the synthetic fur. "You still haven't noticed?"

"I've told you. Chocolate's not my thing."

"So you say." She sipped the hot drink. "Trust me. Milton Hershey would die for my recipe, if he wasn't already…" She shuddered. "Dead."

"Would you die defending it?"

She stiffened. "What? I was kidding. No one's going to *die*."

"That depends. Where do you keep the recipe?"

"Don't worry," she said. "It's safe."

"*In* the safe?" She'd opened the hidden safe for the police, who had been singularly unimpressed by their story of burglars who took nothing and immediately departed the scene after hearing their voices through the grate.

"Not in the safe. In a security box at the bank, but…" She gnawed her lip. "It's not only about the recipe. There's also the supplier. I get a special chocolate made from a particular cocoa bean that's sold only to me. Expensive, but worth it. And the contact info for my supplier is on the computer."

"Would a business rival be aware of this?"

She shook her head. "I don't think so. Debby is my only confidante. But other employees, particularly the kitchen help, probably know since they've been instructed to treat the bulk chocolate shipments and the occasional package of the raw cocoa beans with special care."

"These deliveries—they come the usual way?"

Karina shot him a furious look. She shoved the fur down and set her coffee mug on the table. "What are you suggesting? Debby's in cahoots with Kyle? That makes no sense. She already knows the recipe since she uses it every time she makes a new batch."

"It was only a question. I'm trying to look at this from all angles. Who's this Kyle again?"

Karina nodded, but with reluctance. "I already explained. Kyle is Debby's new guy, our regular delivery-man. They suddenly got the hots for each other—"

"Oh."

"Don't go there, Alex. I trust Debby completely."

"But what about Kyle?"

"You said it wasn't him, getting out of the cab."

"What if I was wrong?"

"Do your binoculars often deceive you?"

"No."

"Well, then." Karina's tone was dry. "It seems to me that you're the only mysterious stranger on the scene. But you don't see me accusing you, even though you're the one with the gun." She shivered again. "I hate that you have a gun."

He tried to pull the fur back over her, but she resisted.

He cleared his throat. "Thanks for keeping quiet with the cops." It had been tense, making himself answer their questions with complete nonchalance when he knew that one slipup could collapse his identity like a house of cards.

"Where is it? If you move too suddenly, will it shoot a hole through my couch?"

"Don't worry. I removed the ammo."

"Wonderful," she said with sarcasm, then sank back down onto the firm cushions and pulled the fur up to her chin, absorbed in thought. After a minute, she looked at him, her eyes narrowed to crescents. "And so…?"

He'd been waiting for her to ask. "The gun is only for protection, like I said. I'm not an undercover cop. Not a bank robber, either. I don't fit any of the crazy scenarios you might come up with." Except the only one she hadn't thought of.

"Uh-huh. Then why were you worried about the police?"

He'd have to give her that one. "The gun's not legal."

She frowned. "Why not?"

"Um, because I'm not into paperwork?"

"This is no joking matter. I want to know the truth."

You can't handle the truth. Hell, I can't handle the truth.

"You weren't in advertising, were you?" she continued. "Did you even live in Arizona?"

"No," he said, and then couldn't make himself come up with a lie to cover the previous lie. He had to tell her some version of the truth—he owed her that.

She turned away from him, hugging herself beneath the fur throw, and he gave in to the impulse to follow her, molding his chest to her curved back, enfolding her in his arms. She shuddered beneath them and said, "Don't touch me," but he didn't stop. He couldn't.

She didn't fight the embrace. The opposite, in fact. She softened against him. "Did you *ever* tell me the truth?"

For once, he was able to say, "Yes."

A minute, maybe two, passed. Then, quietly: "When were you honest?"

"When I was inside you."

She let out a slow exhale. Her head dropped forward, away from his, but then tilted to rest against his arm. "I've been following my instincts with you, trusting you even when my common sense says I shouldn't. This is very unlike me."

He closed his eyes. Honored.

"But I want you to know, I can't keep it up. Tonight, for instance. I had this thought—" She stopped.

He knew what she wanted to say. "You were suspicious of my story about the intruders. Are you still?"

"I should be. I know I should be." Her hand crept out from beneath the fur and took hold of his forearm, where he'd crossed them across her chest. An abiding affection for her shot through him, pure and strong.

"When will you tell me who you are?" she asked.

The last thing he wanted was for any of that ugliness to stain Karina. But asking for her blind faith was too much to demand.

His head inclined beside hers and he breathed the perfume of her hair. "I'm just a guy who's starting his life over from scratch."

"Mmm." Lazily, she rubbed her cheek against his arm. "That's no explanation."

Saying nothing, he clicked off the standing lamp behind the sofa. The sheen of the white curtains softened the glare of the streetlights. A light snow had begun to fall and the flecks danced in the strange silvery-orange glow that filled the windows.

Karina exhaled, her body growing lax. "You promised me…"

"Sleep," he said, and she did.

He drifted off, too, stirring only when the grinding

rumble of a truck on the street woke him with a start. For several minutes, he stayed where he was, treasuring the gift of holding Karina in his arms. Her hair spilled across his shoulder, one smooth cheek turned up near his face. He kissed it before slowly sliding away.

Moving gingerly, he stood and tucked the fur around her again after she'd murmured and nestled against the sofa cushions. She was out like a light, trusting him in spite of herself. A trust he'd done nothing to earn.

Now was the time for him to decide. After Florida, he'd sworn that he'd leave his next life at the first sign of anything out of the ordinary. But rationally, the break-in—for lack of a better word—couldn't be about him. And Karina needed his help. He had to stay.

"A little while longer," he mouthed. Just until he knew she was safe.

Or…he could truly dedicate himself to living a new life. A real one. He'd made a resolution to be normal, after Karina had come to his apartment the first time, but that hadn't lasted long. To do it right, he'd have to commit to more than a haircut and a shave.

Now wasn't the time to decide, with the threat to at least one of them in play. But if he didn't do it now, would he ever?

He walked out. Took the stairs slowly at first, but then faster as decision prickled in his blood. Picking up speed, he emerged from the building and crossed the ice-rimmed road at a fast stride, his breath coming out in vaporous puffs.

Into his building, up the stairs, his pulse drumming. He didn't bother to turn on the light in his apartment or check for signs of intruders, but went right to the windowsill. The binoculars weren't there.

He found them on the floor. Snatched them up. Damned glasses, keeping the world at bay.

He was so consumed, he left his door hanging open and didn't care. The roof was several flights up. He ascended in lunges, two, even three steps at a time. One thought in his head.

To put an end to his fear.

The heavy black tar of the roof was as hard as cement in the cold. He went straight to the back of the building, where there was an opening among the crowded structures, little more than an air shaft.

He hefted the glasses, shoulder-height. Higher. Over his head.

Rearing back, muscles stretching. *Now.*

He threw the binoculars over the edge. Using all his strength, his arms swinging down as if he wielded a sledgehammer. The glasses hit the pavement with a sharp crack. Splitting the cold gray dawn.

He turned away without looking over the edge. Turned toward the sunrise sending an arrow of light onto the chalky red brick of Karina's building.

NIKKI SILK, KARINA WROTE on a notepad the following day, right after she'd hung up the phone. The magazine writer had called to ask for a tour of the shop. She was collecting background information for her article. Karina had tried to put the tour off, but Nikki wasn't taking no for an answer. They'd finally settled on a date later in the week, but the young woman's pushy inquisitiveness had roused Karina's hackles. Although she couldn't see a connection, she added Nikki's name to her suspects list.

All the employees were there, regardless of her trust

in them. Janine and a part-time clerk headed the list, simply because they were the newest. Next was the one worker she'd had to fire earlier that year for pilfering from the till, followed by the rest of the staff.

Reluctantly, she added Kyle's name. And Debby, as his inside connection. Immediately she crossed Debby out with heavy strokes of the pen, and wrote in Alex, and a question mark.

Alex? No, not him. The incident with the intruders made no sense if Alex was in on it. More cross-outs.

Unless the entire thing was a ruse to gain access to her shop. He'd told her not to follow him. If she and Mr. Alonzo hadn't, an expert safecracker might have had time to get in and out before the police had arrived.

"Ridiculous," she said, stabbing her pen on the notepad. "Convoluted. Impossible."

The familiar-looking customer went on the list, even though there was no way for her to track him down. She would question him next time he showed up, *if* he showed up.

Not likely. She decided that he was her prime suspect. Perhaps he'd gotten to one of the employees, promised them a lucrative payoff if they helped him acquire her trade secrets.

Janine buzzed on the intercom, even though Karina's door was open. "Debby Caruso to see you. Don't forget you have that appointment with the wholesaler in twelve minutes."

Debby leaned past Janine's desk, waving.

Karina made a face at the chef, suppressing the urge to giggle as she pressed the intercom button. She intoned, "Thank you, Janine. Please send Ms. Caruso in."

"How can you stand her?" Debby said before she'd quite closed the door.

"Shh. Janine's not so bad. Very serious, that's all. She's a good worker."

"But she's attentive to the point of intrusiveness. That would get on my nerves."

"Seems to me that Kyle's being very attentive."

"Yeah, funny enough, his attentions tend to soothe me." Debby stretched luxuriously before plopping into the visitor's chair. "I was very well attended over the weekend. How about you?"

"Hmm." Karina turned over her notepad. "How's it going with Kyle?"

"Too good to be true. There have been a few moments where I wondered if this was all about sex—"

Karina raised her brows. "You have a problem with that?"

"Are you kidding?" Debby grinned. "But we haven't been big talkers up to now, so I tried to get him to open up. Turns out he likes making model race cars and lives at home with his widowed mother in Queens. Well, in a studio apartment above the garage. The man's a nerd in a muscle suit. Who knew?"

"Does that bother you?"

"Nope. It was almost a relief. I'm a nerd, too. But…" Debby pushed her bangs back. Her mouth puckered. "He did hint this morning that there may be a fly in the ointment. He said he has something to discuss. He actually said *discuss*. You know that's bad, coming from a man. I think he's keeping something from me."

Karina's skin prickled. "That sounds worrisome. What do you think it's about?"

"Oh, you know…whatever." Debby waved a hand,

wearing her brave-soldier expression. "I'll be sure to have a supply of truffles on hand to cure the problem."

Karina shook her head. "A temporary cure…"

"For a temporary relationship," Debby said lightly, although her mouth turned down.

Certain that Debby was more serious about Kyle than she let on, Karina crossed her fingers under the desk and sent up a quick wish. *For Debby's sake, please don't let him be involved in the break-in.*

"It'll be okay, Deb."

"Sure." Debby brushed at her bangs. "Anyway, what did you want to see me about?"

First thing that morning, Karina had gone to the kitchen to check on a few items. She'd asked Debby to drop by the office when she had a free minute. Alex had advised her to keep the attempted burglary quiet for now, so that they could concoct a plan to apprehend the prowlers. But Karina couldn't be compliant. In the unlikely event that Kyle was involved, Debby should have fair warning.

Karina nipped her lip, searching for words. "There's something going on that I wanted you to know about."

"Ooh. Sounds serious."

"Actually, yes. I believe that an unknown employee has attempted to pry into my computer records. After hours."

"What!"

"Looking for the recipe, I expect."

Debby crossed her arms, frowning. "Got to be Janine."

"Shh. Not so loud. She's probably listening at the door." Karina leaned over the desk. "Why Janine? You're just saying that because you don't like her."

"All right, I admit our personalities clash. But she is

new, and frighteningly professional, like the Stepford
secretary. Is there anyone else you'd suspect first?"

"Shelby's new too, and I know much less about her,
where I've worked closely with Janine." Karina made a
helpless gesture. "But really, I have no idea. The thing
is, it appears this person has a copy of the key to the
front door. Or maybe lifted one of the spares. I wanted
to check in with you since you're the only one who has
a set. Have your keys gone missing, maybe?"

"They're always in my purse."

"And your purse is…"

"Always in the kitchen. Oh."

"You see my quandary."

Debby frowned. "Well, what about the recipe?
Everyone has access to—"

Karina raised a finger to her lips. She shook her head.

Debby whispered, her eyes lighting up. "We could
conduct a covert investigation of the likely suspects."

"I don't want the staff all upset, when we're so busy
with the holidays."

"But industrial espionage is a serious issue. You can't
put it off. What if this mystery person has backers who
can buy the Brazilian chocolate out from beneath you?"

"Ugh. I don't want to even imagine that."

Debby was getting excited. "I'm with you, Kare, one
for all. What can we do?"

"For now, keep quiet, but be observant. I'm working
on a plan."

Debby waited expectantly, but Karina shrugged, giving no more details. She had nothing, except her trust
in Alex.

Slowly, a shadow crept over Debby's face. She
shifted in the chair, absently running a finger beneath

her chin. "Are you sure the suspect is an employee? I just can't believe that any of my kitchen workers would be involved. I know them."

Karina nodded glumly. "Unless someone here thinks they can sell the recipe for quick cash, an outside source is probably the instigator. But we have to face that there might well be an employee connection."

Debby jumped up. "I'd better get back to work." With an almost perfunctory, "Don't worry, we'll be just fine," she departed.

Karina's smile faded, along with her confidence. She sat unmoving for several minutes, various suspicions filling her head, vaguely annoyed by the way Janine crossed back and forth through the outside office, glancing at Karina with each pass.

Resolutely, she turned to the computer, typed in her password, opened the supplier file and removed the contact information for her source in Brazil. Trying not to think of the cliché about shutting the barn door after the cow's run away, she changed the password, committed it to memory, then wrote a fake one—KJSTRSTALEX—on a snippet of paper. She added random numbers that simulated the safe combination. Taped the paper under her blotter.

A totally obvious hiding spot, but that was the point.

11

KARINA WAS CERTAIN she'd fallen into a fairy tale. "I've never seen anything so beautiful," she told Alex, her gaze rising up and up and up to the hand-hewn rafters and the four-tiered crystal chandeliers. Everywhere she looked there was the sparkle and shimmer of lavish holiday decor. Evergreen garlands, twinkling lights, richly colored stained-glass wall panels. Flowers in abundance. The soft glow of heavy silver, etched glass, white tablecloths. The shine of brass. "It's magical."

"I thought you could use a treat," he said. "Take your mind off—"

"Oh, let's not talk about that." She reached for his hand, clasping it atop the table and not letting go. After a moment, he relaxed. He smiled. He could use this too, she thought.

"How did you manage this?" she asked. They were seated among the holiday splendor of the Rafters Room at the city landmark in Central Park, Tavern on the Green. When Alex asked a woman out, he really went all the way. "Don't you need to reserve weeks ahead at Christmastime?"

"Bribery." He winked. "It was a challenge. They wanted a credit card just to make a reservation. I had to come in person and use all my—" he coughed "—persuasion to get us a table for the evening."

"You don't have a credit card?" Suddenly she wondered if his barren existence wasn't merely because of the timing of his recent move. "Never mind. We can use mine."

"Of course not." He used such a firm tone that she said no more on the subject.

The setting was so dazzling, she couldn't stop looking. Windows overlooked a snowy garden filled with trees and topiary animals outlined in thousands of tiny lights. She sighed. "Thank you. I'll never forget this."

His thumb moved across her fingers, saying that she was welcome without using the words. "You've never been here?"

"Once, in spring, many years ago. I must have been nineteen or twenty."

He laughed. "Oh, *many* years ago."

"Eight, then." She smiled. "Seems like a long time to me."

"Life is short."

Ah, one of those enigmatic but meaningful statements of his that she had yet to crack....

She forgot the surroundings to study his face. "You're different tonight."

"It's the suit," he said.

She tightened her fingers on his. "Well, you clean up nice."

"You, too."

"I would have dressed up even more if I'd realized what you had in mind." He'd said he was taking her out to dinner, but she hadn't imagined quite such a splash-out. She wore a simple dress of soft gray wool and her leather boots, with her hair caught up in silver combs.

He had on a new suit—charcoal and conservative. But his tie was a surprising ivy pattern in gaudy holiday colors. It made her smile, to think that there was a bright soul hidden somewhere inside him.

"This is a date," she said, suddenly feeling shy.

"I guess so."

"You *guess?*"

"All right. It's a date."

"About time you made an honest woman of me."

"Is that what it takes? You're easy."

She kicked him under the table and they laughed. "We both needed this," she said as a waiter approached the table with their first-course selections: stone crabs and a mushroom dish made with white truffles.

"How was it, at work?" Alex asked.

"We weren't going to talk about that." After a moment, she gave a small hitch of her shoulders. "It was strange. I couldn't help suspecting everyone. Except Debby." When he would have commented—probably to say that she couldn't be subjective—she hurriedly added, "And I managed to come up with reasons that any of them might have to do it, even though I'm not convinced in the least. Shelby is a poor college student, Tara has a sick mother, Richard in the kitchen has been known to place bets with a bookie…."

Alex nodded. "There are always reasons, if you dig."

"I don't *want* to dig. I had a locksmith in, and I changed the alarm code. Isn't that enough protection?"

"You can continue to work with a mole?"

She shook her head. The treachery would eat at her. "But what else can I do?"

"Don't worry." He gave her hand a squeeze. "I'll

think of a way to take care of it. That is, if you've stopped suspecting me."

She kept her gaze level on his face. "It would help if I knew even one true thing about you."

"You know me, Karina."

"Do I?" She looked down at her fork, moving the food around her plate. "I know of you. I know your body and the way you react to questions, or danger and fear, and—and—other stimuli. But I don't know about you. Don't—" She put up a hand to stop him even though he hadn't made a sound. "Don't tell me that's not important."

"It's better that you don't know." Momentarily, his expression turned bleak, but not in the same hard way from before. He *was* different. She'd have sensed that even without the obvious clue of the very romantic date.

"Tell me something," she insisted, for the first time believing that he might really open up to her. "One true thing. About your interests. Your childhood. Anything at all." She gestured at the elaborately decorated Christmas trees, sparkling like jewel boxes in the crystalline light. "Your favorite Christmas."

A wry grin. "It wasn't like this."

She lifted her wineglass. "Go on."

"I was raised in California. An only child. My parents were—they both had good jobs. But there was always time for family."

"Did you have lots—cousins, uncles and aunts and grandparents?"

"No, not so many blood relatives. Many friends though. We had a big house in—on the coast. One of those rambling redwood structures that were popular in the sixties and seventies. It's probably ramshackle by now."

"No longer in the family?"

"Technically, yes. But my father's renting it out."

"What about your mother?"

"She died. Dad remarried several years later to a very nice lady and moved away. He's happy."

"But you're not close?"

"Not anymore."

"I suppose you won't tell me why."

"Right. You said one true thing, and I've given you several."

"Stickler."

He dipped a crab into a pool of hot mustard sauce. "I had a great childhood. Good parents, loads of friends, long summers on the beach. I did well in school. Went on to college, got the job I wanted after graduation." He shrugged. "I had every opportunity in the world."

"But…?"

He tilted his head back and let the crab slide down his throat. "Life happens, you know? Bad luck, bad timing, the wrong choice. Whatever you want to call it. What went down was out of my control, and after a while, I wound up here, starting over."

Although he was trying very hard to be nonchalant, she wasn't buying it. But he'd given her more than before. "Okay. What about women? Now that I know you really were a beach bum, I'm guessing you had bikini babes crawling all over you."

"Maybe the other way around," he said with a teasing lilt.

"Sure. I can just imagine."

The waiter came to clear their plates and Alex caught her hand again, swinging it between their chairs. "I've always been partial to blondes."

She gave him a lofty sniff, imagining him rollicking in the surf with some *Baywatch*-type babe. "And I'm sure they've always been partial to you."

"Your turn," he said. "One true thing about Karina Sutter."

She waited until the waiter had served their entrées. "But you know lots about me."

"I want to know everything."

"Mmm, well…" She tasted the cranberry compote that went with her traditional turkey dinner. Tangy and delicious. "I was the best native dancer at the American school in Papua New Guinea."

Alex gave an astounded laugh. "What?"

"We had sing-sing classes. I picked it right up." She chuckled at his befuddlement. "I didn't tell you about my dad? When I was young, we lived in New York while he was a top executive for an international company. Even then, we traveled a lot. I was nine when he retired from that to become an ambassador for Switzerland. Papua New Guinea was his first posting, but after that we lived all around the world for seven years."

"No, you didn't tell me."

"That's what we get for trying to have a meaningless fling. We've missed all the fun getting-to-know-you part."

"Fun? That depends. You haven't ever been on a bad date?"

She conceded the point. "But with the right person…"

Alex gazed steadily at her. She became flustered, but she couldn't look away.

"You're the right person," he said.

She touched her lips with her tongue. "So are you."

They put their heads together and shared a light kiss. She felt the goodness, the four-square *rightness* of Alex, the feeling setting off a tangled mass of hope and confusion and love.

They separated. Alex dabbed with his napkin. "Ahem."

She let out a shivery sigh. Love? If she was falling in love with him…oh Lord. It might be heavenly, but there was an equal chance that it could be a downward trip to hell. There were so many reasons to have doubts, and only one to believe. And she'd never relied on her heart alone to make decisions.

She touched the burning tip of her nose with her pinkie, then gave it a quick pinch before rearranging her napkin and quietly picking up her knife and fork.

He was smiling at her. "Why do you do that?"

Blink. "Do what?"

"Pinch the end of your nose. It's cute."

"Oh. Well. A habit, I guess. You have them, too, like your penchant for drumming on tabletops." She tried to switch the subject. "How's the venison?" He'd ordered it because he'd never had it before, but she'd teased him that the holidays weren't the best time to start eating reindeer.

He wasn't distracted. "No, it's more than a habit. You did it outside my door, that first time we met, when you came over with the chocolates."

Her brow furrowed. "I did? How am I expected to remember?"

"It was after I—" Alex stopped, looking embarrassed.

"Aha. After you dismissed me."

"You were getting to me. I really needed to be rid of you, and fast, so I was rude. I'm sorry."

"It's okay. I understand. Not *why,* but I know about wanting to keep control. That's what the nose-pinch is.

When I'm getting too, you know, emotional or outlandish, losing my senses…" Her face had grown hot. "I always had to be quiet and well behaved at embassy functions, so I learned to temper myself."

Alex had followed her rambling explanation with his head cocked. "Which was it this time?"

"This time?" Her breath came short. She wrung the napkin in her lap.

"Be honest now."

"You're a fine one to talk about honesty."

He leaned closer, taking her hand again. "Tell me one true thing."

All right then. He'd asked for it.

"I was alarmed that I might be falling in love." Her chest was tight, prickly. "With you," she added, in case there was any question.

Alex didn't speak right away. She was certain he would pull away again, but he gave a small nod.

"That would be the best Christmas present I ever got."

Was that all he meant to say? She waited a couple of seconds before batting her lashes at him. Her mouth made a nipped-in smile. "Then we'll have to wait and see what happens on December 25th, won't we?"

She was thoroughly unnerved when he let go of her hand and straightened up. But he didn't withdraw, as he always had before.

He reached up and pinched the end of his nose.

PLEASANTLY BUZZED by the fermented-cider sauce of a shared gingerbread dessert, they exited beneath the red canopy to a thick dusting of snow that had turned the fanciful gardens into a winter wonderland. "I don't want this evening to end," Karina said, entwining their arms.

"It's not over yet." Horse-drawn carriages were lined up near the entrance, waiting for passengers. Bells jingled as one of the steeds, a dappled gray, stamped a foot and snorted plumes from its nostrils.

Alex waved an expansive hand. "Should we go for a ride around the park?"

"That's so touristy." She moved past him, inspecting the carriages before turning back to clap her gloved hands. "I'd love it!"

Alex approached the driver at the head of the line and gave Karina his arm as she climbed up into a carriage. He followed and pulled the robe over their laps before wrapping her up in his embrace and hugging her close. "Not too cold for you?"

"I like the cold. When I was young, my family spent Christmas skiing at Saint Moritz." Her laugh tinkled on the frozen air. "But you! You're the beach baby." She hugged her arms around his waist. "Too cold for you?"

He smiled down at her, snuggled up against his chest. "Not now."

The carriage took them on a tour of Central Park, peaceful as a picture postcard, under a blanket of snow. Antique street lamps cast halos of light. The horse's hooves clip-clopped to the chime of their jinglebells.

"You're so different," Karina whispered into his ear at one point, still wondering over the change. "I don't know why, but I like it. I like it very much."

He couldn't explain without telling her everything. Maybe one day. For now all she had to know was that he was trying. Every move felt like a risk at first, but slowly he had begun to remember what it was to have a life. Most likely, he'd never be without moments of fear and worry, but even a life shadowed by anxiety was better than the bleak emptiness of his days since he'd fled Florida.

Karina began chattering about the annual holiday party she'd been planning for her staff. The event was catered, a casual smorgasbord set up in her apartment. There would be music and drinks, and a Santa to hand out her gifts, along with the packages from the staff's name exchange.

"You'll come, won't you?"

"I'm not sure."

"What's to stop you?" she asked, as if he would tell her. Her look became sly. "This would be the perfect opportunity for you to evaluate my employees as the mole."

"That's bribery."

She nudged under his jaw with her nose. "You're not above it."

He mulled over his options. "Does the party stick to your place, or do you use the shop?"

"My place. Until we want dessert, then we storm the back entrance and raid the shop for chocolate."

"What's this about a back entrance? You can't mean the emergency exit—that leads outside."

"No, there's another door. It's rarely used. In fact, it's usually boxed off, because it opens onto the corridor where the supplies are stored. I open it for the party—convenient for the guests so they don't have to parade in and out the front door."

Alex inhaled too much cold air; it parched his lungs. "Wait a minute. You're saying this door opens—where?"

"Onto the vestibule for the apartments. But it's hidden under the stairs, and always kept locked, I assure you."

"Still, that's very interesting."

"I know what you're thinking, Alex. But the intruders used the front door, remember?"

"One of them did. We don't know about the other."

"It's not any easier getting into the vestibule."

"I suppose." A plan formulated in his mind. "Who all is invited to this party?"

"My employees, and their significant others—husbands, wives, parents, kids. Some of them bring a friend or two. I invite the tenants in the building too, since we tend to get loud and I don't want complaints—or to leave anyone out."

"Will Debby bring Kyle?"

Karina frowned. "I think so."

"And the rest of the names from your suspect list will be there?"

"All except the one employee I fired. And Nikki Silk."

"Who's that?"

"A nosy journalist. Harmless."

"Invite her."

"Alex! What do you have in mind?"

"It's simple enough." The carriage had circled Sheep Meadow and was now returning to the restaurant, a brick and stone edifice that had once been a sheepfold.

"Tell me," Karina said. Her cheeks were blotched with pink from the cold.

"Suppose that you let it be known this back door is open, ready for the guests to storm the shop for their dessert. I'll hide myself in your office. The mole won't pass up the opportunity to slip downstairs during the confusion and make another attempt at your computer or the safe. Then I'll step out and catch him, or her, red-handed."

"What about the accomplice?"

"We'll let the police worry about that."

"Could be dangerous."

"Nah. I've faced worse."

"Oh, really?"

He shook his head, discouraging the curiosity. "I've already said enough for tonight."

"Actually…" Karina worried her lip. "Your plan could work. Especially because I've planted a fake password in my office." She explained about hiding the slip of paper under her desk blotter. "I was only thinking that it would delay and frustrate the person trying to get into my computer files, but if the mole discovers the codes before the party…"

"The temptation will be all the sweeter."

The carriage slowed. "Ride's over, folks," said the driver, tightening the reins to the chiming accompaniment of the silver bells affixed to the harness.

Alex got out and swung Karina down beside him, his hands on her waist. She rested her hands on his shoulders, moving closer into his embrace. "I don't know. Maybe we should take all of this to the police. Let them handle it."

"You saw how much they cared."

"But what if—"

"I'll be fine." He kissed her, struck by how heightened his senses had become, in a new way. Before, it had been all about keeping his eyes peeled and his reflexes fast. Now he wanted each moment to last. The night was all about the sharp tang of pine, the biting chill, steaming horseflesh, tattered velvet and old leather and cold lips that melted into the warmth of kisses that tasted like apple cider and cinnamon.

"Let's go home," Karina said, puffing warm breath against his ear.

"Will I get to unwrap you?"

"You're supposed to wait until Christmas morning."

She laughed, her cheek pressed to his lapel. "But that's still a week away, so I'll make you a mug of the store's peppermint hot chocolate and, mmm, you know how turned on I get after I've been dipping into the special chocolate. Anything might happen."

"Sounds good to me," he said, even though he was never going to get her obsession with chocolate.

Back at home, she showed him the canister of the drink mix made of dark-chocolate shavings and crushed peppermint. Wondering just how he was ever going to tell her about his allergy to chocolate after delaying for so long, he watched her melt the chocolate concoction in a saucepan, pour the rich brew into mugs and add heavy cream. "Too rich for my blood," he said when she urged a mug on him, but she insisted he take a taste.

"I don't want to drink alone." She tipped her mug back and took a big swallow, coming up smiling as she licked her chocolate-coated lips. "Or get naked alone."

"Magic words." He sipped. "Very good, but you'll taste even better."

She came easily, looping her arms around him and sliding her tongue along his bottom lip. "That's what I like—chocolate and peppermint and Alex, all in one."

Kissing her was a distraction that always worked, and within seconds she'd forgotten about the hot chocolate and was leading him to the bedroom. She mentioned still being cold, and he wished he'd let her down the entire hot chocolate when she hurriedly stripped, put on a pair of flannel pajamas and hopped under the covers.

But matters improved. One hand slipped out from under the blankets and beckoned him. "Come warm me up."

He was out of his clothes in record time. After carefully

placing a couple of condoms in easy reach on the headboard shelf, which made her laugh, he climbed into bed.

"Not so fast," she said when he reached for her. "I want to snuggle."

He moved in closer. "You're really pushing this intimacy stuff."

Laughingly, she pushed his chest. He caught her shoulders and pulled her against him, running his palms over her flannels. "We've got to do something about these pajamas."

"But I'm cold."

"Get under here, then." He lifted the heavy bed coverings up over their heads and they nestled side by side in the dark, soft cocoon, only hugging at first, then more. His fingers brushed across her abdomen, under the pajama top. They found the hard tips of her breasts. He strummed. She gasped.

The air got warmer. Her hands grew more adventurous, sliding along his naked body until they'd homed in on the hard-on that pressed between their bellies. His breathing became more labored, but he went for her mouth anyway, wanting the taste of her on his tongue. They kissed and fondled, murmuring sweet nothings to each other.

"This is almost like our first time," she whispered, releasing him to splay her hands across the clenched muscles below his navel, from hip bone to hip bone.

He made a gap at the top of the blankets, took a gulp of the cool air, then dove back down into their nest. "How's that?"

"We're not strangers anymore."

The defensive part of him—of Alex—wanted to brush off the newly forged intimacy. But Lex was reasserting himself, finding ways to meld the old personality with the new. Karina had no idea how right she was. They were starting over.

"Yes, but I knew you before I met you." His hands were under her pajama top again, stroking the satin skin on her back with one hand, raising goose bumps with the other as he tweaked her nipples. A couple of her buttons popped. He burrowed his head deeper beneath the covers, finding the valley between her lush breasts.

She cupped his head, holding him to her as she wrapped one leg around his hip, even the sole of her foot managing to up the pleasure as she rubbed it over his calf. "Mmm. But I've only just begun to know you."

He nibbled kisses along the fragrant curves, making circles until he'd reached the pebbled center. "Nice to meet you," he said, then sucked her nipple into his mouth, rolling it against his tongue for a few moments before drawing hard.

She squirmed, rocking against him, making soft encouraging noises as she shivered beneath his wandering hand. Shivered, this time, with desire. The heat captured between them had become thick and heavy, fragrant with peppermint and chocolate and arousal.

"I want you now," she demanded, reaching for him again.

He laughed softly. "But we only just met." His hands said otherwise and she exhaled with a deep sigh. He would do anything to please her, and this request was no hardship.

The pajama bottoms slipped past her hips with one tug and then she was open to him, so hot and tender that she jerked at his touch. Her grip tightened on his penis, giving it a tug that nearly blew his mind.

She undulated against him. "Quick," she said, "quick," and he made a blind grab at the condoms as she slid the pad of her thumb across the head of his erection.

He rolled one of them on. "I thought we'd go slow for once."

"Next time."

A much-needed draft of cool air breached their cocoon as he rose up, positioned himself between her open thighs and slowly sank into her welcoming body.

Sweet.

Tight.

Heaven.

Once he was all the way inside her, she let out a moan and wrapped herself around him. Her warm body moved like a wave, drawing him deeper into the relentless stream of pleasure. He rocked in and out of her and she matched him instinctively, moving in perfect sync, giving back with as much energy as she received. They locked hands, riding through the crashing pleasure, coming and coming and coming....

Alex collapsed, completely spent. Karina gasped under his leaden body. She breathed hard against his moist skin, reaching up to claw at the tangled blankets. "Oh, man, I'm so hot. I need oxygen!"

He tipped over onto his side and together they thrust their heads out from the covers, gasping with laughter.

After a minute, he rolled onto her, not finished with her yet, but she held his face away. "Wait, Alex." She made a crooning sound and touched a tentative finger to his mouth. "Your lips are a little swollen."

The chocolate.

He shrugged. "Too much kissing."

"Then we'd better stop." But her thighs clasped his hips.

"Nah. I'm tougher than that." With a lusty growl, he pulled the blankets back over their heads and went in for round two.

12

A COUPLE OF BUSY DAYS passed. The shop was overrun with customers, keeping the kitchen staff working overtime. Karina was barely able to manage quick hellos with Debby and the rest of her employees, which she chose to think of as a blessing. She didn't have time to fret over the identity of the mole. There were presents to buy and wrap, party details to confirm and decorations to finish. After staying up late to deck the halls of her apartment, she'd talked Alex into helping her with the final chore, the Christmas tree. She had played the sympathy card and told him that there was no more sad a task than decorating a tree solo, omitting that for the past year she'd had friends over for a tree-trimming, nog-drinking, girl-talking bash.

The day before the party, she took an hour off work to go with Alex to pick out a twelve-foot blue spruce. They wrangled the tree upstairs to her apartment and set it up near the spiral steps, making plans to do the decorating that evening. Mr. Alonzo was hovering in the hallway when they left the apartment, picking stray evergreen needles off the soles of his shoes. Karina apologized, promised she'd sweep up later and reminded him about the party. Alex cleared his throat. She rolled her eyes at him, but remembered to cheerily add, "And we'll be raiding the shop for dessert again this year, so don't forget to come!"

"You didn't say anything about the secret door," Alex commented as they trotted downstairs.

"How obvious do you want me to be? Besides, it's only Mr. Alonzo. I've made sure that everyone in the shop knows, so the trap is set. I have my doubts that it will be sprung—at least not tomorrow night."

Alex was noncommittal. "We'll see."

She gave him a quick hug outside the shop door. "Will you come inside, just for a minute? You still haven't met any of my co-workers."

He seemed reluctant, but finally nodded. "I want to check the layout of your office anyway."

"That again." She sighed as she pushed open the door. The shop was so crowded, customers had to shuffle about to make way for the new arrivals.

As they made their way to the back, Karina waved at the counter girls, pointing at Alex. "This is him! Alex Anderson."

He hustled her along. "Maybe you shouldn't be introducing me so loudly. We don't want to rouse antennae."

"They don't know you're a…" She glanced back at him and made another wild stab. "Interpol agent?"

"Karina! At last." Janine was on the spot as soon as they stepped into the reception room. "I've got a zillion details for you to approve. First, there's the Santa Claus. I handled that—he's booked. All you have to do is initial the expenditure and sign the check I've printed off…." She shoved a register at Karina before she'd managed to remove her hat and gloves.

Karina glanced over the paper and scrawled her signature. "Janine Gardner, this is Alex Anderson.

He's my—uh, my neighbor. He lives across the street."

Janine blinked owlishly, one eye twitching as she clasped her notebook to her chest.

Alex gave her a head-bob. "Hello."

"Alex was helping me with the Christmas tree." Karina shook the tree's sticky needles out of her hat. "It's a monster. Twelve feet tall."

"Will you be at the party, Janine?" he asked.

Janine's gaze went to Karina for approval. "Wouldn't miss it. Will I see you there, um, Alex?"

"Oh, no," Karina answered. "I mean, I asked, of course, but Alex is busy. He's not staff anyway, so he wouldn't know anyone." Alex pressed his knuckles to the small of her back, steadying her before she ran further amok.

Karina resisted the urge to squeeze her nose. She got nervous around anyone who'd made the top of her suspect list, which was irritating. Shouldn't she be angry with the saboteur?

But she was too giddy to maintain her anger for long. Especially now, with the holidays in the air and the promise of Alex on Christmas morning.

"The caterer is confirmed, as well," Janine said, keeping track of Alex from beneath her lashes as he walked toward Karina's office door.

There's certainly a compelling quality about him, Karina thought, admiring him herself. He had retained his brooding intensity, but ever since their dinner at Tavern on the Green there was a lighter air about him that made him much more approachable. Her feelings grew every time she saw him. Love was inches from her grasp, shiny and alluring as a bauble hung from the high branches of a tree.

Practical Janine continued. "And Nikki Silk is here, with a photographer."

"Oh, no! I completely forgot about our appointment." Karina tore off her coat and tossed it into Janine's arms. "Hang this up, please." She frantically smoothed her hair, which was scraggly from catching on the tree branches. "Where is Nikki now?"

Janine brushed a few more of the stray spruce needles off the coat. "In the kitchen, interviewing Debby. I told her you'd be along any minute."

"You said she brought a photographer? Oh, damn." Karina unclipped her hair, shook it out, then smoothed it back into a tight ponytail. "This was only supposed to be a preliminary interview. She mentioned nothing about pictures."

"I wanted candids of the shop," Nikki said from the office doorway. She wore a big smile, a chunky fake-fur jacket and orange vinyl thigh-high boots. "We're here to capture the inside story on candy-making. But we'll give you time to fix yourself up."

Karina rubbed her lips together. She'd applied a glossy balm that morning, but it had all been kissed away.

"And who is this?" Nikki said throatily, taking several slinky steps into the office. Karina turned. The *Hard Candy* reporter's gaze was pinned on Alex, who stood frozen at the threshold of her office.

"The booty call?" Nikki murmured *sotto voce* to Karina, but not *sotto* enough. Everyone heard, including the photographer, a young man with slouchy shoulders and three day's growth of beard, carefully cultivated.

If possible, Alex became even more tense. Karina felt it radiating off him, but she wasn't sure why. One thing was certain. He wouldn't want to be included in the article.

She touched Nikki's arm. "You promised. My private life isn't part of this."

"Oh, sure, sure." Nikki stroked her long dark hair, still looking admiringly at Alex. "But can you blame me for wanting an introduction?"

"Let me take your jacket first." Karina got it off and lobbed the fur at Janine. She turned toward Alex.

He ducked his head, murmured some excuse or other in a gruff voice, and rudely walked straight out of the room, almost knocking the photographer over.

"Alex, wait," Karina called, although she had little expectation that he would stop. Even their past few days of acting almost like a normal couple hadn't worn away all of his rough edges.

She threw a quick apology at Nikki and ran after him. The customers must have parted for him like the Red Sea, because he'd already reached the sidewalk. "Excuse me," she said, pushing through the crowd. "Make way. Coming through. Thank you."

Too late. By the time she got outside, Alex had already disappeared.

"As God is my witness, I'll never decorate again," Karina said to herself, resting her head in her hands. She sat midway up the spiral staircase, bone tired from the eventful day in the shop and three hours of tree trimming.

She'd given up waiting for Alex one hour in and had phoned Debby to come and help. They hadn't had any time together lately. But Debby had been evasive, muttering something about plans with Kyle before hanging up rather precipitously.

Trouble brewing there. Karina intended to take a few minutes at the party and pin Debby down to ask her what was up. Maybe it was only boyfriend problems. She'd never believe that her friend was the mole, but Kyle…he was another matter. If only because he was new and thus an unknown quantity, like others on her suspect list.

Karina climbed off the stairs. The tree was spectacular—tall and thick, trimmed out the wazoo with multicolored lights, glittery baubles, garlands of copper beads. All lit up, it filled the space with a festive glow and the unmistakable spicy scent of evergreen boughs.

There was still a mound of gifts to wrap and house cleaning to do, but she'd finish those chores tomorrow. Bed, now. After one more look at Alex's place.

She went to the window. Her curtains were open, the shades up, all lights on. No way for Alex to miss her lonesome tree-trimming session. She'd have been ticked off at him if she weren't so worried. Since he'd walked out of the office earlier in the day, her imagination had run overtime.

He'd been featured on *America's Most Wanted*…had changed his name and gotten plastic surgery…was a runaway crown prince….

More and more absurd.

His windows remained dark. There hadn't been even one sign, not a wrinkle in the blind or a single flash of the binocular's lenses to tell her that he gave a flying fig about deserting her.

Fine for him. She tried to harden her heart, but it was no use. He was wrestling with demons from his past and she could only hope that he won, and returned to her a whole man. She'd keep him, somehow she'd keep him, even if she had to feed him a truffle every day and two at night to ensure that he was too aroused to spend time worrying.

LATE THE NEXT DAY, Alex buzzed at Karina's door. It was an hour before the party, and she'd been back and forth between the shop and apartment a dozen times throughout the day, finalizing preparations and seeing to business. Each time, she'd checked his window. If he was watching, he was well hidden. She'd wondered if he'd backed out of his plan to catch a thief.

"Karina." Alex's voice on the intercom was hushed and distant, as if he spoke into a seashell. Appropriate, she thought. "We, uh, need to talk."

She swallowed. At least he hadn't said *discuss*.

"Talk?"

"And make our arrangements."

"Stay there. I'm coming down." She grabbed her keys and ran out the door, brushing by Mr. Alonzo coming up the stairs. They exchanged good cheer.

She tempered hers as she approached the lobby. Sure, Alex was back…this time. But what about tomorrow, or next week? She liked stability, consistency. She couldn't make a relationship with a man who was so unpredictable. So stubborn, so unknowable.

So mystifyingly right.

The vestibule door was open today. Alex was waiting inside when she reached the ground floor. He looked apologetic and her immediate response was to offer him a hug. She was weak.

"I only have a minute," she said, trying to be brisk. "My party supplier was late dropping off the extra chairs and tables, and the caterer is upstairs, getting the buffet ready to go—"

Alex interrupted. "Karina, look at me."

He knew he was asking for too much from her, between his disappearing act and his reluctance to answer any questions, but that was how it had to be.

"Karina," he said again, coaxing her. Finally she brought her face around and stared at him with big solemn eyes. Her mouth quivered at the corners before firming up.

"I'm sorry about yesterday," he said.

The apology got a nod. She was back to being the untouchable princess—hair braided into a tight knot, the serene countenance betraying very little emotion, her posture perfect in a ruby-red party dress that made her bare shoulders and arms look like they'd been carved out of alabaster. But he knew the warmth of her, inside....

"It was the photographer," he blurted, ashamed of himself for letting the old instinct for self-preservation take over. "And the reporter. If they had taken my picture—" The same old worries had come back, as strong as ever. He shook his head, disgusted with himself. "I can't chance being exposed."

She let out a small sigh. "Yes, I thought that might be it."

He steeled himself, but she asked for no more explanation and simply turned away, saying, "Let's do this quickly, shall we?"

He followed her through the small vestibule to a narrow space behind the stairs, ducking his head beneath the slanted ceiling.

"You see why I don't use this door." She sorted through the keys in her hand, unlocked the rough-hewn door and pushed back a rusty bolt. "It also locks from the other side. I had one of my employees clear out the supplies blocking the way so I could get to it."

"You've opened this door for previous parties?"

"Only at Christmastime."

"So it's no secret to your employees and the tenants in the building."

"Not among those who've been here more than a year. But you can see for yourself that the door hasn't been used lately." She gave it a shove.

"Let me help," he said, pushing with her when the door stuck.

It creaked as it opened, and they stepped through to the dimly lit storage corridor running between the kitchen and the office area of the shop.

Karina moved along, speaking crisply. "The children, especially, love entering the chocolate shop through this door. It gives them the feeling of sneaking in, I suppose, and getting to roam through areas they never see. The shop is set up for the visit, of course. Stocked with goodies. The guests are free to wander throughout, choosing as many treats as they like. Some are eaten on the spot, but the remainder go into the goody bags I provide. Otherwise they'd all be sick, going home."

Throughout this, she had given Alex a quick tour of the industrial kitchen, where the workers had departed but left behind the worktable strewn with a variety of chocolates. The candies were lined up on waxed-paper sheets, as if freshly made and not put away.

They wound up in her office, where the desk light had been left on. "Show me the safe," he said.

She went to a particular panel in the wainscoting and pushed her fingertips against the molding. The hidden door sprang open, revealing the heavy steel facing of the safe.

"What do you keep there?"

"It's fireproof, so I store business records, tax and insurance documents, a few computer disks. Nothing of particular value." She shut the panel. "I do have to go. The guests will be arriving soon."

"What's the agenda?"

"We have drinks and music, then the gift opening. I've booked a Santa Claus who arrives with a bag full of presents to distribute. Afterward, we eat, and sometime after that when the party starts to wind down, we come here for the desserts."

"All at once? Everyone?"

"A few of the adults might linger upstairs.…" She gestured to the grate in the ceiling. "You'll hear us when that point comes, I'm sure."

"It's not me I'm concerned about."

Karina's hands clenched nervously. "I don't like you doing this. Please promise that you'll be careful."

"Nothing to worry about." He opened the small coat closet that he'd previously identified as his best hiding spot. "I don't even have to confront them, if you prefer. Identifying who's double-crossing you is what matters, especially as there's nothing for them to steal."

"But—"

He took a couple of swift steps and stroked his hand across her furrowed brow. "Nothing to worry about."

"Say it once more and maybe I'll start to believe you."

"Nothing…" He pressed his lips to her forehead. "To worry about."

She threw her arms around his neck in a tight hug. "Oh, Alex."

His eyes closed. *Nothing to worry about.*

"Come to the party instead." Her small hot kisses peppered his jawline. "Please."

"Too many people."

She inhaled. Stiffened. Stepped out of his arms. "Yes, of course." One palm stroked over the smooth satiny sheen of her hair. She pinched her nose. "Yes. Do what you want, then. I have to go."

Before, he would have believed she was back in control.

Before, he would have believed he was on his own.

TWO HOURS LATER, the party was in full swing. The somewhat disappointing Santa—too short and nasal to be convincing—had finished distributing the gifts. The guests had moved on to enjoy the elaborate buffet stocked with turkey, beef and a huge glazed ham, along with a dozen side dishes. Karina had told the Santa to help himself before leaving, then escaped to the kitchen on the pretense of getting more wine. What she wanted was a moment to think.

As far as she knew, Alex was still hiding in her office, waiting for the mole or his accomplice to return. She'd tried to keep track of anyone who might have disappeared from the party, but that was proving impossible. There were at least fifty people out there, the noise and activity astounding.

Karina gnawed her lip. Should she race downstairs to check on Alex? Or would that be one of those ditzy-heroine moves that she'd sworn not to do?

She peeked around the refrigerator into the party. Debby and Kyle stood nearby. He was chomping his way through a plate loaded with goodies, while she stood by his side, looking distracted. And not eating.

Karina waved to catch Debby's eye, then motioned her into the kitchen.

"Great party," Debby said when she arrived. "What are you doing in here all alone? Where's Alex?"

Karina waved off the question. "You're not eating."

"I'm on a diet."

"Oh, Deb. I thought Kyle likes you the way you are. You know—cuddly."

"Yeah, that's what he *said,* but…"

Karina's tone sharpened. "Has he given you a reason not to believe him?"

Debby let out a huge sigh. "As a matter of fact, yes. For the past few days, I've been trying to figure out if I should tell you."

Karina nodded reassuringly, even though she was stricken with apprehension. "Of course you should tell me. We're best friends. I'll understand. *Whatever* it is."

"Mmm, well, this is about you too."

Oh, God. Karina licked her lips. "The chocolate recipe?"

Debby's nose crinkled. "Sort of, I guess. Do you remember when I told you that Kyle wanted to talk? It turns out that he had a confession to make. He felt guilty because…"

Debby stopped to pluck a piece of tinsel off her black cashmere sweater. Karina grabbed the contoured lip of the granite countertop to stop herself from shaking the story out of her friend. What was wrong with her? Where was her usual cool head and practicality? This urgency was out of character.

Debby blinked at Karina. "I told him about the chocolate, about the sexual side effect."

"I see."

"I went on and on, blathering about how happy I was that he was attracted to me even without the chocolate.

It's not that I'm above using it, you know that, but it was just really nice not to have to. I didn't get it right away, but that's when he started acting funny."

Karina nodded energetically. *Get on with it.*

"So…he finally confessed. That day when I fell off the ladder into his arms? He'd just eaten one of the Black Magic truffles. And the thing is—" Debby pushed the fringe of curls off her forehead and looked at Karina with concern. "The thing is, he got the truffle from Alex. A whole box of them, minus one."

Karina was so taken aback she pulled her head in like a turtle. Alex had given away the truffles, right at the beginning? And she'd wasted her time, back when she'd worried that his feelings were chemically induced…?

She blinked. "I don't get it."

"It was the day after you went over there. Kyle happened to run into Alex on the street, and Alex gave him the truffles as a friendly gesture. Said he was allergic. Kyle didn't realize it was *your* Alex until I started blabbing. Maybe I shouldn't have done that, huh? I'm sorry."

"But…" Karina's mind spun, flipping through all the times she'd mentioned the truffles to Alex. Had he actually said he'd eaten them, or had she only assumed that he had? No, he'd claimed they were delicious at least once. After that, he'd been noncommittal. Now she knew why. "All right. So what if Alex didn't eat the truffles?"

"Don't you see? That means your affair is legit." Debby's shoulders slumped. "And mine isn't."

"That's all?" A wild laugh erupted from Karina. She threw her arms around Debby. "Oh, honey, don't worry about it! Here I thought you had something really serious to tell me, and this was all just about the truffles. I am so relieved, you wouldn't believe."

"Well, yeah. Alex has the serious hots for you. Me and Kyle, we're just—" Debby shrugged. "I know I always said that I wouldn't mind keeping a man in truffles as long as he made me happy in bed, but I was wrong. I don't want a cocoa-bean love affair. With Kyle, anyway, I want the real thing."

"That's not a difficult problem to solve. You cut him off from the chocolate and see what happens."

"Nah. Easier said than done. Kyle's already addicted. He keeps asking me for more of the stuff, and he has very effective means of persuasion. So far, I've been weak." Debby giggled, getting a little of her *oomph* back. "I'm not a drug dealer," she said with a wail. "I'm a chocolate dealer!"

"What's happening here? A little girl talk?" Nikki Silk entered the kitchen and with a natural ease, jumped up to plop her behind on the kitchen countertop. She swung her legs. "What're we gabbing about?"

"Chocolate," Karina said, too elated to care about what Nikki would make of them. Her gut had told her all along that what she had with Alex went beyond aphrodisiac, but now she was certain that Debby and Kyle were innocent. There was still the break-in to deal with, but that was minor to her, in the scheme of things. Love always took precedence.

"Chocolate," Debby echoed. She grinned. "And sex."

Nikki flashed them a toothy smile. "Ooh, my favorite combination. Like I always say, the only thing better than a naked man is a naked man covered in chocolate."

13

THE MECHANICAL FEMALE VOICE drifted down from above: "Give me your hand. I will tell your fortune."

Leaning inside the closet, Alex gritted his teeth. For the past two hours he'd listened to Esmeralda the Gypsy Queen and her plinkety-plonk music play over and over again. Karina would make back the cost of the party on quarters alone.

The Santa Claus's refrains of *ho-ho-ho, Merry Christmas* had trailed off, which meant the guests were moving on to the buffet. Alex had begun to think that he'd guessed wrong and there would be no attempts on the safe tonight. But he wasn't giving up. Not on any of it.

The closet door was open a few inches for air. He put his ear to the crack for the hundredth time, listening for sounds from the reception area. This time, he heard what he'd been waiting for.

Murmuring. A conversation.

Two men? Surprised, Alex pulled the door shut, leaving himself the narrowest crack for spying. Adrenaline raced through his bloodstream. The instincts he'd honed in the year since he'd left California were as sharp as ever. He battled the urge to run, or to leap out and fight, telling himself that there was no reason to believe that these men were after him.

He was here to defend Karina, no matter what terrible images and stark terror the situation made him relive.

The push-button knob on the office door was locked, but anyone with a paper clip could open it with a little effort. Alex stopped breathing when the knob rattled. On the other side, there came more murmuring, then the metallic *snick* of the potential thieves springing the lock.

Alex used the intruders' entrance to cover the small muffled sounds of moving himself deeper into the closet. In case they would think to check the closet, he'd hung up his long coat for camouflage and had positioned himself behind it. Good enough to fool a cursory glance.

"Quickly," said a man.

"Should be right here." Soft thumps and pats came from the office. Alex didn't want to risk peeking yet, but he could tell they were looking for the safe.

"Aha. Here we go." The second man had a cold, humorless chuckle. "Do you have the combination?"

"I thought you memorized it. Be my guest."

"Shh. No talking."

Alex heard the quiet clicks of the lock being turned. He put one hand on the coat hanger nearest him so it wouldn't screech and leaned toward the door. Two figures were huddled at the safe opposite Karina's desk.

The light in the inner office was too dim for him to make out the hunched man working the dial. But the other was...

Santa Claus?

Nice move, Alex thought, remembering that Janine had handled the booking.

"It's not opening," the safecracker hissed.

"Let me try," Santa said. He spun the dial, worked the combination, then pounded on the heavy door when it refused to open.

Inside the closet, Alex smiled. Apparently Karina's ploy had worked.

"It was your girl who got us the combination," the second man said. "What now?"

"I'll try the computer. You keep working on the lock." Santa went to sit behind the desk, barely three feet away from the coat closet. A bald head with a fringe of iron-gray hair was revealed when he swept off the fur-trimmed hat. He rubbed the sweat from his brow, then slipped on a pair of glasses and limbered his fingers. "Heh. Now you'll see what I can do."

Alex pulled back a couple of inches. He'd instantly recognized the man in the Santa suit. It was the same guy who'd been lurking in the store, the customer he'd suspected might be after *him* instead of the chocolate.

Still a faint possibility. But remote, Alex reassured himself. He flexed his fingers before reaching around for his gun. Just in case.

The computer keys clicked rapidly. "Okay, I'm at the protected files. What was that password?"

"Look for yourself. Under the blotter."

"Thought you memorized it, Freddy."

A fist rapped on the wood paneling. "Quit the nit-picking and get on with it, will you? We don't have much time."

Santa moved a couple of items off the blotter and tilted it up. "KJSTRSTALEX," he read. "Or is that A-*one*-E-X?"

"Read it to *yourself.*"

A robotic female voice interrupted. "Give me your

hand." Giggles accompanied the carnival music drifting down through the grate. "I will read your fortune."

Santa jumped. "What the hell was that?"

"Keep your voice down." The other guy pointed at the grate. "It's from upstairs. Remember, I told you. They thought that was why you got away last time. They didn't figure I might have called to warn you."

"Scared me out of my boots," Santa muttered.

"Is the password working?"

Santa typed, then cursed. "No."

The other guy came toward the desk and in the light of the computer screen, Alex finally identified him.

Karina's mild-mannered neighbor, Mr. Alonzo.

"We've been tricked. Dammit." Alonzo flipped up the desk blotter, then tossed it to the floor in anger. "I knew that was too convenient. Both the combination and the password, in one place, so easy to find when they weren't before? And your foolish daughter fell for it."

"So did you."

"Shut the computer down. We're getting out of here."

"Give me ten minutes. I can crack this code and get into the files."

"What good will that do us? The recipe's got to be in the safe."

"You don't know for sure. At least let me try. We may never get back in here again. Tonight's our best shot. My contact is waiting for that recipe. I need it *now*."

"Go it on your own, then," Alonzo said. "I'd rather live to try another day." His gaze scanned around the office, traveling from the safe to the grate to the computer...but lingering on the closet.

Alex, his eye to the thread line of the crack, did not

move. Even in darkness, the slightest shift might be apparent.

"Guard the door," Santa said. "If you leave and I find the recipe on my own, I'm keeping it for myself."

"Bullshit you are. I was the one who found out about the aphrodisiac effect of the chocolate in the first place."

Alex blinked. *Aphrodisiac?*

"So what? The recipe wouldn't be worth squat if I couldn't sell it for a bundle. Those greedy corporate bastards will pay this time." Santa tapped the keys. The screen flashed: *Password Denied.* "Remember, putting Janine on the inside with that fake résumé was my idea."

"I wouldn't be bragging about that if I were you. If she had any smarts she would have been able to get into the safe on her own instead of wasting weeks looking for the damn thing." While Alonzo talked, he walked slowly around the desk until he was standing behind Santa's shoulder. His rabbitlike eyes stared straight ahead.

Alex's instincts prickled. He clicked the safety off on the gun.

He was ready when Alonzo made a sudden grab for the knob. With all his weight, he shoved the door open, knocking Alonzo into the desk chair, which skidded forward, mashing both men up against the computer in a tangle of arms and legs.

Before the yelling pair could sort themselves out, Alex was out of the closet, gun raised. "Hey, guys. I've been waiting for you. Put your hands up in the air and don't move."

Santa said, "What the hell?"

Alonzo's chin jutted. "Are you a cop?"

"No, I'm not a cop," he said. "So there's nothing

holding me back from shooting you for trespassing and attempted burglary." He waggled the gun. "Hands up."

They both complied, though Santa's knees gave out and he collapsed into the swivel desk chair. It thunked against the desk. "Goddamn. This can't be happening. We were so close. Wanda was counting on the recipe bringing us a big payday."

"My sister never should have married a loser like you in the first place," Alonzo hissed. "I told her that at the wedding."

The other man's face twisted with bitterness. "The layoffs at my company weren't my fault."

"Quit the squabbling," Alex said.

The two of them were so hapless, he felt safe in letting his guard down, after he'd done a quick pat down to be sure they had no weapons. He tucked his gun away and picked up the phone.

"Not the cops," Santa whined. "I've got one of the top guys at Royal Foods sweating bullets for this secret recipe. I'll cut you in on the cash."

Alex didn't bother responding. After a couple of rings, a voice he didn't know answered in the apartment above. He asked for Karina. "It's safe to come down now," he said. "Bring Janine. And Kyle."

Alonzo's eyes shifted toward the door. Alex put down the phone and positioned himself to block the way.

Santa stood. "We can take him, Freddy."

Alex shrugged. "Go ahead. Try it."

But Alonzo was thinking it through. "Keep cool, Sam. We haven't done anything illegal."

"Except breaking and entering," Alex said.

"We're guests at this party. We wandered downstairs. The door was open, so who can fault us?"

"The office door was locked."

Alonzo's mouth twisted into an ugly grin. "Got proof?"

Alex had to concede, if only to himself, that there would be very little to charge the pair with.

Karina rushed into the office. Kyle was right behind her, escorting a reluctant Janine. An excited Debby pushed in behind them, pressing Janine forward into the room.

The office assistant gasped. "Dad! Uncle Freddy! What are you doing here? And, uh, why are you wearing a Santa suit?" Janine Gardner was not a good actress.

"Mr. Alonzo?" Karina gaped in shock. "Why are you here?" She looked at Alex. "What the hell—"

He tried to explain. "From what I can figure, Alonzo and this man are brothers-in-law. They picked your lock and entered the office. Tried to break into the safe and the computer—unsuccessfully, thanks to the fake codes you planted."

"Those were fake?" Janine said, genuinely surprised this time.

"Keep your mouth shut!" the bald man, Sam Gardner, said. He ripped off the red jacket of his Santa suit; underneath was a pillow strapped to a rather sunken chest. He aimed a sickly smile at Karina. "You're a nice lady. Why don't you just let us out of here and we won't be any more trouble to you?"

"I know you," she said. "You've been in the store."

Janine frowned. "I *told* you that you didn't need to keep an eye on me, Dad."

Karina had put together the pieces, but her expression remained puzzled. "Why did you want Kyle?" she asked Alex. "If you think he's involved, you're wrong. Debby and I talked—"

Alex cut her off. "Kyle's here as muscle, that's all. I didn't want these two trying to make a break for it."

Kyle nodded and set himself in the doorway, arms crossed over his chest, bulkier than ever in a red sweater knitted with a snowflake design.

"Okay," Karina said softly. She seemed relieved, until her gaze returned to her neighbor. "Mr. Alonzo! How could you?"

"Sorry," he said in a plaintive voice, making his mouth go droopy. "I only did it because of this jerk, my brother-in-law, Sam. He worked in the computer division at Royal Foods for twenty-seven years, but they laid him off with only a measly pension."

Cue the violins, Alex thought.

"He came to me and said that if he could just bring in a big idea like the aphrodisiac chocolates you sell, the company would rehire him. What could I do? I had to help, to keep my sister and niece off the street." Alonzo gave a heaving sigh. "I didn't intend you any harm. I swear it. All we wanted was to find out the secret to your recipe."

The meek-and-contrite act was ruined by his brother-in-law's snarl. "You weasel! Blaming this on *me* when it was your idea all along. Janine will back me up. You came to me!"

Santa Sam reared back to take a swing. Alex stepped in, grabbing the man's arm. He forced it down, then looked at Karina for further instruction. She seemed to be taking everything in stride. Perhaps too calmly. "Listen, Karina, don't be fooled by their excuses."

"You don't have to tell me that. I can see for myself." But she looked sadly at Alonzo. "Janine's betrayal is bad enough, but I'm shocked at you especially, Mr. Alonzo.

My neighbor. How dare you try to rob me—and then have the gall to lie about it right to my face?"

Color flared in the tenant's face. "Go ahead and call the cops then. You don't have anything on us."

"I'm afraid he's right," Alex said. "An attempted burglary is about it."

Debby chimed in. "How about the one who masqueraded as Santa Claus?"

"I hired him," Janine said. "Fair and square."

"Just shut up, Janine," Karina snapped. "You could have had a legitimate job here, a good one."

"You want me to call the police?" Debby asked.

Karina put her hands over her face, took a deep breath, then obviously came to her decision. "All right. Here's what we're going to do. Janine, clean out your desk. You're fired. You—Santa, whatever your name is, you can go with her. I don't want to see either of you ever again, and you can consider yourselves *extremely* lucky that I'm not pressing charges. Mr. Alonzo—your lease is officially broken. I want you out immediately. Tonight."

"But it's the holidays! Where will I go?"

She gave him a grim smile at the absurdity of his statement. "I'm sure your loving family will take you in."

Karina turned to go, but then stopped to make one more pronouncement. "And just so you all know, the chocolate recipe was never here. It's in a safety deposit box. At the bank. Right, Debby?"

Debby nodded vehemently. "Abso-frickin-lutely."

Karina linked arms with her chef. "Come on, let's go serve up some chocolate. I hear the guests arriving." She glanced at Alex, then Kyle. "Can you two clean up the garbage in here?"

"Sure thing," Kyle said. "As long as my girlfriend saves me one of those extraspecial truffles."

Debby stopped short. "What if I can't? Will I still be your girlfriend?"

"Hell, yeah. You're plenty sweet enough for me."

"Oh, huggy bear. I hope you mean that." Debby launched herself at Kyle and the two locked lips.

Karina hovered in the doorway, seemingly only slightly ruffled from the confrontation with the trio of crooks. She smoothed her dress, gave Alex a long look that he wasn't able to decipher, then hurried away to divert the converging guests. If she'd wanted him to stay, she'd given no overt sign of it. Not even a nose pinch.

His initial relief at learning that he was still safe, identity intact, had turned sour. The situation hadn't improved. He remained stuck between the proverbial rock and hard place, knowing that there could be no sweet freedom without Karina at his side.

KARINA WOKE UP ALONE on Christmas morning. She stretched, scratched her head, mumbled to herself. Delaying getting out of bed. There was nothing waiting for her.

Not Alex, anyway.

With a groan, she buried her head under the pillow. She'd wanted a fling, and she'd had a really fabulous one. Nothing to be sad over.

Several days had gone by since the employee party and the discovery of the trio of crooks. Frederick Alonzo had moved out that night as directed, and Karina felt fairly confident that the incident was over. Alex had grumbled at her later about giving them a free pass, but in her estimation, all's well that ended well. The recipe had never been in danger, although she'd learned a valuable lesson about keeping the most important component—the contact information of the supplier of the special cocoa beans—equally safe. Mr. Alonzo and the Gardners would never know how close they'd actually come to the secret ingredient.

A ringing phone finally got Karina out of bed. She exchanged holiday greetings first with her parents calling from Switzerland and an hour later with her brother and his family in California. She then put a pot of coffee on and went to the bathroom.

She washed her hands and brushed her teeth at the pedestal sink. The mirror revealed a sorry sight. Bedhead and pillow creases, rumpled pajamas. Bloodshot eyes. She'd been to a wild office party at *Hard Candy* with Nikki and Whitney, and they'd overindulged in vodka chocolates while taking turns spying on Whitney's alleged "Strangler" and his latest conquest. The man was a Lothario, not a murderer.

She tried to flatten her hair, then gave up with a shrug. What did it matter? Alex had given no indication that he wanted to join her, despite the earlier promise.

He'd wigged out on trimming the tree, too, she remembered. The man was simply not a stayer. Not a keeper. And she had no business feeling so empty inside. They'd had a good time while it lasted.

Karina slumped into the living area and plugged in her Christmas tree. Later, she'd have to put on a happy face. Debby and Kyle were coming over for dinner and drinks. How ironic that they were the couple who were going to last, when they'd been the ones who'd actually founded their relationship on a chocolate-based attraction.

Technically, so had she. Never would she have gone

over to Alex's that first time on her own. But after that, when she'd been so willing to blame their actions on the chocolate…

Her face flushed as she admitted the truth to herself. The lust had been real.

Whether any of it had turned to love remained to be seen.

She looked across the street to Alex's place. The binoculars were long gone, and so was he. Since the staff party, she'd seen him a couple of times. Briefly. He'd seemed apologetic, but distant. Her pride kept her from begging for another chance when they both knew that it was he who had to make a decision.

Gaily wrapped gifts awaited her under the tree, but she had no enthusiasm for opening them. There was only one present she wanted to unwrap—Alex. That evening in Central Park, he'd loosened up and she'd gotten a tantalizing glimpse at who he really was.

Karina pinched her nose. *Get a grip, girl. He's a Chinese puzzle box. You'll never know—*

The door buzzed.

She froze, not daring to hope.

It went off again. *Bzzzz.*

She ran to the door, slipping on her socks, and stabbed at the button. "Alex?"

"Yes," he said.

She dropped her head forward, praying that he was here for the right reasons. "Are you coming to say goodbye?"

Six seconds passed like an hour before his voice crackled through the intercom speaker. "I'm coming to say hello."

With a shaking finger, she buzzed him in. *Please, please, please…*

She had the door open before he arrived. No need for acting cool when she was as jumpy and expectant as a kid on Christmas morning. Alex appeared, looking so good her heart began beating like crazy.

He nodded down the hall. "Alonzo?"

"No sign of him, and the locks have been changed."

"And me?"

She stepped aside to let him in. "You're always welcome."

He looked closely at her flushed face. "Have you been eating chocolate already?"

"Not even a sniff." They hadn't talked about the aphrodisiac, or how she'd attempted to seduce him under the influence, but from a couple of comments he'd made, she knew he'd figured it out.

"In fact, I haven't had any of the special stuff for days." The vodka chocolates from the night before hadn't been from her shop, though Debby had started talking about developing a few recipes to inspire their customers to new heights.

"Maybe you should go eat one of the truffles," Alex suggested. "Make this easier on me."

"No way. I need a clear head when I'm dealing with you."

He opened a hand. "But I was hoping to trade you." A chocolate kiss sat on his palm. "Even up."

She melted. "Oh, Alex…"

He kissed her, and as always she lost herself to the sweetest pleasure she'd ever known. Chocolate be damned. Alex was the aphrodisiac for her.

"I have to tell you." She made herself step away. "That first day, when I came to your apartment with the truffles—"

"Later," he said, skimming off his coat.

"This is important."

"Gifts first." He put a hand on Esmeralda's booth for balance and started taking off his boots.

Karina didn't care. She grabbed him for a hug, laughing at her sudden sense of elation. In the blink of an eye, her world had been wonderfully transformed. "You bought me a gift?"

"Of course I did." Standing on one leg with a boot hanging off his toes, he teetered and grabbed again for Esmeralda, jarring the booth. The light flickered, red, purple, gold. The mechanism whirred.

"Give me your hand," Esmeralda said. Alex kicked a boot at her. "I will tell your fortune."

"Don't be so skeptical." Karina grabbed the card as it emerged from the slot. She stuck it in her pajama pocket without looking. "Esmeralda's always right. On the day that we met, she told me a dark stranger would enter my life."

"Sam Gardner?" Alex teased.

"Uh-huh. Sure." She led him to the sparkling Christmas tree. "Perhaps I fed truffles to the wrong man. Or rather *didn't* feed them...."

"Trust me. You got the right man." He took her hand. "The truffles don't matter a bit when it comes to how much I want you."

"You know, then?"

"Aphrodisiac chocolates? I suppose if people believe in them, they work."

"It's true, I promise you." She stared at Alex, unblinking, her fingers tightening where they laced with his. "I'm going to trust you with my biggest secret. Mr. Alonzo and his brother—they went after the recipe, when all they really needed was to buy out my Brazilian supplier of the bulk chocolate made from some very unique cocoa beans. That's where the magic is, not in a recipe."

Alex shook his head. "There's no recipe?"

"Oh, yes. There is. And it really is in a bank—in Switzerland. It just also happens to be on a card in a recipe box in the kitchen at Sutter Chocolat. Debby doesn't really need it, she knows the instructions and ingredients by heart. It's a good recipe, too, but any other recipe would do nearly as well. The aphrodisiac is in the cocoa beans."

"I can't tell if you're kidding me."

She gave him an enigmatic smile, then stepped closer to smooth a hand over his lopsided collar. "So you're allergic to chocolate, huh?"

His eyes narrowed. "Who told you?"

"Debby, via Kyle. You gave him the truffles."

"Oh, yeah. That's right." He lifted their linked hands and kissed her knuckles. "Forgive me for misleading you?"

She tilted her head. Their eyes connected. The current was as strong and hot as ever. "Forgive me for trying to seduce you with inappropriate measures?"

"That's not something that's necessary to forgive. I prize the day you showed up on my doorstep with your funny hat and fevered face. I thought you were crazy, of course—"

She closed her eyes, expecting to be mortified all over again, but her feelings had changed. Maybe she wasn't as in control, but that meant she was open to a lot of wonderful experiences she would have missed otherwise.

"—but you've never been out of my mind since. As hard as I've tried to get away."

Her eyes welled as soon as she opened them, spangling her lashes so his face was a blur. "How hard did you try?" she asked, but what she really wanted to know was *why.*

He only squeezed her hand, using it to draw her down to the furry white throw she'd placed near the tree. Gifts from her friends and family were piled nearby, but the only one that she cared for at the moment was the small package that Alex pulled from his back pocket.

He sat beside her, offering it without a word.

The gift was wrapped in wrinkled tissue paper and tied with a bit of colored string. No tape. When she scraped off the knotted string, the wrappings fell away. Alex had given her a rough wooden box with painted decorations. Swoops and swirls of once-bright color were now faded by wear. A decal in the center, half-rubbed away, bore the image of a Ferris wheel and the words Orange County Fair.

"It's not new," he said. "Obviously. It's mine, from when I was a kid. I won it at a fair. A carnival."

"Ahh."

"Look inside."

She lifted the lid. Empty.

Alex's eyes glinted at her, and suddenly she understood. She ran her fingertips over the small box, soon discovering a hidden panel that tilted up to reveal a second compartment, flat and narrow. Reverently, she lifted out the small pile of photos it held. Old pictures, slightly discolored. She went through them. A laughing boy romping in the surf. The same boy with what must be his parents, standing on the deck of a sailboat. The father looked like an older Alex, tall and dark, one arm around his wife, the other around the child.

Alex. The next photo was clearly him. A teenager with sun-bleached hair and a big white smile, holding a surfboard and a trophy.

Karina's heart was beating so hard she could feel it. Two more photos. The first was a candid of an adult version of Alex, amid a group of friends, both men and women, most of them with a beer bottle in hand. He was laughing again, his eyes as bright as a sunny sky. He was more subdued in the final picture, posed standing on the steps of what appeared to be a courthouse, wearing a suit and tie. She looked closer. The tie sported a hand-painted hula girl.

So this was Alex. She was meeting him at last.

"That's me, Mark Lexmond," he said.

"What?" She flinched. "Your name is Mark? Not Alex?"

"Now it is. Alex, I mean. I'm going to stay Alex Anderson. It feels right to me. Because—" his hand slid along her arm and she leaned into the reassuring touch "—I like how it sounds, coming from you."

She tested the other name. "Mark Lexmond."

"My nickname was Lex."

"*Lex?*"

"Not as in Luthor. But I did have a Superman complex, until I learned without a doubt that I was no man of steel."

She spoke through numb lips. "What do you mean?" There was something horribly sad in his eyes now and she almost didn't want to know, but this was important. Life-and-death important, she could tell.

"I've lied to you about a lot of things. I was never a writer—I was a lawyer. A defense attorney. I'd had a friend, in high school, just eighteen. He got in trouble, but he didn't belong in prison...." Alex shook his head. "Long story short—I was out to protect the poor and downtrodden, only it didn't take too long before I realized that ninety-five percent of them were guilty as sin. It was the other five percent who kept me going."

She put her hand on his. "And what happened?"

"A couple of years ago, I took on a murder case. The defendant was guilty. I knew it, the prosecutors knew it, the judge knew it. But halfway through the trial, I helped broker a deal between my client and the federal authorities and the charge was knocked down from second-degree murder to manslaughter."

Alex stopped. "I shouldn't be telling you this."

"Why?"

"It's dangerous for you to even know me."

She looked at the photo of the laughing boy on the beach. "Finish the story." Hearing the wrenching pain in his voice hurt her, but he needed to tell all of it. The best she could do for him now was to listen.

"Let me skim some of the details. They don't matter to you." He pulled loose from her to rake his hands through his hair. "What happened was...the father of the young man who'd been killed by the defendant in the case wasn't pleased with the outcome. To put it mildly. He was a powerful man, a kingpin in the drug trafficking trade. He swore that my client would pay, and that I would, too, for brokering the deal. A few months later, the defendant was found dead."

Alex lifted his shoulders, then let them fall, defeated. "The Feds who'd been after the kingpin wanted me to go into protective custody, for a few months at least. I refused. Stubborn, partly, but I also couldn't believe what was happening." He glanced at Karina, with a ghostly smile on his lips. "Even with the uglier aspects of my job, my life up to then had been easygoing—surfing, partying, sports cars and beautiful women. The death threat didn't seem real."

"But it was."

He nodded. "Someone invaded my house one night, but I heard them breaking in and I got away in time. After that, I was convinced. So…"

"No more Mark Lexmond," she guessed.

He nodded. "I said goodbye to my friends and father, still hoping I'd be back before too long, and went into the Witness Protection Program. For a while I was in limbo while the authorities tried to put together a case against Nor—the man who threatened me. They weren't successful.

"So I was given a new identity and sent to Florida. For a time I retained my paranoia. The threat hung over me, making me suspicious of everyone I saw. But eventually I began to believe that I was safe."

His voice was hoarse now. The strain in his face tugged at Karina's heart. She wanted to hold him, love him, tell him that it would be all right. But what did she know?

"I began to relax," he continued. "I had a new name, was working as a bartender. Living the good life in the southern sun. I almost felt like my old self. Then one weekend morning, out of nowhere, a tourist was shot by a sniper. One foot away from me. I'd bent down to pick up a few coins the guy had dropped after buying an Italian ice from a street vendor."

An anguished cry flew from Karina's mouth before she could clap her hand over it to keep her distress inside. She didn't want to add her emotions to Alex's burden.

He went on. "They shouldn't have been able to find me. All I could think was that there'd been a mole in the system who'd leaked information about my whereabouts, so when I left Florida I did it on my own—no more contact with the U.S. Marshals. Completely alone. I figured that's how it'd be for the rest of my life until—" His voice, fissured with cracks, finally broke. "Until you."

It all made sense now. The surreptitious use of the binoculars, the suspicion masquerading as rudeness, his inner struggle. The vivid chapter he'd written. The extreme reaction to Nikki Silk and the photographer. Even his dedication to finding *her* mole.

"I'm trying to…" She waved a hand, at a loss for words. His story was too much to take in. Far more devastating than her silly guesses. "W-what happens now?"

"I've been asking myself that question for the past several weeks."

"Do you think you're safe?"

"So far, yes. I had a few suspicions about your lurker, but clearly I was way off."

"You told me that you might have to leave at any time…."

"Yes. Just pick up and go."

"But that's no way to live!"

He sighed. "I know. If I stay, though, I put you in danger, too."

She placed the photos in his childhood keepsake and closed the lid. "Then this should be *my* choice." Hugging the box to her chest, she raised her eyes to his.

One look and he knew. "Karina, I can't let you sacrifice—"

"What sacrifice? We'll go on as if you're safe, and if ever there's reason to suspect…well, then I'll go with you." Determination surged through her. "Don't bother trying to change my mind. You forget that I served time as an ambassador's daughter. I'm familiar with tight security and emergency plans, and even moving from one place to another. I can handle it."

"No. If you had to give up everything just for me—" Alex's voice broke off. He couldn't stop shaking his head.

Until she pushed the box under the tree and clasped his face between her hands. "That might not happen, right? But if it does—I'd rather be with you, anywhere in the world, than here, alone."

"You're not alone. You have friends and family. I know what it's like to leave people behind and I wouldn't wish that on my worst enemy, let alone..." He turned his face to kiss her palm. "The woman I love."

"Ah." She touched her nose to his. "That's no way to deter me." Her lips pooched out to plant a tiny peck on his mouth. "Tell me, without being a noble martyr, do you *want* to stay?"

She swore she pulled the word out of him by her own strength of will, but finally his resistance crumbled and his body relaxed and he said, with a longing that matched her own, *"Yes."*

"Then you'll stay. As Alex. And we'll be vigilant. You can write, I'll run the shop and we'll live happy, full lives without any fanfare."

"It won't be that easy."

"Nothing ever is." She kissed him again. "Except seduction by chocolate."

His mouth twitched. "I really am allergic, you know."

"That's okay. We'll leave the truffles to Debby and Kyle."

He looped his arms around her waist, pulling her

closer. "Tell me, if there's an aphrodisiac in the choco-lates, how did you dare let your party guests consume so many at once? Children too."

"Oh. Well, the thing is—we get a limited supply of the special chocolate. So the majority of our candies are—" She held up two fingers. "Just a *teensy* bit potent. It's amazing what the power of suggestion will do."

"Don't I know it." He gave a dry laugh, the haunted look lingering in his eyes. She supposed that might never change.

They must always live for the moment, she real-ized. And that meant no holding back. No keeping tight control.

"Alex…" She wanted to kiss him again, but even more, she wanted to say this while looking deep into his eyes. She would drive out the past and replace it with the here and now. "Alex, I love you, with all my heart. And you'd better get used to it, because I'm no fling. There won't be any leaving me behind." To combat the urge to pinch her nose, she took his hand and threaded their fingers together into a knot. "We're bound by a se-cret now, you and I. I'm pretty good at keeping secrets."

"So I found out." He smiled, before leaning in to kiss behind her ear. "About your password…"

"I don't give out my password."

"The fake one. KJSTRSTALEX."

"Just a little message to you." She smiled. "My ini-tials are KJS. TRST—trust. I trust you, Alex, no matter what name you use."

She sensed that he wanted to debate, threaten, scold, anything at all to get her to see reason, but she wasn't having it. Not on Christmas morning, when she'd been given the gift of a lifetime. Alex, Lex, Mark, it didn't matter. The man was hers.

Their kisses were sweet, soft, sacred. After awhile they began to laugh for no reason, except relief, perhaps, and then Alex's hands were inside her pajama top. She tilted her head back, lost in the glimmer and spicy musk and the pleasure moving through her, so good even without the chocolate rush.

Alex stopped. "What's this?" He felt Esmeralda's card in her breast pocket. "Ah, the fortune."

"We don't need that," she said, finally understanding that the future was unknowable.

"Just this once." Alex put his fingers into the pocket, wickedly stroking across her breast before he fished out the card. He looked so serious when he read it that she expected the worst, a dire prediction of doom and gloom.

"Huh," he said. "What do you think of that?"

She read the card he held up. Machine Out Of Fortunes. Buy More At Sanders Carnival Supply Co. 1000 Cards For $10.00.

Humor plucked at Alex's mouth. "What do you think that means? We're out of luck?"

"No." Karina took his hand and returned it her breast. "It means that from now on, our fortune is our own to create. And I think we will do just fine."

"Remarkable, even."

"Spectacular."

"Stellar."

"Stellar," she agreed. "Merry Christmas…*Alex.*"

He stroked her hair. "Merry Christmas, Karina." Kissed the tip of her nose. "And, finally…hello."

Kiss & Tell

ALISON KENT

Alison Kent is the author of several steamy books for Mills & Boon, as well as a handful of fun and sassy stories for other imprints. She is also the author of *The Complete Idiot's Guide to Writing Erotic Romance*. Alison lives in a Houston, Texas, suburb with her own romance hero.

Look out for *Fast, Furious and Forbidden* by Alison Kent, available in February 2010 from Mills & Boon® Blaze®.

To Walt, for TMZ

To Brenda, for Dumbledore

To HelenKay, for making sure I stayed sane

Prologue

April…

"An appellate ruling has paved the way for a retrial in the case of Baltimore businessman E. Marshall Gordon. The CEO of EMG Enterprises was the fifth member of the board of directors to face charges of conspiracy to commit fraud related to EMG's off-the-book partnerships. More on that in our national news segment after the break.

"And coming up in our celebrity beat, we have the latest from Max Savage on Colorado congressman Teddy Eagleton's recent divorce from his wife of twelve years, and his romantic connection to Ravyn Black, the lead singer of the chart-topping emo band Evermore—"

"Enough, already." Corinne Sparks reached to flip off the small television set she kept in the back room at Under the Mistletoe, almost knocking over a glass vase of hyacinths and lilies as she did.

Miranda Kelly, Corinne's employer and owner of the flower shop in the resort town of Mistletoe, Colorado, had been seconds from doing the same thing. Neither one of them enjoyed seeing pieces of their lives on the news, and to be mentioned that way, one on top of the other—first her ex-husband, then Corinne's estranged daughter—was too much.

"Tell me about it." Miranda had been intent on using the quiet spring day for bookkeeping, but the specter of her past impinging on her present allowed room for little else in her head. "I left Baltimore so I wouldn't have to be bombarded by the media's obsession with everything related to Marshall. I sure don't want to think about him while I'm paying bills."

Frowning, Corinne resituated two of the lilies that had slipped in the close call. "I thought you left because the SOB couldn't keep his zipper zipped."

Well, there was that, thought Miranda, swiveling on the bar stool she used at the short end of the long L-shaped worktable that served as a desk. "That's why I divorced him. And seeing his face every time I turn on the news these days reminds me how stupid I was to marry him in the first place."

"He wasn't a cheater when you married him," Corinne reminded her.

"Pfft. He obviously had it in him to be one." Miranda paused and tapped her pencil on the table's surface, feeling an unexpected pang of hurt at the memory of Marshall's infidelity. Logical or not, that pained her more than his criminal acts. "But I can tell you for a fact that the gossip sheets got it wrong. He did not go looking for sex elsewhere because he wasn't getting any at home."

"You're preaching to the gossip-loathing choir here," Corinne said, setting the finished arrangement in the refrigerated storage case for a late-afternoon delivery. "I know firsthand how much garbage gets printed as truth. Then again, in Brenna's case, a lot of the garbage *is* the truth."

Corinne had been working at the flower shop for five years now, ever since Miranda had moved back to the small Rocky Mountain town where she'd grown up, and bought the business from its retiring owners.

She and Corinne had been good friends long enough for Miranda to know the extent of the conjecture printed about her employee's daughter, as well as the grief Brenna Sparks—the very same Ravyn Black mentioned in the Max Savage news segment—had caused Corinne. It was enough grief to bring about mother and daughter's current alienation.

But since the television mention gave Miranda the opening, she took advantage and voiced what had been on her mind. "I'd been wondering when the congressman's divorce was going to be final."

"Such a proud moment, too," Corinne said with a snort, "having to face that your daughter lacks the decency to keep her hands off a married man."

And now Teddy Eagleton wasn't married. Miranda sighed. "Ravyn—Brenna's an adult. She's been on her own for a long time now. And she's the one who'll have to answer for the things she's done."

"Really? Because she hasn't had to answer for much of anything yet." Corinne returned to her end of the worktable and flipped through the rest of the sale tickets to make certain she'd completed the day's most pressing orders. "And, unlike your ex, I wonder if she ever will."

Miranda knew Corinne was talking about the money she'd sent her daughter for college expenses—four years' worth of lab fees, textbooks, tuition for extra classes when Brenna had pretended to change her majors, as well as room and board. The money had been spent instead on funding her band.

Brenna had paid for equipment and instruments, a practice room, stage clothes and traveling, not even completing her first semester, and making Corinne feel like a fool—especially since Brenna had bribed her little sister Zoe to intercept mail sent by the university in Washington State in order to keep their mother from discovering the truth.

Miranda knew, too, that several times over the past six years—since Evermore's first album had hit it big—Brenna had tried to pay back her mother the money she'd stolen, and that Corinne had refused it, wanting nothing to do with what she called her daughter's ill-gotten gains.

It wasn't hard for Miranda to understand Corinne's feelings…except that it was. Brenna's "unexpected needs" had depleted the girls' college fund, and Corinne was now struggling to find what Zoe would require for the basics as a freshman next year. She was struggling, too, with trusting Zoe, who'd been just as culpable as Brenna.

"Will you have to testify at the retrial?"

Corinne's question snapped Miranda out of her reverie and dropped her back into the pit of worry she'd been doing a fairly good job of steering clear of. "I don't know. My attorney says there's a good chance I will, but he's doing all he can to keep it from happening. Trust me, if I have to fly into Baltimore, I'm going to fly out as fast as I can."

"You know, I'm surprised there haven't been more reporters snooping around, seeing how this *is* your family's home."

"You and me both." Not that they'd have an easy time finding her; when she'd returned to Mistletoe, she'd legally taken her mother's maiden name for her own—a protective measure she'd felt necessary at the time.

Corinne went on. "I figured the ones hungry enough for a statement would at least make the effort. Especially considering the scope of your ex's crimes."

A scope that had cost thousands of EMG employees their pensions and almost as many investors everything they'd owned. "Marshall was always a big believer in the grand scale. The more money, the more power, the more covers on *Forbes* the better."

"Or at least he *was* a big believer until he was sentenced to all those big years. I guess that was one grand scale he never saw coming." Corinne tore her copy of the next ticket from the order book and turned to study the shelf of vases, choosing an elegantly flared one of cut crystal. "You think the outcome will be any different this time?"

Miranda turned back to her laptop. Like her employee, she had work to do. "As far as him being guilty or innocent? No. But it better be different in that this time it sticks. I don't want to look up every five years to find a reporter sticking a microphone and camera in my face."

1

November...

IT WASN'T IN Caleb McGregor's bag of reporter's tricks to go after a story by drinking himself under anyone's table, but here he was, at the Inn at Snow Falls' Club Crimson, in the lovers' resort of Mistletoe, Colorado, looking for clarity in the bottom of a glass.

Several glasses actually.

He knew better. Of course he knew better. But knowing better hadn't kept him from recently making the biggest mistake of his life. Neither did it negate the fact that he'd found many an answer to an intriguing question when his nose—or his blood alcohol level—was where it didn't belong.

Even when he was sober, his intuition rivaled that of the female population of Baltimore—the city he called his base of operations rather than home, *home* being a word with too much emotional resonance and Caleb not being a feelings kind of guy.

And that sixth sense had shifted into high gear the minute the lounge singer had taken the stage.

Unfortunately, the Scotch he'd downed had left him with a slippery grip on the instincts insisting he was sitting on top of a big fat scoop—one that might be as big and as fat as the exclusive he'd come here at Ravyn Black's invitation to get.

Whether or not that was the case, one thing was certain.

Club Crimson lived up to its vivid name.

The Inn at Snow Falls' nightclub was a kaleidoscope of reds, from the carpet splashed with sherry, claret and port-wine hues, to the padded bar and stools of scarlet, to the plush sofas and matching wing chairs in patterns of ruby and rose.

The decorative color scheme was not what Caleb found objectionable. After all, he'd yet to meet an Italian or Chinese restaurant he didn't like. Hell, his favorite baseball team had red in its name and wore the color proudly when taking the field at Fenway.

But when the design of a club was calculated to evoke a romantic, sexy mood, and that evocation lacked even a hint of the subtle finesse that made sexy *sexy,* and the entire setup was set up in a town called Mistletoe, well...

Never let it be said that Caleb McGregor didn't embrace his cynicism wholeheartedly.

And then, as if the ornamental bloodbath wasn't enough, Club Crimson had gone so over the top in their efforts to promote romance as to hire a red-haired chanteuse and call her Candy Cane.

A textbook case of adding insult to injury. Or it would've been had she not manipulated the schmaltzy

lyrics into telling a story with the skill of Scheherazade—
and done so with a husky R & B style, and in a voice he
swore he'd heard before but couldn't for the drunken life
of him place.

He was falling for it all—the words that seduced him, the
costume that tempted him, the act as a whole that had him
mentally panting like a randy teen. Or a full-grown man with
more alcohol than reasoning skills at his disposal.

Considering the number of drinks he'd downed, the only
part of this that came as a surprise was the fact that he was
able to recognize the folly of his ways.

At least he'd had the good sense at the beginning of the
evening to claim a back corner booth. He was out of the way,
and in the perfect position to watch. And watch he did,
closely, enjoying himself more than was wise.

She was a looker, Ms. Cane, though considering the pretense of the rest of this place, he doubted her assets were
genuine. That didn't stop him from having a good time ogling
the plunging front of her cherry-colored gown.

He wasn't sure how women did it—kept their tits from
falling out of flesh-baring tops cut from their throats to their
navels. Some, he knew, had little to fear, but not in this case.
Whether Mother Nature or manufactured, she had a lot.

She was curvy, too, her cinched-in waist flaring into real hips
instead of not flaring at all. He liked hips. He liked a woman
with an ass. If he ran the world, women would be required by
law to be more than a pair of breasts on an androgynous body.

He'd amend the Constitution if he had to, put a picture of
Candy Cane next to one of Ravyn Black, the practically her-
maphroditic singer for the emo band Evermore he'd come
to Mistletoe to see, to illustrate the difference between ass
and no ass.

Yeah, that would be the perfect way to make his point. His point being…did he have a point?

Had he ever had a point? Was that the point his crossed eyes were seeing at the end of his nose? Or had his point become all soft and squishy and not pointy at all when he'd upended his glass and swallowed the last of his drink?

O…kay.

It was quitting time, heading-to-bed time. Time to just say no.

Or it would be if he wasn't stuck.

The pianist was playing the introductory notes to the singer's final song, and the crowd that had quieted when she walked onstage, that had done no more than whisper as she sang Frank Sinatra and Ella Fitzgerald and Harry Connick, Jr., had grown deathly still, pin-droppingly silent.

If Caleb got up now, he was likely to be shot.

Candy pulled the microphone from the stand she'd made love to during her previous song, and began to croon the opening lines of her last. Her hips swaying, she crossed the small corner stage and descended the steps into the mesmerized crowd drunk on whiskey, wine and love.

Her hair that he was sure was a wig—long, wavy, strawberry-blond—picked up and reflected the flashes of red thrown by the spinning disco ball, as did the sequins in the dress molded to her curves. So molded, in fact, that if it weren't for the peekaboo slit running up one thigh, he doubted she'd be able to walk.

He watched her wind her way through the gathered listeners, smiling, fingering one man's tie, brushing another's hair from his forehead, cupping a shoulder or stroking her finger along a forearm of their female companions. An equal-opportunity seductress, Caleb mused, finding his eyelids drifting lazily as he, too, fell prey to her spell.

A siren, she moved from table to table, the sultry sweep of her lashes, the alluring touch of her tongue to her lips, making men's knees weak, their palms sweaty, their blood run hot, the front of their pants—once flat against their abdomens—rise like pitched tents. He knew that's what was happening around the room because it was happening to him.

It didn't matter that he was the only person in the room sitting by himself. His reaction would've been the same had he been in the company of his mother, a date or a priest. He wasn't hard because he was alone, or because he was lonely. He was hard because Candy Cane had made him that way.

But the fact that this was a group erection cheapened what he felt—or so he tried to convince himself, since he didn't want to feel anything.

And then something else happened. She turned just so, moved to the perfect spot, leaned against the back of a sofa at the ideal angle with the lights exactly right. The moment didn't last longer than a blink before it was gone, and she'd bowed her body toward another sap in the crowd.

But it stuck with him, wouldn't let him go, and he studied her instead of looking away, stared at her instead of chalking up what he thought he was seeing to too much Scotch on a stomach empty of anything else.

What he thought he was seeing was a familiar face. A familiar face to go with the voice he could've sworn he recognized at the beginning of her set. A recognition he'd then dismissed because of how many times the server had replaced the single malt in his snifter.

Now he really did need a drink, and he needed it to be hot, black and fully caffeinated so he could make sense of the psychedelic swirls and splatters of reds Club Crimson had painted in his mind.

His job depended on rumors. He listened, he verified, he discarded. He'd been doing it for ten years, writing a celebrity gossip column that had started out small and gone into national syndication twenty-four months after launch. It was so popular, it was featured during what one TV network called their "celebrity beat," and had its own Web site to boot.

Caleb McGregor was Max Savage, the notorious "Snoop with the Scoop," loved, lauded and feared far and wide by politicians, society players and celebrities alike for his sarcastic riffs on what his audience demanded and deemed newsworthy about those in the public eye.

Not that anyone at the inn knew who he was, or that he was here by invitation for an exclusive—the very private wedding of Ravyn Black and Teddy Eagleton. Over the next few days, he'd be covering the preparations leading up to the big event. But as always, he was posing as a member of Max Savage's street team. Not even Ravyn knew he was Max.

The only people who knew his identity, who would ever know or have need to, were his agent, his attorney and his editor. When he'd set off down tabloid road ten years ago, he'd made sure his only connection was to the Max Savage machine, not to the alter ego itself.

It was a decision that had turned out to be a sanity-saver, keeping his personal business out of the limelight. And it was going to make it a whole lot easier to transition to life after Max—a retirement that would have him hanging up his gear as soon as he finished this gig.

Yes, he found the energy of chasing down nonstop leads more intoxicating than the boredom of waiting for a big story to break. But he'd never thought he'd end up stooping to the level he had, reporting on celebutantes flashing their bare crotches or finding fame through night-vision sex tapes.

Neither had he thought himself capable of betraying a confidence, so wrapped up in the thrill that he hadn't realized he'd gone too far until it was too late. Until he'd ruined a career by telling the truth. Until he'd lost a lifelong friend because he'd been drunk on the rush of the scoop.

He'd give anything to take back the last month, to think before revealing what his best friend Del, a music star in his own right, had shared in confidence about his Christian pop star fiancée's drug problem…but life didn't work that way.

Caleb couldn't change what he'd done, but he could damn well make sure it never happened again. Right now, however, it was vital that he get his act together. Candy had finished her tour of the rest of the club and was making her way toward him.

Drinking alone and slumped in his seat made him an easy target. Being male made him vulnerable—even knowing her act was a ruse. Last he'd checked, knowledge didn't necessarily work as an inoculant. Especially with his susceptibility to her charms camped out in his pants.

Except for her spotlight, the bar light and the patterns of color thrown off by the disco ball's spin, the club was dark. His corner was even darker, giving him the privacy he needed to adjust his crotch before she reached him.

And then she was there, singing to him, seducing him, the pull in her gaze mesmerizing as she perched her hip against the edge of his table and stretched, draping herself toward him strategically as if she'd done this hundreds of times for hundreds of other men.

Her neckline plunged to tease him. The slope of her shoulder as she leaned close, the movement of her neck, chin and mouth as she sang, teased him more. But what teased him most of all was knowing he should know her, being unable to place her, and sitting here too inebriated to do anything to find out.

He told himself to remember everything about her, to store the sound of her voice in the memory banks he could access most quickly when his wits returned. He didn't hold out much hope for success. She had him stupid, bewitched.

Fluidly, the redheaded chanteuse rolled herself up and off the table, pivoting with an elegance that left him breathless—and therefore, thankfully, unable to groan and give himself away—as she slid to sit in his lap.

It wasn't his lap as much as one leg, but the move put the swell of her bottom against the swell of his fly, and he could only hope the part of him making intimate contact with her wasn't as apparent to her as he feared.

She seemed comfortable, in her element, looping her arm around his neck, looking into his eyes, drawing the song to a close with a breathy, bluesy, brush of words against his cheek as the pianist wrapped up his accompaniment, holding the final notes.

That was when the applause began.

And that was when she kissed him.

He hadn't seen it coming.

He knew the soft teasing press of her mouth to his was part of the act, but he hadn't expected it, and he wasn't thinking straight, and he was running way low on resistance, so he did what any healthy red-blooded male would do with a healthy red-blooded female wanting to lock lips.

He kissed her back.

He caught her off guard. She was bargaining on compliance, thinking he would accept her doing her thing without interfering, interrupting or doing his back. But Caleb wasn't cut from a compliant cloth. And kissing Candy Cane was fun. Or it was until he realized he was the one who was stirred.

Lips on lips was one thing, but this was more. Way more,

and his blood heated and rushed. He opened his mouth to taste her. She gave in, letting his tongue inside to flirt and slick over hers.

He had a vague sense of people around them clapping and whistling, cheering them on, of the pianist's fingers lingering over his instrument's keys, drawing out the moment that had already gone on too long.

But mostly he was aware of Candy's scent like a field of sweet flowers around him, and the touch of her fingers against his nape, the tiny massaging circles she made there too personal for a public display.

He had to let her go before things got any further out of hand, he realized, realizing, too, that he had sobered. He pulled his mouth away and tilted his head back to get the best look that he could into her eyes.

He saw her surprise, then her fear. The first he'd anticipated; he'd felt it himself. The second emotion set the pump on his snoop-and-scoop machine to maximum. Fear? What the hell did she have to be afraid of?

"Who are you?" he asked as she got to her feet, the smile she gave him reaching no farther than her mouth and as much for the crowd as for him.

"I'm the woman you'll never forget," she told him, blowing him a parting kiss before returning to the stage.

Once there, she took her final bow with a flourish, gave props to the pianist then vanished behind the curtain that came down to swallow the stage.

She had it right. He wouldn't forget. But what she had no way of knowing was that, impending retirement or not, big-time screwup or not, he planned to dig up a whole lot more stuff to remember. Stuff he was pretty damn sure Ms. Candy Cane didn't want anyone to find out.

2

WELL. That had been interesting, Miranda Kelly mused ruefully, standing in her dressing room, staring at her reflection and finding Candy Cane staring back.

She had yet to remove her costume—a costume that was more than the dress or the shoes or the colored contacts or the wig. The whole persona of Candy was everything she wasn't.

As Miranda, she wore glasses, though she did accessorize with fashionable frames to emphasize the green of her eyes. Her own hair was auburn in contrast to Candy's strawberry-blond, and cropped close in a wispy elfin cut.

Her skin was nowhere as smooth as Candy's, plus it was ridiculously freckled—a fact that she'd hidden from Baltimore society when she'd lived there behind a cool façade of flawlessly made-up skin, French twists and perfect posture, the veneer of a high-profile life.

She was nothing if not a chameleon.

But, wow. Kissing an audience member? Had she really been so stupidly careless? She'd told Corinne several months ago that her biggest fear about testifying at Marshall's retrial was suffering a repeat of the media madness and losing her sanctuary in Mistletoe as a result. It was imperative that she draw no attention to herself to keep that from happening.

Oh, sure, she flirted and toyed with and played with and teased members of the crowd every night, but she did so as Candy; Miranda was off-limits to the visitors at the inn. That personal touch was part of Candy's act and the only outlet Miranda had to keep her feminine wiles from rusting.

She hadn't dated at all in the five years she'd been here, and hadn't enjoyed more than conversation with the male company she regularly kept. Mistletoe, Colorado, was not a hotbed of sexy, intelligent, available men.

It was a lovers' resort, a place where the people listening to her sing would not be focused on her but on their partners. And that was exactly as it should be. Her rumination was not at all a complaint. Her complaint was that *she* had behaved so rashly, so…thoughtlessly. With Marshall once again in the news, she couldn't afford to stand out, to be noticed.

So who was he, the man she had kissed, the man who had let her, who had kissed her back with a mouth that tasted like aged Scotch and heat? And what was he doing alone in a town that catered to lovers—most of whom had sought out the hideaway specifically because of the privacy it afforded?

She sank onto her vanity bench, still shocked. She could not believe how impressively she had screwed up.

No one passed through Mistletoe by chance, or planned a night out at Club Crimson unless they were staying at the Inn at Snow Falls. The town was off the beaten path, the inn stuck in its own time warp. Visitors were here for a reason.

That meant the likelihood she would see *him* again was spectacular. And with this combustible thing between them having flared in such a sparkling display, her odds of screwing up again were even higher. She couldn't let that happen—not with the publicity from Marshall's trial looming.

Before the career move a decade ago that had taken her

from Denver to Baltimore, and before meeting Marshall and marrying him in the same church where she sang in the choir, she'd spent all but her college years in Mistletoe, growing up an only child of parents who worked in the school district here.

When her life as Mrs. Gordon had soured—not a surprising development considering her husband's indictment for fraud and the dredging up of his affairs during his trial, she'd found herself thinking back to the simple, uncluttered magic of this place she still thought of as home.

In Mistletoe, discretion was paramount. It was even more so at the Inn at Snow Falls. The resort's staff was merciless in vetting credentials, checking IDs and keeping out media riffraff.

She'd seen them in action, and knew that facet of the hideaway's reputation was what brought celebrities and public figures here for intimate trysts, photos of which they didn't want splashed across tabloid covers.

That was the atmosphere she, too, had needed, and with the help of trusted friends, she had escaped the East Coast, leaving the gossips floundering.

For months after, newsmen who followed society scandals had hunted her, wanting the exclusive of her exile. She'd watched from the safety of her snowy cocoon and experienced a flurry of emotions, her feelings ultimately boiling down to one.

She hated the press. H-a-t-e-d reporters and their supposed journalistic integrity. They were vultures. They'd treated her like carrion during Marshall's trial and the divorce. They were as responsible as her ex for making her life hell. But no more.

She refused to spend another moment feeling bared and naked, flayed, exposed to her bones like an instructional cadaver or a plasticized body in a museum display. That's how it had seemed, having the population of the northern Atlantic states knowing minute details of her life....

Her propensity for speeding through traffic lights. How she spent more time on her own charity work than socializing with Marshall or at home. The way an hour of Ashtanga yoga left her smelling as though she hadn't bathed in days. Whether her salon's beauty technician gave her a bikini wax or a Brazilian. And if any of those things sent Marshall into the arms—and beds—of all those other women.

Despite her very public night job she now held, no one had found her, partly because of the disguise she wore onstage—and that was one of the reasons she wore it, to limit any obvious connection between her two selves—and partly because of how well the residents of Mistletoe protected their own.

But the main reason her cover hadn't been blown—besides her legal change of name—was that the only outsiders she mixed with were the customers who came in to order plants and floral arrangements from Under the Mistletoe.

Or such had been the case until she'd fallen all over the gorgeous stranger who'd kissed her until she felt as though she was going to die.

Smart. Real smart. A veritable genius of a cookie.

She dropped her forehead to the vanity's surface and groaned—which only made things worse because it brought to mind all the things he'd made her feel. She'd forgotten how sweet it could be to slide her tongue against a man's seeking to enter her mouth.

Such an exquisite pleasure, that first sweet connection, its wetness, its promise, its warmth. She'd enjoyed a comfortable sex life with Marshall—until he'd begun finding his comfort elsewhere—but she never had seen stars.

She could get used to stars, she told herself, sitting up to study her reflection. She didn't know what she was looking for, something different or new, a visible indication that something within her had changed because of a starry kiss.

She knew that nothing had, that nothing could have. She'd been on her stranger's table and in his lap no more than seconds, and her mouth had been pressed to his, seeking, searching, aching, almost no time at all.

The only thing to change had been her perfect record at staying smart. Five years sober, and she'd fallen off the wagon because of a man. Stupid, stupid, stupid. If her actions became a time bomb and blew up in her face, she would have no one to blame but herself.

"Argh," she roared, surging up off the bench. She needed someone to talk to. Reassurance that she hadn't screwed herself. A reinforcing slap to the head telling her that everything she wanted was *not* in a stranger's kiss—no matter that it had felt as if that was exactly where she would find it.

3

"DO YOU BELIEVE in love at first sight?"

Alan Price, Club Crimson's manager and overflow bartender, stared at Miranda as if she'd grown two heads, which she supposed was about the size of it. She had her Miranda head, and her Candy head, and Alan was one of the few people who knew both well, working with her here at the club, and having lived next door to her when they were kids.

"Was it love at first sight with me and Patrice?" he asked, clipboard in hand while he did his nightly inventory, a shock of his sun-bleached hair falling forward to hide his frown. "Is that what you're asking?"

Miranda settled more comfortably onto the bar stool in the now-empty lounge, leaning an elbow on the bar and propping her chin in her hand. "Tell me about meeting Patrice. I'm in the mood for a good love story."

Alan had calmed her down with a couple of drinks when she'd blasted into the club after her dressing-room panic attack, promising her the crowd had thought nothing of the spice she'd added to her show.

He'd calmed her enough, in fact, that she was almost ready to call it a night, to head back to her dressing room, to strip off Candy…and then hope her ancient import started when she went out in the cold to go home. One of these days, she really did need to spring for a new car.

A reformed ski bum, having shed the *bum* part for re-spectability, Alan shook his head as if too busy cleaning up to humor her. "You know how I met Patrice. I've heard her tell you the story more than once."

Feeling all fluid and relaxed, Miranda sighed. "She's told me, yes. I want to hear it from you."

He took away her wineglass, added it to the crate of dirties destined for the kitchen before he left for the night. After that, he pointed at the clock on the wall at the end of the bar. The hands, shaped like corkscrews, were edging toward 1:00 a.m., the club having closed at midnight.

He yawned for emphasis. "She's waiting for me to get home. If she calls, I'm handing the phone to you."

"And I'll tell her it's your fault, not mine," Miranda said before sticking out her tongue, the back and forth a familiar pattern from their years as friends.

"How the hell in any universe is it my fault?"

"You could be halfway through the story by now, for all that you're dawdling." Men. Why was it so hard for them to talk about their emotional investments? They certainly had no trouble talking about their portfolios. It wasn't like she'd asked him to open a vein and bleed out his feelings for Patrice all over the bar.

Then again, maybe it wasn't copping to love at first sight he was dodging. Maybe it was the embarrassment of not having been on his game when they met, she mused, smiling to herself as she recalled the story Patrice had shared.

"I was skiing," he told her, obviously taking note of the look on her face and scowling as he wiped a rag over the bar, his motions so furious that she thought he'd rub away the finish. "I crashed, broke my leg. Patrice was on the patrol team that rescued me."

The short, to-the-point, testosterone version. She wanted

more. She wanted all the heat and the want and the feelings. "What about the eye contact? The jolt to your heart? The tingle you felt when she pulled off her gloves and laid the backs of her fingers against your cheek?"

"That was frostbite."

Miranda laughed, the sound echoing loudly in the quiet room. "You, Alan Price, are so full of crap. You felt it all just like Patrice did, and you know it."

He stopped scrubbing the already clean bar, and gave her a look, color high on his sharp cheekbones. "Then you didn't need to hear it from me, did you?"

"Sure I did. You've restored my faith that men will be men, and nothing there will ever change." He'd also reminded her that she wasn't missing out by being alone, no matter how magic a man's kiss. "Just the facts. No embellishments. No personalization. No deeper meaning."

His expression was very male and almost angry. "We feel things, Miranda. We may not talk about them, but they're there."

Well. That shut her up. She reached for his hand. "I'm sorry. I'm tired, and tonight threw me off-kilter. I guess I'm the one looking for deeper meaning, though I'm not sure why. Maybe I just need an explanation for what I did."

"And I told you. Candy hit a hell of a groove, that's all. The audience enjoyed it. There isn't any deeper meaning, so stop wasting time trying to find it."

Easy for him to say. He wasn't the one whose lips still felt the kiss, whose pulse had yet to quit racing. She toyed with the seam in the bar's padded edge, picking at threads that weren't there. "Let's hope it was a one-time thing. With Marshall's retrial coming up, Miranda can't afford for Candy to start getting careless."

"Does that mean you haven't changed your mind about singing at the Christmas dance?"

"No. I haven't." She wouldn't take Candy Cane out of Club Crimson, even as a favor to Patrice. She'd reiterated to Alan and his wife all the reasons why when first asked to perform at the Mistletoe County High dance.

"The kids would love it," Alan said, wooing her by wiggling both brows. "All they know is the legend of the sexy redhead who sings at the inn."

And if Miranda had her way, that was all the students would ever know about her. "The kids would *not* love it. I'm an old fart who sings old-fart songs. If anyone needs to perform for them, it's Zoe."

Corinne's younger daughter was seventeen and as brilliant a singer as her sister. Her voice was a deep, throaty alto, incredibly rich and mature for a girl so young.

Zoe was the reason Miranda had used a chunk of her obscenely large divorce settlement to establish the Candy Cane Scholarship for the Arts, and why she continued to funnel into it all the money she made at the club.

Even if Corinne had her reasons for not accepting Brenna's offer to repay the misappropriated funds plus interest, Zoe was too good to be hidden away. A legitimate study of voice and music seemed to Miranda the perfect compromise. The scholarship was her way of putting her money where her mouth was.

Miranda looked back at Alan. "I wish Patrice would add her to the program. Zoe could use the exposure."

"She's going to," Alan said, thrilling Miranda to bits. "But the kids know Zoe. Patrice was hoping for a big-name headliner."

"I heard her sister's in town," Miranda said, thinking about

Corinne and her relationships with her girls. Sooner or later
mother needed to meet older daughter halfway—even if only
for the sake of the younger. "Patrice should try to snag Ravyn."

"That might work if Patrice were willing to forget everything Mistletoe stands for and invade Ravyn's privacy, which
she's not going to do. And if Brenna and Corinne weren't on
the outs. There's no way Patrice is going behind Corinne's
back just to make points with the kids."

Miranda knew he was right. As cool a coup as it would be
for the senior class to have Evermore's lead singer at their
Christmas dance, there were a whole lot of circumstances in
the way of it happening.

Besides, with Ravyn—Brenna—estranged from her family, her visit to Mistletoe sans the band pretty much confirmed the rumors of her romantic liaison with right-wing and
conveniently newly single congressman Teddy Eagleton, who
Miranda had seen in the lobby earlier in the day.

Whatever the two were doing here, mentioning it to
Corinne was nothing Miranda wanted to do. Especially since
the other woman might soon be dealing with the reporters
turned away by security from the inn. Having experienced the
same, Miranda had great sympathy for what Corinne had
ahead of her.

"You finished with that?" Alan asked, looking over Miranda's head.

She started to tell him that he'd already done his conscien-
tious-bartender-and-childhood-friend duty and taken her
wineglass away. Then he realized she wasn't the one to whom
he was speaking.

She glanced over her shoulder and peered into the dark. A
man was walking toward them from the club's far corner, a
coffee cup and saucer in hand.

He was tall, and he rolled with a swagger, his legs long, his hips and waist narrow, his shoulders wide beneath the dark jacket he wore with his jeans…his jeans…

She'd sat in the lap of a man wearing jeans, a man who'd watched her show from the club's far corner. *Crap and double crap*. She turned back quickly, hissing at her ex-friend to get his attention.

"He's been here all this time and you didn't tell me?" Dear God, had she given herself away? Had he overheard Alan call her Miranda? Had she confessed that she was still reeling from the contact of their lips and their tongues? "What the hell is wrong with you?"

Alan smirked his ex-friend enjoyment of her distress. "Patrice said you've been extra moody lately. I figured you might need to get laid."

"I hate you, you know."

"I know. I hate you, too."

Thank God she hadn't taken off her wig. That was the only thought that crossed her mind before the stranger who kissed like a god climbed onto the stool beside her, filling the space as if it had been waiting a lifetime for him to find it. Uh, yeah. This couldn't be good.

"Thanks for the coffee," he told Alan, giving Miranda his profile to study as he handed the cup and saucer across the bar. "I wasn't sure I'd be able to make it to my room, or even remember where I put it."

As hard as she tried not to, Miranda couldn't help a soft laugh; the sound had him swiveling slowly toward her, cocking his head, drinking her in until she forgot to breathe and changed her mind about this being good.

"Laugh at me, laugh with me. I'll take either one."

Oh, he was sharp. And gorgeous. Somehow she'd missed

the full extent of his gorgeousness when she'd been in his lap, but there was still nothing she wouldn't give right now for a big fat hole in the ground.

A hole swallowing her would keep her from looking at his mouth. His mouth, his lips, his tongue, his teeth. She remembered them all. She wanted them all. She wanted more.

She wanted him. She'd been right the first time. This was not good.

"Caleb McGregor," he said, offering her his hand.

After a moment, she took it. "Candy Cane."

"According to the marquee," he said, before letting her go.

Touché, she thought, refusing to confirm his assumption with body language or voice. "I'm not sure if I should thank you or beg your forgiveness."

The mouth that had been all over hers and made her into a marshmallow smiled. "There's nothing to forgive, and I'm pretty sure I'm the one who should be thanking you."

He was smart. Smooth. Cutely self-deprecating rather than smarmy. Or maybe that was the kiss talking, and she should be listening to her survival instincts instead. "You were a good sport, and I'm sorry if I embarrassed you. I don't usually get that...personal with the audience."

He paused a moment, taking her in. "Then I'm glad I was there when you decided to change things up."

Spice, Alan had called it. Adding spice to Candy's routine. If only it were that simple, adding, changing, but the truth rarely was. And this particular truth wasn't easy to admit.

There had been no conscious decision in what she'd done. Her brain had had nothing to do with her sliding into his lap. Hormones and lust were responsible for her pressing her mouth to his and giving him her tongue. She'd seen him. She'd wanted him. She'd taken him.

And now here he was, sitting beside her, close, his knee brushing her thigh when he swiveled on the stool, a whiff of Scotch and coffee reaching her nose along with the scent of something earthy and warm.

She needed to excuse herself. To go. She was in so much trouble here. So, of course, she went ahead and made it worse. "What brings you to Mistletoe, Caleb? You're not here alone, are you?"

"Actually, I am," he said, bursting that insulating bubble.

Kiss or no kiss, his having a companion would've put him off-limits. Now he wasn't, which was going to make it hard to say no—to him, to herself…especially with Alan's comment about her needing to get laid echoing with more veracity than she liked.

She pushed aside the noise of that echo, focusing on Caleb's hand that rested flat on the bar. His fingers were long, thick, the backs broad and dusted with golden hair. She closed her eyes, opened them slowly, hoped he couldn't read her mind because, oh, there were so many places she wanted his touch.

"Alone? Really?" She cleared her throat. "I'm surprised."

He glanced over, arching a brow, questioning, curious. "Surely you get the occasional single up here."

She stared at him, studied him, liked too much what she was seeing…his stylishly mussed hair, a warm brown toasted with highlights…his eyes that were a gorgeous blend of gold and bronze…his mouth that she was certain did more things than kiss well.

Good. Not good. She didn't know the difference anymore. "I don't mingle enough with the guests to be sure, but I can't say I've seen anyone not part of a couple."

"Well, now you have," he told her, teased her. "Seen someone who's not, and mingled."

She looked down, went back to picking at the bar. "I'm just breaking all sorts of rules tonight."

"Must be the company you're keeping."

"I can't think of any other reason." It was hard to think of anything with her heart in her throat, choking her, cutting off her ability to breathe.

He watched her hands, then looked up, his eyes saying more than his words, saying that he knew what she was feeling, the extreme pull she was fighting. That he was fighting the same. "Can you think of one that would keep us from getting a drink?"

She nodded. "The bar's closed."

"That's a hard one to get around," he said, adding, "though I can think of one solution."

"No," she told him. Absolutely not. "I won't come up to your room for a nightcap."

"Rules?"

"Rules," she said, and nodded again.

"Too bad about the rules," he said, and she laughed. And then she stopped because he leaned close to say, "You're a hell of a kisser."

Well. She'd been hoping to hear him tell her goodbye. Or hear that he wasn't much for obeying the rules. He seemed the sort, a bit brash, a bit dangerous. He'd obviously convinced Alan to let him hang out long after closing.

"It was all part of the act," was what she finally said, ignoring the flutter of her pulse as he breathed her in and sighed, and the tongue of flame in her belly when he came back with, "The hell it was," a response that begged the question, *Where do we go from here?*

Alan clearing his throat pushed her to answer. "If you can stomach the mess, I have a bottle of Drambuie in my dressing room."

He didn't respond right away, looking her over, staring into her eyes. His were hard to read in this light, but that didn't lessen the impact of his gaze, or the heat simmering in the air around them.

She wasn't sure if she should take back the offer, if she'd been too forward in making it. If he had wanted nothing from her. Or had just wanted an acknowledgment that the kiss had been way out of line.

That wasn't how she'd read him, but she was so out of practice with men—

"A man in your dressing room. That's not against the rules?"

"I don't know," she said, sliding from her stool, unable to stop herself from giving in to this very big wrong that had her nape tingling, other places doing the same. "You're the first one I've ever invited to join me."

4

CALEB COULDN'T BELIEVE his good fortune. First, that the bartender had told him to take his time with the coffee. Second, that Candy Cane had so easily fallen prey to his charms.

Especially when he had so few.

If what he did have qualified as charming at all.

Not many people thought so.

As she'd gestured in the direction of her dressing room and turned for him to follow, he'd watched the subtle exchange that had passed between the redheaded siren and the bartender.

The man who'd served Caleb the coffee he'd so desperately needed hadn't seemed insulted or injured that she'd invited him back for a drink. Neither had he gone into protective, big-brother, hurt-her-and-I'll-kick-your-ass mode.

So far, so good.

Having witnessed the conversation the two had shared earlier, Caleb assumed the bartender and Candy were good friends. Not that he'd heard any of what they'd said, but he had noticed the casual nature of their exchange and the comfortable intimacy between them.

All that was to say…either the man behind the bar with the ski-bum look knew Candy could take care of herself, or knew Caleb was the one heading into trouble. Judging by the sway of her hips as she walked through the club and his body's primal reaction, Caleb heading into trouble was true either way.

He told himself to look up, to look away, over her shoulders, above her head, down at the floor. But her hips had been in his lap at the same time her tongue had been in his mouth, and that was all he could think about. That, and wanting more.

Or so it was until he reminded himself of why he was here, why he'd wanted the coffee in the first place. The recognition he'd needed to be sober enough to place. Yes, he was getting out of the biz, but he couldn't give up his curiosity any more than he could cut off a leg. If he figured her out and found her story worth telling, well…he'd cross the bridge of what to do when he got to it.

She led him through the bar, across the stage and to a door down the hallway behind the wings.

There was no name, no star, nothing to indicate where they were. It could just as easily have been a broom closet for the lack of signage. But she opened the door, and like a beast in rut, he followed her in.

"Like I said," she reminded him as she flipped on the lights. "A mess."

It didn't look any worse than his place, he mused, walking inside as she shut the door behind him. The floor was covered with the same red carpeting as the rest of the club. The walls were painted off-white with a pink tinge—or else the semi-gloss was reflecting the floor.

A closet with a six-foot rod took up the wall opposite one with six feet worth of mirrors. The accordion doors were open, showing red tops and bottoms on and off hangers, dresses draped over the pole, other items of clothing puddled on the floor and covering dozens of shoes flung here and there.

He turned toward the mirror, and she pushed in behind him, closing the doors as if to hide her shame. He wondered if her house was in the same disarray, and how she could look so put together when she dressed in a danger zone.

"I promise, I'm much neater than this in the rest of my life. For some reason when I'm here, I tend to let down my hair—as it were," she tacked on, nodding to a shelf of wigs he hadn't yet noticed.

"You didn't fool me for a minute," he told her, reaching for the strawberry strands where they caressed her bare shoulder. He allowed his fingers to linger on her skin, her soft skin that in this light was obviously freckled, leaving them there, tempting himself. Testing himself.

She was warm, smooth, and he couldn't help but think about the rest of her that was still covered, wondering how soft she'd be elsewhere, thinking, too, about her mouth and the touch of her tongue to his, wanting that again, wanting her taste, wanting another jolt of that unexpected heat.

It took her several seconds to move, and his gut tightened while he waited. He watched her face as it broadcast the push-pull conflict driving her, push winning out in the end and demanding distance and space between them—though pull sizzled in the air that had grown sharp with expectation.

She opened one of the lockerlike cabinets stacked next to the closet doors. "I have a bottle," she said, showing him the Drambuie and the single glass tumbler she had. "But I only have one glass."

He took it from her hand, took the bottle, too, uncapped it and poured. He drank, then offered the glass to her. "So we share."

She took it and sipped without hesitation. He closed up the bottle and set it on the vanity next to a pair of narrow-framed eyeglasses. A contact-lens case and a bottle of solution sat nearby, as did a brush with several strands of short dark hair caught in the bristles.

Caleb smiled, and turned back to the mysterious faux-redhead, thinking how much he'd like to see her in nothing but her freckles and her real hair. He swallowed hard, fighting the rush of blood through his veins, and asked, "What do singles do around here for fun?"

"Leave?" she suggested, and laughed softly, looking into the tumbler and avoiding looking at him. "The only place to get a drink besides Club Crimson is Manny's, but it's more a local watering hole. There's Fish and Cow Chips—"

"Seafood and steak?" he asked, cutting her off with a grimace at that mental image.

She held the glass close to her chest as she finally met his gaze. "Yes, it's very poorly named. Though the food is amazing."

"No theater with dinner?"

"Nope," she said, handing him their shared drink. "And if you want a movie, well, you drive down the mountain into Golden, or you get a satellite dish and be happy that you're only six months behind the pop-culture curve."

He wondered what she'd think if she knew he swung the bell for that curve. He leaned back against the edge of the vanity, swirled the herb-flavored liqueur in the glass, enjoyed the waft of aroma. Enjoyed even more being in close quarters with this woman he very much wanted to figure out.

"What do you do when you're not Candy?"

She gave him a teasing smile. "I'm always Candy."

"Then what does Candy do when she's not onstage?" he asked taking a step closer, feeling the crackle of electricity

burning fiercely between them, a live-wire connection he
swore he could reach out and touch.

This time she gave him a shake of her finger, a school-
teacher scolding a pupil for his impertinence, with a wickedly
sexy gleam in her eye. "Ah, that's something I only share with
friends and family."

"Hmm. In a town this size, that must cover everyone."
And then because he needed to know… "Including the man
in your life?" Or the men who once were.

She shook her head, sat on one end of the vanity bench,
took the glass when he offered it and allowed his fingers to
linger against hers. "No lovers, current or ex. Not for a very
long time."

"That's a shame." He joined her on the bench. The seat was
only so long, and their thighs brushed. She stayed where she
was. Even when he shifted to touch her hip, her arm, she
didn't move. "You're a beautiful woman."

At the base of her throat, her pulse jumped, but that was
her only response. She sat still, the glass of honeyed Scotch
liqueur held between both of her hands in her lap. The
walking slit in her skirt had parted to reveal the length of her
stocking-covered thigh. The deep V-neck in her top highlighted the inner swells of her breasts.

It was hard to keep his gaze on her face with all that bounty
to feast on, but her face along with her voice would help him
figure out if he knew her—though he had to admit he was
quickly forgetting he'd ever had such a hunch. He was much
more interested in exploring the rest of her, and doing so for
very selfish reasons.

"You never did tell me why you were here," she finally
said. A hitch in her chest when she breathed in revealed the
state of her composure.

He liked that she reacted to him, that he wasn't the only one here caught up by anticipation and need. "I'm attending a wedding."

She gave a nod, a smile. "Another celebrity off the market?"

"It's a private gig, but, yeah. It'll be a pretty big deal when it makes the news." He raised a brow, raised the drink. "I'm sure you could snoop into what's going on, if you really wanted to know. A perk of working here and all."

That caused her chin to come up, a frown to crease her brow—a response he hadn't expected, and one he filed away. "I don't think so," she said. "People come here because they don't have to worry about being stalked or hounded by the media, or by the staff."

He made a mental note not to reveal the hounding he had done, the stalking, definitely not the betrayal. Reaching for their shared glass, he set it on the floor beneath the bench, then shifted to better face her before cupping his hand to her cheek. "I'm sorry. Offending you is the last thing I'd ever want to do."

"What's the first?" she asked, her lashes drifting down in a soft sexy sweep before she raised her gaze in invitation.

The heat he'd been feeling grew to engulf him, and the surface of his skin fairly burned. "Are you sure you want to know?"

She nodded, the look in her eyes one of hunger, of craving, one that caused him to ache. When he leaned toward her, he wasn't a journalist. He was only a man. A man who hadn't been able to stop thinking about her since melting into her kiss.

And so he kissed her again. This time he didn't have to be still or discreet. He was able to close his eyes and give in to the desire that rolled through him the moment their lips made contact.

He continued to hold her face as he slanted his mouth over hers and coaxed her to open. She turned toward him, leaned into him, allowed him the access he wanted, and met him with her tongue.

The kiss was tentative, a gentle exploration. He didn't want to rush her or push her or frighten her away. She didn't want to give in too quickly or show him too much of her need. He felt it, though, in the tense way she held her jaw, in the tautness of her neck as she kept her head straight.

She'd admitted to having no lover. He had a feeling it had also been a while since she'd had something as simple as a kiss. Not that this kiss was any simpler than the one in the club, any less arousing or potent.

The difference was in being alone and able to complicate things as thoroughly as they wanted, with no one to interrupt, with nothing to keep the kiss from becoming more.

She pushed forward, exhaled tiny moans into his mouth, used her teeth to nip, her tongue to bathe the damage, her lips to play catch and release with his.

Then she shifted her position, turning her body toward him instead of the vanity, and looped her arms around his neck, raking the fingers of one hand up his nape and into his hair. Her hunger was a match lit to his.

The hand with which he'd been cupping her face moved to cup her slender neck. His other hand found its way to the slit in her dress, and to her thigh. He slipped his fingers between her legs, and she parted them in invitation, whimpering as she did.

He stroked down to her knee, up to the seam where the sequined fabric split, but no farther. As much as he wanted to go there, he needed a sign that she was ready to take things that far.

She gave it to him with a softly whispered, "Please," and

with a hand that guided his higher between her legs. Before he'd even cupped the mound of her sex, he felt her moisture and her heat.

He used the edge of his index finger to play her, pressing it against her, rubbing it back and forth over her clit. She jumped, shuddered, blew short, sweet panting breaths against the edge of his open mouth.

"Good?" he asked.

"So good," she answered, the words more moaned than spoken. "Can you—"

"Make you come?"

"Yes. Oh, yes." This time the words rolled up from the back of her throat, a growled order as much as a plea.

He smiled, covered her mouth, bruised her with his kiss until his erection strained against his fly. When he pulled away, she urged him back.

But first… "Your hose—"

"Get rid of them."

He loved a woman who knew what she wanted. One brave enough not to let propriety get in the way. He found the seam between her legs, dug his fingers against it and tore the fabric free, finding a scrap of a thong covering her sex, and scooping it aside.

She was smooth and damp, and she gasped when he touched her. He moved his lips to the base of her neck and parted her folds with his finger. Her throat vibrated with the sounds she made as he toyed with her, sliding a finger inside her, flicking his thumb over her clit.

She tucked her chin to her chest, closing her eyes, gouging her fingers into his shoulders hard enough to leave marks, and rode his hand, pumping her hips where she sat, sliding on and off his finger.

He ran the flat of his tongue along her collarbone, kissed his way back to her throat, moved to the swell of her breast and pushed her dress aside. He found her nipple and sucked, penetrating her sex with a second finger, rolling the tip of her breast with his lips. She was close now.

He'd hit the right rhythm, found the right combination of pressure and motion, and he kept it up, stroking, rubbing, in and out and around. She tensed, grew wetter. Her breathing quickened, becoming labored and shallow and damp.

And then she cried out, tossing back her head as her orgasm consumed her. He watched the fierce sweep of emotions cross her face, felt her sex contract around him, found himself awash on an amazing high at being able to give this to her, share this with her. At pleasing her so completely.

She came down quickly, shaking, her hands sliding from his shoulders to his biceps, color rising to her cheeks as she dipped her head. "I can't believe—"

"Believe." He didn't want her to feel self-conscious, or awkward at what she'd allowed him to see. He wanted her to bask in the lingering sensation, not embarrassment.

"But you didn't. It's not right—"

He smiled, leaned forward to nuzzle the skin beneath her ear. "If you want to do something about that, I won't say no."

5

TEN MINUTES LATER Miranda and Caleb were sneaking into the Inn at Snow Falls' kitchen, ready to feed their hunger with leftovers since the lack of a condom had kept them from feeding it in more intimate ways.

Miranda was still smiling at Caleb's lack of preparedness. Her own lack was just as sad, but then she never expected to cross paths with eligible men. She'd resigned herself to a life of having sex with herself and her vibrators, and poured out her sensuality onstage.

But a sexy, gorgeous and extremely persuasive man like Caleb—for him not to have a condom at the ready for the women he must meet… She glanced back at him, her smile widening and taking over her face.

"Are you laughing at me or with me this time?" he asked from behind her as she waved at the dishwasher, Earnesto, who winked back a promise not to tattle to the boss about her bringing company along on her kitchen raid.

"I'm not laughing at all." At least not outwardly. Inside she was like a kid on an amusement park Tilt-a-Whirl. "I'm giddy because I can't wait to dig into the chipotle tomato cheese spread I heard Chef made up today. He always keeps snacks around for us late-nighters."

In the smaller of the kitchen's three refrigerators, she found the cheese spread and a bottle of wine; the latter she handed to Caleb. After grabbing two saucers, she pointed him to the rack of wineglasses and a bag of seasoned bagel crisps. Then she led him toward the corner of the kitchen where a folding table with four matching chairs was tucked away in a small alcove for the inn's staff to use.

She sat facing the kitchen, which was probably a mistake since it left him to sit facing her and the wall, and left her to deal with his scrutiny. It wouldn't have been awkward had he not just fingered her to orgasm. But he had, and she could hardly ignore how close they'd come to taking things all the way.

Caleb went back to the utensil cabinet for a corkscrew while Miranda removed the cover from the cheese spread and opened the bag of bagel crisps. By the time he had the wine opened and poured, she had used one of the sturdiest chips to scoop cheese onto their plates.

"Do you do this a lot?" he asked. "Midnight snack in the hotel kitchen?"

"Of course." She laughed, dipped a chip half into her cheese. The light in the alcove wasn't as bright as in the main part of the kitchen, making it hard to read his face. "A perk of the job. And a good one since the town is short on all-night convenience stores."

He watched as she popped the bite of food into her mouth. "That's one of my favorite things about New York. The bodegas. Need a sandwich or a roll of toilet paper or batteries at 4:00 a.m.? It's a one-stop shopping trip."

"Is that where you live? New York?"

He shook his head, reached for his wine. "Not anymore."

She noticed he didn't volunteer where he was from. "Do you miss it?"

"Not much to miss." He held her gaze while he drank, and

returned his glass to the table. "I'm there a lot. And I'm in L.A. a lot."

"Is all that travel for work or pleasure?" she asked, doing her best not to look away. His attention was so focused on her, his expression so intense.

"A little of both. I work in…the arts," he said, and she picked up on his hesitation.

The arts could mean books or movies…or music. He'd said he was here for a wedding, one that would be a big deal. She'd gathered from the staff's whispers while they scurried to do Ravyn's bidding that the singer was home. As far as Miranda knew, Brenna had not been in contact with her mother. But with the congressman here as well…

Could Brenna and Teddy be tying the knot? Could Caleb be here because he knew Brenna as an industry insider, or was a friend? She wanted to press for Corinne's sake, but if Brenna didn't want her mother to know what was happening, well, it wasn't Miranda's business anyway.

In fact, she could be totally off the mark. And she was not going to ask questions that could start hurtful rumors. "An interesting line of work, I'll bet."

"It is. It can be. It can also be a pain in the ass."

Now *that* she could relate to. "Show me a career that doesn't have those moments, and I'll show you someone who's not working very hard."

His eyes flashed with a teasing heat. "I know you work hard. I've seen you."

He'd seen things she didn't want to think about right now. She was trying to get beyond the frustration of their aborted encounter, and she never would if every look he gave her reminded her of what they'd done as well as made her regret what she'd missed.

She needed a drink, and took one. "And you want to know what there is about being Candy Cane that could possibly be a pain in the ass."

He popped a bagel chip into his mouth and nodded.

"The wigs make me sweat."

"So why wear them?"

"Because I don't have long red hair, and red is a theme here, in case that's slipped your notice. And, yes, the wigs are well-made and breathable, but that doesn't help much when I'm onstage. Those lights are brutal."

"Then spend more time offstage with the audience."

Funny man. "You'd like that, wouldn't you?"

"Me and the rest of the men watching you. Some of the women, too."

And again the suggestive innuendo, the heat in his eyes, the want. It was hard to look away. "That's what I'm afraid of. And why I don't mingle more than I do. This is a lovers' resort. I don't want to come between the lovers."

"Why did you mingle tonight?"

She'd been trying to figure that out for herself ever since draping herself across his table. Using a broken chip, she toyed with the cheese on her plate.

Instead of eating it, she told him, "You looked lonely."

He paused with his wineglass halfway to his mouth. "A pity kiss?"

"Not hardly," she said, the gruff accusation causing her chest to tighten. "More like a sense of familiarity. Not to sound totally pathetic, but I know that feeling well."

Without drinking, he returned his glass to the table. "And you thought you'd cheer me up."

"To be honest, you weren't the one I was hoping to cheer. My motives were much more selfish." She felt the heat of a blush on her face and fiddled with her food to try to hide it.

"It was my pleasure."

"No," she said, laughing quietly. "I'm pretty sure it was mine. You were the one left hanging."

"Being left hanging never killed a guy." He gave her a look that left her unable to breathe.

Oh, this was going so many places she wouldn't have expected when singing for him tonight, places she wasn't sure she was ready for. "Not according to the stories I've heard."

"Old wives' tales. Trust me. But just to be on the safe side…" He shifted forward, leaning toward her with an intent that wasn't threatening, but unnerved her because of what she sensed he was going to say. "I'll come prepared to tomorrow night's show."

"Thanks. Now I'll never be able to perform," she said, sighing as she popped the chip and cheese into her mouth. It kept her from having to say anything more, and gave her a chance to catch the breath she still hadn't found.

He didn't press, gave her the time, finally asking, "Were you a performer before coming here?"

Reaching for her drink, she cut her gaze sharply toward him. "Is this the man who works in the arts asking?"

He shook his head. "Just the man who kissed you."

And thank goodness he left his comment at the kiss. "Then, no. Not a performer. Unless you count singing in the shower and the church choir."

"A soloist?"

"From time to time. Always at Christmas."

"Do you do anything special for Christmas here?"

"Besides my regular shows? No. Though I do change up the set. Christmas isn't Christmas without Bing Crosby.

Alan's wife is trying to get me to sing at the high school's holiday dance, but I just can't."

"Why not?" he asked, refilling both of their glasses. "Afraid some of the boys might be lonely?"

"Oh, that is so not funny," she said, though she couldn't stifle a laugh. "But, no. I don't take Candy out of Club Crimson. Except to raid the fridge."

He studied his plate, picked up a bagel crisp. "I would think a local celebrity would be in demand."

"In demand for what?" she asked, curious as to how he saw her alter ego. "Mistletoe doesn't have political fund-raisers or charity events. It's too small a community—one of those places where everybody knows your name. Besides," she went on, "I like my privacy. And Candy's not real. She's a fixture here at the inn just like the huge stone fireplace in the lobby and all the knotty-pine tables."

"I disagree. You're not huge or knotty."

"Very funny," she said, tossing a wedge of bagel at his chest, wondering whether to put an end to their evening, or forget sleep and talk to him until morning. She was exhilarated, exhausted....

When he lifted the bottle to pour her more wine, she found her hand coming up to cover her glass. And there she had her answer. "It's late. Beyond late. And unfortunately, I'm not a woman of leisure."

"Meaning your real self needs to get home so tomorrow you won't fall asleep during brain surgery, or while coming in for an emergency landing, or plowing the back forty, or whatever it is you do when you're not a redhead."

"And that depends on the day of the week," she replied teasingly, wondering what he'd think if he knew about her pedestrian life as a florist. "But, yes, I need to go. This has been the best evening I've had in ages. Thank you."

He followed suit as she got to her feet. "Will I see you tomorrow?"

"If you're in Club Crimson at showtime you will." *You and your condom*. She closed up the bagel crisps, covered the cheese spread, stacked their plates and reached for the wine. "Take this with you."

"Consolation prize?"

She held on to the bottle. "If you're going to be like that, then I'll take it with me and celebrate."

He tossed back his head and laughed. "You, Candy Cane, or whoever you are, are some piece of work."

Good. She was glad he wasn't taking her for granted. "I wouldn't want you to think you could have me without putting in some effort."

He hooked a possessive arm around her neck. "C'mon, mystery woman. Let me walk you back to your dressing room."

She stopped first at the refrigerator, then at the baker's rack, then at the sink where Earnesto took the plates and glasses before waving her and Caleb on their way.

Wearing her sequined gown, her long wavy wig, a warm pair of sheepskin Uggs on her feet and Caleb's jacket over her shoulders, Miranda walked beside him down the hallway from the kitchen to the club. Neither one of them hurried, neither one of them spoke.

It was as if Caleb didn't want to let go of her any more than she wanted to tell him goodnight. They fitted so well as they walked, fitted, too, as they talked. She was certain it would be no different when they made love.

When. She was assuming it would happen, rather than accepting they might have nothing but tonight. Counting on more, looking forward to more wasn't smart. Doing so was tantamount to throwing away the past five years she'd spent making a new life. She couldn't do that to herself. She wouldn't do it for a man about whom she knew nothing.

Then they were at her dressing room, the trip over too soon, the silence lingering as she reached out to punch the code into the keypad lock. Caleb stopped her, covering her hand, turning her and pulling her arms above her head as he backed her into the door.

He spread his legs, captured her hips between them, leaned his lower body into hers and rested there. His eyes were fierce, bright, and she was almost unable to draw a breath for thinking about all the things he might want. She scared herself with all the things she wanted.

He lowered his head to the crook of her neck and kissed her there. She raised her chin to give him full access, her nipples tightening with the thrill of the contact. The scratch of his late-night beard over her skin had her sex clenching as she thought of it scraping her belly, her breasts, the skin of her inner thighs.

His mouth was warm, his tongue warmer still, and wet. His hands around her wrists were tight enough to keep her from moving. His erection bulged between them and pressed against her belly.

She wanted to see him naked, to feel him, touch him with her fingers and her lips. She thought about the weight of his cock, the length, the girth, and squirmed where he'd pinned her to the door.

He chuckled, the sound a low rumbling vibration that tickled in the pit of her stomach. She was frustrated, she was aroused, she wanted him, and wiggled her hips to let him know. He laughed again, continued to kiss, to lick, to nibble.

She couldn't take any more. "This isn't enough."

"It has to be," he murmured against her skin, his whiskers and his teeth both torture and bliss.

There were things they could do, ways they could give each other pleasure that wouldn't require a condom. "We can—"

"No, we can't," he said, bruising her at the base of her neck. "Not tonight."

He was doing this on purpose. Making her miserable. Making her ache. Making her wish she had it in her to be reckless. "This isn't fair."

"Life never is."

She groaned. "Don't you want—"

"I do, but I can wait."

She didn't want to wait. She wanted him, and badly enough that throwing caution to the wind, taking a chance…surely it was worth it. There were other options—

Putting an end to her musings, Caleb stepped back, his touch lingering on a lock of her hair. "Good night…Annie."

She rolled her eyes. "It's not Annie."

"Belle."

"Hardly."

"Daisy," he said, skipping from B to D, since Candy filled the C position.

"Uh-uh," she said, grinning to herself as she turned to open the door.

"Erin."

Shaking her head, she laughed. "Nope."

"Fanny."

"Good night, Caleb." And with one hand on the doorknob, she stood on her tiptoes, kissing him on the cheek before backing into her dressing room and closing the door.

She leaned against it, taking a deep breath and trying to remember the last time she'd had this much fun, realizing it had been so long the memory no longer existed.

It was time to change that, to make some new memories that would hold her long after he was gone. She just had to figure out how to make that happen without giving herself away.

6

CALEB TOOK THE bottle of wine Candy had given him in the kitchen back to the nightclub's stage and waited just off the hallway in the wings. Best he could tell, there was no exit from Club Crimson other than this one and the main one into the inn's lobby. He figured whoever Candy Cane was, she'd head back through the kitchen to leave.

From here, he could catch a glimpse of her as she made her escape. He wanted to see what she looked like in her glasses and short brown hair, certain from seeing the hairbrush and contact-lens case in her dressing room that she was making the transition from her stage self to her real self even now.

He wasn't going to stalk her or follow her home—he'd be hard-pressed to do the latter since he was here without wheels. And the former, well, showing up for tomorrow night's show was where he drew the line.

But after the time they'd spent together tonight, he was more curious about her than ever. He wanted to glimpse the woman who had turned him on, the woman he knew he was going to have trouble getting out of his head. This rarely happened. No, it never happened, he mused, lifting the wine bottle and thinking back over his thirty-seven years.

Sure, there'd been women, lovers who'd lasted for months,

one in college he'd stayed with for almost two years. Nix that. One who'd stayed with him for almost two years. He hadn't made the change, she had. She hadn't liked that he'd had a mistress—journalism—that had demanded his time, his energy, his love.

He'd been obsessed with learning the world of news reporting, with researching, finding one lead and following it down a rabbit hole to another, with pushing public and private boundaries, while serving both his audience and the subjects of the pieces he wrote.

Women he'd dated after his college sweetheart dumped him had felt the same way about his split loyalties, so he'd quit dating and settled for one-night stands, the occasional fling, and sex with his own right hand.

Instead of fighting the Mars–Venus wars, he'd poured his emotions into his work. No need putting himself through the wringer when it was obvious he was worthless at balancing the things he loved.

Caleb was just about to fall into a pit of self-pity when he heard Candy open her door. Leaving the wine bottle on the floor against the wall, he edged as far as he dared toward the steps that descended from the wings into the hallway.

The light in front of her dressing room wasn't the greatest, but it would've been bright enough for him to see her by— if she hadn't already pulled the hood of her parka over her head and been looking straight down, her face completely obscured.

Carrying a small red gym bag and wearing her padded boots, what looked like insulated sweatpants and the coat, she checked that the door had locked behind her, then headed toward the kitchen as Caleb had hoped.

He'd pulled off his boots while waiting, knowing they'd

make too much noise should he have to follow to get the look he wanted. He set off now to do just that, keeping his distance while keeping her in sight.

The kitchen was empty and dark save for one light left on at each end. He breathed in dish soap and floor cleaner and the lingering odors of fresh fruit and garlic, hanging back as she hugged the perimeter of the room.

On the other side, she hit a button that opened a secured door. She walked through, and Caleb rushed forward, his socks sliding on the floor as he caught the handle before it latched. He waited several seconds, finally slipping into what turned out to be a large storage room where a big red exit sign glowed on the far wall.

This room was colder, filled with shelves of boxed supplies, freezers, laundry carts and crates of booze. The way out—to which Candy was headed—looked as if it led to a delivery bay where trucks could pull in at the rear of the inn to unload, and Caleb assumed the staff parking lot was adjacent. He could hardly follow her all the way outside, but he saw a window in the heavy steel door he could look through.

He ducked behind the closest shelving unit and listened to the pad of her footsteps echo in the cavernous space. Since she'd kept his jacket, leaving him in his shirt sleeves, he rubbed his hands up and down his arms for warmth while waiting for her to reach her destination.

Once she'd slammed her hand against the red button that released the exit's lock, Caleb took off after her. By the time he got to the door, it had closed, and the room was again secure. He eased up to the window and peered through.

Snow swirled lightly in the parking lot. He could see her form as she hurried toward her car, and he watched her fumble to get her key in the lock, then fumble again to get the driver's-side door open.

After starting the engine, she let it warm, turning on her headlights and sitting there for several minutes. Caleb imagined her cupping her hands together, blowing into them, her breath frosting the air.

Just thinking about it made him cold. Standing on the concrete floor in his socks didn't help. He tugged on his boots then looked out in time to see her drive away, the older import jerking as she shifted the gears, exhaust belching out in wispy clouds.

Shivering, he continued to stand there until she disappeared into the night, then stuffed his hands in his jeans pockets, hunched his shoulders and hurried back to the other side of the room.

He returned to the door that led into the kitchen—and that's when he saw the keypad on the wall beside it. He tried the handle, got nothing. He looked for a phone, found one that rang directly to security.

It was either call for help and look like a fool, spend the next few hours in here until the kitchen staff arrived for the morning shift, or leave the same way Candy whoever-she-was had done and traipse in his street clothes—no jacket, no hat, no gloves—around to the front of the inn.

None of the options thrilled him, but the third would get him back to his room a whole lot faster. He glanced in the laundry carts and lucked out, finding a blanket wadded up in the bottom of one.

Wrapping it around his shoulders like a super-reporter's cape, he damned himself for being so nosy, and headed out into the frigid winter night for a much deserved—and self-inflicted—comeuppance.

IT WAS NEARLY 3:00 a.m. when Miranda climbed into bed. She couldn't remember the last time she'd been so exhausted. The shows she did four nights a week tired her already. Adding to the mix the extra hours spent tonight with Caleb, her sexual release and her mad dash to escape, well, she barely had the strength to set her alarm.

She had no idea why Caleb had waited for her, or why he'd followed her, especially when it was obvious that he had no intention of catching her. That left her wondering, as she drifted between wakefulness and sleep, if he'd discovered what he'd been after. Wondering, too, with no small amount of amusement, if he'd found a way out of the warehouse. Or if he was still huddled up somewhere in the room.

She was so glad she'd considered the possibility of his being there—whether to give persuading her to come up to his room one more shot, or to convince her that it would be worth her while to take him home—and had pulled up her parka's hood before stepping out into the hallway.

She would've preferred that he respect her privacy and her wish to remain incognito, but she understood his testosterone-driven need to be in control. That didn't mean she was going to let him find her out, or to score more points in this game than he had with his promise to come prepared to tomorrow night's show.

How in the world she was going to get through her performance… She shivered, pulled her comforter to her chin and settled back on her bed's mountain of pillows, refusing to borrow trouble and think about that now.

She borrowed trouble of a different kind instead. Last-minute thoughts of how much differently the night would've played out had one of them had a condom meant her dreams were filled with graphically detailed images—his body, her body, fingers and tongues, and, oh, how he kissed.

She woke late and not the least bit rested, her body way oversensitive as she showered and dressed. Breakfast was a cup of coffee in a travel mug and a toasted English muffin that, by the time her car had warmed up enough to make it to the shop, was as cold as the blackberry jelly topping it.

The snow flurries that had swirled around her during last night's drive home were gone this morning. The sun was shining brightly, reflecting off the blanket of white and forcing her to reach for the sunglasses clipped to her visor.

The town's one plow had been out early, and the trip from her bungalow to the store was uneventful—a good thing since she was having trouble letting go of last night and focusing on the roads. Running a half hour late didn't help.

The part of her brain not thinking about Caleb was thinking about the work she had ahead. A fairly large order had come in last week, well, large by Under the Mistletoe standards. And now that she thought about it…

The flowers had to be for the same wedding Caleb was here for. There were two standing floral arrangements, one for either side of the altar in the chapel at the inn, a bridal bouquet and one for the single attendant, as well as an exquisite corsage for the mother of the bride, and boutonnieres for the groom and best man.

The name on the order was neither Eagleton nor Black, nor was it Sparks, but if Brenna and the congressman were here to get married, that would make perfect sense. They'd be keeping their plans as hush-hush as possible, using assistants to run errands and see to the details of the event.

And though most brides were very hands-on when it came to the decorations for the ceremony, Miranda understood Brenna keeping Corinne in the loop by having her mother help with the flowers—even if Corinne didn't know that's what she was doing.

Brenna had made it more than clear that she wanted to reconcile, sending birthday and Christmas gifts—which Corinne gave away—trying to reimburse the money she'd taken—money Corinne, as generous as she was, couldn't see beyond her pride to keep—calling and leaving messages Corinne never returned.

It came as no surprise that Corinne was already at Under the Mistletoe when Miranda sneaked in the back door at ten-thirty. The older woman looked up from where she was trimming stems and arranging red roses in a delivery box with silver and gold ribbons. "Late night?"

Her employee's simple question cleared Miranda's mind of everything but her time with Caleb, and she couldn't help blurting it out. "I met a man."

"Oh, really?" Like Miranda, Corinne was divorced and held out little hope that as long as she lived in Mistletoe, her marital status would change. "Long-term potential or short-term fling?"

"Definitely fling-worthy," Miranda admitted. "But since he's just visiting, I'd have to say—"

"A fling is all it will be," Corinne finished for her.

And such was Miranda's lot in life. She sighed, tucked her purse away in her locker and pulled on the red and green apron she wore to protect her clothes.

"If I were a less practical woman, I'd say the Fates were playing an unnecessarily cruel joke. I mean, I hardly need to be reminded that I'm living in a town that caters to lovers, and have little chance of having one of my own. Or having one for longer than a fling anyway."

She stopped as the truth consumed her. "Not that I've even had one of those since I've been here—"

"But one can always hope," Corinne said as she assembled the top of the flower box and fitted it over the bottom, tucking the order ticket between the two parts. "Did he say how long he'll be in town? Or what he's doing here? I need to know how many mornings I'm going to have to take up your slack."

"Ha." Miranda stuck out her tongue in response to her friend's teasing. "He didn't say how long, no, and I won't be late again. As for what he's doing here—" All her speculation about Brenna returned, but since she had no proof, or any business gossiping about the girl to her mother…

"Well?" Corinne prompted, her brown eyes curious, the blond highlights in her shoulder-length hair making her look younger than her fifty-three years.

Miranda forged ahead, sharing none of her thoughts so as not to influence any conclusions Corinne might draw. "He said he's here for a wedding."

"The same wedding we're doing the flowers for?"

"I have a feeling it could be. He did say the ceremony was private, but it would be a pretty big deal once word of the nuptials got out."

Color rising on her cheeks, Corinne shoved the box of roses at Miranda, averting her gaze as she moved from the worktable to her order book, set next to the phone. "Then I'd better get busy, hadn't I? Wouldn't want our flowers to reflect poorly on any big deal."

Miranda looked down at the box she held. She had no way of knowing what Corinne was thinking, but judging by the other woman's reaction, it was quite likely word had reached her that Brenna was staying at the inn.

Miranda set the box on the table, and pulled open a drawer beneath the work surface where spools of ribbon hung on built-in dowels. "I'm hardly worried about your work reflecting poorly on anything or anyone, but if you'd rather I tackle the wedding, you can work on Mayor Flynn's dinner party."

Corinne didn't respond. She stood and watched Miranda measure a length of Christmas plaid ribbon to tie around the box. "Marvetta Chance told me yesterday that Barry picked up Teddy Eagleton at the airport."

"Hmm."

"I asked Patrice when she dropped off Zoe after choir practice last night if it was true that Brenna was in town."

"What did she say?" Miranda asked, expecting Alan's wife to be more circumspect than the inn's shuttle driver.

"Nothing, but then we both know that Patrice treats the comings and goings at the inn the way a priest treats his confessional."

Miranda didn't want to butt in on Corinne's personal life, but the two of them had been friends long enough that she felt she owed it to the other woman to say her piece. "It's not any of my business, but isn't it possible that if Brenna is marrying Teddy, she's having the wedding here because she wants you to come?"

"More like she wants to rub my nose in it. 'Look, Ma! I can take money from you and take Teddy from his wife and there's nothing you can do to stop me.'" Shaking her head, Corinne moved closer to hold the ribbon in place while Miranda fashioned the bow. "I just pray to God her sister doesn't find out that she's here."

At that point, Miranda figured it was best to move on. "When's the last time Zoe saw her?"

Corinne gave a careless shrug. "Brenna picked her up after school on her birthday last year. She took her to Denver for the weekend. Spoiled her rotten." Corinne grabbed the box of flowers and headed from the back room to the front of the shop, tossing over her shoulder, "But trust me—if I have my way? She'll never see Brenna again."

Frowning, Miranda followed. "You can't mean that."

"I can. I do. Zoe has her whole life ahead of her. She doesn't need to get involved in her sister's, or end up being dragged through the mud Brenna seems to enjoy wallowing in."

The gossips had had a Britney-esque field day with Ravyn Black's comings and goings. Having suffered similarly, Miranda believed Brenna might truly be in need of her mother's understanding.

But with Corinne still nursing the old hurt, it was hard to imagine anything but a miracle bringing the two Sparks women together.

7

STILL TIRED, still cold and still hungry, Caleb followed the hostess to the quiet table he'd requested against the back wall of One in Vermillion. The pub was the more casual of the inn's two restaurants, the other being Will Ruby Mine.

This whole red thing was still getting on his nerves, but today his pique had less to do with the resort thematically exploiting the concept of love and romance, and more to do with a woman who was hiding behind red costumes and red hair.

He had a feeling Candy whoever-she-was had known exactly what she was doing when she'd led him into the storage room and left him locked in there. And he'd deserved it. He should've left well enough alone. Any other man would've done so, would've respected her privacy and waited for her to reveal herself in good time.

Caleb wasn't any other man. He was a journalist. Curiosity was in his blood. And he didn't have good time. He was due, in fact, to leave immediately following the Saturday-evening wedding. Or, he had been until, on his way to meet Ravyn, he'd stopped by the front desk to extend his stay.

Not an easy feat to accomplish with the inn booked solid so near the holidays, but possession being nine-tenths of the law and money being no object, he'd managed to hang on to his room through the weekend, though only by the skin of his teeth.

Come Monday morning, it was either hit the road for the airport and his rescheduled flight, or head down the mountain, find less colorful lodging, and rent a car to get him back and forth, since he doubted Candy whoever-she-was would be inviting him to her place for home cooking anytime soon.

Home cooking he could do without. Hell, if it came right down to it, he'd even survive not taking her to bed. He wasn't looking forward to things going that way, but, as he'd told her, no man ever died from being hung out to dry when the sex thing didn't work out with a woman.

It was leaving here without knowing who she was that was giving him the true hard time. And not because of thinking he knew her. He wanted to know the woman who had kissed a stranger in a nightclub as if that moment meant more than the rest of her show.

The kiss, the intimacy, the near miss in her dressing room. He still couldn't believe she had given herself to him so freely. He wanted to chalk it up to being an extension of the whole lovers'-resort thing, but Candy whoever-she-was had seemed knocked for a loop of her own.

He couldn't leave here without discovering more about her—which presented a real problem. He no longer trusted himself to keep private what was told to him in confidence, to separate the personal of Caleb from the business of Max. And with his believing that Candy had secrets...

"Mr. McGregor?"

He looked up, expecting his server with his coffee, frowning that it hadn't arrived. Instead he saw a young woman, a kid really, dressed like so many others in low-rise jeans, brightly colored insulated boots, her hair caught back in a bandana, not a hint of makeup on her face.

"Yes?"

"I'm Brenna Sparks. We have an appointment."

"We do?" He wasn't firing on all cylinders, but he knew he should be able to place the name.

She rolled her eyes, then stared, waiting, as if his study of her would bring recognition. When it didn't, she tossed back her head, reached for the neckline of the top she wore layered over several others and ripped it with the loud banshee wail made famous online in bootlegged Evermore concert videos.

Okay, not a kid. Not a typical congressman's wife either. Brenna Sparks was Ravyn Black. Hard to believe this woman who looked about twelve years old was to Congressman Teddy Eagleton what Marilyn Monroe had been to JFK. Was more, actually, since they were about to become one.

"Sorry," he said, getting to his feet, and gesturing toward the chair opposite his, glancing at the other patrons, who were obviously not banshee fans. "Please, sit. I'm still trying to wake up."

She gave him a look that was decidedly maternal and not kidlike at all. "It's almost noon."

He shrugged, amused to have a rock star criticize his sleeping habits. "One of those nights. What can I say?"

She plopped into the chair, reached for his water glass, and downed half of it before looking up. "You can say I'm not making a big mistake by telling my story to a half-wit."

He caught sight of the server approaching and signaled for another coffee before taking his seat. "You're not, and I'm not. I was just lost in thought, trying to find a solution to the problem that kept me up so late."

The server returned then, setting cups and saucers and a pitcher of cream on the table, handing them both menus and explaining the specials of the day while Brenna studied the appetizer section.

Listening with only half an ear, Caleb reached inside the jacket he wore, finding his digital recorder in that pocket, his pen and notebook in the one at his hip.

"I'll let you look over your menus, and be back in a few for your orders," said the young man in black pants with a white shirt and red tie.

He had just turned to go when Brenna stopped him. "Would you go ahead and bring an order of crab cakes?" She looked at Caleb, who shook his head. "That's all for now."

"I'll get that turned right in."

Caleb waited until they were alone, then asked, "Do you mind if I record our conversation? I take notes, but a recorder makes for better accuracy."

She reached for the device, activated the record function and brought the microphone to her mouth. "And we know reporters are always accurate."

He didn't want to have that argument now. "You've given him the exclusive and Max takes that seriously. He doesn't want any mistakes. Having your voice on a digital file detailing your relationship with the congressman is about as accurate as it gets."

"Whatever." She handed back the recorder with a shrug. "Let's just get this done. I've got a facial and a massage at three."

Caleb took the device and left it running, studying his companion while she spent longer than he would've expected focused on the menu. The server returned then with Brenna's crab cakes and took her order for a large baked potato with the works. Caleb didn't care what he ate, so he ordered the same.

She insisted Caleb share the appetizer. He did, and once he'd bit in, was glad. "This is what I love about being on assignment."

"Having crab cakes for lunch?"

"Breakfast, lunch, dinner or midnight snack."

"I'm assuming you travel with a gastroenterologist?"

"Just a pharmacy's worth of meds."

She snorted, forked up another bite of her food, and they chatted about nothing for several minutes. Brenna finally asked, "So where do you want to start? What do you want to know? How Teddy and I met, or wedding details, or juicy news on the next album?"

He wanted it all, but waited while the server delivered the football-size potatoes with pools of melted butter, sour cream, cheese, chives and bacon. His stomach rumbled. "I saw the congressman in the lobby yesterday."

Her look said he could do better than that. "It's a wedding. I'm the bride. He's the groom."

"Is he still not crazy about a media witness to your vows?" Caleb asked, dredging a bite of potato through the reservoir of melted butter.

She sipped at the soda she'd called back the server to get her. "Not crazy about the media being Max Savage, no. But he agrees it's better to do it this way than to have helicopters hovering over a beach in Maui, or to have dozens of half-assed contradictory reports springing up and causing him unnecessary grief. Not that it won't happen anyway—"

"But at least there will be digital proof if you need it."

"Exactly."

"I'm sure he gets as much of that in his position as you do in the band."

Placing her fork on the edge of her plate, she sat back and rolled her head on her shoulders as if gathering her thoughts, sorting through, shaking off those she didn't want to share. When she faced him again, he saw confusion more than confidence, and that intrigued him as much as her confession.

"We love what we do," she said. "The band and I. We're devoted to what we do. We believe in the messages of our songs. It's a heart-and-soul thing for us."

She looked down at her plate, a little girl with hurt feelings. "But that's not what gets written about in reviews. That's never the focus of articles about the music. Sound bites are always played back in a negative context. And, yes, I know that's what I signed on for when I chose this life."

She might have expected some of what was written about Evermore, but he doubted she or the band members had anticipated the vitriolic charges that their lyrics encouraged drug use, casual sex, teen rebellion and even suicide pacts. Nothing new in the world of rock 'n' roll, but amplified because of their explosive Internet presence.

As Max Savage, Caleb had written about all of these things. He'd also quoted disillusioned fans who said Ravyn's affair with the charismatic conservative congressman was akin to selling out. That it proved she didn't stand by her message of being true to oneself at all.

"You know the public thinks the only reason you're with Teddy is to legitimize your act. Make it acceptable to the mainstream. How can parents complain about their children listening to Evermore if Congressman Eagleton, their contemporary, puts his stamp of approval on the band?"

"That's such bullshit," Brenna said, shaking her head. "Teddy's generation grew up with Def Leppard and Poison as their music idols. My generation grew up with Marilyn Manson and Nine Inch Nails. They turned out fine, we turned out fine. Today's kids, my sister's age group, they'll turn out fine, too. It's not about the music. It's about knowing yourself, who you are, what you want."

He couldn't believe she was that naive, or even worse, that

he was feeling a twinge of something uncomfortable over his part in the grief she'd suffered from the reports in the press.

He shook it off, asking, "And you think kids in your sister's age group know those things? Who they are? What they want? That they're not influenced by Evermore singing about putting an end to the pain?"

Having picked up her fork earlier, Brenna now tossed it to the table and plopped back in her chair. "I love how those lyrics are the ones everyone pulls out of context without paying any attention to what comes before or what follows."

"More negative sound bites?"

"What do you think?" she asked, holding up one hand to keep him from answering.

Caleb watched as she closed her eyes, squirmed in her chair until she was comfortable, then reached for the torn edges of her top. She held tightly to the fabric, her knuckles nearly white, her chest rising and falling.

And then she sang, pouring her emotions into the lyrics she'd written, telling her audience that life was hard and lonely, that escape was just moments away. That an end to the pain could be had by reaching out, and that if one did, the loneliness would all go away.

She fell silent then, took a deep shuddering breath and then opened her eyes. They were red, her lower lids brimming with tears, the emotional resonance of the words she'd poured out unmistakable, undeniable—to her, and to the crowd who got to their feet and applauded.

Caleb couldn't help but be moved.

Looking down at her plate, Brenna reached for her fork again and whispered, "I sing about reaching out. How can anyone say those lyrics are destructive?"

He had no answer. But as the noise in the pub died down,

he realized that what he'd said earlier about the parents of her fans had hit a deep nerve. And with Brenna mentioning her younger sister…

"Did you and Teddy get together because you thought a relationship with the congressman would persuade your mother to accept what you're doing with your life?"

"If my mother and I were estranged because of my music, taking Teddy home for Christmas dinner might have softened her up, but since my music isn't the problem between us, I'd have to say no."

Interesting. "What is the problem between you?"

Bristling, Brenna cut him off. "If you want this interview to continue, don't ask me about that again."

So there *was* more to that story. He'd come back to it later. For now… "Then let's talk about your groom. The first time you met. The heat you've both taken over the months. The impact that has had on your relationship. The impact your relationship has had on the band."

They spent the next two hours talking about the things the public was going to be glued to their televisions to find out. A lot of what Brenna told him, Caleb already knew to be fact. Other things he'd suspected, but had not been able to verify.

But there was even more that surprised him. Her vulnerability, for one thing. He didn't know why. He did know it shouldn't. The impenetrable, unflappable persona of Evermore's lead singer was an act the same way Max Savage was an act. The same way Candy Cane was an act.

Why he expected the woman who wore Ravyn's hard shell to be anything but who she was, singing her heart out in the middle of the pub, digging into her baked potato and crab cakes and then ordering key lime pie for dessert, made no sense.

He knew there was very little of importance in what he

8

"WHO IS IT?" Miranda called in response to the knock on her dressing-room door. She was still wearing her sweats and her glasses, not to mention her own head of hair. After her successful escape from Caleb last night, there was no way she was opening the door to him now and undoing that victory.

"It's Patrice."

Thank goodness. "Hey, sweetie. C'mon in."

Alan's wife pushed open the door, came inside and leaned back, making sure with a quick test of the knob that it locked behind her. Miranda noticed, but didn't comment. Patrice obviously wanted privacy.

The other woman's nearly black hair hung in a long braid over one shoulder. She wore leather work boots, faded jeans and a cable-knit sweater in a herringbone pattern of black and green. The look was as much a uniform as the one she wore on the slopes as a member of the ski patrol team.

"What're you doing here so late in the day?" Miranda asked, getting a closer look at the flush on her friend's usually creamy complexion as she sat on the bench beside her.

Patrice's eyes went wide. "Tell me about your new man. I want to hear everything. I am starved for gossip. There has been nothing going on at work. No avalanches. No crashes. No one to rescue. No lost hikers to find."

Gossip. On one hand, the bane of Miranda's existence, on the other, a source of fun between girlfriends that she glee-fully—if hypocritically—participated in. "Who have you been getting your info from? Alan or Corinne?"

"Both, actually, though Corinne didn't know enough to juice things up, and Alan's a man and thinks juice comes in a jar." Patrice nudged her shoulder against Miranda's when she laughed. "So? Is he juicy?"

Miranda met the other woman's reflection in the mirror. "Juicy enough, but there's not a lot to tell. I kissed him during my set—"

Patrice gasped. "You what?"

"Tell me about it." Miranda gave a moan and a nod. "It was so strange. It was the end of the night, I was in the crowd for the last song and there he was. Alone. The only person in the club alone. One of the only people I've ever seen in there alone."

"So you kissed him? Because he was alone?"

And how stupid did it sound to hear it said? "Trust me. I've tried to find an answer that makes more sense."

"No luck, I guess?" Patrice leaned forward and grabbed one of Miranda's lipsticks, twisting it open and frowning at the shade. "What do you think?"

"I think it would look great. And, no. No luck." She watched her friend lean closer to the mirror and carefully apply the dark coral. "A man alone is no reason for me to risk ruining the life I've built here."

"Who says? A man alone is probably the perfect reason to risk it. I mean, it's a fling. It's not like he'll be here long enough to ruin anything." Patrice pursed her lips, smiled, pressed them together and made a loud pop. "I wonder if Alan will like this."

Knowing the other woman rarely wore makeup at all,

Miranda considered her visitor's complexion. "You could add some color to your eyes for balance."

"Are you calling me unbalanced?" Patrice asked with a frown.

Miranda grinned. "Just your face."

"Gee, thanks." Patrice found one of Miranda's headbands and pulled her long wispy bangs away from her eyes. "But I'm serious, you know."

"About the risk?"

"Sure. You've been here five years. You haven't dated. The East Coast divorce gossip has surely died down by now. What's the harm in having anyone you once knew find out that you're living here? If anything's ruining your life, it's you being so careful." Patrice cut her gaze to Miranda's reflected one. "I mean, five years without getting laid? How can you stand it?"

She'd stood it because there hadn't been men here to date, and because she stayed too busy to leave and find one. True, she had probably taken being cautious way too far. At the beginning it had been a necessity. Then it had become habit. Now it was a rut she didn't see a way out of—especially with this new looming threat of the retrial.

Looking back with twenty-twenty hindsight, it was easy to see that she could've handled things with less emotion and more logic. But here she was. And things really hadn't been *that* bad. Or if they had been, she'd done a good job of lying to herself. She turned back to Patrice.

"Now that Marshall's in the news again? If it were made known that the ex-Mrs. Gordon was living in a lovers' resort in the Rocky Mountains, reporters would fall all over themselves booking flights and rooms."

"But I still don't get what that has to do with you having a fling here in Mistletoe."

"I don't want the man I have a fling with to leave here, see coverage of Marshall's trial, and when the mystery of the ex-wife who's dropped out of sight comes up, to then call the press and say, 'Hey, I know where she is. I just boinked her silly.'"

Patrice stopped short of rolling her eyes. "Do you think that's what will happen?"

"Am I borrowing trouble, you mean?" Miranda shrugged. "Probably, but I've been doing the better-safe-than-sorry thing for so long, it's instinct. And knock on wood, it's worked."

"Worked to keep you from getting laid, anyway." Patrice picked up an eyeshadow quad, then discarded the selection of blues for one with greens. "Doesn't it get to you?"

"It does. At times." Too many to name. "Like when watching Bridget Jones kiss Mark Darcy."

Patrice, a hater of anything labeled romantic or comedy, groaned. "Back to your better-safe-than-sorry lifestyle. *My* instincts are telling me that you need to ditch it and have an affair with the juicy one while he's here."

Juicy. The thought had everything in Miranda tingling. "Since it was only the lack of a condom that kept us from doing it last night, I'd say there's a good possibility."

"You!" Patrice pointed at Miranda's reflection with the eyeshadow brush she held. "What have I told you about buying condoms when you buy tampons?"

Ridiculously, Miranda's face heated. "If I bought condoms every time I bought tampons, I'd have enough to keep me through menopause."

"And if you'd bought them at least once, you'd be all kinds of sore and hobbling around today." Patrice finished dusting on a glittery sea-green shadow before adding a darker pine color in the creases of her lids. "I'm hoping Alan will start tearing off my clothes once he sees the new me and then I'll be all kinds of sore and hobbling. He does know the code to your door lock, right?"

"Uh-uh. No way. If you're planning on getting naked in my dressing room while I'm singing, stop. Having Caleb in the audience will be enough of a distraction. Thinking about you in here with Alan would put me over the edge."

"Caleb," Patrice said, as if weighing the name on her tongue. "I like it. What's he like? Where's he from? What does he do? Why's he here all alone?"

"I don't know where he's from. He never said, though I'm thinking the East Coast. As far as what he's like, well, he's attentive and sexy and very nice. Not pushy. A great kisser. A great flirt. And, I hope, a good sport."

"Why's that?"

"When I left last night, he followed me."

"All the way home?"

Miranda shook her head. "Just down the hall, through the kitchen and warehouse to the parking lot."

"To your car?"

"Not quite that far," Miranda said, remembering the blur of Caleb's face as he'd watched her drive away. "The last time I saw him, he was looking out the window of the exit door. I left him there."

"You left him in the warehouse?" Patrice asked, and when Miranda grinned, nearly screeched. "Oh my God! Do you think he stayed in there all night?"

"I'm going to guess that when he realized he couldn't get back in the way he'd come out without calling security, he walked around to the front of the inn."

"And froze his ass off." Laughing, Patrice closed up the eye-shadow and found a new mascara in the vanity's top drawer. She pumped the wand in and out of the tube then swept the brush over her lashes. "You know, when you sleep with him—"

"You mean *if.*"

"*When* you sleep with him, you're going to have to consider more than having enough condoms. Do you wear your contacts?" One stroke of mascara. "Do you wear your glasses?" Another stroke. "Do you wear a wig?" A third stroke. "Do you wear your real hair?" A fourth.

"Yeah. I've gone over all of those a thousand times."

"And?"

"Do I want a one- or two-night stand?" Miranda opened one palm for one option, opened the other for a second. "Or do I want more? I mean, if sex is the goal, why get out of any more than my underwear?"

"Because nothing beats full-body contact?"

"Okay, so I get out of everything but my hair." She flipped the ends of the wig she would be wearing tonight; it sat on the vanity, still fitted to its foam head form. "We can have sex in here up against the wall or on the floor or on the vanity bench."

"True."

"But if we have dinner or drinks and get to know each other, and things look promising, do I sleep with him as Candy? Or as the real me? And how much of the real me do I really want him to know?" Miranda felt her voice and her blood pressure both rising. "Miranda Kelly who owns Under the Mistletoe? Or the ex-Miranda Gordon who lived in Baltimore and was married to Marshall, the crook?"

Patrice wrapped an arm around Miranda's shoulder and hugged her close. "Why don't you play it by ear, sweetie? Take it a day at a time."

"That's all well and good, except I can't think he's going to be here for very many," Miranda said, deflating.

"You never told me *why* he's here," Patrice said, getting back to her makeup.

"He's here for a wedding."

"Do we know whose?"

"No." Miranda paused, waited until she had her friend's attention, and added, "But Teddy and Brenna are both here."

Patrice's eyes widened. "Are you kidding?"

"Corinne knew. I thought you probably did, too."

"Nope. I've been wrapped up with the Christmas dance plans. And trying to get someone to sing. Someone besides Zoe," she added before Miranda could make the suggestion. "She's already on the program. I wanted someone with a little more...cachet."

Which Patrice thought Miranda had. "So ask Brenna."

"Are you kidding? Corinne would defriend me forever. God, I can't imagine what she must be going through. This whole congressman–rock-star thing has been a nightmare since the beginning. I can't believe they might be getting married."

Miranda reached for her sponge and foundation to get started on her face. "Actually, having both of her daughters onstage at the dance might be the very thing to bring about a reconciliation. Unless there is a wedding and it magically happens there."

"If only life was that easy."

"Worth giving it a shot?"

Patrice got to her feet, and with Miranda's nod of permission, pocketed both the eyeshadow quad and the mascara. "Let me run it by Alan. And thanks for the makeover."

"If there's anything else you want, run it by him while you look like a runway model."

"More like a sportsman's catalog model. But then Alan

does like a woman with a bulls-eye for his arrow to hit," Patrice said, laughing as she opened the door.

"Just keep all that shooting out of my dressing room," Miranda called after her friend who yelled back, "Break a leg, and then you won't have to worry about it!"

9

AN HOUR BEFORE THE SHOW, Caleb was at the bar in Club Crimson nursing a glass of sparkling water with lime. No more booze for him until he had a better handle on Candy. He was going to be one-hundred-percent sober for tonight's show.

And as far as how things would go down after the show? For that, he'd come prepared—and then some. They could make love until his plane took off on Monday without having to worry about being protected.

Strangely, he hadn't thought a lot about Candy this afternoon. He'd been focused on writing the copy for the wedding story, and on Brenna Sparks and her estrangement from her mother. He'd wondered what that might have to do with her choice of Mistletoe for the event. He couldn't see any other reason for the venue.

For a ceremony so small, she and Teddy could have found the same privacy in any judge's chambers, and then dealt with the media aftermath similarly to how they'd be dealing with it now. But as curious as he was, he let it go. Brenna had told him to drop it, and he had a newfound respect for boundaries.

Only when his stomach had reminded him that his brain needed more fuel than a crab cake and stuffed baked potato had he pushed away from his laptop and ordered room service. After eating and noticing the time, he'd showered away the exhaustion of his work, dressed and headed down to Club Crimson.

He was too early for Candy's show, but that was fine. It allowed him time to really see where she worked. He'd been too tired from traveling and too toasted from drinking to notice much of anything last night.

Er, anything except the overwhelming and sappy color scheme which hadn't improved with either time or sobriety. When he arrived, the club was already half-full, the patrons lulled by piped-in mood music—instrumental pieces, classic crooners, even sexy R & B tunes and pop ballads. Servers worked the room, their trays laden with cocktails, bubbly champagne, even mugs of beer.

Partners in hushed conversations cuddled closer on love seats and sofas. A group of three couples had pulled club chairs into a circle, and were sharing several bottles of wine while boisterously discussing a recent bestseller, politics, the chances of the teams headed for the Superbowl.

Other couples sat in the more privately situated booths—the last in the row the one where Caleb had sat last night—and if they were talking at all, no one could hear. Neither did anyone pay them attention unless they signaled for service.

Tonight, Caleb sat at the far end of the bar, choosing a stool on the short side of the L and putting his back to the wall. From here, he could see the stage and all of the room, save for the few tables behind him.

But the best part was that unlike the back corner booth, the bar was too tall for Candy to drape herself over should she want to slide into his lap and kiss him. Yeah, he wanted her to kiss him, but he didn't want her to start something here in public that they'd have to put on hold.

When she kissed him, when he kissed her, he wanted privacy, no audience, no reason to stop or pull back because the time and place were wrong. Her dressing room was fine. His room upstairs was fine. If she wanted to take him home with her, that, too, was fine. Club Crimson, the lovers' lounge in the lovers' resort in the lovers' town of Mistletoe was not in the least bit fine.

"Can I get you a refill on that? Something stronger, maybe?"

He looked up at the bartender who seemed to be considering him too closely. "The water's fine, but a refill would be good, thanks."

The other man, probably close to Caleb's age with a skier's ruddy tan, returned with the drink himself rather than sending it with one of the servers in their short flirty red skirts. "Here ya go."

"Appreciate it," Caleb said, then waited for the man to walk away. He didn't, and it wasn't hard to know what was coming. The bartender had been hovering last night even before Candy had invited Caleb back to her dressing room. Might as well set his mind at ease. "I left her as safe and sound as I found her. No need to worry, okay?"

The bartender laughed, held out his hand. "Alan Price."

"Caleb McGregor. I'm going to guess that you and Candy whoever-she-is go way back, and you enjoy playing big brother."

"We grew up here, next door to each other. But as far as playing big brother, I'm a friend. That's all."

Hmm. Then this was her home. "A friend who wants to make sure she doesn't invite the wrong creep to her dressing room."

"Last I looked, that's what friends were for."

Nodding, Caleb reached for his water. "She's…not what I expected."

Alan arched a brow, and slid a new napkin beneath Caleb's drink. "What did you expect?"

Caleb shrugged. "A lot of performers continue their act offstage. I didn't find that to be the case with her at all. She was very down-to-earth. Very real. Very nice." And very, very sexy.

"She is. All of that."

"And you want to make sure I don't hurt her. That all my intentions are good."

Alan leaned a hand on the bar and looked down as if fighting a smile. "I doubt, in Candy's case, you and I would agree on what makes a good intention."

Caleb was pretty sure the other man had that right. He was pretty sure, too, that his intentions were his own business. "Do you call her Candy in private?"

Alan laughed. "If you think I'm going to tell you her name, think again."

"I don't think that at all," Caleb hedged, since he had indeed been digging.

Alan's expression made it clear that he wasn't buying it. "My wife and I have known her a lotta years, so yeah. We call her by her real name."

"Has she been headlining here long?"

"A while. When she moved back a few years ago, she was desperate for a second job, something to keep her from going stir-crazy after sunset, she said. I think she was more of a mind to serve drinks, but we'd just lost our regular act, and she thought it would be fun to fill in till we got someone new. She's still filling in."

Filling in as a second job. Meaning her day job left her evenings free. Caleb wondered how big a town Mistletoe actually was, and if he made a trip down the mountain, how long it would take him to stroll the main streets and find her?

And then he thought back to the rest of what Alan had said. That a few years ago Candy had moved back. From where? "She said her only previous singing experience was with a church choir."

"Yeah. That was hard to believe when she got up onstage the first time. It was like she was born to perform."

"Whose idea was the costume?"

"Both of ours. She wanted to keep her two lives separate, and I wanted something to fit with the theme of the inn."

Candy Cane. Club Crimson. One in Vermillion. Will Ruby Mine. And the theme didn't stop at the color red. Just this morning when at the front desk convincing registration to let him stay the weekend, he'd seen a delivery from a shop called Under the Mistletoe.

He wouldn't be surprised to find Santa living in town. "She said your wife wanted her to sing at some school dance."

"She does, but it's not going to happen, which is fine. There's a girl in town who's going to perform. Zoe Sparks. She's amazing."

Brenna's sister sang? Caleb wondered how her mother felt about that, and if meeting the girl might answer his question about their estrangement. Then he wondered if Brenna's family even had a clue about the wedding. He picked up his glass, swirling the ice in the water. A trip into town might be in order after all. He'd have to hire a car...

"Lights are going down. Do you want anything else before the show starts?"

Already? He'd been so lost in thought he hadn't noticed the music he was now hearing was the pianist who'd taken the stage to warm up.

"No, I'm good," he told Alan, realizing the time he'd spent talking to the bartender was the time he was supposed to be getting a better handle on Candy by taking in the place where she worked, the mood of those who came to see her.

Alan had given him some of that, but Caleb was suddenly struck with the urge to go. This wasn't where or how he wanted to see her again. He didn't want to share her with the bartender, with the pianist or with the crowd.

When he was with her again, he wanted it to be just the two of them. Sitting and listening to her sing, watching her as she strolled through the club flirting and touching was more than he could handle. After what they'd shared last night, the thought of her being so close without having her...he couldn't do it. He couldn't stay.

He patted his jacket pocket, found a pen and his notepad, then scrambled for a way to leave her a note that no one at the bar could open and read. "Hey, Alan, you wouldn't happen to have an envelope, would you?"

"An envelope?" Alan walked the length of the bar, digging through drawers and stacks of papers near the register. He came back a moment later with a window envelope meant for bill payments. "Will this work?"

"Sure, thanks." Caleb jotted his note to Candy whoever-she-was, slipped that along with his room key inside, and considered adding a condom, but thought better of taking his invitation that far.

He scratched her first name across the back, drew a cane for her last, smiled at the sap he was for falling for the schmaltz. He waved Alan to come back. "Can you give this to her after the show?"

"You're not sticking around?" the bartender asked, taking the envelope from Caleb's hand and studying it as if he could see through the paper to the contents.

"Can't. Something's come up." Caleb boosted himself off

the stool, then hurried out before Alan asked for details and he had to lie. "Just see that Candy gets the note."

AS SHE DID EVERY NIGHT following her show, Miranda—still decked out as Candy—climbed onto a bar stool to unwind while Alan closed up the club. Unlike every other night following her show, she didn't see much unwinding ahead.

She'd poured out her heart tonight, had lost herself in the lyrics as she'd sung. It had been hard to wait for just the right moment to step off the stage and walk into the crowd.

Too soon, and the audience wouldn't be receptive. Too late, and they'd be anxious to get back to their rooms with their lovers. Strange that she'd waited till her final song last night. She never waited that long.

What had been different? Why the blip in her routine? She didn't want to think what she would've missed out on had she not changed things up.

But that was then. Tonight was tonight. She'd tried not to think of Caleb while singing, but it was hard to separate the emotions inspired by the love songs from the spiral of feelings she'd been riding all day. She didn't love him; of course she didn't love him, but the high of lust and infatuation was undeniable.

What she couldn't understand was why he hadn't been there to hear her. And then to return to the club and find out that he hadn't even come downstairs to meet her after the show? "I want the largest appletini you can make. And then I want another."

Alan started in mixing the drink. "How 'bout you finish one before I waste the makings of a second?"

Oh, yeah? "Just because I was stood up, you think I can't handle two drinks?"

"You weren't stood up," he said, adding apple schnapps to the vodka, apple juice and Cointreau. "Not exactly."

She whipped her head around to search the club. It was empty. Even the back booth where Caleb had sat last night. "What do you mean? What are you saying?"

He reached into the pocket of his apron, pulled out an envelope with her name written across the back, waved it at her like a flag. "He left you a note."

"Caleb?" Caleb had left her a note? And Alan thought he was going to play keep-away? This was so not funny.

"Were you hoping for one from someone else?"

"Well, give it to me already," she said, her heart pounding as she leaned across the bar and snatched it, tucking it into her cleavage for safekeeping.

Her ex-friend laughed like a hyena as he poured her drink into a large martini glass and handed it to her. "Who knew we were still in high school?"

"I think I'd prefer to read my note in private, thank you very much," she said, swiveling her stool away from the bar, her hand holding the drink in the air as she eased down.

"Hey! No taking drinks out of the club," Alan called from behind her as she wound her way through the tables, sofas and chairs toward the stage.

"Call the manager," she tossed back, climbing the steps and making her way to the rear exit. "Tell him I'll be in my dressing room."

She couldn't get there fast enough. The envelope was itching and scratching and tearing at her skin. It wasn't really, she knew. It was her anxiety, her wanting to know what Caleb had said, what excuse he'd made, if he'd left the Inn at Snow Falls and Mistletoe without a word of goodbye except for what she held in her hand.

She dropped to her bench, swallowed a quarter of her drink before setting it on her vanity, and caught her reflection in the mirror when she did. Makeup aside, her cheeks were flushed, her neck, too, the high color an outward display of the rush of blood through her veins.

Why was she letting Caleb leaving her a note get to her? They did not have a relationship. They'd met twenty-four hours ago, and could barely call themselves friends. Yes, he had told her that he would come to the show tonight, that he'd be prepared to finish what they'd started last night.

He could've changed his mind, gotten a better offer, been called away on business, gone to bed early with the fever and cough he'd come down with after she'd forced him out into the snow. But holding the envelope with a shaking hand while staring at her reflection and borrowing mental trouble was not going to fill in the blanks.

She reached for her glass, took another big gulp, then slid a finger beneath the envelope's flap. Inside she found a sheet torn from a pocket-size notebook and a room key.

Miranda held the key, her heart racing, her head pounding, her stomach tossing and turning. And then she unfolded the paper and read the single word Caleb had written.

Come

10
___

HEADING BACK TO HIS ROOM to wait for Candy hadn't been the best idea after all. Caleb swore he'd paced a trough to China during her set. At the end of the hour following her set, when the knock on his door finally came, he twitched hard enough to snap his spine.

He'd given her a key; was it somebody else outside? Had she come to return it instead of use it? Could he be any more relieved that he hadn't been a jerk and included a condom with the key and the note?

He glanced around the room, made sure nothing of Max had been left out, then went to answer. He didn't even bother with the peephole. If it wasn't Candy whoever-she-was, well, he wanted the surprise either way.

He pulled open the door to find her standing there wearing her sheepskin boots, his blazer from last night, her wig and the long slinky gown she'd obviously performed in. She had her parka draped over one arm. In her other hand, she clutched the handles of the same red gym bag she'd been carrying when he'd followed her through the kitchen.

He didn't want to try to interpret the expression on her face. She wasn't smiling or frowning. He couldn't tell if she was calm or scared stiff. All he knew was that if she stayed out in the hallway, he wasn't going to find out any of what she was thinking.

Holding open the door, he stepped back to give her room to enter. She took a deep breath, and did. He let the door close, and saw her jump when the latch caught and clicked.

She was nervous. He was nervous.

Whether they slept together or not, they needed to get nervous out of the way.

He walked up behind her, cleared his throat so she'd know he was there, took her parka and her bag from her hands. He tossed the small duffel to the floor of the closet and hung up the coat next to his.

She turned then, shrugged out of the blazer he'd left her wearing last night, and held it out in offering.

He waited, staring, knowing they had to break this ice or the night—whether they had sex or stuck to conversation—was going to be a disaster. When he saw the corner of her mouth quirk and one brow begin to lift, he moved.

His chest tight, he took the jacket, tossed it to the floor, held her face between his hands and kissed her.

She clutched his biceps and whimpered, leaning into him and parting her lips. His heart beat like a hammer as he slanted his mouth over hers and groaned, breathing her in, tasting her, wanting so much more of her than he could get with the two of them still fully clothed.

It was Candy and what she wanted that kept him from pushing things further. He was ready for anything, ready for it now, but he sensed that for her it was too soon. That she had things she needed to settle, things she needed to say.

He was right.

She eased her grip on his arms, pulling her mouth from his and backing away. A shy smile crossed her face. "You know I can't think when you do that."

"Guess that means I'm doing it right."

"Oh, you're doing it right," she said, laughing softly. Then she took another step away and wrapped her arms around herself. "Aren't you wondering why I didn't use the key?"

He moved his hands to his hips. "I am, but I figured if you wanted me to know, you'd tell me."

"Honestly? I'm not sure me being here is a good idea."

Right now, he couldn't think of a better one unless it was the two of them getting naked. "And you thought if I didn't answer you'd be off the hook?"

"No. Nothing like that."

"Then why did you come?" he asked, confused.

"Because I want to be here."

"You want to be here. You're just not sure it's a good idea. Got it." Yeah, this was going well.

"I had the best time with you last night. The dressing room. Sneaking into the kitchen. Your goodnight kiss. And condom or not, if you had pushed, I wouldn't have said no," she said, and he saw color bloom on her cheeks.

If he'd only known that then, he mused with no small amount of sarcasm, before admitting to himself that he had known it. That he'd had to force himself to walk away and leave her at her dressing-room door.

He scrubbed a hand down his jaw. "Look, Candy—"

"It's Miranda."

"What?" Stunned, he whipped his gaze up to meet hers.

She took a deep breath and rushed out with it again. "My name is Miranda. And that's why I'm not sure being here is a good idea."

That didn't make any sense. "Because your name is Miranda?"

"No," she said, her voice soft, patient. "Because I can't be with you as Candy. And being with you as myself is not an easy thing for me to do."

Once she got out of her clothes, he'd show her how easy it was. But he knew that was not what she meant.

"Okay...Miranda." He paused, searched for a new tack to take, since kissing her hadn't turned out to be such a brilliant idea. "Are you hungry? Should I order room service? Do you want a drink?" He sure as hell wanted one.

She shook her head. "No. All I want is you. To make love with you. But now that I've had time to think, I know that I can only do it as myself."

The drink could wait. "Does that mean you're going to tell me all of your secrets?"

"I don't think so," she said with a laugh. "Only my name, and this."

As Caleb looked on, she reached up and pulled off her wig. Her hair beneath was the short dark color he'd guessed from the strands caught in the bristles of her brush. Or so he first thought.

When she reached up to fluff it, pinching her bangs into wisps and shaking the rest of the layers, he realized it was more red than brown.

"You really are a redhead."

"Of a sort," she said, and blushed.

"Do you have freckles on your nose?" he asked, tickled by this whole discovery process.

"My nose, my cheeks. My forehead. And if you'll give me five minutes to wash off my makeup, I'll let you see for yourself."

He was all over seeing for himself. He didn't say a word, just gestured toward the bathroom and bowed. She walked by him and shoved his shoulder, knocking him back to the bed.

He laughed, but he didn't look away, only propped himself

up on his elbows far enough to see her grab his jacket from where he'd tossed it before closing the bathroom door.

He lay there for several moments, listening to the water run, then jumped up and got rid of his shoes, socks and shirt, keeping his pants on for now. He turned off the light nearest the bed, leaving on the one nearest the window, then sat down in one of the room's two wing chairs to wait.

He was still sitting there, leaning forward and staring at the floor, his elbows on his knees, his hands laced and his head hanging, when the water stopped, the bathroom door opened and Miranda came out.

He didn't care about her last name. He didn't care about her secrets. He didn't care that everything up until now had been awkward, tense and the bad idea she'd suggested. All he cared about was getting her clothes off and showing her with his body all the things he was feeling but was too tongue-tied to say.

She stood at the edge of the bedroom, the light of the bathroom behind her, seeming almost uncertain, hesitant, as if she needed his approval before taking another step. If he could've found his voice in that moment, he would've have given it a thousand times over. His voice, his heart, his brain…none of it was working.

He was looking at the most amazing creature he'd ever seen in his life. As Candy, she was gorgeous, classy, seductive. As Miranda…words failed him—a sad state for someone who made his living using them. But this wasn't gossip or a story for the hungry hordes. This was the two of them acting on an attraction that had him struggling to make sense of blindsiding emotion.

She was naked except for her panties and his blazer. Her face was scrubbed clean, her hair fluffed in layers and bangs. The lapels of the coat hung open, baring a long strip of skin from between her breasts to her sex that was covered by a triangle of white cotton. The look in her eyes was one of longing—and hope.

His hands on the chair arms, he pushed to his feet and walked toward her, slid his fingers beneath the jacket where it covered her shoulders and pushed it down her arms. It fell to the floor and left her standing in a scrap of a thong.

Running his hands down her arms, from her shoulders to her elbows, he tried to drink her all in, her green eyes, her freckles, her hair, still feeling a tug of familiarity but no longer trying to put his finger on the source. Right now? He didn't care.

She was here. She was beautiful. She was his.

Again, he struggled with words. "You are absolutely perfect, did you know that?"

"I'm absolutely terrified, does it show?"

He moved to her hands, found them shaking and held them. "I don't see anything but a long night ahead."

"I'm not too freckled? Too plain?" She looked down at herself. "Too small?"

She was talking about her breasts. She didn't have a lover, hadn't had one in how long? And she was worried he would find her breasts too small? Who had told her they were? Who had told her she was anything but incredible?

He brought up his hands to cup her, catching her nipples with his forefingers and thumbs, rolling the tight tips and leaning down to kiss the crease between her shoulder and her neck.

She sucked in a sharp breath, covered his hands with her own, guided him to touch her the way she wanted, shuddering when he did as if he'd given her the world.

"Good?" he asked, his mouth at her collarbone.

"Oh, yes. So good."

He wanted to make it even better, to show her what she'd been missing, and drifted lower, kissing his way down the slope of one breast, tugging at her nipple with his lips. She made tiny sounds in her throat, wiggled and squirmed, threaded her fingers into his hair and pulled.

He looked up, met her gaze, ran the tip of his tongue around the tip of her breast while she watched. Her eyes grew smoky and wicked hot, she bit at her lower lip, slowly shook her head and said, "Let's go to bed."

The bed, the floor, up against the wall, the chair and the desk…anywhere was fine with him as long as he could have her. And knowing she wanted him, too? He was afraid this first time would be over as fast as it started, but there was nothing he could do.

He stood, began to wrap her in his arms and tumble them both to the mattress, but stopped. He wanted her out of her panties.

He didn't ask. Just pushed his hands beneath the strip of elastic that held them in place and shoved them to her feet. He remembered touching her last night, how smooth she was, how wet on his fingers. He wanted to know that she was just as ready for him now.

She stepped out of the fabric and reached for his fly, un-buckling, unbuttoning, unzipping while he slid a finger into her folds, separating the plump lips of her pussy, finding her clit hard and bold.

And then her hands were holding him, the sac of his balls, his rigid shaft, lifting him out of his shorts then letting him go while she pulled his pants down. That was when he finally tumbled her, grabbing her up and falling with her to the bed.

She giggled as if she couldn't imagine having more fun, and he found himself smiling, too, loving the foreplay because of the joy reflected in her face. But he could only stand the teasing touches of her fingers and her mouth so long. Enough had become enough.

He pinned her down and moved on top of her, rose up to his knees and rolled on a condom while she watched. Her eyes were hungry, and he hurried, bracing his hands above her shoulders while she guided him into place.

He surged forward, driving into her. She gasped, thrust upward, settled back onto the mattress and closed her legs around his hips, her arms around his back.

She pulled him down, and he lowered his weight to his elbows, riding her, rocking against her, filling her with every slow, smooth stroke. He wanted to take hours, knew they only had minutes. The heat of this connection was a fiery one, consuming them.

She took him in, clenched her muscles and held him, grinding hard. He wanted her to stop, to be still, to let him go. This was happening too fast. He wasn't going to be able to hold on. He needed to know she was getting what she wanted, that he wasn't letting her down. But he couldn't wait, he couldn't wait. He had too much need.

"I can't—" he started to say, then lost the words in his throat.

"It's okay," she told him, breathless, her voice breaking. "I can't either."

He closed his eyes and gave up his control, spilling himself as she ground her sex to his shaft and cried out. He came quickly, fiercely, felt her spasms at the same time. The sensations rocked him physically, but a strange pulse of emotion followed.

He didn't want to deal with it now, but he couldn't push it away. His body was still humming, his desire still winding down. So he allowed the sense of rightness to wash over him as he pulled out of her body and spooned close to her side.

She cuddled back against him, but only stayed a minute or two before excusing herself and heading to the bathroom. He discarded the condom in the room's wastebasket, listening to the water running, the toilet flushing, and realized how intimate it was hearing Miranda clean up after sex.

Miranda—and, yeah, he liked that name so much better than Candy—opened the bathroom door, switched off the light, and wearing nothing but her skin, crawled beneath the covers and rested her head on his shoulder. He was surprised at how perfect it felt to have her there, how comfortable he was holding her close.

"You staying the night?" he finally asked.

"I can. Most of it anyway. Unless you want me to go."

"Hell, no. I'd like to get in a round two and three at least." Rounds during which they would take their time exploring instead of exploding. He wanted to know what it was he was feeling with her, why he was feeling anything at all.

She tugged at the hair on his chest. "Awful full of yourself, aren't you?"

"I'd rather you be full of me."

"I'd like that. Maybe a marathon this time instead of a sprint?"

Ouch. "Hey. Who're you calling a sprinter?"

She rolled toward him, rose over him on one elbow. "The man who sprinted?"

He crossed his arms beneath his head on his pillow. "I'm pretty sure that race was a photo finish."

"I like a photo finish. It's exciting. Especially after a marathon."

A one-track mind, this woman with the freckles on her nose. "How 'bout I lie back here and give you a head start?"

"Wouldn't that be giving you the head start?"

"If you want to get technical…"

But that was all he got out before she climbed on top and straddled him. His cock stood at attention against her belly, and it was the biggest fight of his life to keep his hands beneath his head. He wanted to pull her down, press her breasts together, tongue his way from one nipple to the other and make her squirm.

Instead, he closed his eyes and let her play, lying as still as he could as she started at his collarbone, moved to the dip in his throat, kissing and licking her way down his chest, to his belly, to his cock.

She kissed the full head, flicked the tip of her tongue over the slit, had him muttering silent curses when she wrapped her lips around him and sucked.

She ringed her fingers at the top of his shaft, stroked them up and down his glans as she pulled at him with her mouth. His balls drew up tight against his body, and it took everything he had in him not to come.

But everything wasn't enough. He tried to warn her, reaching down to pull out, but she shook her head, pushed his hand away, and sucked him harder and faster until he bucked his hips and came.

She took all of him, stayed right there with him, only letting him go when he groaned to let her know he was done. *Done* wasn't even the half of it. He was spent, exhausted. He wanted nothing more than to sprawl across the bed and sleep.

He'd promised her a marathon, however, so he flipped her to her back, knelt between her spread legs, and with a rumbling growl as he went down on her, said, "My turn."

11

MIRANDA'S INTERNAL CLOCK went off before her cell-phone alarm could ring and wake Caleb. She rolled away from him as quietly as she could, realizing as she stretched that Patrice's predictions had come true.

Her muscles were all kinds of sore, her skin rubbed raw and bruised, and if she managed to get out of bed in one piece, she would definitely be hobbling like an old woman all the way to her car.

She had no idea what had happened to the thong she'd been wearing, and couldn't worry about that now. Instead, she crept to the closet and found her gym bag. Tugging gingerly on the zipper pull, she opened the duffel and dug through her things for panties, socks and a bra.

After reading the note, no, the *word* Caleb had left for her last night, the only thing she'd wanted to know was why he hadn't come to her show. The more she thought about it, however, the more she appreciated his not being there.

Looking for him in the crowd had been distracting enough. She couldn't imagine the distraction if she'd found him. Maybe he'd anticipated that and stayed away to save her performance from swirling down the tubes.

She'd meant to ask him about it when he'd opened the door. She hadn't meant to seize up with nerves and forget everything except telling him her name.

But he'd stood there staring at her, looking all disheveled and unhinged as if the wait had been driving him mad, and her long list of questions had dissolved into nothing but wanting to hear him call her Miranda.

She should be glad she'd managed to do that much, she mused, tugging on her socks before digging for her sweatshirt and pulling it over her head. The rest of the answers she wanted could wait. She figured he had a few things on his mind, too. Funny how nothing else had mattered to either of them when faced with a marathon of sex.

She was just starting to pull on her thermal bottoms and sweatpants when the light beside the bed clicked on. She cringed, stepped forward, peered around the corner to see Caleb propped up on his elbows, frowning as if looking for what woke him.

"Sorry," she whispered. "I was trying to be quiet."

"You *were* quiet." He sat up, scrubbing his hands over his face. The sheet fell to his lap and left her looking at the chest that she'd come to know so well, the hair in the center that was silky and soft. "I got cold. Where are you going?"

"Home." He was gorgeous, all warm and sleepy-looking. She didn't want to go. "I have work, remember?"

That sobered him. He tossed the sheet out of the way and wearing absolutely nothing but the stirrings of a hard-on, walked toward her. He didn't smile or speak or give her a chance to catch up. He just backed her into the wall and brought his mouth down on hers.

Oh, this was so not fair, this way he caused her to forget everything but his body and what it could do, the magic he could make her feel. She had not had this in so long—if she'd had it ever. He'd taken her over so completely, she couldn't remember any other men at all.

He held her shoulders, kissed his way from her mouth to her ear then down her neck to her sweatshirt. He stopped there, grunted, reached for the hem and pushed the fabric up over her breasts. He grunted again at finding her wearing a bra, but the garment didn't stop him from sucking her nipple into his mouth.

She threaded her fingers into his hair. "I've got to go."

"I've got to come."

She laughed. "Again? I can't believe you have anything left in you."

"A machine, baby. I am a machine."

She tugged up his head, forced him to look at her. "I have one of those at home. It's called a vibrator."

"Sorry. Half asleep. Not thinking with my big head."

Being a man, in other words. "You go back to bed. I'm going home."

"Why don't you come back to bed with me, then I'll go home with you?"

She closed her eyes, moaned in pleasure as he pinched both nipples, tugging and rolling them while sucking on the skin at the base of her neck. It was a good thing she had more than one costume with a banded collar neckline. She was going to have bruises to hide.

And then she remembered it was Thursday. Tonight was her night off. The thought of not seeing him... "Why don't I go home now, and you come later? For dinner."

He stopped with his hands only halfway into her panties. Then pulled them out, and looked up. "You want me to come to your house? Like, Miranda's house, not Candy's house?"

She cocked her head to the side. "Candy doesn't have a house. She has a dressing room."

He frowned. "I didn't think you wanted me to know who you are."

"Not all of it. Not yet." She paused, considered everything she knew about him, considered all the things she still didn't. "You scare me."

"Really? I didn't think my cock was that big."

It was hard to keep a straight face. "Please. Not that kind of scared. Though if I don't get away from you, I am afraid I'll never walk without hobbling again."

He scratched his chest, his grin all cock-of-the-walk proud.

She pushed him away, fighting an answering smile. "Move so I can get my pants on."

"You look a lot better with them off."

"That's because you're looking with your southernmost eye." She didn't even want to think about how good he looked out of his clothes or she'd never get to the shop in time to avoid a scolding from Corinne.

He leaned a hand on the wall next to her head, whispering into her ear as he nibbled her lobe, moved down to the skin of her neck, "What time do you want me to come?"

She was not going to play this game of double entendre. She was not. It didn't matter that just the right touch and she'd melt all over him.

Since she was usually home from the shop by six… "Eight?"

"Where do you want me to come?" he asked, nuzzling her neck.

She was not, she was not, she was not going to play. She ducked out from under his arm, shoved her feet into her Uggs and grabbed her parka and duffel from the closet. "Second Avenue. Twelve-oh-five."

"Miranda?"

She turned back. The way he said her name… She wanted to weep from the beauty of hearing it. Her heart thundered in her chest. "Yes?"

"After dinner, can I come? Can I make you come? Can we have another photo-finish marathon of coming? Or take turns all night long?"

As if she could turn down a man who begged as beautifully as he made love. "After dinner, you can come until the machine won't come anymore."

"TEN-THIRTY YESTERDAY. Eleven today. By next week you'll be showing up at closing time."

"I know, I know. I'm sorry." Miranda stashed her purse in her locker, pulled on her apron, wondered if she'd remembered to brush her hair. She hadn't bothered with more than mascara, running as late as she was. "I spent the night at the inn. I forgot how long it can take to get down the mountain with the sun glaring off the snow."

"You spent the night at the inn? With him?"

"That's not all."

One of Corinne's brows went up. "You told him who you were."

"Only my first name," Miranda said, holding up one finger. "But I did invite him for dinner tonight."

Clucking like a hen, Corinne went back to work. "When all of this blows up in your face, I don't want to hear about it. You've got too many secrets to make a relationship work, unless you're planning to come clean."

An understatement if Miranda had ever heard one. "Right now, it's just sex. It's not a relationship. There's nothing to blow up or any need to come clean."

"Tell yourself that now," the other woman said, using a pair of scissors as a pointer. "And I'll remind you of it later when you realize you're over your head and drowning."

Knowing the subject of relationships was a touchy one for

Corinne, who'd been alone years longer than she had, Miranda switched to something a little more pressing. "What should I make for dinner?"

"What does he like?"

They hadn't exactly gotten around to sharing their favorite foods. "I have no idea. I don't know if he's a vegetarian or a vegan, or a meat-and-potatoes guy."

"Meatless lasagna, salad and bread sticks," Corinne suggested.

Easy enough, but… "What if he doesn't like veggies? Or what if he's allergic to wheat?"

Still brandishing the scissors, Corinne turned to face her. "Why don't you call him and ask?"

"Now that's an idea," Miranda said, heading for the phone. She dialed the switchboard at the inn, booting up her laptop while waiting for the operator to answer. "Room two-eighteen please."

Muttering to herself, Corinne got back to cutting stems from filler carnations.

"McGregor," Caleb said, picking up after four rings.

Hearing his voice brought back all of last night in a mental slideshow. Miranda tucked the phone close to her chin, feeling her cheeks flush. "Caleb? Miranda. Are you a vegetarian? Do you have any food allergies? Is there anything you won't eat? Broccoli or bacon or béchamel sauce?"

He laughed, the sound echoing richly through the line. "If I knew what that was, I might turn up my nose, but I'm good with grilled cheese or a PB and J."

"I'm not going to feed you a PB and J, but I don't want to feed you shrimp if you're going to break out in hives."

"No hives. No worries. But while I have you…what're you wearing?"

"Goodbye, Caleb," she said, and hung up before he could respond. Fanning her face with one hand, she turned to Corinne. "We're good to go with anything."

"What's this *we* business? You're the one jumping from the frying pan into the fire. Though judging by your face, I'd say you already made the leap."

She'd made some kind of leap. She just hadn't yet figured out where she'd landed. In a relationship or in a fling? Back to the food. "Italian?"

"Too much garlic," Corinne said sagely.

"Steaks and stuffed baked potatoes?"

"If you want to be the ones stuffed." Again, more sound advice.

"I want to make a good first impression," Miranda said, humbled by the fact that she, who had worked with caterers on events feeding hundreds of strangers, couldn't decide what to cook for a man she'd spent a very long passionate night getting to know.

Corinne snorted. "If the burn marks on your jaw are any indication, I'd say you've moved beyond first, to a second or third at least."

Crap. Miranda headed for the bathroom and peered at her reflection in the mirror above the sink. She turned her head left, then right, finding a spot scraped red by Caleb's whiskers.

She hadn't bothered with foundation this morning, already in a hurry to get to the shop, and obviously she should have. Good thing she kept a bag of makeup samples in her locker.

She was covering the red marks when Corinne appeared in the doorway behind her. "Make it simple."

Miranda froze with her hand halfway to her face. "I was only using foundation."

Corinne shook her head. "Not your makeup. Dinner. Stuff

some chicken breasts. I've got a great recipe using spinach and goat cheese. Or forget stuffing. That's not exactly simple. Just bake. If he turns out to be handy in the kitchen, put him in charge of a salad, or at least the wine. You can talk while all the prep is going on, get to know him better. He could be the one, and I don't need to be putting an old-hag damper on things."

"You're not putting a damper on things," Miranda said, frowning as she turned away from the mirror to look at her friend. "Why would you even think that?"

Standing just inside the bathroom, Corinne closed her eyes and dropped her head against the door. "Because I've been such a grump these past few days."

"Oh, Corinne. Being a grump does not make you an old hag," Miranda said, laying a hand on the other woman's arm, sensing the source of her unusual show of emotions. It couldn't be easy working on flowers that were more than likely for her own daughter's wedding. "We're all allowed to be grumpy from time to time. And some of those times can be really, really hard."

Corinne opened watery eyes and met Miranda's gaze. "I shouldn't have given away all the gifts Brenna sent. I've been so angry with her for so long. But giving away the things she sent was just cruel. I never meant to hurt her feelings."

"Of course you didn't," Miranda said, turning and drawing her friend into a hug. "And being cruel wasn't your intent. You were hurt—"

"Which is why I should've kept the gifts." Corinne pulled away. "I wasn't thinking straight."

With Corinne's guard down and her regret running high, Miranda decided to give her employee a push in the direction she was certain Corinne was ready to go. "You could always call the inn and talk to her."

Corinne stopped in the act of running her fingers beneath her eyes. "Apologize?"

"Not apologize. Explain. Open a dialogue."

"I don't know. I don't want to make things worse."

"Then think about calling her." Miranda was not giving up. "Thinking's harmless enough, isn't it?"

Corinne shrugged. "I guess if you can invite a stranger home and cook him dinner, I can think about settling things with my daughter."

12

BARRY CHANCE, the Inn at Snow Falls' shuttle driver, seemed to think Caleb was a tourist wanting a rundown on the resort and the town, when the only thing he wanted was to get to 1205 Second Avenue at eight o'clock on the nose.

From behind the wheel of the minivan warmed to near suffocation, Barry prattled on. "Twelve-oh-five Second Avenue. Isn't that Miranda Kelly's house?"

Miranda Kelly. Caleb stared out the side window into the darkness made even darker by the shadows cast by the thick evergreen forest on either side of the road.

Miranda Kelly. Nice, but not a name he could place in the context of freckles, green eyes and short auburn hair. Either he was thinking of someone else and he didn't know her at all, or she'd changed both her name and her looks.

He settled back, bracing his arm across the seat. "You know her then?"

"Everyone in Mistletoe knows Miranda. But then everyone in Mistletoe knows everyone in Mistletoe." That tickled the driver, and he cackled like a witch throwing newts' eyes into a cauldron. "She owns Under the Mistletoe, the flower shop. But then you probably know that, being friends with her and all."

"Sure," Caleb said as if affirming Barry's assumption,

wondering what else the other man knew and might share without Caleb having to dig.

"Corinne Sparks works there with her." Barry caught Caleb's gaze in the rearview mirror. "Her daughter Brenna's that singer Ravyn Black, though you probably know that, too. She's up at the inn. So's Congressman Eagleton."

Caleb figured he knew more about Teddy and the rock star than Barry did. But the rest was interesting. The sister at the high school. The mother at the flower shop. Maybe he could get to the secret of Brenna's family estrangement through Miranda.

Miranda Kelly. Nope. He didn't know the name.

"Here we are," the driver announced moments later, pointing out a tiny bungalow that sat back from the road, its long front walk and driveway shoveled, its yard a blanket of snow. "Do you need me to come back for you later?"

Caleb glanced through the windshield toward the light diffused by the front window's curtains. No way was he going to share his plans to stay the night with this gossip. "If Miranda doesn't want to drive me back, I'll call the inn."

Barry flung his arm along the seat, turning to look at Caleb sitting behind him. "I get off at midnight, so don't wait till the last minute or you'll be stuck here all night."

That was the idea.

"Thanks for the ride," Caleb said, climbing out into the street and waving as the minivan pulled away. He made his way to the end of the walk that led to her house, studying the small Craftsman structure, the smoke rising from the chimney, the welcoming glow of the porch lamp.

Heading up the front walk, he imagined her inside, all warm and cozy as she fussed with dishes and food, setting the table, lighting candles, arranging flowers she'd brought home from her shop. And then he wondered what the hell he'd been smoking, painting that domestic scene, and ignored the strange aching tug in his chest as he rang the bell and waited for her to answer.

She pulled open the door moments later, a flurry of sounds and scents coming with her, her eyes going wide when she saw that he was wearing only a blazer with his dress shirt and jeans, and had his sheepskin coat in one hand.

"Aren't you freezing?"

"Only marginally," he said, and when she didn't invite him in, added with a forced chatter of teeth, "Though the longer I stay out here, the worse it gets."

"Oh, geez. Sorry. Come in." She stepped back, let him pass, then closed the door, taking his coat and hanging it in the front room's closet. "I was so busy ogling you, I forgot my manners, *oomph*—"

He crushed her to him, his mouth coming down to cover hers in a punishing kiss, though he didn't know who he was punishing. Himself for being so besotted with her, or her for besotting him the way she had.

And then it didn't matter because she was kissing him back, her hands on his shoulders, her tongue in his mouth, her legs wound up with his, her breasts pressed to his chest. He groaned. She groaned. She whimpered and squirmed and then shoved him away.

"Dinner first," she told him breathlessly, her eyes sparkling with the heat of the kiss as the fire leaped in the fireplace behind her.

"What if I want to skip dinner and go straight for dessert?" he asked her, his chest rising and falling as he fought back his desire.

"Then you can follow me into the kitchen and have a slice of Italian cream cake while I finish stuffing the chicken

breasts." And with that, she turned, not looking back to see
if he was coming with her.

He didn't have much choice, and cake sounded good, so
he followed.

"I didn't think you were really going to cook," he said,
climbing onto a stool on the other side of the center island
from where she worked. "I thought it was all a big pretense
to get me in bed."

"You may live on sex and grilled cheese," she said, grabbing a small plate and a cake knife. "But I like a more
balanced diet."

He looked at the colorful array of food laid out, inhaling
herbs and spices and something…sharp. "Veggies, protein,
sex and sugar?"

"Plus singing, working and spending time with friends."

"So I'm a friend, huh?" he asked, grabbing a wedge of bell
pepper and popping it into his mouth. He crunched down, felt
the tang and the crispness, and reached for another.

Miranda set the cake plate aside and offered him the handle
of the small paring knife that had been lying on the island.
"You're welcome to work on the salad."

He took it with a teasing grumble. "Not only do I have to
wait for sex, now I have to work for my dinner."

She turned around, reached into her pantry, came back
with a loaf of bread and jar of peanut butter, and set both in
front of him. "I happen to think the best things are worth
waiting for. If you don't, feel free to make a sandwich with
your left hand, and use your right as you wish."

Oh, he liked this woman. "Saucy tonight, aren't we…Mi-
randa Kelly?"

She froze in the act of mixing cooked spinach with
chopped onions and some sort of pasty white cheese, and was

slow to lift her gaze. "How did you find out my name? The Kelly part."

"The shuttle driver was a talker," he said, reaching for the salad bowl of lettuce and other greens and pretending not to notice the panic that flashed through her eyes.

"Did he tell you anything else?"

"He did, yes."

"Like what?"

"That you own a flower shop. That you employ the mother of Evermore's Ravyn Black. That he gets off work at midnight, and to call before that if I need a ride back." He added the last part because he was no longer sure that she'd want him to stay.

She didn't say anything at first, just got back to stirring and stuffing, arranging the chicken breasts in a shallow glass dish and putting them in to bake. Then she chose a bottle of wine from the small built-in rack above her refrigerator and set it on the island with two glasses.

"Barry's a sweetheart, but he does like to make conversation when he drives." She climbed onto the stool beside him, picked up a second paring knife.

Since she didn't stab him with it or ask him to leave, he figured so far so good. "Did you not want me knowing your last name? Or about Under the Mistletoe?"

"It's not that," she began, then shook her head. "That's not true. It is that. My life here is private, and I want to keep it that way."

The curiosity was killing him. "Miranda, I don't know who you are, so I don't know who I'd tell about you or the flower shop even if I was inclined to do so, which I'm not. So relax. Please." He reached for the wine bottle. "Now, did you want a drink? Or were you planning to bash me in the head with this and hope for amnesia?"

She gave him a weak smile, obviously still a bit hesitant to accept him at his word. "A drink would be nice, yes, thanks."

He poured a glass for both of them, watching her swallow half of hers before he'd taken his first sip. He didn't think his being here was making her nervous as much as his knowing her last name, and he found that extremely telling.

They both knew he could easily do an Internet search and most likely discover the story she was hiding. He supposed he could set her at ease by promising he wouldn't pry, but he'd already written a mental note to do just that when he got back to his laptop and the inn's wireless connection to the Web.

So he didn't say anything. He just waited, watching as she cut a red pepper and a yellow pepper to go with his green, deciding, when the silence lingered, to change the subject. "I'm surprised you can get all these vegetables so readily. The grocery store I saw in town looked like the small-canned-goods type."

"I cheated," she said, smiling. "I had Alan get them from the inn's kitchen. The goat cheese, too."

A big *eww* went though Caleb's head. "Goat cheese?"

Miranda chuckled. "Oh, don't be turning your nose up now, Mr. I'll-Eat-Anything. You had your chance to give me a list of food deemed off-limits."

"It wouldn't have occurred to me to mention it," he said, leaning away from the bowl with the leftover white lumps clinging to the glass. "I mean, is goat cheese a food?"

"Yes, it's a food, and you're going to eat it and love every bite."

He started to say something about eating her and loving her instead, but he had a feeling that discovering her name— no matter that he'd been given the information without asking—had sent him back to square one in the sex game.

Good thing he had Barry the shuttle driver's card. It was a hell of a long walk back to the inn. "Barry who likes to talk. He does know you're Candy Cane, right?"

"He does, yes."

"And Alan and his wife."

"Yes."

This time he went further. "Alan said he's known you a long time."

"He has," she admitted, her mouth quirking.

"Has anything bad happened with having them know about you being Candy?"

"No, but they're friends. They're not going to turn my dual identity into a human-interest story the way a reporter who got hold of the information might do," she said pointedly. "I don't want to risk having Candy's picture show up next to mine in the newspaper."

Because then someone who was looking for Miranda might see the article about her and Candy Cane, and boom. End of privacy. Now he wanted to know everything. "Who's looking for you, Miranda? Who are you hiding from?"

"What do you mean?" she asked, stalling, evading, clearly knowing exactly what he meant but obviously hoping to throw him off track. "All I said was that I didn't want my picture in the paper next to one of Candy."

Fine. She wanted him to spell it out? He'd spell it out. "People who know you wouldn't need the side-by-side pictures. They'd recognize you just from your name and identity as a florist. That means there's someone else out there you don't want making the connection."

She waved him off, reaching for extra spinach leaves that she hadn't cooked for the chicken. "You're thinking about this way too hard."

"Am I?" he asked, not easily dismissed.

"Yes. I'll take back what I said about the pictures, okay? If that'll quell your suspicions? I don't want my name linked to Candy's by some reporter wanting to write an article on her or Mistletoe. I like my privacy. Is that better?"

Better for her, maybe.

He shifted on his stool, reached for the wine and refilled both their glasses. "But outside of Mistletoe and the resort, who would care? Unless you're notorious in some way…"

"I'm not notorious," she said, her words tinged with a touch of desperation. She held up one hand. "I had a bad experience with the press and I don't want to relive it, okay?"

"Is there a reason you would have to?"

She set down the knife, and used the stem to slide her wine-glass closer, but didn't drink, gathering her thoughts without ever glancing toward him. "Are there any reporters actively looking for me? I don't know. Are there reporters who would jump all over the news of me being here?" She nodded.

"The ones you had the bad experience with?"

"Yes. And it's those reporters I don't want seeing my picture or my name next to Candy's in the news. Satisfied?"

He should've been, but satisfaction wasn't what he was feeling. He was feeling that hunch again, the one telling him this story was big. "You know all I have to do is plug your name into Google and click go."

"I do. I'm just hoping you won't." The timer on the oven dinged. Saved by the bell, she jumped from her stool to pull the chicken from the oven. "Now. Let's eat."

13

DINNER WAS A VERY quiet affair. They ate at the small table in the alcove off Miranda's kitchen. The bungalow didn't have a formal dining room, so the entertaining she did was always as casual as tonight—though the menu was usually much simpler.

Parties of drinks and hors d'oeuvres for the holidays. Burgers on the backyard grill in the summer. Big kettles of soups and stews with bread from the inn's kitchen the rest of the year. A casserole shared with Corinne.

They had bread from the inn's kitchen tonight, too. A crusty artisan loaf that she served with a crock of real butter alongside their salad and stuffed chicken. The wine flowed freely. Very freely. More freely than was wise considering the conversation they'd had before sitting down to eat.

If she wasn't careful, she was going to spill everything about her past to Caleb just to get it off her chest. And because for some reason she didn't understand, she wanted him to know. She was obviously running on alcohol and hormones, but she got the feeling his curiosity was born of caring more than prurient nosiness.

His questions about her past showed his interest, and it felt so good to have that attention from a man. She knew he wouldn't be here long, making a relationship between them highly unlikely. Yet a part of her was unwilling to discount the possibility and was prepared to tell all. It was a part of her she had to keep in check.

"You're a great cook," he said, interrupting her thoughts, and gesturing toward what was left in the serving dishes. "This was wonderful."

"I'm great at following recipes. I'm not so sure that's the same thing as being a great cook." She placed her knife and fork on her empty plate. "I got this one from Corinne. It's not bad. Goat cheese and all."

"I was teasing about the cheese, by the way," he said, finishing off his wine.

What he was doing was trying to make her feel better. "Sure you were."

He frowned, shook his head, swallowed. "I swear. It's one of my faves."

She laughed, moving her napkin to the table from her lap. "You are so full of crap."

"What I'm full of is dinner. I have no idea where I'm going to put dessert."

"We can save it," she suggested, loving the disheveled style of his light-brown hair, the sexy stubble covering his jaw. Loving even more how he looked in her kitchen, how right it felt having him here.

"Are you kidding me? Save Italian cream cake?"

Laughing, she got to her feet, stacked their plates, and gathered up their utensils, feeling incredibly nurturing and enjoying it more than she should. "Why don't I make coffee? We can have dessert in the living room."

"In front of the fire?" Caleb stood and pushed his chair beneath the table. "Like a date?"

"Since that's what this is, yes," she said, then carried the dishes to the sink. When she turned to head back for the rest, he was there behind her, trapping her against the edge of the counter.

"What are you doing?" she asked, feeling the flutter of her pulse in her throat.

"Dating."

She looked down to where he'd pressed his lower body against hers, the flutter moving lower and turning insistent, urgent. "It's been a while, but I'm pretty sure this isn't the dating I remember."

"It's grown-up dating," he said, grinding against her, reaching for the buttons of her blouse and pressing his lips to the base of her neck.

"I see," was all she could get out. She was too focused on the way her skin zinged beneath his hands and mouth to say more, and instead of reaching for him the way she wanted, she held on to the counter's edge by her hips.

She longed to touch him, she did, but she ached with the way he touched her. He stroked and pleasured and made love to her, revered her, with every movement of his fingers, every ministration of his lips and his tongue. His touch made her want to cry. She hadn't felt this treasured, this desired in so long.

She closed her eyes, dropped her head back on her shoulders, shivered when he reached under her short skirt and slipped his fingers beneath the leg opening of her panties. He rubbed the bare lips of her pussy, bumped his knuckles back and forth over her clit.

She spread her legs wider, wanting his penetration, needing to feel him moving inside of her, but he continued to tease her, his hand in her panties, his mouth moving down to kiss the swell of her breasts above the lace edge of her bra.

She couldn't take this. She needed more skin-to-skin

contact, more friction, more heat, and less—she couldn't believe she was thinking it—foreplay. She parked her hands on his shoulders and shoved. "I'm tired of dating. If you don't mind, I'd rather just go to bed."

His eyes sparked when he laughed, a deep rumbling growl of a sound that told her he was all for playing along. "What about coffee and dessert?"

She kicked off her wedge heels, reached back and unzipped her skirt. The garment fell to her feet and she kicked that away, too. She left her blouse hanging open, and stood there in her panties and bra. "You can have cake and coffee, or you can have me."

She didn't give him a chance to do anything but narrow his eyes and devour her with a look. She lifted her chin and walked by him, leaving her shoes and skirt in the kitchen, dropping her blouse in the hallway, unhooking her bra and draping it over the knob of her bedroom door.

She had just shimmied out of her panties and crawled up the bed on her hands and knees when Caleb caught up with her and covered her body with his. He was as naked as she was, and didn't ask or pretend not to know what she wanted. He mounted her from behind, his sheathed erection sliding into her, and she was wet and swollen and ready.

She groaned, pressed her forehead to the mattress, clutched the comforter as if she needed the anchor to keep her from flying off the bed. Caleb held her hips, pushing in and pulling out with maddeningly slow thrusts, causing her senses to spiral wildly, her arousal to consume her.

He leaned over her, slipped one hand from her hip to her belly, then lower still to her clit. He pressed against the knot of nerves coiled there, caught it between his forefinger and thumb, pinched, rolled and tugged until she whimpered and writhed. She couldn't believe he was giving her this, that he was so focused on pleasing her.

"Come, Miranda."

She shook her head on the mattress. She wasn't ready. "Not yet. This feels too good."

"There's always more of this to be had. Anytime you want it. Come for me, Miranda. I want to feel you let go."

Oh, but how she wanted to do just that. She slid forward until she was flat on the mattress. Caleb slid with her, his cock still inside her, his hand caught between her body and the bed. She lifted her hips to give him room to move, but instead of pulling free, he continued to touch her, his fingers playing while his cock stroked.

She wanted to turn over, but later. When they were done here. When he didn't have the upper hand. When she wasn't feeling this mad rush of emotions. She'd turn over then, wrap her legs around his hips, and search his gaze for what he was feeling…

He had to be experiencing at least some of the same sense of rightness overwhelming her, didn't he? Or was she truly feeling all of this alone? This connection, this perfection. This powerful thing they had found that was growing too large for her heart to contain.

She shifted her position, moved one hand down between her legs to join his, spreading her fingers in a V around his cock where it entered her. He groaned, thrust, muttered sexy threats and sexier promises under his breath.

"Come for me, Caleb. I want to feel you let go."

This time he didn't mutter, but spewed a string of raw words and curses into the air as he pumped his hips, filling her, stretching her, pleasuring her until she couldn't hold back. She cried out, shuddering, her muscles contracting to milk him as he came, too.

It was bright and brilliant, explosive and fast. She was still shaking when he pulled out and flipped her over, shoving inside her again while they lay face-to-face. Tears rolled from the corners of her eyes. She hadn't meant to release them. She'd tried so hard to keep the things she was feeling tucked away.

But he cupped her face in his hands and smiled at her, brought his mouth down to kiss her, and she was lost. She wrapped her arms around his neck and held him close, fighting one sob, then another, until everything she was feeling spilled out in the most ridiculously loud hiccup.

She couldn't decide whether to laugh or to weep with joy that what had started to feel like a monster intent on ruining the rest of the night, dissipated with that ungodly sound.

"Sorry about that," she said, then hiccuped again and laughed when it wouldn't stop. "I think that was all my veggies being tossed around."

"Bell peppers, definitely," he said, rolling away now that he'd softened.

She brought up her hand to cover her mouth. "Oh, gross."

"Hey." He propped up on one elbow, comfortable in being naked beside her. "Not gross. Just the same thing I'm tasting."

"Note to self. No sex after salad."

"How 'bout sex before dessert?"

"Coming right up," she said, pushing into a sitting position, not quite as comfortable as he was, fearing her emotions were as exposed as her skin.

Caleb grabbed her arm before she could scoot off the bed. "Miranda. It's okay."

"No, it's not." She didn't want to talk about this now. Not the truth, anyway. "I'm a terrible hostess with terrible manners."

"Maybe so," he said, dragging her back for a long earthy kiss. "But you're a hell of a date."

14

CALEB LAY SPRAWLED on his side on the Persian rug that covered the living room's hardwood floor. He'd set Miranda's coffee mug on the low table, and was sipping at his own while waiting for her to follow with the cake.

He'd pulled on his socks for warmth, and his jeans, boxers and dress shirt for propriety, but had left the latter unbuttoned just in case she got an itch to scratch him.

Instead of dressing in the clothes she'd been wearing, Miranda had put on skinny black pants, socks and a sweater, and had scooted around him in the kitchen while making coffee as though she was skating on a floor of ice.

He'd been afraid she was going to fall down and break an arm or a leg, but not half as afraid as he'd been of her heart breaking while they'd made love. He'd been well aware of the hitch in her breathing, the way she'd been reluctant to put distance between them but had. Just because he wasn't keen on emotions didn't mean he was clueless about feelings.

Especially women's feelings.

Especially women's feelings about sex.

Miranda hadn't been with a man in a while. He didn't know anything about her history, whether she was divorced or had never married, whether she'd gone through a bad breakup or parted ways amicably with the men she'd dated at the ends of their relationships, whether short-term or long.

He didn't know any of that, but he didn't have to. All that mattered was how right it felt for her to be with him. And the fact that it did made his leaving on Monday a good thing for them both. She didn't need a man in her life with the means to expose whatever it was she didn't want known. And he could do that in a very big way.

He wasn't planning to, but then he hadn't been planning to with Delano Wise either—though it was Del's fiancée Caleb had really screwed over, betraying a confidence to tell the world about the Christian music phenomenon's cocaine addiction and stint in rehab. Thanks to his Max Savage exclusive, she'd lost her recording contract and a deal for her own clothing label with a national department store chain.

And Caleb? He'd lost the best friend he'd ever had, a massive chunk of his self-respect and the blinders he'd been wearing, ones that had kept him from seeing that over the years he had, indeed, done harm. That there was a line, and he'd crossed it. That there were boundaries, and he'd gone beyond them, changing himself in the process.

"Are you sure you're in the mood for cake?"

He hadn't heard Miranda come into the room, and he looked up to see her standing with two plates in her hands. He swung up into a sitting position and reached for one. "I'm always in the mood for cake."

"You looked lost in something pretty intense," she said, neatly folding her legs and dropping down beside him.

He shook his head, dug off a bite of the top layer with his fork. "Thinking about a book I'm working on."

"You're writing a book?"

This was probably as good a time as any to reveal one or

two of his true colors. Since she'd had a bad experience with the press, he knew what he did would make a difference to anything that might happen between them. "When I said I worked in the arts, that was a bit of a stretch. I work in entertainment news."

She froze. Her eyes went wide, and he caught a glimpse of the fear he'd wondered about before. "You're a reporter?"

He nodded.

"You said you worked in the arts."

"I know. The arts just sounded less…"

"Tawdry? Shallow? Mindless? Cheap?"

He feigned collapse. "Way to cut out a man's heart."

"You expected kudos and admiration?" she asked, staring at her cake before brutally stabbing at the slice with her fork.

Why did he feel as if she would rather be stabbing him? "I write a mean story."

"*Mean* being the operative word," she said, finally cutting off a bite.

He took a swallow of his coffee, needing a bit of distance before responding. "I write an entertaining story, then."

"And you use the most entertaining details whether they're true or not."

Firing back wasn't going to earn him any points, but damn if having her pin him like a butterfly didn't sting. "You really know how to stick it to a guy, don't you?"

"I'm sticking it to what you do, not who you are," she told him before popping the cake into her mouth.

He couldn't separate himself from his work that easily. He'd be surprised to find out that she could. "So if I were to call Candy a karaoke hack, Miranda wouldn't wince just a little bit?"

"Maybe a little," she admitted, then sobered, her brow

furrowed as she went back to thinking, drinking her coffee, thinking, eating her cake, before finally asking him, "Why entertainment news, then? Why not Capitol Hill or the Middle East—"

"Instead of Hollywood and New York? Since what I report on isn't really important? Or even news? No matter how many people gobble it up?" Yeah, he'd heard it all before.

She nodded, avoided making eye contact. "What you do hurts people, Caleb."

He knew he was feeling too defensive over something he was walking away from, but he still viewed the work he'd done as having value—even if he'd made a mistake and lost his taste for it, lost his ability to draw the lines.

"All reporting has the potential to hurt people, Miranda. I reveal a scandal on Capitol Hill, someone's going to get hurt. I report on American deaths in the Middle East, someone's going to get hurt."

"But it's not the same. Not at all. Don't you see that?" she asked, punctuating her insistence with a sharp stab of her fork to her plate.

"It's not the same because you were hurt in your former life by some journalist, is that what you mean?" he asked, sensing he was close to tripping over the root of her anathema for his brand of news.

"My divorce, yes. I was humiliated, made out to be a pitiable figure who either couldn't keep her husband satisfied, or whose charitable works were to throw investigators off the scent of his fraud. Take your pick, and add an icy-cold bitch to the list while you're at it."

So there *was* another name to go with Miranda Kelly. A name, a divorce, an ex-husband accused of fraud. "It's human nature. People want to see the mighty fall. It makes it easier for them to feel better about their own situations. And you're not icy or cold."

"A thought or two for the mighty who share that human nature would be nice." She took a deep breath. "Sorry. That sounded arrogant and pathetic all at the same time."

"Something only one of the mighty could accomplish," he said teasingly, watching the play of the firelight as it caught the lighter strands of red in her hair.

"Trust me," she said with a snort. "I was never mighty. I happened to marry well. That's all."

"Doesn't sound like that's the case. Not if he cheated."

"The cheating came later. He developed an inflated sense of self-importance and the entitlement that went along with it. What he wanted, he made sure he had."

"But he quit wanting you."

"No. I quit wanting him. I'd become the dutiful wife, busy with my own causes, with running our household…I never knew about the other women until his philandering came out in the trial."

"The trial?"

She waved him off with her fork. "I've said too much. How's the cake?"

"The cake is great." And to his way of thinking, she hadn't said enough.

"Finish telling me about your book," she said, obviously hoping to derail his prying.

But her reaction to what he did had him feeling rather protective of his future plans. "I'm not sure that I want to."

"I promise, no sticking it to you, or to what you do. I want to hear about what you're writing. Really."

He doubted that, but talking about his study on the tabloids' impact on society should keep him off her hit list.

He just wasn't sure how much of his plans for the future he wanted to share with anyone.

He surprised himself by starting out with a full confession. "Considering everything I just said, this is going to sound really strange, but I'm actually working at getting out of the industry."

She gave him an appropriately stunned look. "Is this book how you'll do that?"

He nodded. "I'm putting together a proposal for my agent to shop. He's already giddy at the prospect of an auction."

For several tense seconds, she stared at him thoughtfully, then said, "I think there's something you're not telling me about who you are."

Uh-oh. "Why would you think that?"

"You seem awfully confident this book is going to be big."

With the information he had at his disposal? He knew it would be big. "We'll have to get together one day and trade secrets."

She blew out a huff of breath. "Probably not a good idea. I can't imagine anyone who'd want to clean up after that explosion."

He laughed. "I'll just send you an autographed copy of the book before it hits the shelves. How's that?"

"Can I ask you something?"

"Sure."

"It's none of my business, and I have absolutely no right to expect you to answer—"

"Ask me, Miranda. If I don't want to answer, I won't."

"If you had the choice, would you rather be writing for CNN or the *New York Times?*" She paused to let him assimilate what she'd asked him before adding, "Instead of covering celebrity weddings, which I'm assuming is what you're here to do rather than just attending the event?"

And here she'd said she wasn't going to stick it to him again. "I am, yes, and I'll answer the first part if you'll answer a question for me."

She stiffened, but she met his gaze directly, her green eyes sparkling from the firelight and the sizzling heat of her emotion. "What do you want to know?"

"Why did you move back here?"

"What do you mean?" she asked, frowning. "This is where I grew up."

"But you left, you got married and divorced, and you came back. Why?" He reached for his coffee, brought it to his mouth.

She shrugged as if she thought the answer should be obvious. "I like it here. It's quiet, peaceful, wonderfully stress-free."

He pushed harder. "And there's no press hounding you?"

"That's part of it, yes," she said, nodding. "But I don't expect you to understand what it's like to be hounded. You're on the wrong side of the microphone."

He thought back to what she'd asked him, back to what she'd told him about her divorce before that. "Would it make a difference if my microphone were recording for CNN or the *New York Times?* Is it just the entertainment part of what I do you don't like?"

"It's hard for me to take in, that that's who you are or what you do. You represent everything I hate about the media. And yet…"

"And yet you can't find it in you to tell me to go."

"I can't. I enjoy your company. I like being with you. I thought… Never mind." She shook her head, tears glistening in her eyes. "It doesn't matter."

It did matter, but he wasn't going to argue or say anything else to upset her. If she didn't want to see him again, he wasn't going to push. But he couldn't help but wonder how she'd react if she knew the whole truth instead of the sanitized version he'd given her.

"If you don't mind, I'm going to turn in. I suddenly have a terrible headache," she said, then set aside her plate and got to her feet, hugging herself tightly. "The guest room is all yours, or there are pillows and blankets in the closet if you'd like to sleep in here with the fire."

"Sure," Caleb said, wondering if screwing up the important things in his life was karma biting back because of the way he'd screwed up the lives of so many others. "I'll see you in the morning. Good night."

15

WHEN CALEB FINALLY dragged his butt off the couch the next morning and made his way to the bathroom, he found a note from Miranda propped up on the back of the commode. She'd prepped the coffeepot, all he had to do was turn it on.

There were eggs and hot cereal if he wanted to cook breakfast, cold cereal if he wanted to keep it simple. She was at the flower shop, but would see him tonight at Club Crimson if he felt like making up for last night. That made him smile. Then it made him cringe and feel like the jerk he was.

Since she hadn't offered him use of the shower, he skipped doing more than washing his face and using his finger for a toothbrush. He should've come prepared to spend the night, but he'd only come prepared for sex and dinner.

He did, however, take her up on the coffee, drinking almost the full pot while standing in her open kitchen door and freezing his balls off. It was one of those pleasure-pain things that was hard to explain. The hot coffee made the icy cold bearable—if anything about where he found himself this morning was.

First things first. He'd decided before drifting off last night to pay a visit to Under the Mistletoe and send Miranda a bouquet to thank her for the wonderful meal and an evening he wouldn't soon forget. The irony of her having to send flowers to herself was hardly lost on him.

Either she'd appreciate the gesture as the mea culpa it was, or he'd be further inflating his jerkitude factor in her eyes. And in that case, he doubted there would be any making up going on.

First he had to figure out where the flower shop was and how to get there from here. He found the phone in her kitchen, with a business directory in a drawer beneath, and Under the Mistletoe listed as the only local florist.

The address was on First Street, which according to the tiny map at the bottom of the ad, really was the next street over from Second Avenue. Unfortunately, the number of the address was 102 which, if Mistletoe's numbering system ran like those in most cities, put him walking ten blocks in the cold.

He had his boots and his coat, but he didn't have a hat or pants warmer than his jeans. He'd have to move fast, rely on his circulation to keep him warm and hope, in the process, he didn't lose his ears and nose to frostbite.

Once he got started, he realized it really wasn't that cold. Or maybe he was too busy trying to come up with a way to repair the damage he'd done last night to notice. Even though she'd smacked on him, his doing the same to her had been unconscionable.

She wasn't the cynic he was. She believed in love and romance and no doubt in happily ever after, too—even after going through what had sounded like the sort of divorce that cured most people from believing in fairy tales.

It didn't surprise him, not really, that she still did. She was kind, smart, sweet, an optimist—all the things he wasn't.

Well, he *was* smart. And intuitive; he wouldn't be the success he was if he didn't have a brain—though that might be hard to prove based on this cold-weather trek he was making.

Boy Scout material he was not, he mused, looking down at the snow crusting the toes of his boots.

He still couldn't believe she'd left him to find his own way out of the inn's supply room. It was more understandable that she'd made him sleep on the sofa, though that had gotten to him, too. After all, he thought, as a gust of wind smacked him, not two hours before giving him the boot from her bed, she'd given him her body.

She could sing, she could cook, she could run a business. She was every man's dream in bed and was gorgeous to boot. If he wasn't careful, he mused, cupping his hands and blowing into them to keep his fingers from falling off, he was the one who was going to start believing in relationships and other L-words than lust.

Five minutes later he reached the one-hundred block of First Street and found Under the Mistletoe tucked between Orsy's Donuts and Hardware by Frank. He reached up to smooth down his hair, then reached back and messed what he'd straightened.

When he stepped through the front door he heard two female voices—one Miranda's, the other most likely Brenna Sparks's mother. The one he didn't recognize was saying something about Zoe staying after school to meet with the Christmas dance committee and Patrice giving her a ride home.

Caleb tucked those tidbits into his mental file and headed for the counter, the chime over the door silencing in mid-ring as the door shut behind him. It was the Sparks woman who came out of the back to help him with a cheery "Good morning."

"Good morning." She looked a lot like Brenna around the eyes, but her mouth was pinched and aged, even while her smile was welcoming. "I need to order some flowers. Do you deliver to the Inn at Snow Falls?"

"We do, yes. Do you know what you want? Can I help you decide on something?"

Though he was sure she could hear him, Miranda kept herself hidden. All the better to tease her with his dastardly plan. "Do you know Candy Cane? The singer at Club Crimson?"

Corinne stared down at her order pad, tapping with a pen as if trying not to give too much away. "I do, yes. Is that who you're sending this to?"

He nodded. "I'm not so good with knowing what a woman might want. Uh, when it comes to flowers, I mean. Roses seem too over the top, and plants seem too…funereal. What would you recommend? What do you think she would she like?"

"Well, that depends on what you want to say," she said, doodling a cane at the end of Candy's name. "'Enjoyed the show' or 'Thanks for the memories' or 'Same time next year'?"

Caleb struggled to keep from revealing any more than Miranda might have already shared of their affair. "Maybe all of the above with some added—'Sorry for being a jerk'?"

"'Enjoyed the show,'" Corinne quoted back as she scribbled on the pad, adding, "'Thanks for the memories.' 'Same time next year.' 'Sorry for being a jerk.'" Then she met his gaze, her eyes twinkling. "Anything else?"

"Yeah. 'You made me love goat cheese.'"

"Got it," she said, almost laughing now, reaching up and nudging one knuckle against her nose. "Let me think what would best convey all those sentiments."

They talked for several minutes, Corinne suggesting a variety of flowers to go into an exotic arrangement, and Caleb whipping out his credit card without a care for the cost. It would be worth whatever they billed him to imagine Miranda assembling her own flowers or watching her employee arrange the bouquet, knowing it was for her.

As he looked up from signing the receipt, a movement caught his eye, and he cut his gaze to where Miranda stood in the entrance to the shop's back room.

She had her arms crossed over her chest, a shoulder propped against the wall, and was wearing blue jeans, a sunflower-yellow turtleneck and an apron embroidered with her shop's logo. She shook her head, her look as she met his eyes telling him she could not believe what he'd done.

He winked back, stuffed the receipt into the bill compartment of his wallet, and turned to Corinne. "The donut shop next door. Do you know how late they stay open? Or is there another place close by where I can get a cup of coffee while I wait for the inn's shuttle?"

"Orsy is open till noon at least. Sometimes later, depending on the crowd." She motioned him closer, leaning across the counter. "Don't tell him I told you, but he's good about throwing together sausage biscuits for people who need more in their stomachs than pastries."

"Thanks," Caleb said, waving at Corinne as he headed for the door, but looking at Miranda as he said, "And your secret's safe with me."

Orsy's Donuts gave Caleb a sugar high the minute he walked through the door. The small eatery was obviously a gathering place for locals taking midmorning breaks. The customers were mostly male, mostly dressed in aged denim and thick down, and mostly over sixty.

At the long Formica counter, Caleb climbed onto a stool that swiveled when he sat. He clenched his fingers, blew into his cupped hands. That got him the attention of the wiry man behind the bar who walked toward him with a large white mug and a coffeepot.

"I've learned to ask before I pour," said the man with a badge that read Orsy pinned to his apron. "Some people who come down from the inn want juice or tea instead."

"Coffee. Cream. Sugar. I love all the things that I shouldn't," Caleb said, nodding his head toward the mug and inhaling the fragrant steam as the other man poured.

"What about something to eat?" Orsy asked, leaving room in the cup for Caleb's extras. "Donuts, Danishes, turnovers. Pick your poison."

"Anything with cream cheese would be great." Caleb reached for the sugar shaker, cutting his gaze toward the other man while adding two teaspoons worth of sweetener to his drink. "Maybe a sausage biscuit or two?"

Orsy snorted and set a handful of individual creamers next to Caleb's mug. "You've been talking to Corinne, haven't you? I make biscuits one time for her as a favor, and she tells everyone she sees they're an off-menu item."

Caleb dumped three of the creamers into his coffee and stirred. "Hey, a cream cheese Danish is fine. I was thinking to knock out both breakfast and lunch with one stop, but I'll find a burger later."

"Oh, I'll get you the biscuits," the bakery owner said, dismissing Caleb's decision with the wave of his empty hand. He returned the coffeepot to the warmer, coming back with a Danish the size of the saucer he served it on. "Only good place for burgers is Fish and Cow Chips, and Finch doesn't open till four. Unless you want the fast-food type down at the McDonald's. I'll get you those biscuits. You just hold on."

Caleb picked up the Danish and bit in, then picked up his

coffee and drank, reaching, as he did, for a paper that turned out to be Mistletoe's weekly local news.

He flipped through the ten or so pages to get a feel for the content, then started at the beginning and read through. There were a couple of national stories, some county political flare-up, a report on Denver's crime lab and a lot of snowfall predictions for local ski runs.

He found an ad for Miranda's shop in the classifieds, and wondered how much of her business stemmed locally as opposed to from the Inn at Snow Falls. He had to think the lovers' resort would provide a good chunk of her revenue, because in a town as small as Mistletoe he was surprised to see a florist at all.

Then again, he supposed people honored birthdays, anniversaries, births, deaths and holidays everywhere on the map. Just because he wasn't much of a flower giver didn't mean there weren't others who spent a fortune on the things.

Listening to the chatter around him, he found himself smiling as he thought about the card accompanying Miranda's bouquet. He doubted many florists were asked to include notes about goat cheese, though there were probably a lot who were asked to include apologies.

Next time he saw her, he'd offer another via voice. Her smile as she'd watched him pay for the order was enough to let him know his point had been made. Still, he would prefer delivering his mea culpa face-to-face.

This whole incident was a big fat perfect reminder of why emotions got in the way of good times, he mused, thanking Orsy with an acknowledging nod when he delivered his food and topped off his coffee.

Here they were, he and Miranda, having known each other three days, having shared dinner, drinks and sex—and she was already banning him to the sofa, while he was already sending her flowers to make up for doing her wrong.

It bugged him even to go into rights and wrongs, a situation he mulled over as he bit into the sausage biscuit and swore he'd died and gone to breakfast heaven. Caleb was being himself. That was all.

Miranda liked him well enough in bed, seemed to enjoy herself when the conversation stayed in the shallow end of the flirtation pool, but when things moved away from the easy and the safe into the deep and the dangerous…

He'd meant what he'd told her. Any news story published had the possibility to hurt someone somewhere. He understood she was operating from a place of having suffered that hurt, but her blaming those who did the reporting without addressing what the public considered newsworthy didn't sit well with him.

And that fundamental difference in outlook—even though he wasn't particularly proud of how he'd gone about telling every story he'd put on the page—was going to be what kept them apart in the end.

16

"OKAY, SPILL," Corinne said, spinning toward Miranda the second the door closed behind Caleb and the chime stopped. "What's the deal with the flowers? And does he know who you are?"

Miranda leaned a forearm on the wall, leaned her forehead on her forearm. "He knows, yes."

"You told him?"

"No," she said with a snort, looking up and gesturing with one hand, not even sure who she was most aggravated with: Caleb, herself or Barry. "It was Barry, fancying himself as tour guide to Mistletoe, Colorado's stars or something."

Corinne picked up the order pad and read from the notes she'd written while Caleb had talked. "Goat cheese and sorry for being a jerk?"

"It's a long story." Miranda turned back to the work room. She wasn't sure she wanted to go into it with Corinne, and have her friend lecture her on getting so deeply involved with Caleb in such a short amount of time when she'd sworn off getting involved with strangers at all.

And they *were* deeply involved. As much as she hadn't wanted it to happen. As much as she knew *he* hadn't wanted it to happen.

"Well, since I've still got the wedding flowers to finish on top of everything else, you talk and I'll listen." Corinne set Caleb's order aside and got back to an arrangement of two-dozen red roses also slated for delivery to the inn. "I'm going to take a wild guess and say the stuffed chicken turned out okay?"

"It was more than okay," Miranda assured her, boosting up to sit on her bar stool. "And the cake I bought at Ida's? Amazing."

"Italian cream?"

Miranda nodded, her accompanying moan near orgasmic.

Corinne sighed her own appreciation. "Mm-mm-mm. I swear, I owe at least thirty of my extra pounds to Orsy and Ida. And yet I keep going back for more."

"You're not the only one." Miranda booted up her laptop and waited while the accounting program launched. "I want to know how the two of them stay so thin. Their kids, too."

"It's all in the G-E-N-E-S. As opposed to being in the J-E-A-N-S, which seems to be more of a problem for you," Corinne said, and Miranda gave her a look.

"That was a terrible segue."

"Yeah, but it got us back on track."

Miranda pointed to the computer screen. "I'm doing payroll. You might want to rethink what track you're on."

"Just for that," Corinne said, one eyebrow arching, "Candy Cane is going to get the most hideous arrangement Under the Mistletoe has ever designed. There won't be a single flower in it she likes. In fact, it's going to be filled with the ones she most hates."

At that, Miranda had to laugh. "I guess it's a good thing she's not allergic to much of anything or one sniff and she'd end up in anaphylactic shock."

"I was just wondering about that," Corinne said, shelving the roses in the cooler. "But since I can't afford to get fired if I want to fund whatever part of Zoe's education her scholarships won't cover, I guess I'll put together something nice."

"You haven't mentioned if she's decided where she's going to go." Miranda knew Zoe had been accepted by all three schools to which she'd applied. All amazing universities. All on the East Coast. All very far away from Corinne. "I know it's going to be hard on both of you, wherever she goes."

Corinne brushed off Miranda's attempt at comfort, sorting through the vases kept on hand for the more exotic arrangements. "Zoe will be fine. Zoe will be super, in fact. She's looking forward to leaving Mistletoe and getting a taste of the real world, as she calls it."

"And you?" Miranda asked, not surprised by the deflection.

"Me?" Corinne asked, once again considering herself as an afterthought. "I'll survive."

Miranda wasn't having it. "You'll do more than survive. You'll do all the things you've been putting off because of the demands on a single parent rearing an exceptional child."

Corinne responded to that with a snort. "You mean like cleaning out the garage and grouting the bathroom tile? Yep. Can't wait."

"You said you wanted to spend a week with your sister in Boston. And you and May Potter were talking about an Alaskan cruise." Corinne had always put her girls first, but to have nothing of her own to look forward to was new, and a change that concerned Miranda. "You have paid vacation time, you know. I mean, if you're worried about losing the hours."

"I'm not worried about the hours."

"Then what?" Miranda asked, turning to sit sideways on the chair and giving her friend her full attention.

Facing the shelf of vases but staring off into space, Corinne released a sigh that shook her whole body. "I'm worried that I've screwed up so badly with Brenna that Zoe won't forgive me for it, and neither one of my daughters will ever come home again."

"What are you talking about?" Miranda asked, sliding from the chair and crossing to where her friend stood. "Of course Zoe will come home."

Her eyes damp, Corinne cut a questioning gaze in Miranda's direction. "And Brenna? I mean, I haven't exactly showed her open arms, but what if she eventually stops trying?"

"Then you'll go to her and you'll make the effort. She's here now."

"At the inn, yeah," Corinne said, shaking her head and reaching for a squat vase colored an iridescent coral. "But I only know that because people have seen her and told me. It's not like she called and let me know."

Brenna could've chosen anywhere in the world for her wedding to the congressman. Miranda couldn't believe her coming to Mistletoe was about anything but wanting her family with her on such an important day.

But she was still practically a girl, one with a formidable force of a mother. "Maybe she's afraid to come any closer."

Corinne frowned, hugging the vase to her chest. "Why would she be afraid?"

"I don't know. Maybe because you've given away her gifts and refused to take her money." Miranda wrapped an arm around her friend's shoulders. "Maybe she believes all the gossip about you hating her lifestyle."

"I do hate her lifestyle." Corinne pulled away, moved to set the vase on the table. "That doesn't mean I hate her. I could never hate her."

Love the person, loathe their deeds. Learn to compromise. Advice Miranda could afford to take to heart. "Maybe she needs to hear that?"

"I've told her that very thing God knows how many times," Corinne said, her tone cracking under the weight of her internal struggle.

"You could always say it again," Miranda suggested, returning to her computer, smiling as she added, "Maybe this time with flowers?"

"You'll do anything for a sale, won't you?" Corinne asked, but she did revisit the shelf and choose a second smaller vase to go with the one she'd already selected for Caleb's order.

There are days, Miranda thought, *when nothing speaks as eloquently—and elegantly—as flowers.* "With the way things have been going today? It sure looks that way."

SINCE HE WASN'T UP for the two-mile walk to Mistletoe County High School, Caleb phoned Barry, the shuttle driver, before leaving Orsy's, and asked if he had time in his schedule for the detour before heading back to the inn.

Barry had nothing lined up, and was glad to play taxi for the tip Caleb offered—as long as Caleb understood he'd have to turn back if dispatch got a call.

He also wanted to know, inquiring once Caleb had climbed into the minivan's backseat, what business Caleb might have at the high school. Not that Barry wanted to cramp Caleb's style—Caleb understood that, right?—he just wanted to be sure there wasn't anything hinky going on with Caleb visiting a high-school campus to see a girl.

Caleb told Barry to rest assured, his visit was strictly work-related, but since he didn't have an appointment, he would appreciate Barry hanging around to make sure he didn't get stuck walking up the mountain to the inn. It was cold, it was getting dark…

Barry was good with all of that, and pulled to a stop at the gymnasium entrance. He'd heard from his wife Marvetta who was friends with May Potter who cochaired the Christmas dance committee with Patrice Price that they held the meetings in the gym so they could work on decorating the place once they were done going over their planning.

Caleb thanked the driver for the scoop, struck with the realization that the information Barry provided for free and in this case to an audience of one, wasn't that much different than what Caleb was paid to provide every day to millions.

It was all a matter of perspective, he mused, stuffing his hands in his coat pockets and heading up the recently shoveled sidewalk to the gymnasium's door. He pulled on the handle, found the door unlocked, and realized again how insulated from the outside world the town of Mistletoe was.

Once inside, he was greeted with a scene from his high-school days, one he knew almost anyone looking back to their teenage years spent in public education would recognize. Crepe-paper streamers and construction-paper cutouts, tempra paint, glitter and glue were spread across the folding tables set up along the far walls.

Students scurried from one table to the next, giggling and chattering as they worked, their athletic shoes squeaking against the glossy wood surface, and the big room amplifying all the noise. It smelled like school, too. Floor wax and sweaty leather and ink on paper and cafeteria grease.

The only thing that had changed since Caleb had been in school was that a man walking into a gym unannounced wasn't left to his own devices but was challenged.

The woman approaching him now was dressed like a lumberjack but built like Marilyn Monroe. Her long brown hair, pulled back in a braid that hung nearly to her hips, swung when she walked. "May I help you?"

Might as well play this one straightforward. "My name is Caleb McGregor. I'm working on a project for Brenna Sparks and staying up at the inn. I was wondering if her sister might have some time to talk to me."

"I know you," she said, considering him with a frown that said she wasn't sure that was a good thing.

He figured she was Alan's wife, but didn't voice his suspicion. "You do?"

"You're the guy Mir—" She caught herself and started over. "You're the guy my friend who works there was talking about."

Might as well let that cat out of the bag. "Would your friend be Miranda Kelly?"

"I wasn't sure if she'd told you her name. I'm Patrice, by the way," she said, offering him her hand. "Patrice Price."

"Nice to meet you, Patrice. And, yeah. She told me the Miranda part. The shuttle driver added the Kelly."

Patrice shoved her hands to her hips. "Damn Barry. Has to have his nose in everyone's business."

"Don't give him too hard a time," he said, shoving his still-cold hands into his jeans pockets for warmth. "He's the one who knew I could find Zoe here."

"I'll never figure out how he does it," she said, shaking her head, her braid popping back and forth. "Knows who's doing what with whom and where all of the time."

An ability Caleb recognized. "It's an ear-to-the-ground thing."

"Ah, yes." She went back to looking at him as if not sure she wanted to like him. "You're a reporter. I forgot that part."

Word got around fast. He'd only confessed all to Miranda last night. "If only everyone could forget that part."

"You mean Miranda? Your kind gave her hell. Take a look in the mirror before you go blaming her for making you jump through hoops."

"No jumping through hoops yet." Just sleeping on the couch, which he supposed was the same thing. "If you're in the middle of things here, I can go. Maybe you could have Zoe call me at the inn?"

"We're done for the most part," Patrice said, glancing back to where several students had ditched the decorations and were passing a cell phone back and forth and giggling at whatever was on the screen. "Zoe!"

A girl with dark hair and huge blue eyes looked up. She got to her feet and came over in answer to Patrice's wave. "Zoe, this is Caleb McGregor. He's a reporter, and was wondering if you'd have some time to talk to him."

"Me?" Zoe looked from Patrice to Caleb, her stance hard to read, her expression emotionally evasive. In other words, a teenager. "What about?"

Being straightforward had worked with Patrice, so he took the same tack with Zoe. "I'm doing a story on your sister."

At that, her eyes brightened. "My sister?"

He nodded. "I talked to her yesterday and wanted to get your take on some of the things she told me."

"You talked to her?" Bright eyes and bright smile. "Here?"

He nodded. "She's staying up at the inn."

"Oh my God! I can't believe she's here," the girl said, shaking her head frantically, her hair flying around her shoulders as she looked at the coats and backpacks piled against the far wall. "I can't talk now. I've got to go."

Patrice reached for Zoe's arm. "You're riding home with me, remember?"

"I'll ride with Deb. She said she's gotta get to work like ten minutes ago." Zoe turned to Caleb to explain. "She works in the gift shop at the inn."

Caleb didn't want to lose this chance to talk to Brenna's sister, and knew he was crossing a line, but... "Actually, if you want to go to the inn, the shuttle driver's waiting for me outside. I'm sure he won't mind driving you home later. He said he doesn't have anything going on today."

"That would be great," she squealed, nearly leaping into the air. "Let me get my stuff. Oh my God. Oh my God. I can't believe Brenna's home."

With Patrice beside him, Caleb watched her go. Or he watched until Patrice stepped in front of him and snarled, "You're some kind of instigator, aren't you?"

And...here it comes. "I thought I was doing her a favor."

Her eyes shooting sparks, Patrice dropped her voice. "Did it occur to you that her mother might not want her to talk to her sister? Or run up to the inn by herself?"

Caleb pulled his cell phone from the holster at his waist and flipped it open. "Do you know the number to the flower shop? I'll call and ask."

Patrice hesitated, as if Caleb had called her bluff. He kept the phone in sight, but pressed on. "She's what? A senior? Six months from now she'll be a graduate, two months after that heading for college."

"That's six months from now. Eight months from now," she added, as if he couldn't do the math. "It's not today when she's supposed to be working on plans for the dance."

"I thought you said you were done here."

"Look, Mr. McGregor," Patrice began, rubbing at her temples. "Zoe is very special. To all of us. She's got an amazing future ahead of her."

"And no one here wants her to spiral out of control like Brenna has allegedly done. I got that. But she's obviously made up her mind to go," he said, then played the trump card he'd just realized he was holding. "Would all of you looking out for her rather she make the trip with her friend Deb there rushing to get to work? Or with reliable Barry in his minivan?"

Patrice crossed her arms, and turned to look at the students on the other side of the gym, obviously fighting an internal battle between protecting her cubs from the predators and letting go of one who was ready to step into the wild.

When she finally looked back, it was easy to see that she wasn't happy to have come to her decision. "Don't be logical and make me like you."

"I try to make sure nobody likes me," Caleb said, exhaling his pent-up hope. "It makes it easier to do my job."

"Should I mention that to Miranda?" she asked, one eyebrow cocked.

"You can tell her anything you'd like," he said, though he couldn't deny the pang that hit him with the admission.

Zoe returned then, wearing her coat, her backpack strap hooked over one shoulder. Patrice walked with them to the minivan, shutting the back door behind Zoe and chatting with Barry while Caleb climbed into the front next to the burly driver.

On the drive to the inn, Zoe and Barry did most of the talking, shooting the breeze like best friends. Since questioning the girl was impossible in front of the local rumor mill, all their talking gave Caleb time to think how best to get what he wanted from Zoe before her reunion with Brenna blew his chance.

By the time Barry pulled into the inn's circular drive and

the young valet, Jacob, opened the door, flirting with Zoe as he escorted her inside, Caleb had come up with what he thought was a workable plan.

Keeping his eye on his charge as she and Jacob stood close and talked near the concierge's station, Caleb picked up the house phone at the end of the front desk and asked for Brenna's room.

Five rings later, the singer picked up. "Yeah?"

"It's Caleb McGregor. Could you meet me at One in Vermillion in thirty minutes?"

"I don't know. Do we have anything else to say?"

"You and me? I think we're good. But I thought you might like to talk to Zoe."

Brenna sucked in an audible breath. "She's here? Zoe's here?"

"She just rode up with me from town."

"Does my mother know?"

"Not that I'm aware."

"Okay. I'm coming down."

"Thirty minutes."

"Screw you and your thirty minutes. I'm coming now," she said before slamming the phone into its cradle.

So much for his plans, he mused, spying a very large arrangement of exotic flowers next to a vase of red roses, and another one of daisies and baby's breath on a table behind the clerk.

He thought about Miranda finding the arrangement in her dressing room when she got to work later. Then he stopped thinking about Miranda altogether. He had to think about Zoe and Brenna and his Max Savage swan song so he could get this story done right, and get this monkey off his back for good.

17

TEN MINUTES INTO PACING her dressing room and waiting for the club to clear after her show, Miranda realized she was wasting time. Caleb knew her as herself, so thinking she had to sneak back and rejoin him as her alter ego was silly.

If anyone else was still there, well, none of them were likely to know her, but she'd make sure no vestiges of Candy remained just in case. Besides, the person she most feared making the connection to the ex-Mrs. E. Marshall Gordon was the person she was on her way to see.

She tugged off her wig and washed off her heavy stage makeup in the dressing room's private bath. Only after running a brush through her hair's short layers, applying a fresh coat of mascara and adding gloss to her lips was she faced with a conundrum—what to wear to join Caleb in the bar?

The clothes she wore to commute up and down the mountain—boots, insulated sweatpants and layers of tops beneath her parka—were hardly appropriate for Club Crimson, which left her with Candy's wardrobe to dig through.

She sang four nights a week, and over time had added enough things to her closet that she could go a whole month before she'd cycled through all the outfits she had. That didn't mean they weren't all recognizable as costumes belonging to Candy Cane, being glitzy and one shade or another of red.

But since she didn't have a choice…

She considered the three dresses she owned with a knee-length hem, deciding on one that would be perfect for a night out. It was strapless with a twist bodice and the appropriate boning to keep it in place, and was made of a rich ruby silk.

She found Caleb sitting in the bar's back booth, the same one from that first night and that first kiss. The one she'd avoided approaching earlier at the end of her show, not certain she could resist his temptation.

She still had some self-preservation instincts—though they were quickly becoming things of the past—and she had to admit with each one she shed, she felt as if she were emerging from a confining cocoon. It was a sense of freedom she'd never expected because she'd never thought herself confined.

Caleb looked up when she slid into the booth opposite him, a cherry martini in her hand. His hair was disheveled, the stubble on his jaw a noticeable shadow around a mouth that wasn't smiling.

"What's wrong?" she asked, lifting her drink to her mouth.

"You didn't kiss me," he said, his expression caught between tormented and teasing. "I thought if I sat here again, I'd get the same action as before."

Ah, that. She returned the glass to the table, laced her fingers and rested them in front of it. "I was afraid I wouldn't be able to stop. Your kisses are rather…addictive. And Candy can't play favorites."

"Says who?" he asked, thanking Alan as the other man replaced his empty glass with a full one.

Miranda waited until they were once again alone. She had several things she wanted to say, but had to get the biggest one off her chest first. "I've been thinking a lot about my reaction to what you told me last night, about you working in entertainment news. I owe you an apology."

He gave a sharp huff. "For what? Being honest?"

"For being rude. Your profession is your choice. I may not like it, but it's obviously something you're good at, and my making a stink was uncalled-for. So I'm sorry. Truly."

"No, Miranda. If there's an apology to be made here, I'm the one who needs to make it."

"You already did. And the flowers were lovely." Beyond lovely, though Miranda was certain she thought that partially because he had sent them. "Corinne wouldn't let me see the arrangement. She hid it until she went out on her afternoon delivery run. I had to wait until I got here to get a look at what she'd done."

"And?"

"They were gorgeous. And you shouldn't have spent all that money. But thank you. I can't remember the last time someone sent me flowers."

"You should have flowers every day."

"I do," she said, plucking the cherry from her drink by the stem. "They're just not mine."

Caleb smiled, looked down, turned his glass in a circle on the table. She watched his hand, studied the length of his fingers, remembering having them on her skin, and was extra glad she hadn't kissed him earlier when just that thought caused her stomach to buzz.

He finally spoke. "Had you planned to open the shop before moving here?"

She shook her head, realizing how decidedly unprepared for her new life she'd been upon leaving Baltimore. She'd come here without a single plan, only the need to come home.

Looking back, she couldn't help but be amazed that she hadn't fallen flat on her face.

She wondered if Caleb could sense that amazement when she shook her head. "No, I honestly didn't know what I was going to do. I had my divorce settlement and my savings, and when I discovered the shop was for sale, I jumped. It just seemed so…safe. So normal. So uncomplicated."

"Did you have experience as a florist? Or running a business?"

"Only if working with caterers counts." Volunteer work was called *work* for a reason. "I used to plan fund-raising events for the charities whose boards I served on. It often felt like a full-time job, but I loved it. It was one of the things I missed most after settling here."

He picked up his glass, took a drink. "Yeah, I can't see a lot of charities around here in need of volunteers."

"Exactly. That's why I established one."

He frowned, obviously curious. "Come again?"

"My divorce settlement was rather…substantial," she said, realizing she'd given him another piece of the past he could use to find her out. Realizing on top of that that she was no longer as worried about him doing so as she had been when they'd first met.

Right now, however, she wasn't going to take the time to figure out why. "After realizing the struggle Corinne was going to have putting Zoe through school, I set up a scholarship fund. There are several stipulations, but basically it assists one student each year who plans to study music, art or creative writing."

"Wouldn't that put you in the news? Make you a local celebrity of sorts?"

Ah, but this was the best part. She grinned. "Not me. Candy. It's the Candy Cane Scholarship for the Arts."

"See?" He lifted his glass, used it to gesture toward her. "I knew you loved the arts."

"My arts, not your arts. But you're right. I do." Drink in hand, she sat back, crossing her free arm over her middle. "It's why I took the job singing. I use the money I make at the club for the fund."

"You're quite the woman, Miranda Kelly. Entrepreneur, entertainer, patron of the arts. And that's not even taking in all the rest of the things you're good for."

"What I'm good for?" She kicked out, found his shin beneath the table. "You're walking a fine line toward never experiencing any of that good stuff again."

He sat up straight and saluted. "Consider me back on the straight and narrow."

She did consider him, wondering about other paths he was walking. "Have you used all your reporter's sources and instincts yet to find out who I am?"

And then *he* considered *her,* his gaze intensely curious as it crawled over her. "I thought about doing a Google search, yeah. But the inn's wireless was out when I got back to the room. I started working, forgot about it, and the next thing I knew, it was time for your show. I never checked again."

That wasn't what she'd expected. She'd thought he would be obsessive about digging in the dirt, wallowing until he'd rooted out the tastiest morsels he could find. Either he wasn't that into her…or she had it all wrong, and he wasn't the bottom-feeder she'd pegged him to be.

She wondered which it was. "You get that involved, do you? In your work?"

His expression softened as if he were indulging a child. "Those columns you see in newspapers and magazines? They don't get written without a lot of involvement. And focus. And discipline. Even when the stories are nothing but entertainment news."

"I recognize curiosity is human nature, but whatever happened to minding one's own business?"

"Where do you draw the line between what's public and what's private? Your charity work obviously made you a public figure, as did your divorce—"

"Right there? Those two examples? That's where I draw the line. I want, I *need* my causes to be in the public eye. But my divorce?" She pressed her palm to her forehead then ran it back over her hair in frustration. "I mean, c'mon. Speculation about what I had done during my visits to the spa? For God's sake, one reporter talked to my waxing technician. She didn't say anything, of course. But what right did he have even to ask her such a thing?"

"The rights granted by the first amendment? Freedom of speech? Freedom of the press? You don't have to like what he asked, but he had the right to do so."

She didn't like it. She didn't like it at all. "Then where do ethics come into play? Or is anything fair game in this age of blogs and YouTube? What about an individual's right to keep her personal hygiene routine out of the news?"

"I'll need a history refresher. I can't remember a personal hygiene amendment."

"You're not funny."

"I'm not trying to be. I'm trying to get you to see that you're drawing a line based on your comfort zone."

"And the media doesn't have one, I know."

"The media may not, but there are journalists who do."

"Are you one of those journalists?"

He took longer to answer than she would've expected. She would've thought he knew himself and his work so well that he could draw a line in his own personal sand with his eyes closed and his hands tied behind his back.

"I haven't always been, no," he finally said, his voice low, gruff. "And I haven't always worked in…the arts. I was that college graduate with the journalism degree who was going to save the planet from global warming. Or at least from turning a blind eye to what was happening around the globe. The poverty. The hunger. The religious oppression."

"What made you switch course?"

"I couldn't catch a break. Granted, I was impatient. I wanted my Pulitzer *now*. But every time there was breaking news, I was on the wrong continent, or tied up on assignment in another state. A classic case of always being in the wrong place at the wrong time. What I was bringing to the table in comparison, nobody gave a crap about reading. And then along came Delano Wise."

"The country-music star? That Del Wise? You know him?" When Caleb nodded, Miranda gasped. She remembered the flurry of publicity that had helped launch the singer to stardom. "What does Del Wise have to do with the direction your career took?"

"We grew up together. Played Little League. Punked each other in school. Shared our first cigarette and hated it. Shared our first beer and loved it. Must've been all of twelve."

"You're kidding."

"God's honest truth. When he was on the verge of hitting it really big, I used what resources I had available to keep his name in the news. The more popular he got, the more I did to get him that exposure."

"So it started with Del and now here you are with Teddy and Ravyn. And in helping a friend, you found something that got people's attention, and you offered them that instead of the global warming reports."

"That about sums it up," he said, taking one sip then another before returning his glass to the table.

"Must be a trip to be able to make or break a career with what you keep out of the papers and what you expose."

He shifted, then leaned forward. "You may not like it, but sensationalism sells. Add sex to the mix often enough, you've made yourself a name as the go-to guy for the best gossip to be found."

"How did that make you feel?"

"Honestly? I felt great. I'd made it. On top of the world, and all that."

"And yet…"

"Who said there was a yet?"

"You did. You're a journalist with a comfort zone, remember?"

"It's newly found, trust me. It hasn't always been there."

That sounded like a story she wanted to hear. "It's never too late to make a new start."

A corner of his mouth quirked. "Now you're quoting platitudes?"

"No. I'm speaking from experience," she told him honestly.

He looked down. "I'm sorry you had to go through that."

"Why? I've loved starting over," she told him without a moment's hesitation.

"Not the starting-over part. The public revelation of things that should've been kept private." He said it as if making an apology. As if he'd been responsible for what had happened to her. Or for a similar wrong.

"Well, thank you," she said, a part of her that should've been stronger, melting. "But I'm pretty sure you wouldn't have cut me any slack if you'd been the one there doing the snooping."

"Like I said," he said with a shrug. "In the wrong place at the wrong time every time."

"It's much better this way." And that was another absolute truth. "If you'd revealed my waxing secrets to the world, we wouldn't be dating. And I would really have hated to miss out on dating you."

"I was just sitting here thinking that it was time for more of that." He pushed out of the booth, reached for her hand and helped her to her feet. "Your place or mine?"

18

THOUGH THE DRINKS were on the house, Caleb left a sizable cash tip on the table before following Miranda from the club. Alan, who Caleb had learned was Club Crimson's manager, had stuck around long past closing rather than put an end to their conversation.

The tip wasn't about paying him for his time as much as it was a thank-you for respecting their privacy and giving them the space. It was unexpected, especially since Caleb had seen the wife Alan had waiting for him at home.

He and Miranda crossed the stage and headed first for her dressing room. He got that she wanted to grab her clothes and keys and other personal things before going to his room. He got it, but he didn't like it because it meant a delay in getting her into his bed.

He wanted to get her into bed. He was having all these… feelings, and needed the sex to forget them. Miranda had him thinking about the choices he'd made, had him wondering about where he'd gone wrong, why he'd gone wrong, what had triggered the rush of power that had driven him to step over the line. He didn't like feelings. He liked facts. They were clean. Simple. Feelings were messy and got in the way.

Then again, ignoring what he didn't want to feel had probably been the root of his downfall. He hadn't stopped to consider the people involved because he couldn't. He'd had to think objectively about the stories he told. But if he'd remembered he had a heart and not just a head, he and Del might still be friends, or at least still be speaking.

"See? What did I tell you? Corinne did this whole gorgeous arrangement without letting me even peek."

The flowers on her vanity were the ones he'd seen behind the inn's front desk this afternoon. "Nice."

"They are nice," she said, kicking off her heels then twirling around and launching herself at him to give him a hug. "Thank you again. You really didn't have to."

He hugged her back, enjoying the sensation of her arms around him, her hands in the middle of his back, her breasts pressed to his chest, his heart…tingling enough to make him wonder what it would be like to feel more of this, and to feel it all the time. "Can we not talk about the flowers anymore?"

She pulled back to look into his eyes. "What would you like to talk about?"

"Nothing."

"Nothing?"

"I like to think of myself as a man of action."

"Did you come prepared?"

He held up three fingers like the good Boy Scout he was.

"Then don't think," she said, her green eyes begging. "Act."

Caleb didn't have to be told twice.

He kept one arm wrapped around her, threading the fingers of his other hand into her hair's short layers that he loved seeing so much more than her longer and supposedly sexier wigs. To him, nothing beat the real thing.

And that was his last thought before he lowered his head and slanted his mouth over hers. She tasted like Miranda and her cherry martini. She tasted like he could get used to her. She tasted like he wanted her every day, like having her would make him a better man because she made him think—about what he was doing, about what he'd done.

She moved her hands to his chest, slid them up to his shoulders, slipped her tongue into his mouth. She smiled as she did so. He felt her lips on his, saw the sparkle in her eyes just before she closed them, knew that he was in a world of trouble because he lacked what it would take—strength, will-power…the desire?—to walk away.

And so he quit thinking. He just shut down his mind and let his body take over because, right now, being with her was all that mattered, the only thing he wanted, what he cared about most in the world. She meant more to him than she should after such a short time, and that realization left him wondering where things might go with half a chance.

He found the zipper pull beneath her shoulder blades and tugged it to her rump, coming back up to grip the fabric and ease it down her torso. With her dress bunched at her waist, she shimmied her hips and sent the bright-red garment to the floor, then she started in on his buttons.

Once she reached his belt, she tugged his shirttails free from his pants, and finished with the buttons there before moving to his cuffs. She pushed his shirt away much as he'd done with her dress, leaving her wearing nothing but her panties and strapless bra, leaving him in his boots and jeans.

"You're so amazing," she told him, leaning back and looking him over, though staying in the circle of the arms he'd looped around her neck as she did. She ran her palms across his shoulders, down his chest, over his ribs to his abdomen. "Did you know that?"

He resisted sucking in his gut. "You're blinded by all those martinis you drank."

"Am not," she said, shaking her head, her eyes tellingly damp when she met his gaze. "Your body's perfect. I love that your hair is always a mess. And that most of the time you need to shave."

He reached up, rubbed at his chin and jaw. "That's because most of the time when you see me, my beard's had several hours to grow."

"I like it. I like this hair, too," she said, nuzzling his chest, finding his nipple, flicking it with her tongue. When he jumped, she moved to the other and did it again. Then she rubbed both of them with her thumbs.

He closed his eyes and groaned, sliding his hands down to release the clasp of her bra. With that hindrance out of the way and her breasts bared, it was his turn to torture her—though first he had to get rid of his boots and jeans.

That done, he backed up until his knees made contact with her vanity bench, then straddled it and sat, pulling Miranda around to straddle him. She spread her legs and did, lacing her hands at his nape while finding her balance.

He looked at her then, her short hair, her freckles, her breasts tipped with nipples the color of pink roses, her sex covered by nothing but a scrap of red mesh that matched her bra. "If anyone's amazing, it's you, Miranda Kelly. You're goddamned beautiful."

She dropped her head, tucked her chin to her chest, began to shiver as he stroked the skin of her neck, her shoulders, his fingers tracing the lines of her collarbone before circling the globes of her breasts.

Her gaze was still lowered when she said, "You make me ache, Caleb. You make me want so many things."

He swallowed hard, wishing he knew how to give her more than this, wishing he knew what it was she longed for as he cupped her neck and pulled her toward him, kissing her until neither one of them could see straight.

It didn't take long for his erection to make itself known between her legs. She squirmed, reached down and stretched the elastic waistband of his boxers far enough for him to spring free. Then she scooted up farther on his lap, capturing his cock between them.

"One of us is wearing too many clothes," she said. "And I think that person is me."

He agreed. He also realized he could easily pull her panties out of the way, and that if she was wearing too much, he wasn't wearing enough. "My pants. My wallet. My kingdom for a condom."

She reached down, tugging his wallet from his jeans' pocket. He dug for one of the condoms he'd stashed inside. She took it from him before he'd even tossed his wallet to the floor, tore the packet open and rolled the sheath from the head to the base of his shaft. Then she planted her hands on his shoulders and pushed him back until he was lying on the bench.

With his hips at one end, his head at the other, he fitted, but just barely. He certainly didn't have room to play acrobat or make like a monkey in the jungle. Miranda didn't seem concerned. She swung one leg over and away so she could get rid of her panties, then swung it back and stood with her sex positioned over his.

Wrapping her hands around the sides of the bench just above his shoulders, she lowered her body, sliding the head of his cock through her slick folds until he was wet with her moisture, then taking the full length of him inside herself, grinding her clit against the base of his shaft as she sat.

He watched as she closed her eyes, parted her lips, caught at her lower one with her teeth. And then she began to move, rotating her hips, groaning as the friction between them heated and increased. He held on to her forearms, bucked his hips, crunched his abs and thrust upward.

She hit a rhythm, up and down, up and down. He countered with his own steady strokes, driving in and out until his heart was racing and sweat broke out in the small of his back, the center of his chest, the palms of his hands. He couldn't remember sex ever being this fierce, this close to the bone.

He watched Miranda's chest rise and fall as she panted, her breasts jiggling inches above him, her nipples just out of reach of his mouth. He wanted to taste her, lick and suck her. He wanted to kiss her tits, kiss her lips, kiss her between her legs. He wanted to know all of her. He wanted years to learn her. He couldn't get enough.

She tucked her chin to her chest, pressed her lips together. He felt the change inside her, the tightness, the contractions, the electrical charge. And then she came, tossing her head back, crying out, shuddering above him. She was the most beautiful creature he'd ever seen, and he couldn't hold back.

He surged into her, gripped her thighs, gritted his jaw and came apart. His muscles burned, his chest ached, his orgasm exploded through him as if ripped from his soul. The intensity seared him, the fire roaring through his veins. It took him forever to return to the moment, and when he did, he knew nothing would ever be the same.

Miranda groaned as she moved off him and crumpled to sit on the floor. "As much as I'm a fan of after-sex cuddling, I think I've just ruined my thighs forever."

Caleb sat up. "Your thighs, my abs. I'm too out of shape for gymnastics."

Miranda laughed, reaching for his shirt and slipping it on as if suddenly worried about modesty. "You are not out of shape. I told you. Your body is amazing."

"My body is old and quickly becoming decrepit," Caleb said, getting to his feet and heading for the bathroom to dispose of the condom, snagging his boxers off the floor on the way. He pulled them on before coming back.

Then he stood above her, staring down. "Do you think we could take this party up to my room? Or do you have to rush home to water the plants or something?"

She cocked her head to the side and considered him while she crossed her legs, tugging the tails of his shirt into place over her sex. "I don't have plants to water, a pet to feed or a stove to clean, no. But we're going to have to stop in the kitchen because it's too late for room service and I'm starving."

Caleb's own thighs were feeling rubbery, so he backed up and sat on the bench, reaching for his socks, then his jeans. He held his pants in his hands as he said, "Let me make something for you while you get your things together. Earnesto saw me the other night. I can tell him you sent me."

"You'd do that?" she asked. Her voice was soft as if she was having trouble placing his offer in the context of their relationship.

He was having the same trouble. Especially since he didn't know what that context was. "Sure, why not? I figure after the show, the booze and the sex, the starvation's half my fault."

He wasn't too crazy about the way she was looking at him, so rather than squirm beneath her scrutiny, he put on his pants, found his wallet on the floor, returned it to his pocket.

She didn't move, or offer up his shirt so he could finish getting dressed. No, she went back to playing with the buttons and the placket, giving him glimpses of her body that caused his cock to rise. "You'd better be careful. I might take that as you caring."

That was the biggest problem of all. He did care, but he wasn't ready to let her know. He was having trouble enough admitting it to himself.

And so what he told her when he helped her to her feet and stripped his shirt from her body was, "I care about getting you fed and into bed. Why don't we leave it at that for now?"

19

MIRANDA DIDN'T WANT to move. She was warm, relaxed, sated, incredibly comfortable and loathe to leave Caleb. He was spooned around her, his knees tucked up beneath her bare bottom, his arm draped over her torso beneath her breasts, his head next to hers on the pillow.

His slow measured breaths stirred the hair above her ear. It tickled, but she stayed where she was, wondering if she'd ever woken after a night spent with a man—her ex-husband included—feeling as if her life was perfect.

And not because of the sex. Or at least not solely because of the sex. It was so much more. It was…everything. An everything that frightened her for a very good reason.

If she wanted things to move forward with Caleb, she had to come clean, and she did want them to move forward— because she was coming to care for him deeply.

In a million years, she would never have believed it possible for her to give anyone in the media the time of day, much less her body, and now it seemed, her heart. She knew it was too soon, logic said it was too soon. But when did logic have anything to do with love?

Oh, God. This couldn't be love, even if her heart was about to burst in her chest. Love grew out of affection and friendship and caring respect. It did not grow out of sweaty sex in bedrooms and hotel rooms and rooms with nothing to lie on but a bench or a floor.

Yet even as she mulled over that thought, she knew she and Caleb had shared more. They had talked, their conversations going into how she felt about her past more deeply than she'd gone with Patrice or Corinne. And last night?

The man had actually come back from the kitchen with the best club sandwich she'd ever had in her life. Okay, it was just a sandwich, but having him go to the trouble to put it together for her? Then adding a side of bagel crisps and the chipotle tomato cheese spread she loved?

When had anyone other than one of her best friends been so thoughtful? And when was the last time anyone made her wonder if she really was doing the right thing, avoiding the sordidness of what she'd gone through instead of accepting it as the history it was? With Marshall again in the news, wasn't it the perfect time to stop hiding?

Yes, Caleb held fast to his beliefs, but he let her hold fast to hers, challenging her without demeaning her, questioning her without ridiculing her. He let her be herself. Better yet, he liked her as herself.

Marshall had wanted to mold her, to turn her into his ideal. Caleb might not embrace her same causes or share her same views, even like the same books, food or movies, but he hadn't made a single effort to change her.

He hadn't even pressed to find out why she'd hidden herself. And that was the one thing that was troubling her the most. Why wasn't he pressing? Why wasn't he digging? Not that she wanted him to, but why wasn't he trying to figure her out? It was who he was, what he did. Yet he wasn't doing it with her.

Was he trying to protect her? Respecting the boundaries she'd set? Would he put his own curiosity aside and do that?

She couldn't think about it anymore. Not now. She had to get up. The tickle of his breath above her ear was getting to her, and then there was the screaming of her bladder that no mind-over-matter thinking would silence.

She scooted out from under Caleb's arm, found her panties and his shirt, and carried both to the bathroom where she suddenly realized she was freezing. Instead of washing her face and brushing her teeth as she'd planned, she left the garments on the counter and climbed into the tub.

She knew the shower would finish the job of waking Caleb her sliding from bed had started, but since she thought he might want to tell her goodbye, she didn't feel terribly guilty. Besides, the idea of him joining her in the shower, warming her, washing her—

At the sound of the shower curtain's metal hooks sliding back on the rod, she startled, then turned to stare at a very sleepy Caleb as he stepped into the tub. She stared too long. Shampoo ran from her forehead into her eyes.

"Ouch," she yelped, lifting her face to the spray. Caleb came close while she rinsed, wrapping his arms around her middle and nuzzling her nape. She pulled back, swiping her hands down her face. "If you're not careful, you're going to get a mouthful of lather."

He reached up and adjusted the shower to spray over her head and onto his, sputtering as he cleared the soap from his mouth—and then keeping the water for himself. She had to turn and face him, staying in full body contact to keep warm. It was no hardship at all.

"I didn't mean to wake you up," she said, cuddling close to his chest. "At least not at first."

His hands roamed from her nape to the base of her spine. "What changed your mind?"

She shivered. She didn't want to have to leave him and go to work. "I needed someone to wash my back."

"I see."

"You don't believe me?" she asked, breathing him in, rubbing against the wet hair that had matted in the center of his chest.

"Who washes it when you're at home?"

"No one."

"So it never gets washed?" he asked, using his fingers in ways that definitely qualified as dirty.

Warm water and a warm man with warm hands. She could stay here forever. "I've been thinking of hiring someone. A cabana boy maybe."

"They have those up here in the mountains?"

"A ski bum then."

"If you want, I can help you write an ad for the classifieds."

"And here I never thought having a reporter around would come in handy."

"Reporters are handy for more things than you can imagine," he said, and spent the next thirty minutes showing her.

Once they had both caught their breath, soaped, showered, rinsed and dried off, he asked, "What're you doing today?"

She looked over from running a comb through her hair. "I work Saturdays so Corinne can be home with Zoe, though tonight they're both going to be at her daughter's wedding. I'm going to miss it because of the show, so I'll want a full report."

Caleb frowned. "They made up?"

"Who?"

"Corinne and Brenna."

She nodded, reached for the blow dryer, but ended up setting it aside when she saw the deep V of concentration furrowing his brow. "Last night before closing, Zoe came into the shop. She'd been up to the inn, and she brought Brenna back down the mountain."

"That must've been after I talked to them then."

"You talked to Brenna and Zoe?" The Brenna part didn't surprise her. The Zoe part did, though only because she didn't know Caleb had met the younger of the girls. Then she wondered if they'd talked before or after the delivery of Corinne's flowers. "What about?"

He gave a lazy shrug. "Work. Background stuff for the wedding story. The human-interest side."

She bit down on asking him if he really meant the sensationalist, tabloid side. "Did they tell you they were coming to see Corinne?"

Shaking his head, he said, "Last I heard, they were going to Brenna's room to catch up."

Looking down, Miranda toyed with the controls on the blow dryer. "Corinne sent Brenna flowers yesterday. It's the first gesture she's made this whole time."

"It got Brenna to come to her. It obviously worked."

"Corinne was in tears. Sobbing. All three of them were." Miranda smiled. Her eyes misted as she thought back to the group hug that had taken the small family to their knees in the store's back room. She'd felt like an intruder, and knowing Corinne had her own set of keys, Miranda had locked up and headed home, leaving them to their reunion. "I honestly wondered if it would ever happen."

"Zoe told me what Brenna had done. That was a lot to put on her mother."

"It was," Miranda agreed. "But I guess it's true that time heals all wounds."

"It definitely wounds all heels. I know that much."

"Some heels deserve it," she told him.

"We do indeed," he said and before she could insist that she had not been talking about him, he went on. "If you're working today, what are you doing tomorrow?" He stood with one shoulder on the bathroom doorjamb, his arms over his chest, a towel knotted around his hips like a sarong.

She almost couldn't answer for drinking him in, the stubble he hadn't shaved from his jaw, his biceps that bulged where his arms were crossed. "Since the shop is closed, grocery shopping, cleaning, the usual."

"That can wait."

"Says you." She turned back to the mirror and rubbed the moisturizer she'd taken from her dressing room into her face.

"Yes, and me also says for you to pack a bag and bring it with you tonight."

"Where am I going?" she asked, and met his reflected gaze.

"We're spending the night away. I'll make the arrangements."

Away? He was going to take her away? God, just the idea had her hands shaking. "What about the wedding?"

"I'll be finished there by the time your show's done."

"I need to know what to pack. Casual? Dressy?"

"Casual."

"Outdoor casual or indoor casual?"

"You don't need a snowsuit, but bring a jacket."

"Is this like a real-world date? Not a Caleb McGregor date?"

"It's a real-world Caleb McGregor date. How's that?"

"It's perfect. I love…it," she said, barely catching the slip. "I haven't been out of Mistletoe in forever. I'm excited. And feeling incredibly spoiled."

"Spoiled?"

"First you send me flowers. Then you get me food. And now you take me on a date. A real date. Watch out," she added, reaching for the toothpaste, "or I'll start to expect this treatment."

"Don't," he said, shaking his head.

Uh…gulp. What was that? "Don't start to expect it?"

"Not from me," he said, his gaze fierce as it held and studied hers. "I fly out of here on Monday."

Her throat clogged immediately. She almost couldn't find her voice to speak. "To another assignment?"

He shook his head. "Home. To Baltimore. I figure it's time I check my mail, clean the fridge of whatever leftovers were in there when I flew out and have since built competing bacteria colonies. Air the place some before getting to work on my book."

Oh, God. She took a step back, sat hard on the toilet, appreciative of the lid being down, but surprised since everything around her had just flushed away. "Baltimore? That's where you live?"

He nodded. "I've been there about five years, why?"

"No reason."

Except that seven years ago she'd been the queen of the city's charity balls. And that six years ago her husband had been indicted by its courts. And that five years ago, while he was on trial, she'd started divorce proceedings there.

Could Caleb really not know her from any of that?

She jumped back to her feet, finished brushing her teeth and rinsing, then packed her kit of toiletries. "I've got to get out of here."

"What's wrong? Miranda—"

"Nothing. It's just that if I'm going to have time to pack before going to work, I need to hurry home." She said it while thinking that going away with him after the show tonight was probably the worst thing she could do.

Then again, she'd already stepped off that cliff several times, opening herself up, sharing details of her past that he would have no trouble using to find her out.

That he hadn't tried to nail down her identity by now confounded her, but she knew sooner or later he would—just as she knew the smartest thing to do would be to tell him about the ex-Mrs. E. Marshall Gordon herself.

NOT LONG AFTER Miranda left, Caleb's plans to spend the day preparing for the evening's wedding hit a snag. His concentration started giving him hell the first time through listening to his recording of Brenna Sparks, his efforts to focus derailed by a ridiculous distraction, one that hit him at the most inopportune times.

He could smell Miranda everywhere in the room.

He'd ordered room service after she'd left, hoping the aroma of the coffee, of the bacon and the maple syrup he'd poured on his pancakes would make it impossible for him to smell anything else.

It hadn't worked.

Neither had letting maid service in to clean.

Every time he turned to check the written notes from his conversation with Brenna, or got up to pace and listen to the recording of his conversation with the sisters, he would catch a whiff of something sunny and flowery and warm, and his head would wrap itself around Miranda and the things she was making him feel.

It was so bad, and he was feeling so much, that he still hadn't done anything about searching out her true identity. She'd told him she would tell him when it was time, and for some reason he'd decided that was good enough. He was waiting, letting her call the shots—which he supposed was the right thing to do. It was her life after all.

Thing of it was, he'd never cared about the right thing or the wrong thing, only about getting the scoop. Work had been everything since the moment he'd seen his byline on his very first story. Or it had been until the power Miranda had mentioned had gone to his head and he'd crossed a line into territory where he had no business being.

Speaking of stories… He rubbed the back of his neck as he paced, turning over what Zoe Sparks had told him about the hard feelings keeping her mother and Brenna apart. He wondered if Corinne had shared the whole truth of her thieving daughter with Miranda.

Caleb couldn't imagine that being any fun for the younger daughter, to be torn between sibling and parent. That was one dynamic he had yet to witness, the one his research still lacked: the one between Brenna and Zoe and Corinne.

He stopped pacing, thought a moment. If he set up in the chapel even earlier than he'd planned, he might catch the family still celebrating their reunion.

He set about closing up his laptop, securing his notes and recorder in the same case, then hurried to get dressed and cart his audio and video equipment downstairs.

While he was rolling his cases through the lobby on the way to the inn's chapel, Caleb saw Alan Price walk through the front door. He called out, and met the other man halfway. "I need to get my hands on a car. Anywhere to do that around here?"

"In Mistletoe? No." Alan shook his head. "You'll have to get one of the bigger agencies to deliver."

"I was afraid of that."

Alan shook back the shock of hair that covered his forehead, and hefted higher the pack he carried on his shoulder. "You can't get Barry to take you where you need to go?"

Not if he could help it, Caleb thought to himself. "I'm taking Miranda down to Golden for the night. I'd rather not have Barry along."

Price snickered, obviously at the idea of the local gossip sharing the date. Then he grew sober. "Do you think that's a good idea?"

Yeah...that's the reaction he'd expected. "Taking her out of town?"

"Getting her hopes up."

Was that what he was doing? "I haven't promised her anything but a date. I figured it's been a while since she went out for dinner and a movie. And it's not like I'm going to be here for anything long-term."

"You've told her when you're leaving?"

Caleb nodded. "Told her this morning that I fly out on Monday."

"She was okay with that?" Alan asked, his expression a mix of concern and curiosity.

"Why wouldn't she be?" Caleb realized she hadn't reacted much at all except to drop to the toilet lid and sit. "I know you're just looking out for her, but give her some credit for knowing what she wants to do."

"And who she wants to do it with?"

"Yeah. That, too."

"Here," Alan said after a long moment of eye-to-eye contact. He tossed Caleb his key ring. "An electric-blue Toyota FJ Cruiser. I'll get Patrice to come pick me up when the club closes."

"You sure?" Caleb asked, wrapping his fingers around the bundle of keys, warm in his palm.

"As long as you don't go breaking Miranda's heart," Alan said, bringing his hand down on Caleb's shoulder to enforce his warning with his heavy grip.

Caleb doubted that was a promise he'd be able to keep. So he didn't make it. He just said, "Thanks for the use of the SUV."

20

IF MIRANDA HAD BEEN asked to regale friends with the details of her last date, she wasn't sure she'd have been able to do more than assure whomever was asking that there had been no intimacy involved beyond that of friendship.

Though she'd hardly been in the mood for romance, much less sex, she had agreed to have dinner with one or two single men after filing for divorce from Marshall. But since every move she made was paparazzi fodder, she'd either cooked at her new apartment—where no one could get past the doorman to prove what company she was keeping—or she'd included other friends, and they'd gone out as a group.

And all of that had been before her move to Mistletoe. In the five years she'd been living here, she hadn't had a single date. She hadn't even been interested in going out with any of the few men she had met. Not until she'd lost her mind and kissed Caleb McGregor in front of her Club Crimson audience to a round of deafening applause.

Having him pick her up after work on Saturday had saved them time in getting to where they were going—a boutique hotel in Golden within walking distance of all the shopping, eating and artsy things she could imagine crowding into one day.

She would've given anything to have more.

They'd arrived long after midnight, but Caleb had told the front desk to expect them late. Their room had been ready and waiting. They'd fallen into bed and asleep spooned together and clothed in their underthings, making love once the sun had risen to bathe their room in a toasty yellow glow.

Breakfast had been an extraordinary affair of berries and chocolate, syrup and whipped cream, laughter and kisses topping off Belgian waffles, served with hot coffee and bacon in the restaurant around the corner at ten.

They'd done a lot of window-shopping, as there were only a few stores open on Sunday. She had copied down the contact information for a jewelry store displaying a black Akoya pearl necklace that she coveted, and bought an ivory cashmere cardigan from a clothing boutique she'd had to drag Caleb into.

He'd had to drag her into a stationer's where he'd bought himself a limited edition fountain pen. It had an ivory-colored barrel and sepia-toned scrimshaw artwork that depicted Herman Melville's *Moby Dick,* and he'd given her the matching roller ball to use in her shop.

She'd started to tell him that she couldn't accept the gift, that it was too expensive, that when she used it she would think of him and be sad. In the end she took it because she wanted the reminder of their time together, this stolen week that she would never have again.

Though things between them were far from settled and would no doubt remain so even after he left Mistletoe, she had needed the break from her routine, and time with the man who'd seen that need and taken her away. The man she was quite sure she was coming to love.

She'd been thinking about her fast-growing feelings for him and whether or not she could trust them to be real. Of course they were heat-of-the-moment. Of course they were thrilling. Of course they were causing her a lot of sleepless nights.

But just because she was reveling in the excitement of what she was feeling didn't mean she'd lost her ability to distinguish between reality and fiction.

Fiction was the lies that had been printed about her life with Marshall. Reality was living through the resulting humiliation and being careful not to do anything, to say anything that would ruin the safe—if somewhat lonely—life she'd carved out for herself after the end of her other one.

She knew that, but she also knew she had to tell Caleb the truth about who she was if she wanted what they had found here to grow. They had just sat down for their second meal of their day away in Golden when she made the decision to do so. Once they'd finished here they'd be driving back, and she didn't want to have this conversation in the dark with both of them facing the road any more than she'd wanted to have it in bed.

The booth in which they were sitting in the casual restaurant offered just enough privacy. She reached for the margarita their server set in front of her, and once Caleb had his beer, she took a deep breath, found her courage, and began.

"Did I tell you that I was born in Mistletoe? Even went to business school at the University of Colorado in Denver and majored in marketing? My parents both worked for the school district before retiring to Arizona."

"Hmm. But you lived out of state before moving to Colorado."

"Right. I left here not long after graduation to work for an ad agency on the East Coast." She paused, returned her glass to the table and added, "In Baltimore."

Caleb's gaze came up. He'd been studying his menu,

drinking his beer, but with those two words, she had his full attention. "You were living there before I moved there then."

She nodded. "And you were there when I moved away."

She left her admission at that for the moment, reaching again for her drink which she knew wasn't going to be enough to get her through their meal. She was tense, stiff, frightened. She was about to give up her safety net to a man who had never promised to catch her.

Caleb, who had been leaning forward, suddenly sat back as if pinned to his seat by a blast. His eyes went wide. The expression on his face was the shock of a man poleaxed. "Gordon. You were married to E. Marshall Gordon. You were Miranda Gordon."

Just as she'd thought. He knew exactly who she was. "Maybe say it one more time to be sure?"

"Oh, I'm sure," Caleb said, shifting forward again, shaking his head as if to help his suppositions fall into place. "That first night in Club Crimson, I knew I'd seen you, or at least that I should've known you, but I never could put it together. You…distracted me."

"In a good way, I hope," she said, toying with the stem of her glass.

"Considering I never let anything distract me…"

"I'll take that as a yes," she said, even though she could see that he was distracted now. He was blinking rapidly, giving her no more than a weak smile before getting back to whatever destination his mind was racing toward. "Caleb?"

"Hmm?"

"Caleb?"

He shook free from his thought-filled daze and reached for his beer. "Sorry. I was—"

"Lost in thought. Weighing the implications of me handing

you such a scoop and the ramifications of using it. Especially now, with Marshall's new trial coming up and speculation about what happened to me no doubt running rampant."

"I have heard of a renewed interest in finding you."

She pulled her drink closer. "I know. And I knew that's what you would do once you figured it out. At least I hoped that's what you would do. That you would think about it for a while."

He waited as a laughing foursome walked by their table. "Instead of pulling out my phone and e-mailing my editor, you mean?"

She nodded. "Or writing the headline before you knew the whole story."

"Does that mean you have more to tell me? Or more you want me to know? Because you've told me a lot, and I'm pretty good at cobbling all those different parts into something—"

"Big and juicy and guaranteed to make you a name?"

"Something like that," he said, but he looked away as if there was something he was holding back from her. A big juicy something he didn't want her to know.

She canted her head to the side and considered him as someone with a secret of his own. "So? What do you want to ask me? What are you curious about?"

This time, he was the one who considered her, frowning as if he didn't understand what she was asking. "I'm curious about all of it, but I didn't think you wanted me digging around."

"I don't. But I'm offering the information freely," she said just as their server returned to take their order. She went with a Cobb salad. Caleb chose a gourmet burger and home fries.

They both ordered a second drink and once the waiter gathered up their menus with a promise to be right back, they were left staring at one another across a table that seemed a whole lot wider than before.

Caleb was the first to speak. "I'm not so sure about that freely thing. I don't think those wounds are healed. I think if I started asking about what I want to know, you would bleed."

"That's ridiculous." Why would he think such a thing? "I've moved beyond all of that. It's ancient history."

"It's not that ancient. And moving to another state doesn't mean moving beyond. It's still there, Miranda. It's why you hate what I do. It's why you don't want the media connecting Miranda to Candy. Especially now. It's part of who you are. And it's why I think I—" He stopped in the middle of his sentence, reached for his mug and drained his beer.

Miranda didn't know how to react. Their server arrived with their second round of drinks, giving her a bit of breathing room. What had Caleb been about to say? That he loved her? That he enjoyed her company? That he had to leave Mistletoe before he got in too deep?

She could hardly believe it was any of those, and yet… "It's why you think you what?"

"It's why I never did put a lot of effort into finding out who you were. I like who you *are*. You said you'd tell me when it was time. And now…" He reached for the stack of coasters on their table, and tapped them on the tabletop the way he would a deck of cards.

"And now you wish I hadn't told you?"

"Yeah. In a way," he admitted, avoiding her gaze. "I mean, me liking you doesn't change the fact that I'm an entertainment correspondent."

"And now that Miranda Gordon is once again in the news

as scandal fodder…" She brought her drink to her mouth, swallowed, licked the salt from her lips. "Since I'm not a private citizen but a public figure and newsworthy, you've got to decide how to handle what I've told you."

"What do you want me to do with it?" he asked. "You had a reason for telling me. You had to have thought about what I'd do with the information."

"I wondered how you'd react, yes. Whether you'd rush off to make a call to meet a deadline."

"That's all? No other scenario?" he asked, cutting his gaze upward.

"Such as?"

"That I would respect your wishes and keep what you told me in confidence?"

She wondered—if she made that request, would he give her his word? "I guess not. I know your type. And I knew by telling you, that I was risking the information leaking out."

"And if it did, if I leaked it, were you going to leave Mistletoe and remake yourself somewhere else?"

That question was one she had no trouble answering, and she shook her head. "No. I'm staying where I am. I have friends, a business, my singing gig. I have a wonderful life."

"What about having Miranda Gordon's picture showing up in the paper next to Candy Cane's?"

She waited for the server to set their meals in front of them, reaching for her fork before going on. "If my name ends up in the paper, I'll deal with the fallout then. And if I'm lucky, people will still call me when they want flowers. If not, well, I'll cross that bridge when I come to it. Honestly, I'm more worried about Corinne."

He took a bite of his burger, studying her while he chewed and swallowed. "How so?"

Miranda realized she was going to have to walk a fine line between giving him her thoughts and giving him a lecture. She was pretty sure he wouldn't go for the latter. "I'm saying that gossip is damaging to more people than those it's about."

He nodded, but it wasn't a sign of agreement. That was obvious from the tightness of his mouth, the hard line of his jaw. "So if I write about you being in Mistletoe, it could hurt your business and take out Corinne as collateral damage. Is that what you're saying?"

He was close, and she expounded. "And if I were forced to sell or close the shop and Corinne were forced to find another job, it could impact Zoe's scholarship, especially if they had to move away for Corinne to get work. Mistletoe's not exactly a town with a lot of prospects."

"What would you do? If you had to leave?"

There was something she wanted to know before she answered. "Is my response going to influence what you do with my revelation?"

"Why did you tell me?" he asked, rather than giving her an answer. "You didn't have to. I didn't ask you to."

"You haven't for a couple of days, no."

"Then why? Knowing what you do about me—"

"What *do* I know about you, Caleb? That you're an entertainment correspondent writing a book. That's not a lot. I don't know if you have a column in *People* magazine or if you write for *TMZ*."

He looked down, grabbed a thick French fry and swirled it through a pool of ketchup. "I do have a column. It's syndicated. Nationally. Just not under my name."

And things just got better and better. "So you have a Candy Cane persona of your own?"

"More or less, yeah."

"And what would happen if I exposed you?"

"Do you know who I am?"

She shook her head. Until now, she hadn't thought he was anyone with an alter ego she might recognize. "No, but I know how to use Google. I also know a couple of private investigators who would love to hear from me again."

He sat back, ran his napkin over his mouth and tossed it to the table before reaching for his mug and draining it. "What do you want me to do with the information, Miranda? Sit on it? Write about it? Give it to the Baltimore press?"

"I want you to add it to what you already know about me and see if it changes anything."

"Such as?"

"Your feelings," she blurted out, because right now that was the only thing that mattered to her. She ached with wanting him, loving him, needing to know he shared the incredible high she'd been riding this past week.

He obviously didn't. "I'm not much for feelings."

"Then you're lucky that you can push them aside," she said, tossing her napkin to the table. "Most of us aren't able to do that so easily."

"It's not about pushing them aside."

"Then what is it?"

"I can only do what I do, the type of reporting I do, by keeping my distance. I can't get personally involved. Things get…fucked up when I do."

"With me, you mean."

"With anyone."

"Then thank God I didn't tell you how I really feel," she said, scooting to the end of the bench seat and getting to her feet before they shook out from under her. "I'm going to the ladies' room. Could you settle the check so we can go?"

THE DRIVE BACK WAS MADE in absolute darkness and silence. Caleb didn't want to leave things with Miranda any worse than he sensed they were, and figured his best shot at doing that was shutting the hell up.

He'd come so close to telling her that he loved her. He'd almost blurted it out in the middle of their conversation. Judging by the look on her face, he was pretty sure she knew he'd caught himself in the nick of time.

And then he'd compounded the error by denying he felt anything at all. Such a smart guy he was. Such a brilliant piece of work.

Funny thing was, he'd been ready to tell her that no woman had ever meant to him what she did, that he woke up in the mornings wanting her there, that when he thought about their time together, the simplest things made him smile, that their knowing each other only a matter of days made no difference at all.

The look on her face when she'd caught him ordering her flowers. The way she'd taken over the inn's kitchen the night they'd sneaked in for a snack. Her leaving him to discover the only way to get from the warehouse to his room was to trek outside the building through the cold and the snow.

All of those things—and others, dozens of others—were at the heart of his inability to get his work done and get out of here, and he didn't even care. Leaving tomorrow was eating at him. Unbelievably so.

He could see himself sticking around, bunking in with Miranda, working on his book on the sofa or the kitchen island, while she curled up beside him to read or put a pot of coffee on.

He'd been having thoughts of home and hearth…and then she'd dropped her Baltimore bomb into his lap. He had no idea what he was going to do with it.

The Caleb he'd been a month ago, before the fiasco with Del's fiancée, would've done the very thing she'd wondered about, pulled out his cell phone and e-mailed his editor a sound bite for WBAL-TV's evening news.

The Caleb he was now, the one who found himself seriously considering a recent offer to buy his Max Savage empire, that Caleb was fighting a battle between his feelings for Miranda and the power trip of telling all.

"What did you say?"

At Miranda's question, he glanced over, seeing nothing but her profile lit by the glowing dashboard lights. "Did I say something?"

She nodded. "It sounded like a curse."

"It probably was."

"What were you thinking?"

He wasn't going to tell her that. Once he figured out what he was going to do, he'd let her know, whichever way it went, but he wasn't going to talk about it now. Instead, he turned to something that was still weighing on his mind.

"About work. About reporting. About the stories we hear, how much we never know of what's behind them."

"But it's that way with all news. Not just celebrity gossip. In cases of national security, we're given what the reporters and correspondents are allowed to make public. It's the same with the criminal justice system, or even human-interest stories. We may hear about someone losing two hundred pounds, but we don't know if it was really done for health reasons or because their spouse threatened to leave."

"Doesn't say much about the spouse, does it?" he responded without really thinking.

"I was speaking hypothetically, but, no. A lot of couples do fine through the better, but fall apart through the worse."

They weren't officially a couple, but they had come to a better-or-worse crossroads. What he did with her story would determine whether he'd be welcome in Mistletoe, whether he'd switch his home base from Maryland to Colorado, or whether he'd never see Miranda Kelly again.

That was Caleb's final thought as he pulled the borrowed SUV to a stop in front of her bungalow. He left the engine idling, but neither one of them made a move to get out. This could be the last time they ever saw one another, both of them knew that, and he was gripped by a sadness that was hard to shake.

"Do you want to stay the night?" she finally asked.

"I do, but I can't. I have to pack, and Barry's meeting me in front of the inn at four-thirty. My flight leaves at seven."

"Gotta love all that airport security adding hours to the process," she said, and they laughed together awkwardly.

Miranda took a deep breath. "This is goodbye then."

"Only for now."

"Does that mean you're coming back?"

"That means we'll see. I've got some things to do, to work on. Things to think about."

"The book?"

"Yeah. There's that."

"And what I told you."

"There's that, too."

She opened her door then, so Caleb did the same, retrieving her overnighter from the backseat once he'd climbed out. He circled the vehicle to walk her to her door. She was already halfway up the walk when he got to her side, so he did the only thing he could do and followed.

She dug in her purse for her keys, unlocked the door. He pushed it open far enough to set her luggage inside, but stayed on the porch, feeling that he'd worn out his welcome over the dinner neither one of them had eaten much of.

"Thank you for the day away," Miranda said, turning up her face and meeting his gaze. "I can't remember the last time I had so much fun. And it was even better with you there to share it."

"I had a great time, too," he said, knowing he had to go, that there was nothing to be gained by standing here telling her goodbye in a dozen different ways when there was only one way he wanted to say it.

He stepped closer, brought up his hand to cup her face, guided her close to his body with his other one in the small of her back and kissed her. It was a tentative, questing kiss, a gentle pressing together of their lips, of hers parting, of his tongue slipping inside to find hers.

He knew she was crying before he heard the hitch in her breathing and felt her tremble against him. Hot tears ran down her cheeks and wet his. He tasted their saltiness, used his thumb to wipe away what he could reach. She curled her fingers against his chest, holding on to the fabric of his sweater.

That was when she pulled away. "Where is your coat? Aren't you freezing?"

If he was, he hadn't noticed. "I'm fine. The heater's on in the SUV."

"I guess you'd better get back to the inn so Alan doesn't have to walk home."

"Yeah. I guess I'd better."

"Thank you again. For the minibreak."

"Thank you," he said, wondering if he was about to have a heart attack, his chest hurt so bad. "For everything."

21

MIRANDA HAD NEVER HATED a Monday morning more. She got up, got dressed, skipped breakfast and got to work early, and did it all without having slept during the night.

She'd tried. Over and over, she'd tried. But she'd tossed and turned, paced from the bedroom to the kitchen and back fifteen times, finally sitting in the hot shower until her water heater spat out its last drop of warmth.

A prune by then, she'd given up the bed and built a fire, then curled up on the couch and nursed a mug of soothing herbal tea that hadn't done such a good job of soothing. She didn't blame the tea. She was beyond being soothed.

She'd had an amazing six days with Caleb—six days that seemed like six weeks, six months even, but it was over. He was gone, and he'd taken her secret with him back to the very city where her life had fallen apart. Now all she could do was sit here in her hideaway and wait for the backlash.

When four o'clock had rolled around, she'd thought about calling him before he left and asking him if he'd decided what to do with the news. She hadn't, her pride rising up and smacking her before she could make that mistake.

She'd chosen to tell him the truth of her identity, now she had to face the consequences of her actions. That meant she had to go to work without having slept a wink. And for the first time in a long while, she beat Corinne to the shop.

The other woman stopped inside the back door, looked at her watch, looked up at Miranda where she stood at the work-table sorting carnations. "Am I in the right place?"

Miranda scowled. "You, mother of the bride. Don't try to be funny. I'm not in a funny mood."

"Well, you're in some kind of mood." Corinne tucked her purse in her locker and pulled her apron over her head, looking cheerier and younger than she had in ages. "Couldn't have anything to do with the love of your life leaving town, could it?"

"He was not, is not, will never be the love of my life. He was just…a guy," Miranda said, cringing inside at how false her statement sounded, how wrong it felt. "We got back from Golden pretty late, and I didn't sleep, and here I am, grumpy and tired."

"Go home. Take a nap," Corinne suggested, checking the order book for what needed doing first, finding the season's usual requests for poinsettias and the like. "There's nothing going on that I who have no worries and a wonderful new son-in-law can't handle."

As happy as she was for Corinne, Miranda couldn't stand the thought of being alone the day Caleb was leaving town. "If I go home, I'll pace and fret like I did all night."

"And you'd rather do that here. Inflict your pain on an audience."

Miranda threaded her fingers into her hair, took a deep breath, and forced it out loudly. "No pain. No inflicting. I promise."

"He's not such a bad guy, you know. For a reporter," Corinne said, heading to the bathroom to wash her hands while Miranda stared at her aghast.

"And you're telling me that now because…"

"He wasn't sticking around." Corinne shook the water from her hands before pulling three paper towels from the dispenser. "Does it matter when I gave you my opinion?"

"It's not the same opinion you gave me when you found out what he does."

"That's why they're called opinions," Corinne said, patting Miranda's shoulder as she walked by on her way to the front of the store. "They're subject to change."

"And what changed yours?" Miranda called before Corinne disappeared from the back room.

She stopped in the arched walk-through. "I spent some time with him on Saturday, before the wedding. He's got a good heart. Good intentions. He made doubly sure that he got everything about Brenna's story right."

"Are you saying he's one of a few good newsmen? A reporter who knows where to draw the line?"

"He stepped over a time or two, but was a good sport when I pushed him back."

"Then maybe I don't have to worry about the Baltimore press descending like the plague?"

The front door opened then, putting an end to her musings and their conversation. Since she wasn't getting much of anything done, she followed Corinne to the front.

It was Orsy from next door with a box of donuts in one hand and an envelope in the other. Orsy always offered his neighbors freebies when they came in, but he never delivered.

"Hey, Orsy." Miranda leaned her elbows on the front counter. "Is it a special occasion? Or are you just teasing me before you take those somewhere else?"

The bakery owner laughed as he set the box in front of her. "Nope. These are for you. Guy who came in last week and wanted the sausage biscuits told me to bring 'em over when you and Corinne got in."

"Caleb?" she asked, knowing the answer, her heart racing, her thoughts speeding ahead.

"Didn't give a name. Had Barry drop him by first thing. Did give me this, though. Asked that I made sure you got it." Orsy handed her the envelope, before turning for the door. "You ladies have a good day."

"Thanks, Orsy. You, too," Miranda said, glancing over at Corinne. "Donut?"

"I think I will," the other woman said, opening the box. "What's in the envelope?"

"A Dear Jane letter, I'd imagine." She wasn't about to admit that her stomach was in knots. She was having enough trouble hiding the tremors in her hands.

"So open it already," Corinne said, gesturing with her donut and dropping sugar crumbs everywhere. "See what the reporter has to say."

Miranda reached for a letter opener and slit the top. A strip of newspaper fluttered out to land on the counter. It was the most recent Max Savage column. And it was signed.

"Oh my God! Your reporter is Max Savage!" Corinne grabbed the article away from Miranda. "And look here. He says he'll be doing a weeklong feature on the newly married Ravyn Black and Teddy Eagleton."

Miranda couldn't even think about Corinne's daughter. Caleb was Max Savage! The Snoop with the Scoop! Dear God, the man had the ability to smear her from here to Baltimore and around the world.

The question was, would he? Or had he already? Was her name slated to appear in tomorrow's column?

She leaned her elbows on the counter and buried her face

in her hands. Max Savage. She never would have imagined things would turn out this bad.

"Hey, he wrote you a note. Here. On the back." Corinne stabbed a finger against the newspaper.

Miranda hadn't seen it. All she'd seen was the heavy black signature scratched above the column's headline.

She picked up the paper and turned it over, unable to groan or laugh, afraid she was going to throw up. She was screwed. So incredibly screwed.

And then she read what Caleb had written…

> You were honest with me. This may be a chickenshit way of returning the favor, but never let it be said that I wasn't an honest chickenshit.
> Caleb

"Well, there ya go," Corinne said. "Can you believe it? You were sleeping with Max Savage. What a hoot! Now if he tells the world who you are, you can out him back."

Somehow, that didn't make Miranda feel any better. Right now, she didn't think there was anything that would.

CALEB'S FLIGHT FROM Denver to Baltimore was amazingly uneventful and even on time. If he was a suspicious man, he would've taken that as a sign that he was meant to forget Mistletoe and Miranda, and reclaim his life from the strange week he'd spent at the Inn at Snow Falls. But it wasn't going to happen, and he knew it.

He would always remember the redhead he'd found living on the mountain. The redhead he'd fallen in love with.

Leaving her his most recent column on his way out of town hadn't exactly been a fair way to tell her who he was—not when she'd come out to him twice, first as Candy Cane, then about being the ex-Mrs. E. Marshall Gordon.

All he'd done was sign a newspaper. Not hard to figure out which one of them had the balls. At least Barry's chatter during the drive to the airport had distracted him from thoughts of further professional hara-kari.

Once he was in the air, he'd pulled out his laptop and his earbuds, plugged in and tuned out everyone else on the plane. He'd spent the flight looking over the notes for the week's worth of columns he'd drafted about the romance of the congressman and the rock star, then pulled up a new document to put down random thoughts on his book.

It hadn't been easy deciding how to start the study of his observations on the tabloids and society until he'd realized that his own decade spent reporting entertainment news, and the impact doing so had had on him, would make a perfect preface. Yeah, he'd be putting himself out there as Max Savage, but it was time to own his mistakes as well as his successes. He had a lot of both. He was proud of the bulk of it, but not all.

While crossing the continent at thirty thousand feet, he'd discovered his story wasn't particularly difficult to chronicle. By the time the plane began its descent into BWI, he had the first draft of the preface polished within an inch of its life.

He shut down his laptop, grabbed his computer bag and his carry-on and disembarked, heading to the cab stand. He gave the driver his address, then settled back for the trip to his town house, his brain engaged with where he'd be picking up in the book once he was home.

He'd need food delivered, coffee, milk and cereal to see him from one Chinese takeout to the next. But this felt right, this buckling down and digging in to get it done. It needed to be said, to be shared, to serve as a warning or a lesson, or, hell, even as entertainment to those who would take it that way. And when he *was* done, when he'd bled the words he wanted to say all over the page, he'd send it to his agent and to Miranda.

He wanted her to know what he had written. But most of all he wanted her to know that he loved her, and that if she couldn't love him back because of who he was, what he had done, the things he stood for, he'd live with that.

And with Max Savage being laid to rest, neither she nor anyone else would have to suffer his bite again.

22

MIRANDA WAS IN NO MOOD to go onstage. She'd thought about calling in sick this last week of December, coming back after the new year was well under way with a new attitude and list of resolutions and goals.

But this week was the busiest of the year at the Inn at Snow Falls, and she had too much pride in the reputation of Club Crimson and too much love for Candy Cane to bail on the show and her friends.

The new year would be here soon enough, along with the whole new outlook on life she was determined to have. There would be no more hiding and worrying about being found out. If she wanted to fly to Baltimore and visit old friends, fly to Baltimore she would.

She'd done enough waiting around like a lump on a log and hoping for things to happen this past month, waiting for Caleb to get in touch, hoping he would call and tell her what he had decided to do with what she'd told him about who she was.

Hoping more for him to call and say that he missed her. That he loved her. And then she realized how much time and energy she was wasting with her passivity, and she'd given herself a lecture that was long overdue.

No, from now on, whatever she wanted or hoped for, she

would go after. She was done with hiding, done thinking privacy and anonymity would protect her from the ugly things said by people who didn't know her.

Cloistering herself away in a small mountain town was not going to stop the gossip any more than had keeping a low profile while living in the city. People who wanted to talk and speculate were going to talk and speculate.

All she could do was hold her head high and go on living her life. And that meant letting what she'd shared with Caleb fade into a wonderful memory, no matter how painful that was for her to admit.

His parting *we'll see* had obviously been his way of letting her down easy, when telling her he'd enjoyed the week for what it was would've been a much kinder kiss-off.

Sure, she could've called him. She didn't know if he was listed, but her contacts in Baltimore would've had no trouble finding him—once they got over the shock of hearing from her. But the thought of chasing him down after leaving the ball in his court seemed so…desperate.

Sitting on the vanity bench in her dressing room, she stared at her reflection. Before Caleb McGregor had come into her life, she'd experienced bouts of loneliness, had griped to Corinne and Patrice about the lack of eligible men in Mistletoe until her friends had tired of hearing her whine.

But she'd never let herself fall into a pit of desperation or depression. The fact that she was so close to doing so now—

"Miranda? You in there?"

At Patrice's voice, Miranda turned from facing herself to facing the rest of the world. "It's unlocked," she called, reaching for the band that held back her hair. "Come in."

Patrice opened the door. "I knocked, like, three times. I guess you were in the bathroom."

"No, I was here. Thinking. I didn't hear you, sorry."

"I'd ask what you were thinking about, but since Caleb has been the only thing on your mind lately…" Patrice let the sentence trail off as she perched beside Miranda on the bench. "Maybe this will help."

She handed Miranda a manila envelope addressed to her with nothing in the upper left corner but a block-printed CM. There was no postmark to show that it had come from Baltimore. In fact, there were no stamps at all.

She touched her fingertips to the initials, her pulse quickening. "Is he here?"

"Not that I know of," Patrice said, stabbing the center of the envelope with one finger. "I'm assuming that came with the rest of today's FedEx packages. Alan said he tried to flag you down when you came in—"

He had. She'd ignored him. "I heard him. I was too busy having a pity party to want to talk."

"Aw, sweetie." Patrice wrapped an arm around Miranda's shoulders. "What's the pity for this time?"

Miranda elbowed her friend in the ribs. "This time? Just for that, I'm not telling you."

"You don't have to tell me. It's written all over your face."

Miranda looked up to check her reflection. "I see a frown that's easily remedied with a smile, and some under-eye circles that I'll need makeup to get rid of. But nothing written there except my lack of sleep."

"You know what I see when I look at you?" Patrice took the large envelope from Miranda's hands and held it up. "I see this. Him. You're in love with the man and you're not doing anything about it."

"What am I supposed to do?" Miranda asked, flailing one hand. "He told me he'd be in touch, and he hasn't been."

Patrice waved the envelope. "What do you call this?"

Hmph. "A month late?"

"He's a guy, Miranda. A month of sorting out his feelings is nothing."

Miranda stared at the packet. She was certain it contained the decision he'd made in one form or another. What she couldn't figure out was why he thought she would want to read about it this way rather than hearing it firsthand.

Patrice patted at the envelope. It was almost a half-inch thick, and stiff, as if it held cardboard. "Aren't you at all curious?"

"Of course I'm curious."

"Well, then? Open it and see what he has to say," Patrice said, peeling back the adhesive flap to get Miranda started.

Miranda took it from there, sliding out a small sheaf of three-holed paper bound together with metal fasteners. A handwritten note was paper-clipped on top.

The opening to my book.
I wanted you to be the first to read it.
Caleb

"Ooh," Patrice said. "I've never been able to resist a sneak peek."

"If this is what I think it is, he's written about me," Miranda said, even though she couldn't figure out why Caleb would put her in a book about pop culture. It didn't make sense, but why else would he send it?

Patrice was quiet for several seconds, then said, "Maybe you shouldn't read it until after the show then."

"No, I have to know what it says."

"Do you want me to flip through and give you the highlights?"

Miranda shook her head. She was going to be strong. Nothing he had written could hurt her, whether a lie or the truth. "Why don't you read it to me while I do my face?"

Patrice gave her one more chance to back out. "You sure you don't want to look at it while you're alone?"

"So I can have an even bigger pity party?"

"If you're sure…"

Miranda nodded. She wasn't sure at all. "I am."

"Okay." Patrice opened the cover page to read.

In 1995, Caleb McGregor graduated from the New-house School of Public Communications at Syracuse University. Having interned at the *New York Times* in his senior year, he was ready to find and report "all the news that was fit to print"—as stated in the logo found in the paper's masthead. Things didn't go as planned, and several years later he discovered his true calling, rein-venting himself as Max Savage.

All he had to do was play Faust to Max's devil, and he had a guaranteed ride to the top. He was arrogant. He was impatient. He was greedy beyond belief. And so, like the brash and impatient young fool that he was, he sold his soul and said yes, digging into the lives of celebrities, politicians, society's movers and shakers, and feeding their stories to a public starved for his brand of news.

Patrice stopped, and met Miranda's gaze in the vanity mirror. "Sweetie, I'm not so sure this is about you at all."

"Let me see it." Miranda flipped through the pages, reading tidbit after vignette after recountal about Caleb, and not a word about Miranda Gordon or Candy Cane. She looked back up at Patrice. "This isn't about me. It's about him."

"Why him?"

"He's Max Savage."

Patrice's eyes went wide. "The gossip columnist? You've got to be kidding me."

Miranda shook her head. It had been a month since she'd received the signed column at the flower shop, but she hadn't breathed a word to anyone else, and knew Corinne would never repeat what she'd been told in confidence.

"He told me with a note after he left."

"And you didn't spill?"

"I didn't think he wanted it known."

"Well, if this is the opening to his book, I'd guess that he's changed his mind. I wonder why."

Miranda was wondering, too. "Listen, do you mind if I read the rest of this alone?"

"Sure, sweetie." Patrice dropped a kiss on the top of Miranda's head as she stood. "I know where I'm not wanted just the same as I know where I am wanted. I've got a hot date with an even hotter bartender."

"I was wondering what was up with the shoes," Miranda said, glancing down to the low-heeled pumps Patrice had co-ordinated with dress pants instead of wearing her usual blue jeans and boots.

"We're going out to dinner at Fish and Cow Chips, if you can believe it," Patrice said, waving goodbye as she opened the door, then nodding to indicate the manuscript pages. "You'll let me know what he says?"

"Of course. I just need to get through it on my own first."

"Okay, but don't forget you go on in an hour."

"Yes, Mrs. Club Manager. I'll be on time."

And then Patrice was gone, the door closing behind her, and Miranda was left with Caleb's story and the realization that he hadn't written his pièce de résistance about her. Had it been arrogant of her to think that was what he was going to do?

She looked at the top of the last sheet, saw that there were only fifty pages. She had an hour and would be cutting it close, but she didn't care.

She started at the beginning and read through to the end, seeing in his words so much of the Caleb she'd come to know, learning things about him she hadn't had time to find out in their six days together. Discovering what a complicated man she'd fallen in love with. Accepting that anyone wishing to make a life with him would have her work cut out.

He was not an easy man, a simple man. He was full of complexities and contradictions; she knew from her experience that he was set on things going his way.

And then she turned the last page, and she found a note that wasn't meant for his agent or editor or the scandal-loving public. It was meant only for her.

And it made her smile as her heart began to thump with a new beat in her chest.

You owe me an end-of-show kiss.

23

It had taken Caleb a long time to figure out how to pull off the biggest romantic gesture he'd ever made in his life. The only one he'd ever made, if he were being honest.

And since it was time to be honest about everything, well, yeah. He'd never done anything like this before, or even had the desire or the need—until he'd been smart enough to fall in love with Miranda Kelly.

The day Caleb had left Mistletoe and flown out of Colorado, he'd tipped Orsy well enough that he had no doubt the baker had delivered the donuts and the signed Max Savage column to Miranda at Under the Mistletoe.

Now it was almost the new year—meaning Miranda had had almost a month to deal with Caleb being Max. The same month Caleb had used to exorcise his alter ego from his life.

He'd had to do it. He had to be free before he returned to grovel for Miranda's forgiveness, and beg her to share the rest of his life.

His first romantic gesture had been to call the flower shop and talk to Corinne. Fortunately, he'd only had to hang up on Miranda twice before her employee had answered the phone.

Corinne was good to play along and keep his plans to herself. He had no idea how she would fill his order without Miranda catching on, but that he left up to her.

Next he'd called the inn and talked to Alan. Caleb knew Club Crimson's manager was the best hope for pulling strings and getting him a room at the inn. He was also Caleb's best hope for a ride from the airport that would avoid using both Barry and the front door once he arrived.

Unfortunately, all Alan could provide was the ride; the inn was booked solid. Caleb had made the trip anyway. If things went well, he'd be sleeping with Miranda. If not, well, he'd bunked down in worse places than the inn's lobby while waiting to get out of one town or another.

He'd originally planned to overnight the section of the manuscript to Miranda. But he didn't want the pages arriving without him there to explain should his flight be delayed due to the holiday crush. So he'd tucked the FedEx envelope in his computer bag and given it to Alan after the other man had parked behind the inn in the employee's lot.

He'd also brought a copy of his final Max Savage column to show Miranda before it ran on New Year's Day. Signing off on the sale of Max Savage had been one of the sweetest moments of his life.

But nothing would compare to the moment when he laid eyes on Miranda again.

Walking into Club Crimson had been like walking into a rose garden. Dozens of the red flowers sat on every table in the nightclub save for one. His table. The one where he'd been sitting the first night he'd seen her.

Now he sat exactly where he had then.

Tonight, however, he was sober.

The glass in front of him contained nothing but water, ice and a slice of lime. He didn't need the clarity of mind to figure out who she was the way he had that first night. But neither did he need the crutch to get him beyond the hard-sell color scheme.

He still hated the red. He hadn't changed his mind about the whole concept of a lovers' resort as ridiculous. And if it hadn't been Miranda singing the songs, he wouldn't have stuck around for the sugary-sweet set.

But since it *was* Miranda, and he was involved on a level felt by no one else in the club, the moment the pianist began warming up, Caleb jumped in his seat, certain his heart was attacking for real.

It got worse when she came onstage. And it intensified as she sang, that feeling of his chest exploding, his lungs crushing him, his spine snapping as he broke. Through it all, she ignored him.

Not once did she look toward where she knew he would be sitting. Oh, no. She gave her attention to everyone else, stopped at every other table and leaned close to smell the flowers. His flowers. The flowers he'd had put there for her.

He bristled when she touched the men, grunted when she touched the women. He wanted her touching him. He wanted to be touching her. From the corner of his eye, he caught Alan at the bar gesturing his offer to break the rules and bring Caleb a real drink.

He came close to taking it, but that was when the opening notes to her final song floated through the club, and Miranda began walking toward him.

Not a single word of the lyrics registered. All he knew was that she was there, then on his table, draped across it as she sang, teasing him with flirtatious smiles, with the tip of her tongue as it wet her lips, with her teeth as she bit at the corner of the bottom one and caught it.

Her eyes teased him, too, tears glistening in the corners, the moisture reflecting the joy he saw there. The same joy he couldn't keep out of his own.

She straightened then, slid from the table into his lap, giving him a glimpse of both breasts as she moved and the scooped neckline of her sequined dress gaped.

And then she finished the song, drawing out the final note as she looped her arms around his neck, before whispering, "I love you," against his mouth, and kissing him.

He crushed her to him and kissed her back, not asking, not pleading, just sliding his tongue into her mouth the moment she parted her lips. Exquisite. Her taste. Her texture. The warmth of her mouth on his. The scent of flowers that was hers and had nothing to do with the roses.

He could not believe he had flown away and left her behind. He could not believe she was taking him back, that she was loving him, that she loved him, that she was going to let him love her. He didn't deserve her, but he was here for as long as she would have him.

Too soon, she pulled away, breathing deeply as if she'd forgotten she needed to. He knew breathing had slipped his own mind and he, too, inhaled, filling lungs that had finally remembered how to work.

When Miranda got to her feet and took a bow, the crowd around them clapped wildly.

Caleb also stood and, tears bright on her cheeks, Miranda reached up and laid her hand along his jaw. "I missed you."

"I doubt half as much as I missed you," he got out, his voice only cracking once. He suddenly couldn't see so well, his own eyes watery.

"We'll have to debate that later," she told him, stepping closer and pressing her body to his. "On our date."

He groaned. "Since I'm here without a room, I was hoping you'd say that."

She laughed, shook her head, then fluffed at her short auburn hair. "Did you notice I'm not wearing a wig?"

"I noticed. I also noticed you're not wearing a bra."

"That was just for you."

"Good. I'm a big fan of secrets."

"I was wondering about that," she said, and all he could do was drink her in as she added, "You know, not that I care so much anymore, but it's good to know you're not the kiss-and-tell type."

"Are you kidding me? Kissing and telling is what I do best." And before she could respond, he took her microphone, brought it to his mouth and stared into her shimmering eyes.

"I love you, too," he said, silently adding, "Miranda," before bending her backwards, following her down, and while the audience whooped and cheered, kissing her with every bit of that love.

* * * * * *

millsandboon.co.uk Community

Join Us!

The Community is the perfect place to meet and chat to kindred spirits who love books and reading as much as you do, but it's also the place to:

- **Get the inside scoop from authors about their latest books**
- **Learn how to write a romance book with advice from our editors**
- **Help us to continue publishing the best in women's fiction**
- **Share your thoughts on the books we publish**
- **Befriend other users**

Forums: Interact with each other as well as authors, editors and a whole host of other users worldwide.

Blogs: Every registered community member has their own blog to tell the world what they're up to and what's on their mind.

Book Challenge: We're aiming to read 5,000 books and have joined forces with The Reading Agency in our inaugural Book Challenge.

Profile Page: Showcase yourself and keep a record of your recent community activity.

Social Networking: We've added buttons at the end of every post to share via digg, Facebook, Google, Yahoo, technorati and de.licio.us.

www.millsandboon.co.uk